Home TO Tomorrow

JOYCE BARTON

CHAPTER ONE

Colorado plains July 7, 1873

The crack of distant gunfire straightened Cole Adams in his saddle. The buckskin horse bobbed his head, his powerful muscles bunched for action. The large dog alongside glanced first in the direction of the sound then up at Cole as if waiting for orders.

Was it the rustlers? Had they doubled back?

Cole pulled out his rifle and looked around. Other than the cattle tracks he'd been following since dawn, only dirt, sage and heat waves glimmered across the Colorado plains. He double-checked the rifle to make sure it was loaded then slipped it back in its sheath. Sensing Cole's nerves, the dog whined and the horse began to dance around. "Easy boys, only one shot, probably some fellow getting himself some supper."

He glanced at the layer of dust covering him and his animals, blending them into one hue. He'd taken on this task as a favor to Austin, but once he helped get his friend's brood stock settled in their new mountain home, Cole was hightailing it back to Georgetown, his favorite mining community. Give him the mountains, a deck of cards, and a pretty woman on his knee any day over all this heat and sweat.

Another gunshot echoed across the prairie, followed quickly by three more. Cole groaned. Definitely trouble; hot on the heels of a second stampede in as many days. The first had been caused by a lightening storm. The very next evening, six men created no end of trouble when they rode in, guns firing, in an attempt to steal the herd. Fortunately the rustlers only succeeded in getting a couple of themselves killed. The four remaining turned tail and ran. Austin and his cowhands were left with the task of bunching the cattle and heading them east again. And Cole began this sweltering search to round up the strays.

Trouble seemed to follow them like a grizzly after fresh meat.

Cole pulled his hat on tighter and nudged the horse into a gallop. The big dog kept pace close by.

Within minutes the parched flat land dropped away to form a deep, wide ravine. Cole drew rein and jumped from the saddle. Off to his right, four saddled horses stood ground tied. He did the same with Storm, then slipped his left pistol out of its holster and peered over the crest of the hill. Just below him on the side of the hill crouched the four remaining rustlers they'd dealt with last evening.

Apparently they'd found easier prey. They were shooting at three men huddled together behind a fallen tree at the bottom of the abrupt incline. The threesome looked like travelers. A heavily loaded packhorse and their saddled mounts grazed nearby. The rustlers' attack must have caught them off guard. The travelers didn't appear to have any weapons to defend themselves from the continuing gunfire.

Cole motioned for the dog to lie down and stay and then stretched out flat behind a clump of sagebrush. His first shot effectively drew the rustlers' attention. They scrambled for cover before aiming their guns at him. A bullet kicked up dirt near Cole's face. Clearing his eyes, he fired again and flattened the outlaw closest to him. Just as quickly, he dropped another. The remaining two ran up the hill behind a volley of gunfire. Cole rolled to his side and squeezed the trigger again. One of the men screamed and grabbed his booted foot before scrambling into his saddle. It was over in a matter of seconds.

Cole let them ride away while he checked on the two he'd shot. They were both dead, so he mounted Storm, retrieved their horses and signaled the dog to follow as he headed down the hill.

At the bottom, a lazy river snaked through a widespread band of thick grass and several stands of cottonwoods. Cole picked a shallow spot to cross, and as he got closer to the travelers, he could see a man propped against the fallen tree, his shirtfront wet with blood, his white hair matted with dirt and sweat. A much younger man squatted next to him, pressing a blood soaked cloth against the old man's shoulder. Light blonde hair fell over his eyes. He brushed it aside as he watched Cole approach.

City folk, Cole decided after a quick assessment of their clothing. He glanced around for the third one and saw him on the side of the hill cutting leaves off of a broad-leafed plant. He looked to be no more than about thirteen and wasn't dressed as neatly as the other two. A black, wide-brimmed hat rode low over his ears, and his slight frame was nearly swallowed up by a tan shirt and gray pants. His movements were slow but deliberate, and he stopped now and then to wipe sweat out of his eyes.

"Thanks...for your help, mister." The older man drawled through gritted teeth. Pain drew his shaggy white brows into a heavy column across the top of faded brown eyes.

Cole swung down from the saddle. "How bad is it?"

"The bullet went right through." The younger man answered, openly studying Cole from head to toe.

Cole ignored the younger man's stare, now fixed on the two pistols belted around his hips. He'd already noted the only weapons these men carried were rifles still sheathed in new-looking scabbards on their saddles. Greenhorns, he assessed. A gun didn't do a man much good tucked away out of reach. His scrutiny moved back to the boy, now busy with something at the river. "What are you doing out here? This is pretty dangerous country for sight-seeing."

The old man's eyes squeezed shut in pain a moment before he spoke. "We're from North Carolina on our way to the mountains. Don't know what we would've done if you hadn't...come along."

As if just remembering his manners, the young man stood and thrust a hand out to Cole. "I'm Dalton Tate. This is my grandfather, Zebediah Pettigrew. He likes to be called Zeb."

Cole leaned forward to accept the slim hand, surprised by the firm grasp. He nodded to the grandfather before glancing back at the boy, wondering why his name had been left out of the introductions.

"That's a great dog," Dalton said. "He looks like a wolf. What's his name?"

Cole scratched the top of the dog's black head just above the tan hair half encircling his right eye. "Ring."

"That's fitting." Dalton grinned then dropped back down to fuss with the bloody cloth on his grandfather's shoulder, folding it over in an attempt to find a cleaner side.

Before Cole could speak again, the boy walked up and knelt by the old man. He deftly cut away the bloody shirt using a knife he'd removed from a leather sheath tied around his waist. The blade was thin and looked lethal, the bone handle was carved to fit a small hand.

After doing away with the shirt, the boy began to clean the raw, bleeding wound with a pungent-smelling liquid. Cole couldn't quite grasp what it was about the boy that bothered him, but he didn't seem right. He looked as weak as the old man, although it didn't stop him from doing a competent job with the old man's wound.

"Looks like you've done this before." Cole spoke his thought aloud as he watched the boy apply a poultice made from something he'd taken out of a leather bag, along with some of the leaves he'd mashed.

The youngster's only acknowledgment of the comment was to glance up briefly, giving Cole a glimpse of eyes the color of storm clouds.

Dalton suddenly stepped in between them and again boldly eyed Cole up and down. "I've never seen a firearm worn with the butt facing forward. Are you a gunfighter or something?"

Cole shoved his left hand into his belt, checking the impulse to teach the younger man the risk of such brash behavior. The West didn't suffer fools. A challenging tone like that out here could get a man killed. "I know how to use them."

"Dalton didn't mean any offense," the grandfather intervened, giving his grandson a terse shake of his head. "We're grateful for your help, Mister…"

"Adams, Cole Adams." Cole made himself relax a notch. These three weren't a threat to him. Only a nuisance, he decided, eager to be on his way.

"Happy to meet you, Mister Adams." The old man offered him a feeble smile before speaking to his grandson. "Dalton, please take care of the horses."

Cole handed over the reins of the two rustlers' mounts and pinned the younger man with a firm look. "I'll take care of my own."

Dalton had the good sense to look chagrined before he led the other two horses away to stake them in the tall grass and remove their saddles. Next he unloaded the bags on the packhorse. The boy finished bandaging the old man's shoulder, stuffed the unused necessities into his leather bag and followed after Dalton. Cole watched him struggle to unsaddle a bay mare that looked to be nearly sixteen hands tall. The big horse affectionately nudged the boy in the back with her nose as he led her to the river to drink. The rustlers had obviously intended to salvage their losses by cashing in with these horses. The mare and packhorse would bring top dollar in Denver, as would the dun and roan geldings.

"The pain is letting up some." The old man struggled to a sitting position. "That youngster is truly blessed with a healing touch."

Cole agreed the boy's work was impressive, but it would take more than skill at treating gunshot wounds if these men hoped to survive out here. The three of them together hadn't come up with enough sense to grab a gun when bullets started flying. "Where in the mountains are you headed?" He asked.

"To a glacier lake just below the headwaters of the Grand River."

"Spirit Lake. Cole said. "It's a favorite camp ground of the Arapaho."

"Indians," Zeb spat, then winced and grabbed his shoulder. "A bunch of them attacked my youngest brother and his companions up there some years back. Murdering savages. The world will be a better place when we get rid of the whole lot."

Cole wanted to caution the old man that not much had changed to better the situation since his brother had ventured west. They had no business heading into that remote area without the aid of several armed men. But Zeb Pettigrew had a mulish look about him that said the only reasoning he listened to was his own. Look at the chance he'd taken traveling all the way out here with a still-wet-behind-the-ears grandson and a kid doctor who looked like he needed doctoring himself.

Cole eased away from the subject of Indians. "A friend of mine just built a ranch up there in Middle Park, only a day's ride from the lake. I'm helping him drive a herd of brood stock up there. That's how I happened along. The men who attacked you tried for our herd of cattle earlier."

"Lucky for us you were close by. Any chance you could stay the night? I sure would rest easier if you did. I'm happy to pay you for your trouble, and you could get an early start tomorrow."

Cole removed his hat and brushed at the dust, leaving a noticeable streak on the brim. When was he going to learn to mind his own business? Babysitting three greenhorns ranked right up there with driving a dirt-dumb bunch of cattle into the high country. He slammed the hat back on his head and said, "Right now I have to round up those strays. I hope to be back before dark. We can talk more then."

His frustration caused Storm to dance sideways when he jammed his boot into the stirrup and settled himself in the saddle. Anxious to share this unwanted responsibility, Cole turned toward Zebediah Pettigrew and said, "The main herd should catch up sometime tomorrow. You might give some consideration to joining it for a few days. Give your shoulder a chance to mend a bit before you strike out on your own again."

He flicked the reins and headed Storm toward the river, then spun him back around. "Do you have a shovel in your gear?"

"Yes."

"Have your grandson dig a couple of graves. Those bodies will get rank real fast in this heat and attract critters you won't want to deal with. And keep a gun handy. I doubt we'll see those two rustlers again, but you never know."

The moon was near full and the prairie sky alive with stars when Cole took his turn at watch in the wee hours of the next morning. He pulled the makings of a cigarette from his pocket, wishing for one of the cheroots he'd run out of last week. A mournful call from one of the calves broke the hush of the early morning. Cole listened and waited, but the dozen strays seemed content with the grass beside the river. He came close to sharing their contentment. Except three hours sleep hadn't been nearly enough. And in spite of a quick wash in the river, he still felt dirty.

He thought of the big claw foot tub in his rooms above the saloon. And the sumptuous warm meals served by the cook. And the even warmer women who worked there. Soon, he told himself, soon.

As he tapped a line of tobacco onto the creased paper and began to roll it between his fingers, a movement in camp stopped him. It was the boy, creeping like a thief in the night as he followed the riverbank downstream. Probably going for a quick pee.

Cole's youngest charge still made him uneasy. Earlier in the evening, as they sat around the fire talking, the boy stayed way back in the shadows so quiet Cole didn't even notice he'd gone to sleep. But Dalton noticed and immediately got up and covered him with a blanket. Maybe he's mute, Cole decided. Or simple-minded, but if that was the case, how could you explain the good job he'd done with the old man's shoulder?

Something was wrong with him though. Cole would bet his last winning poker hand on it. The boy didn't fit with the other two. In fact, the three of them together made an odd lot. Cole wasn't sure which one was greener. It had to be sheer luck they'd made it this far in one piece. Dalton especially. Cole had come close to killing the inexperienced fool just a few hours ago.

After instructing the younger man to take first watch, Cole had settled down for some much-needed sleep, never thinking Dalton would be foolish enough to wake him by grabbing his shoulder. Cole had bolted upright and shoved the business end of a forty-four in Dalton's face, shocking them both. Hopefully the younger man had learned a lesson.

That thought brought his mind back to the boy. He'd been gone too long. Maybe he needed a lesson, too.

After a short walk along the riverbank, Cole rounded a bend and came to an abrupt halt. Standing waist deep in the middle of the dark water was a goddess, head thrown back and arms aloft as if reaching for the stars. She softly chanted words Cole couldn't make out. Moonlight glistened on her wet stomach and high, round breasts, and bathed her face in a pearly glow.

Boyhood legends of mermaids rising from the depths of the sea flashed through Cole's mind. He thumbed his hat off his forehead and stepped close enough to see this was neither mermaid nor goddess. She reclined in the water now, a flesh-and-blood woman. The tips of her breasts were barely visible at the surface; the shimmering current tugged her long hair in its tow. Cole felt an immediate tightening in his groin, quickly followed by a gnawing apprehension in his gut. Where the hell had she come from? He looked around for the boy before realizing with a jolt that this was the boy.

He watched as she moved to the shore to get something from the riverbank, exposing nearly every inch of herself in the moonlight. For several minutes he drank in the sight, his groin heavy and tight as she turned back to wade deeper and begin lathering all that hair, her narrow shoulders, arms, breasts and small waist. Finally she moved her hands on down to just beneath the water where her rump and femininity were hidden from view.

When she abruptly sank completely beneath the water to rinse off the soap, Cole regained some control. And the situation inflamed him in another way. He suddenly felt like the brunt of a bad joke.

Who the hell were these people? What kind of game were they playing? He glanced at a small pair of leather moccasins and neatly folded shirt and trousers laying on the shore and decided to return the favor.

A sliver of pink light streaked low across the eastern horizon by the time she finished bathing and waded toward the shore. Partway there, she stopped. "There must be leprechauns about, they've taken my clothes."

Cole stepped from behind a tree, holding her pants and shirt in front of him. "Looking for these?"

Gasping, she covered her breasts with her hands, stumbled backwards, and sat down with a splash. "How…how long have you been standin' there?"

"Long enough." Cole stared at her, still trying to comprehend that the person he'd thought was a thirteen-year-old boy was actually a woman. A beautifully put together, full-grown woman.

"Would you please put my things down and leave."

Cole wasn't budging. "Why are you pretending to be a boy?"

"I'm not… pretending. Not really. It just…makes things easier."

"What things?"

"Mister Adams, please… It's really not your concern."

"Come out of there and get dressed before you get a chill." Cole realized how ridiculous that sounded, as if she'd get a chill in this July heat. He dropped her clothes on the ground and turned his back.

"Mister Adams…."

"I'm not going anywhere," he shot over his shoulder.

A long minute passed before he heard her leave the water.

As he listened to her muffled exclamations, he easily imagined the struggle she was having, trying to shove those lovely wet limbs into dry clothes.

"Are you finished?" He wasn't sure whether the agitation in his voice stemmed from his physical response to her or the fact that her charade made him feel like he'd been the one caught with his pants down.

"Nay, just a moment, I'm not finished with the buttons."

Her voice was intriguing. Besides the slight Irish lilt, there was a trace of something else he couldn't make out. He counted to ten and turned.

She stood as motionless as the prairie air and was close enough for him to smell the lingering scent of her soap. Lilac? Her dripping hair hung past her waist, soaking the baggy shirt and making it very obvious she wore nothing underneath. The top of her head came just to his shoulder, so she had to tilt her head up in order to look him in the eye. Which she did with a boldness that didn't quite mask her nervousness.

There was enough light to see clearly now, and Cole took his time getting his first good look at her face. It was as pale as the moon, except for those enormous eyes. No wonder he'd thought of storm clouds when he first saw them. They were the color of purest silver, outlined with a ring of dark charcoal. Drops of moisture clung to her long lashes and winged brows, and Cole had trouble forcing his gaze to move on to the high cheekbones, straight nose and full mouth. Sensuous, he thought, and fought a sudden urge to kiss away the lingering dampness on her upper lip.

Instead he pried his attention back to her eyes, wondering what was so disturbing about them. He noticed the grim shadows on the delicate skin beneath. Had she been ill? The look in her eyes reminded him of the young doe he'd come upon years ago, it's leg caught in a trap. The animal was in obvious pain and terrified. He'd worked as fast as he could to free it, but in the end, its foreleg had been so mangled, he'd had to end its misery with a bullet.

"Matt?" Dalton called out, walking toward them. "There you are, Matt. I was worried when…"

"It's all right, Dalton. I'm fine, and I think Mister Adams has figured out my name isn't Matt."

Cole's focus remained on her. "What is your name?"

Her chin came up almost defensively. "It is...I am called Cassie." She backed away and found her hat. "Come on, Dalton. It's getting late. We'd better fix some breakfast."

Cole caught her hesitation over her name. And he didn't like the way she was dismissing him. "Cassie." He waited until she turned and looked at him. "You never answered my question. Why are you dressed like that?"

"I answered, Mister Adams. I told you it's not your concern."

Watching her walk away, Cole became seriously worried about his observation skills. Even with baggy trousers, any fool could see she was a woman. He grabbed a fistful of Dalton's shirt as the younger man started after her. "What's going on?" he demanded.

"What do you mean?

"You know exactly what I mean. Why is she dressed like that?"

"It...makes things easier."

His unintentional parroting of Cassie's response only riled Cole more. He had to force the snarl out of his voice when he ground out, "Makes what easier?"

"Look, Mister Adams, if Cassie wants to explain anything to you, that's fine. But it isn't up to me." He pulled free and took off like a shot, leaving Cole standing there gaping, and wanting very badly to hit something.

CHAPTER TWO

Cassie ignored the pain gripping the back of her head and started a cooking fire. With practiced ease, she assembled the items for their morning meal. Thoughts of Cole Adams unnerved her, but she refused to be embarrassed by his watching her at the river. He was the one in the wrong. Was he raised with no manners at all?

From the moment he'd come riding to their rescue, her instincts warned her not to let him get too close. Now she knew why. From a distance, he was truly fascinating; the perfect depiction of an imagined man-of-the-west, approaching life head on as if knowing no one or nothing would dare defy him.

Up close was another matter altogether. He was at least three inches taller than Dalton's six feet and broader by several inches. And there was a raw power about him so tangible she felt it could suck the air right out of her lungs.

Which is why she'd been surprised at the unexpected urge to give him her Indian name. She must never do that. Her Irish father had insisted from the time she was big enough to understand. 'You look white and you are to always think of yourself and present yourself as white.' Her Choctaw mother had agreed, thinking it might save Cassie from the harm and bigotry she and her people had suffered.

But Running Deer, her great-grandmother, had gone along with them only to save peace. Whenever the two of them were alone, the old healer used every opportunity to pass on the pride of her heritage to her precious great-grandchild, along with her healing skills.

Oh what tangled webs we weave, Cassie thought, loathing her deception every bit as much as she was grateful to her father for insisting on it. None of these men would even consider helping her if they knew she was a half-breed. Especially Zeb; Indians were responsible for the death of his brother, and his resentment ran deep.

She added another stick to the fire and set a pan of water over the small blaze. Drops of moisture spit and sizzled in the heat. Wisps of smoke curled upward, a painful reminder. Cassie turned away from the terrifying memories. She quickly walked to the edge of the river and pictured instead the wide muddy waters of the Mississippi behind her family's small Kentucky farm. She could almost smell the musty earth and hear the muted sounds of the surrounding forest. Oh how she longed to return to the quiet isolation of her farm, to slip back into the sheltered embrace of her family's love. But it was impossible. Like the river at spring flood raging out of its banks, she had been violently shoved into the outside world, and there was no turning back.

A hand touched her shoulder, and she whirled around. Dalton smiled down at her. "I'm sorry, Cassie. I didn't mean to scare you. Are you all right?"

She nodded and swallowed the ache and fear in her throat. Her fingers sought the strand of beaded stones beneath her shirt. The reaction was automatic, something she wasn't even aware of anymore. The necklace had comforted her since she was small, when her great-grandmother tied it around her neck with the promise it would keep the smoke-and-fire-breathing monster in her nightmares from hurting her. She didn't know then that the old healer believed the dreams to be prophetic visions, or that her father had been angry with Running Deer for maintaining that conviction.

But it was true. The monster was real. And one day he left her dreams and came shrieking to life to destroy her entire world.

"Hello in there." Dalton waved a hand in front of her face.

She took a deep breath and made herself focus. "I'm all right. Thank you for asking."

Dalton was wearing his I'm-going-to-protect-you-from-the-world look. She was used to it. He had assumed the role the moment he and Zeb found her, badly injured, near the woods by her farm. "I saw the water boiling on the fire and made some porridge. That's what you intended, isn't it?"

"Aye, it is. I'm sorry. I…"

"You need a break, Cassie. Paps has been pushing us too hard."

"That he has, but I understand," she said, although she didn't, not really. Zeb was on a quest to retrieve a cache of gold his youngest brother left behind during an Indian attack. The gold had been buried for years. What could a few extra days or weeks matter?

"I'm looking forward to taking part in a real live cattle drive," Dalton confessed, with a reddening face, as if a man of twenty shouldn't be making such a statement. But it didn't stop him for long. He began chattering again about the herd, wondering how big it was and how many cowboys he'd get to meet. Cassie had always found Dalton's excitement endearing whenever he pointed out new sights along their journey. This sudden change in plans was a way for him to live out one of his fantasies about the West.

All at once, he stopped rambling, put his hands on her shoulders and bent his head to look closely in her face. "You don't look very good today."

"Why, thank you, sir," Cassie attempted a light-hearted tone. "Every girl likes to hear things like that."

"You know what I mean. Is it another headache?"

His concern made her regret her sarcasm. For weeks now, he'd been doting on her like a mother hen with its chick. At first, when she'd been too weak to ride alone, he had supported her in front of him on his big roan. When she was stronger, he purchased Lady for her. He had become her champion, and she would be forever in his debt.

She cupped his cheek with her hand. "I'll be fine. We have to wait for the herd, so maybe…" The rest of her thought tumbled to a halt when Cole Adams stalked into camp with the long-legged suppleness of a panther. His leather clothing fit him like a second skin, making him seem even more like a wild animal. She watched him saddle and bridle his horse, then lead him their way.

At some point, he'd rid himself of the dirt and dust he'd worn yesterday, but a shadow of dark beard still covered his square jaw and sharply angled chin. His unruly black hair looked like it rarely met up with a pair of shears as it curled behind his ears and over the back of the blue bandanna knotted around his neck. He had an arrogantly straight nose, except for a slight ridge on one side where it might have collided with one too many hard fists. His lips were smooth, well defined and fixed in an unyielding line when he stopped just inches in front of her.

She looked up at him, and his cobalt gaze rendered her breathless. Time seemed to stop, along with the awareness of anything or anyone outside of the whirlpool of emotion swirling through her insides.

It could have been seconds or hours, but the spell was finally broken by his rough, uncompromising command. "Stay close to camp until I return with the herd."

She was released from his scrutiny when he turned and mounted his horse. Cassie sucked in some air and watched him ride over to Zeb who was just sitting up and rubbing his eyes.

"I should be back by late afternoon. Make sure someone stays on guard at all times." He looked pointedly at the rifles in their scabbards on the other side of camp. "Get those guns and keep them close," he ground out as if scolding errant children. In the next moment, he spun the horse and cantered away.

Dalton scowled at the top of the hill where the horse and rider disappeared from sight. "He certainly has no problem issuing orders."

"I'm sure it's just his way, Dalton." Cassie agreed with him, but she didn't want to encourage her friend's irritation. Cole Adams seemed like the kind of man who could chew up softer men like Dalton and spit them out with no remorse.

By late afternoon, Cassie's headache was worse. She made no attempt to hide her irritation with Zeb as she untied the bloody bandage on his shoulder. "Hold still and let me check it," she snapped.

This was the first time she'd had a chance to get some real rest since they'd left Kentucky, but Zeb's stubbornness was making it impossible. Throughout the entire sweltering day, he'd insisted he was well enough to be up, forcing her to practically wrestle him back down. This time, he'd fallen, making his wound bleed and her patience snap. She mopped her brow with the back of her hand and batted at the relentless flies. There wasn't so much as a breeze to help keep them away. Her head hurt so bad she could hardly hold her head up. She'd tried every remedy she could think of, but nothing helped. She felt as feeble as a sick kitten.

"The bleeding has finally stopped." She dabbed at the area around the wound with a clean cloth then applied a small amount of the poultice. "But you have to stay still. Do you hear me?"

"I hear. But that doesn't mean I have to like it." Zeb peered at Cassie from beneath his shaggy white brows. "You know, girl, you look like a ragamuffin. I think it's high time you started dressing like a lady. You're safe now, we're a long ways from Kentucky."

Cassie frowned at him, unsure that she'd ever feel safe again. She began to wrap Zeb's shoulder in a fresh bandage. "The britches are fine. They make it easier for me to keep up with you."

"Yes, yes." Zeb dismissed her scolding. "Nevertheless, it's not proper, especially since other men will be around. I should never have given in to Dalton on this matter."

Cassie cringed inwardly, not wanting to remember the fierce argument she'd caused between Zeb and his grandson when she'd begged to be taken with them. Zeb hadn't wanted to be saddled with her or her problems. He'd argued that they should take her to the nearest town where the law could deal with her situation. Thankfully Dalton had disagreed and adamantly refused to go on without her. Then he'd angered his grandfather further by giving her some of his clothes.

"Well, don't fret about it today." Zeb patted her hand in a rare show of compassion. "We'll discuss it later. Besides, I'm obliged to you. This is the second time you found some useful vegetation to help me out. That...uh... little problem I had a few weeks ago just about did me in. What was it you called that medicine?"

"Slippery elm bark. And you let that 'little problem' go on too long, Zeb." She remembered the old man's reluctance to mention his constipation. By the time she coaxed him to talk about his ill behavior, he was nearly too sick to ride.

"Ah, yes. Slippery elm. You still have some of that tea?"

Cassie paused from buttoning his shirt. Why? Are you feeling poorly again?"

"No, I just wondered. In case. You know a lot about medicine, ah...plants and such. Don't you?"

"I know a little," she hedged. This wasn't the first time he'd poked at her about her healing skills. But she could never explain. He bristled at the mere mention of Indians. There was no telling what he'd do he if found out her knowledge came from a Choctaw great-grandmother. She tied off the ends of the bandage and patted his shoulder. "There, I've got you all put back together."

The old man reclined back on the quilt and squinted up at her. "You don't look so good, Cassie. Why don't you rest awhile? I'll behave. I promise," he emphasized after she gave him a doubtful look. "I know I've been a nuisance today, but it's your own fault for doing such a good job. My shoulder quit throbbing minutes after you doctored it. Made me feel like I wasn't hurt bad enough to lie around like a lazy old hound."

Cassie shook her head at his roundabout apology. "I know you hate to slow down, Zeb. But the quieter you stay now, the faster you'll heal." She slipped her knife back into its sheath and wrapped the rest of the poultice in a piece of cloth and placed it in the deerskin bag with the rest of her medicine-makings.

"Here they come," Dalton announced, walking up from the river to join Cassie and his grandfather.

The July sun glared intensely off the dust cloud bearing down on them and made her head hurt worse. Within moments, the air was filled with the clamor of bawling cattle and shouting men. As the herd rambled over the ridge and down the hill, they broke apart and spread toward the river. Cassie shaded her eyes with her hand and made out the tall figure of Cole Adams atop his rugged horse, the huge dog alongside. The three of them seemed to belong together; one as disreputable looking as the other.

By the time Cole dismounted, another man joined him. They left their horses ground-tied and strolled together into camp. The new man was as tall as Cole Adams, but had a slighter build. He was as fair as Cole was dark. His eyes were also blue, but they were lighter, like the sky on a sunny day. Cassie thought maybe it was because they were friendly eyes, not intense and probing like the dark-blue pair that made her insides quake.

"Austin, this is Zeb Pettigrew, Dalton Tate, and… Cassie." Cole pointed to each one as he introduced them, but his eyes lingered a little too long on her, making her face burn. Finally he turned and cuffed the other man's shoulder with his gloved hand, stirring up a puff of dirt. "Folks, this is Austin Barret. He's the man responsible for all this dust."

The owner of the herd shook hands with Dalton then bent to take Zeb's hand where he rested on the blanket. He started to offer his hand to Cassie then hesitated, pulled back and tipped his hat. Cole Adams had the audacity to look pleased by his friend's confusion. Cassie wanted to crawl behind the nearest tree.

Dalton saved the moment by asking a battery of questions about the herd. Austin and Cole patiently took turns answering. All the while, Cole's eyes drifted back to her. She ducked her head to block his penetrating gaze with the brim of her hat. Right now she didn't have the energy to deal with the strange effect he had on her. In truth, the heat robbed her of the energy to deal with much of anything. Her head was pounding, and she was feeling worse by the minute.

As the conversation droned on, the men's voices began to fuse with the incessant hum of the flies. She strained to stay focused on what they said, but the buzzing in her ears grew louder. She needed to sit down. It was so hot...

Cole watched Cassie begin to wilt and moved quickly to catch her, knocking her hat off in the process. Dalton reached out at the same time, but Cole's threatening glare stopped him. He carried her a few short steps to the river's edge then knelt and rested her head and shoulders on his lap. She was completely still, the slight rise and fall of her chest her only sign of life. He untied his bandanna, rinsed it quickly in the water and pressed the wet fabric against her forehead.

There was no response. He dipped the bandanna again and stroked the cool water down each side of her face and neck. There wasn't so much as a flicker from those dark lashes.

Dalton squatted beside Cole and took one of Cassie's hands in his. The others waited silently while Cole worked to bring her around. He opened the first three buttons of her shirt and noticed a coral and turquoise necklace, each small stone intricately inlaid in silver. Pushing it aside, he doused cool water over the soft skin and slender bones that formed a delicate V at the base of her throat. Still no response. Cole's heart rate jumped up a beat. He gently shook her shoulders. Nothing.

His gaze locked on the thick braids wound tightly around her head. He searched for and pulled out the pins and leather ties holding them in place, then loosened the long plaits with his fingers to spill around her shoulders, over his knees and onto the ground. This was the first time he'd seen her hair dry and in full daylight. The sun turned the dark mass the color of fine burgundy wine. Which made her skin look that much paler.

She was deathly white.

Just like Victoria when she died. Cole's thoughts rushed to the past. He'd just turned fourteen when his two-year-old sister succumbed to the cholera that had already killed his mother, father and two brothers. He'd begged God not to take the baby too. But God wasn't listening. And when the villagers sealed her body in the tiny wooden box and lowered it into the dark hole, he'd wanted to climb in with her.

Damn it to hell. Cole yanked his mind back to the present. What was wrong with this woman? Why wasn't she coming around?

"She's never done this before," Dalton whispered. He stroked her fingers, looking like he ached to take her away from Cole. "Cassie? Cassie, it's Dalton. Open your eyes."

Cassie was floating in a cool, dense fog. Her head was clear and free from pain. She felt safe. She wanted to stay here forever. Especially when she saw her great-grandmother appear in the mist. The old woman opened her arms and Cassie sailed into her embrace with a sob.

"Hush little one, don't cry."

Cassie clung to her comforting presence. "Oh, Grandmother, I've missed you so much. I've been so frightened."

"There is nothing to fear, Red Dawn. You are safe. Remember when I gave you the necklace?"

Cassie's fingers closed around the precious stones. "Aye."

Her grandmother pulled back and looked at Cassie with eyes like black-jeweled orbs. "The necklace holds Great Medicine. It belonged to your ancestor, a powerful Alikchi with very strong Medicine."

"As strong as yours?"

The old woman gave her a slow smile. "Yes. She was my teacher." Her wizened features grew serious once again. "The stones are your Allies. The turquoise will keep you safe from Bad Medicine. The coral is to remind you of your connection to the Earth, and to all things of the Earth. The Stone People know the secrets of the Earth, Red Dawn. They know the way. They will assist you in your search for your truth."

The old woman began to fade away. Cassie reached for her. "What truth, Grandmother? I don't understand."

"I must go now. Do not be afraid. The Great One is always with you. Follow the sun, Red Dawn. You will know. You will understand."

"Please don't leave me," she begged. But the old woman was gone.

"Cassie." Someone called her name from far away. She didn't want to answer.

"Cassie." The voice grew louder, stronger. It pulled her out of the safe, cool place into heat and pain. She opened her eyes to see Cole Adams staring down at her. He didn't seem especially pleased. She tried to make her mind work, but her thoughts were sluggish. Cole brushed the pad of his thumb across her cheek. The tender gesture confused her more.

She felt a tug on her hand and turned her aching head to see Dalton's familiar smile. Over his shoulder, she saw the owner of the herd and another man staring at her. The concern on their faces finally penetrated her bewilderment. She struggled to get up, wishing she could suddenly disappear.

Cole helped her to her feet. "You'd better go slow." His voice was huskier than usual.

She shaded her eyes from the painful glare of the sun and looked up at him. "I...I'm sorry for all the fuss. I don't normally... It must have been the heat."

The short, wiry man standing next to Austin Barret elbowed his way through the others. "You can all quit your gawking, now. This young lady will be just fine." He slipped a bony arm around Cassie's back and gently propelled her to the shade of a cottonwood.

"The name's John Brewster, little lady. "I'm the cook for this outfit and all round handy man." He nodded toward Cole and Austin. "Those two pups couldn't make it through a day without me."

Her rescuer wasn't much taller than herself, but his wiry arms were rock solid as he settled her on the ground. "Head hurt?" She nodded. "You stay put. Ole Brewster has just the thing to fix you up."

He sauntered over to a wagon at the edge of camp, a decided hitch in his bowed legs. He returned in less than a minute to place a tin cup filled with dark liquid into Cassie's hands. "Here you go. This will fix you up in no time."

Her head hurt worse now that she was upright. She fought off a wave of dizziness and nausea as she took a sip of the thick mixture. It was both bitter and sweet, with a hint of molasses. She swallowed more, wondering what it was. Not that it mattered. Her head had been throbbing for hours, and, at this point, she'd drink lamp oil if it would help. She drank more and wiped her mouth with the back of her hand, trying not to think about the group of men standing back a ways in a loose semi-circle, watching her every move. Cole's glare was the most intense. The others were trying not to be so obvious. But even with his hat pulled low over his forehead, she could still see his cool, assessing eyes.

"Drink it down, now." Brewster urged, his gentle voice softening his gruff manner. "You'll feel better. That's a promise."

Cassie swallowed the contents and coughed. "What is it?" The mixture was puzzling; her great-grandmother had never given her anything like it.

"Ah, now that's a secret." He winked at her. "A man can't be giving away all his secrets now, can he? At least not today." He chuckled, took the empty cup, affectionately ruffled the top of Cassie's hair and left her alone.

To Cassie's immense relief, the others did the same. She sagged back against the tree and closed her eyes. Remnants of the vision came back to her. Her great-grandmother's presence had felt so real, her comfort so achingly familiar. But it wasn't real, she reminded herself. Running Deer was dead. They were all dead. Cassie choked back a sob, still not wanting to believe it. Her great-grandmother's death had been difficult enough to accept, even at her advanced age. But barely a month later, her father had suffered a fatal stroke, and the second death, so soon after the first, had turned her sorrow to shocked anguish.

Yet it was the third death, only three weeks to the day after her father's that threatened to shatter her sanity. It was the brutal death of her mother that brought the terrifying childhood nightmare into reality and left her teetering on the edge of a darkness that threatened to suck her into its deep unknown.

Stop it! Cassie scolded herself. If she didn't stop thinking about it, she would go mad. If she let the tears come, they'd never stop.

Her fingers felt for the necklace. She must focus on something else. What had Running Deer said? Something about finding her Truth. What did that mean? She had no idea. Nothing made sense anymore. Nothing was the same.

Here she sat, in the middle of the Colorado plains, completely dependent on a group of strangers. One of them wanted to be her knight-in-shining-armor. One of them completely beguiled her whenever he was near. The others were kind to a fault. But in spite of their care and protection, in spite of Running Deer's assurances, she felt afraid, and lost, and terribly alone.

CHAPTER THREE

C ole left the herd late that evening and returned to camp guided by the flicker of the low-burning fire and brilliant starlight. Dalton had taken first watch along with Dan Mores. Buck and Charley would take over at midnight. Cole and Austin would break them around dawn. The herd rested easy, and Cole hoped they stayed that way. He had schooled Dalton on how to keep the cattle quiet, and put him on Sparky, an old cow pony that had sharper eyes than any of the others and wasn't inclined to shy at shadows or sudden noises. Throughout the weeks on the trail, she'd had a calming effect on the herd. Maybe she'd do the same for Dalton.

Cole unsaddled and brushed Storm, fed him some well-deserved oats and turned him into the rope corral with the rest of the herd. When he entered the campsite, he noticed that Austin was already asleep. He took the plate Brew handed him and sat down to eat alone.

Austin's three other cowhands were scattered around Cassie. Twenty-one year old Buck Kendrick, the oldest, was involved in some silly argument with seventeen-year-old Charley Snyder, the youngest. Both were preening for Cassie's attention. She rewarded them with an occasional smile. For some reason, their youthful rivalry irritated Cole. He forked a bite of beef and beans into his mouth and tried to look away, but his curiosity pulled his attention back to the group on the other side of the campfire.

Cassie was hatless for once. Her long hair drifted loose around her shoulders, reflecting the fire's red glow. Sensing his gaze, she glanced his way. Their eyes met and held for a moment, sending a heated response to his groin.

Disgruntled at how easily she could arouse him, Cole shifted away again and leaned against the spokes of the wagon wheel, directing his focus to the tiny insect trailing its way through the powdery soil. He didn't want to think about Cassie, the scare she'd given him when she fainted, the pain in those incredible eyes, the way she'd felt in his arms. Or the way he felt every time he revisited that corner of his mind where he kept a moonlit vision of her bathing in the river. Nor did he want to listen to Austin's randy cowhands competing for her attention.

He got up, handed his empty plate to Brew and shook out his bedroll. He hadn't been able to string together six hours sleep in the past four days and was sure he would pass out the moment he was prone.

Two hours later, sleep still eluded him. He tossed restlessly from one side to the other, silently cursing the hard ground. But he was only kidding himself. It wasn't the ground keeping him awake. He rolled onto his back and stared into the star-filled heavens. It had been a long time since he'd let a woman move him in any way other than mere pleasure. And this woman touched him in ways he didn't want to think about.

Never mind that she was too damned beautiful for her own good, or anyone else's, for that matter. No, he convinced himself, the thing that ate away at him was all the unanswered questions. Why all the mystery? Why did she seem so frail? What or who was she hiding from?

Why did he care? That was the question he should be asking. "Damn!" he grumbled aloud, then flipped over and prodded Ring off the blanket with his foot. The dog grunted, shifted slightly, then curled up and went back to sleep.

The problem was he did care. There was an air about her as unsettling as the mists on the moors near his boyhood home in England. You should take that as a warning to stay away from her, he cautioned himself. He'd already learned what obsessing over a woman could do to a man. He didn't need any more of that kind of heartache.

Cole never remembered falling to sleep, but Charley woke him with a quiet word a few hours later. When he saddled one of the extra horses and joined the herd, some of the cattle rose to their feet at the changing of the watch, but settled back down with minimal fuss. Cole slowly circled the entire herd then nosed the piebald mare up next to Austin's appaloosa. "Looks like we might make it through an entire night without a hitch."

"Hope so," Austin replied, then stretched and yawned. "Everyone's worn out. The herd was still so spooky last night we spent the entire night in our saddles."

Cole grinned at the image he'd just gotten of his friend, the ex-lawman, now branding cattle and growing hay. "It's going to be a different life for you."

Austin smiled, shrugged his shoulders and sighed. "Yeah, big change. But worth it."

The two men sat in silence for a minute, each lost in their own thoughts. Then Cole spoke again. "You thinking about Ginny?"

"I can't quit thinking about her. I hope she's okay up there alone."

"She's not alone. Ollie is with her, and that new man, Kane. Art...?"

"Arthur."

"You checked him out."

"Yeah. I wired the manager of the spread he worked for near Dallas. He wired back that Kane was a hard worker. He'd been with them a couple of years and quit because of a family matter. Kane told me he was on his way back to Texas when he heard I was looking for help."

"Well, don't worry then. Ollie wouldn't let anything happen to Ginny. You just miss her that's all."

Austin glanced at the sky and exhaled a deep breath. Cole shook his head at the naked longing on his friend's face. "Married life has you spoiled, Austin. You don't like sleeping on the hard ground when there's a soft bed and an even softer woman waiting at home."

"You say that like a man who might long for the same thing."

"Humph. Not me!" Just the thought felt smothering to Cole.

Austin laughed at the quick denial. "No? Your behavior with a certain young woman back in camp says different. Down right possessive, if you ask me."

"Nobody's asking you." Cole shifted in the saddle and hooked a leg over the pommel.

"Yes sir, down right possessive," Austin repeated, ignoring Cole's burst of surliness. "You jumped in there real quick when she fainted."

"Anyone would've done the same. She's nothing to me. I was just being helpful."

"Helpful. Right." Austin chuckled again. "Why is it, when you showed up yesterday and told us about rescuing that trio of greenhorns, you failed to mention that one of them was a woman?"

Cole had asked himself that same question a dozen times. What was it about Cassie that made him want to keep her to himself? She was definitely pleasing to look at, but so were countless other women he'd met and they'd never sparked this fierce protectiveness in him. So what was it then? Her air of frailty? Absolutely not! Fragile women had the complete opposite effect on him.

"She's so secretive," Cole grumbled, locking on the trouble he sensed around Cassie. "Has she told you anything about herself? Has Zeb or Dalton told you anything?"

"No, but it's easy to see that young Dalton doesn't appreciate your attention to her."

Cole had noticed that too. "I wonder what she is to those two. They're pretty open when it comes to discussing themselves, but they clam right up at any mention of Cassie. Nobody's even gotten around to mentioning her last name. And the way she dresses... I'd like to know what or who it is she's hiding from."

"Like I said, you're mighty interested."

Cole shrugged off the goading. "I don't like mysteries."

"Mysteries? It's not that unusual out here for a person to go by one name or no name at all. And ranch women often wear men's clothing. This is hard country." Austin's grin broadened. "I think your attention runs along a different line."

"What line?"

"I think you've taken a fancy to her."

"I `take a fancy' to a lot of women," Cole drawled, suddenly wanting to end the conversation. "I like women. That doesn't mean anything."

Austin wasn't buying it. "You may have done a pretty fair job at keeping females from getting too close up till now my friend, but I think this one slipped inside your barriers when you weren't looking."

"And I think your longing for Ginny is clouding your judgment. Besides, Cassie will only be with us a little while longer. I'll probably never see her again."

That statement was left hanging as a calf started bawling. The mother bellowed an answer and others began to stir. Austin nudged his horse one direction, and Cole turned Storm the other, humming in his deep baritone. The cattle quieted as he circled the herd, and he soon found himself thinking about Austin's remarks.

What would it be like to have a home and a loving woman like Ginny waiting there at night? Unbidden, the vision of Cassie in the river sprang into his mind; moonlight glistening on her wet skin. He ran a hand over his face, determined to keep his physical desires from controlling his thoughts.

The next image came from his childhood, his mother's frail figure, wasted away by poverty and hard work. Besides caring for her large brood, she had often worked late into the night, stitching quilts and other things for the villagers in order to supplement his father's meager fishing income. If the cholera hadn't killed her, something else would have soon enough.

That's why Cole had been determined to have plenty of money when he asked Ramona to marry him. No woman should have to live that way.

A wife should be pampered and protected. She should live in a fine house with the finest of luxuries, the way Ramona and her mother lived, thanks to her father's money and care. Cole had learned a great deal about the way life could be from that family. But that was all water under the bridge now. Ramona had married somebody else and Cole had grown up.

Spending this much time with the newly married Austin was stirring up things he didn't need to be thinking about. Cole reached for his tobacco pouch. He'd been alone a long time. And he intended to stay that way.

CHAPTER FOUR

Cassie woke slowly the next morning. The breeze in the pre-dawn air caressed her face and tickled her nose with smells of animals, wood smoke, coffee and bacon. She reveled in each separate impression. Until the sounds of the camp filtered in, and reality smothered her tranquility with leaden grief.

Yet there was one good thing, she reminded herself as she climbed out of her bedroll, no headache this morning.

Brew turned down her offer to help with breakfast. She thanked him again for relieving her headache and insisted he let her do something to help with the chores. He pointed to the calf hide suspended under the wagon and told her if she wanted to be useful, she could fill it with twigs and broken limbs from the cottonwoods. "Prairie coal burns real good when you mix it with bacon rind," he explained, "but I still like to collect wood whenever possible."

"She sipped on her coffee, careful not to burn her tongue on the hot edge of the tin cup. "What's prairie coal?"

He glanced at her sideways, grinning through his scraggly beard and moustache. "Cow and buffalo dung."

She wrinkled her nose and grinned back. The camp began to stir. The cowhands knelt one by one at the river, splashing water on their faces and over their heads. Charley used the same large rectangle of cotton Dan had used to dry himself, then demanded the comb when Dan barely had his brown, shoulder-length hair slicked back flat against his head.

Brew gaped at them, "Having a woman in camp sure changes things." He cupped his hand over his mouth and bellowed, "Your breakfast is ready. Come and git it before I throw it in the goddamm river." The moment the words were out, his face turned the color of his crimson underwear. "Pardon me, missy. I try not to swear around the ladies."

Dan walked over and poured himself a cup of coffee. "Forget it, you old coyote." He gave Cassie a look of feigned seriousness. "Swearing takes a strain off his liver, you know. He'd probably turn yellow and keel over dead if he gave it up."

Brew scowled at the young cowhand and swatted at him with a long-handled spoon.

"Please don't worry about offending me, Brew," Cassie offered. "My father's language could be very colorful at times."

Brew grunted something unintelligible and stooped to dish up a plate of beans and bacon for her. She thanked him, smiled at Dan and walked over to the fallen log to eat with Zeb and Dalton.

A few minutes later, Cole and Austin came in from the herd. Brew dished them up some breakfast, and they ate near the back of the wagon. When they finished, Austin walked over to praise Dalton on the good job he'd done with his turn at watch. Dalton blushed with pride and listened carefully as Austin told him what he'd expect if Dalton wanted to help out today. Zeb was told it would be best for him to ride in the wagon with Brew.

Cole leaned against the wagon, his scrutiny directed toward Cassie. Did he know how intimidating his look could be? Aye, he knows, she thought and kept her gaze steady as it locked with his. What are you thinking, Cole Adams? Do you use that intensity to keep people from knowing who you really are?

"Cole," Austin called.

Cole lazily broke eye contact with her and looked toward his friend.

Austin shook his head and smiled before turning to walk away. "We're heading out," he called over his shoulder.

Cole remained where he stood. His gaze drifted back to her, and Cassie felt heat rising in her cheeks.

"Cole." Austin's voice took on a teasing note as he called from the far side of the camp. "Are you coming? We've got a herd to move."

When Cole finally strolled away, Dalton scowled at his back. "I don't like the way he looks at you."

"It's all right, Dalton. I'm sure he looks at everyone that way." Cassie's whole body was on fire from the intensity of Cole's stare, but she couldn't seem to stop defending the bigger man to Dalton.

"Cole means her no harm, Dalton," Zeb agreed. "Austin told you what he wants from you today. Now you go on and do your job."

"Better shake a leg, boy," Brew put in as he lifted the cook box into the wagon. "It's not a good idea to keep the trail boss waiting."

"I'm not a boy," Dalton grumbled, turned on his heel and sulked off.

Brew helped Zeb settle on a pile of blankets near the cook box. And after a quick wink at Cassie, he climbed onto the seat, picked up the reins and clucked his tongue to the two-horse team.

Cassie found Lady saddled and waiting for her. No one had instructed her where to ride, so she pulled herself into the saddle and followed after the wagon.

The cowhands prodded the herd into a ragged line four or five abreast. The few steers shifted to the head of the developing column. The cows and their young fell in behind, calling out to each other as they topped the ridge and resumed their trek across the prairie. Dalton and Dan were positioned at the rear. Both men wore bandannas tied tightly around their faces to ward off the building cloud of dust. Buck and Charlie rode on either side. Austin and Cole led the way. Austin waved as Cassie passed them by. Cole merely glanced at her, his face a stoic mask. What a strange man, she thought. One minute, he warmed her all over, the next, he seemed as cold as winter.

The wagon soon left the herd behind and Cassie did the same with her thoughts of Cole Adams. In the east, the sun erupted grandly out of the flat horizon. Up ahead, the dark outline of the mountains thrust their grand peaks into the sky.

Cassie focused on that jagged, deep purple line and felt a stir of excitement. When she'd first seen the mountains, they'd looked like mist rising out of the prairie. Each day's journey had given them more substance. Today they seemed closer than ever, and gazing at their lofty peaks brought to mind her great-grandmother's telling of the Choctaw migration legend.

Our people once lived beyond the great mountains. In time, their numbers grew so large it was difficult to exist there. The prophets told of fertile land and abundant game in the southeast. So they gathered behind Chahta, their leader, and began a great journey.

At the end of each day, a sacred pole was planted. The next morning, it would be found leaning in the direction they should go. One morning, after a long and arduous journey, the pole stood straight and tall. Chata declared this place as the sacred burial spot for their ancestors. They had found their new land, their new home.

Cassie didn't know if the mountains up ahead held any answers for her, but they beckoned her, nonetheless. Their very magnitude seemed to offer a sort of sanctuary. In a strange way, she almost felt like she was going home.

Throughout the morning, her enthusiasm increased. She hummed along to the odd melody made up of the soft cadence of the horses' hooves, the creaking of the wagon and the clanging of the Dutch ovens tied to the back. It seemed like only moments had passed before they pulled up for their noon meal.

Brew started a small fire. Cassie climbed into the back of the wagon to look at Zeb's shoulder. She was pleased with the way his wound was healing and used that fact to persuade him to stay quiet and rest a while longer. She applied another poultice of herbs and re-bandaged the wound, then decided to walk a little and stretch her stiff limbs.

The land was not as flat now. There were dips and rises dotted with brush and occasional stands of trees. A steady breeze kept the heat more tolerable, so Cassie removed her hat and increased her pace. It felt good to move her legs after sitting in the saddle for so long.

She wandered into a shallow gulley and was lost in a game of hide and seek with a family of prairie dogs when the Indians appeared. Her surprise turned to delight when they stopped their horses in front of her.

"Good day," she greeted, putting her happiness into her smile.

The five men sat rigidly on their ponies. The most savage-looking one was around Cole and Austin's age. Two others appeared to be slightly older. The youngest one seemed barely out of his teens. He was the only one who returned her smile. The eldest had a copper face deeply creased and seasoned with experience. His long ebony hair was streaked with gray and held off his face by a beaded headband. He reminded her of Running Deer.

"Do you speak English?" she asked.

The fierce one edged his spotted pony closer. His black hair hung loose along each side of his heavily muscled chest. He was naked except for his leather leggings and breechclout. His dark eyes gleamed like a wild animal as he inspected her from the top of her tightly wound braids to the tips of her moccasins.

When his harsh gaze moved back to her face, she met it with her friendly one. She knew very little about these western tribes, but she had read enough in the few newspapers her father had received to know that many of them were being forced off their land onto reservations, just as her mother's people many years before. At first, she'd been startled by their sudden appearance, but she wasn't afraid. In truth, she was glad to see them and wished she could communicate with them.

"I'm sorry you can't understand me," she tried again. "I don't...

"We want food," the fierce one said.

"Oh, you do speak English." Excitement brought her words out in a rush. "I'm traveling with a cattle drive. Mister Barret, the owner, will surely be able to spare something for you. The herd should catch up with us soon and you can…"

"Cassie!"

She jumped nearly a foot and spun around as Cole galloped up and reined his horse to a halt right next to her. His large dog stopped too, fangs bared, but not making a sound.

"Are you all right?" Cole's eyes never left the Indians, but she could feel the intensity of his glare as if it were aimed at her.

"Aye. Everything is fine, Cole. These men need food. I was just telling them about the herd."

"Go back to the wagon, Cassie, I'll make sure they're taken care of. Ring, go with her." He signaled to the dog with a finger, and the large animal moved next to Cassie.

Cassie gave him a pleading look. "Cole, please…"

"Go!" The hard command offered no compromise. She scowled up at him then raised her hand in farewell to the Indians.

As she turned and walked away, oppressive grief rose up from the deepest part of her and settled around her like a shroud. Of course Cole had no way of knowing the instant feeling of kinship she'd had with the five men. How their sudden appearance had pleased her. No, he wouldn't know, and she couldn't let him know.

Her mixed blood had never been a problem tucked away on her family's small farm. Her father's obsessive need for her to look and act white had always been diluted by her mother's quiet, reassuring manner and Running Deer's strong influence. But she no longer lived in isolation. And this continued pretense made her feel as if she were slipping into a crack between two worlds.

Cole listened to Cassie's retreat, his heart still in his throat. He'd seen the Indians earlier and had been waiting for their approach. When he'd ridden ahead to check on the safety of the wagon and found Cassie gone, his fear had nearly knocked him out of the saddle. The moment he'd seen her, looking so small as she stood before the five braves, he'd wanted to yank her into his arms and hold her long enough to right his senses. Or shake her until she came to hers.

What in the devil had gotten into her, taking off alone like that and then standing there visiting with a renegade group of Cheyenne as nonchalantly as if she were at a Sunday social?

The five braves watched him, their dark eyes showing they were primed for anything. He recognized one of them. Long Arrow; he'd been a vicious foe to all whites ever since Colonel Chivington and his troops massacred a large band of Indians at Sand Creek, nine years before. The fanatic soldier hadn't stopped until they'd slaughtered over a hundred Cheyenne and Arapaho, mostly women and children. In a frenzy of revenge and grief, Long Arrow and others like him had wreaked vengeance on every eastern Colorado stage stop and ranch between Julesburg and Denver.

Now, like the Arapaho, Comanche and Kiowa of the area, the Cheyenne were in the process of being banded to reservations and not getting the food and clothing they needed to survive. Small groups like this still roamed the area stealing cattle and horses.

"Adams drive cattle now." Long Arrow spoke first.

Cole's tenseness eased slightly. "Only this once. Long Arrow remembers me."

"Long Arrow remembers white vigilantes cowards before Adams' guns."

Cole recalled the scene, too. A little more than two years before, he'd come upon six white men preparing to hang a severely beaten Indian. When he'd asked what was going on, the liquored-up group bragged about finding the 'redskin' after his horse had fallen and broken his neck. They intended to see that the 'Injun' died the same way.

Cole hadn't appreciated their reasoning or their treatment of the brave, so he made quick work of breaking up the lynching party, then took the injured man back to his people. "Your wounds healed well," he said, pointing to scars on the brave's neck and upper body.

Long Arrow slammed a fist against the muscled wall of his chest. "Outside wounds heal. Inside no heal."

Cole nodded in empathy, knowing he'd feel the same. He cautiously changed the subject back to food. "I can give you beef to ease the hunger in your people's bellies."

Long Arrow was silent for a tense stretch of time. Then he gestured in the direction Cassie had gone. "Woman wears clothing of man. Eyes like smoke hold no fear of my people."

Cole frowned, afraid of where this was headed. His words sounded stiff when he offered the same lame excuse Cassie had given him. "Yes... men's clothing make things easier for her. Come, I will give you beef."

The Indian refused to be put off. "I wish to trade for woman with fire in hair."

Cole's insides bunched into a tight knot. The Indians wanted and needed food; Cassie must have made quite an impression for Long Arrow to offer to trade for her. "She cannot be traded," he stated in a flat voice.

The Indian's dark eyes narrowed dangerously. There was another long silence. "Woman belongs to you?"

"Yes, she is mine!" Cole kept his tone even. "I will give you beef. No trade. A gift."

The brave turned slowly to the others. The old man made a slight motion with his hand. Long Arrow spoke rapidly back in his own language. The old man shook his head once and grunted something only Long Arrow understood. He faced Cole again and nodded curtly, acknowledging that Cassie would not be part of the deal.

The knot in Cole's gut eased somewhat, but the trickle of sweat running down the back of his neck did not. A battle with Indians such as these was something he preferred to dodge, but there was no way it could have been avoided if they'd insisted on taking Cassie.

As he led the five Indians toward the herd, the words he'd spoken to Long Arrow kept coming back to him. 'Yes, she is mine.' Without thought or hesitation, he'd claimed Cassie as his woman. His purpose was to discourage the brave's interest, but once the words were out, he realized he'd meant them. Which was loco. He needed to rid himself of thoughts like that. He'd be glad when his commitment to Austin was over. He needed to get back to Georgetown and get on with his life.

A short while after Cassie returned to the cook wagon, the cowhands rode in to eat. After they left, Cole and Austin arrived. Neither man offered any explanation about the Indians. They quickly ate their small meal, and the drive was once more on its way.

Cassie let Lady have her head and soon gained distance from the wagon and slow-moving herd. With each step, Cassie found it increasingly more difficult to bear the sorrow pressing in on her. She hated the idea of not seeing the Indians again. She couldn't stop thinking about the old man. In spite of his age, he'd sat his horse as ramrod straight as the four younger men. His obsidian eyes had held a wise, ancient look, so like Running Deer's.

Cassie wished she could have spoken to him, spent some time with him. Maybe it would have helped to ease the band of grief round her heart. As she gained some distance from the wagon and slow moving herd, the solitude made it impossible to hold her feelings inside any longer. Weeks of repressed pain welled up, catching in a massive clot in her throat. She swallowed repeatedly between gasps for air, fighting to keep the memories from surfacing, fighting the panic. But the tormenting sounds and images, smells and terror refused to stay buried any longer. And when they erupted, it was with such force that Cassie fell forward with a wail and buried her face in Lady's mane.

In vivid clarity, she lived it all again: Hearing her mother's screams. Running from the river to the house as fast as she could. Seeing Barnaby Noley's horse. Running up the porch steps and through the front door.

And then everything slipped into slow, ragged bursts of awareness as she tried to comprehend the scene in front of her... Noley bent over her mother's lifeless body, his large, bare buttocks glaring white in her vision.

She shrieked and lunged at him from behind. He grunted in surprise and fell to the side, half draped over her mother's body. She hurled toward him again, screaming and clawing at his face. But even in fury, her small frame was no match for the huge man. He shoved her, and she fell back against the iron stove, hitting her head with a loud crack.

Everything went black. When she came to, she felt herself being dragged across the floor. Her eyes opened to see Noley looming over her; his pants down, his stiff penis jutting out like a weapon. "Well, well. Isn't this nice. I like my women fighting and kicking. Your ma didn't put up much fuss at all. I only had to hit her once."

Cassie looked over at her mother. She willed her mind to clear, to think past her terror and the pain in her head. Her mother's dress had been torn off. She was sprawled naked. Blood seeped out of her nose and left ear and pooled on the floor beneath her head.

Before she could move, Noley straddled her, weighing her down with his bulk. "She's a gonner." He snickered. "Didn't mean to kill her. Wouldn't of had to if she'd cooperated." He reached out and ripped open the top of Cassie's dress. "Well now, lookie here. You got much more to grab onto."

Abruptly the pain and fear melded together into crystal clear rage. She growled and pounded at his chest and tried to role over. He laughed, grabbed both her hands in one of his and forced them over her head. Then he yanked up her skirt and shredded her under things. Cassie managed to pull a hand free and swung ineffectively at him. He hit the side of her face with the back of his fist and shoved a meaty thigh between her legs.

Cassie stilled.

"That's a good girl." Noley rutted against her, trying to find entrance, his large fingers probing painfully at her opening.

She reached for her knife and, with all the strength she had left, rammed the blade into his shoulder. He howled and leaned to the side. Cassie pulled out the knife and wildly slashed again and again while furiously kicking her legs. The razor-sharp blade punctured his shoulder once more, then his face. It sliced through his left eye and down his cheek. Her knee smashed into his groin, and he rolled off of her.

She crawled away from him and over to her mother. Her hand trembled so violently she had difficulty feeling for a pulse. She put her mouth close to her mother's, willing her to breathe. "No!" she screamed. "Momma, please. No!"

Noley's hand closed around her ankle. She jerked out of his grasp and staggered to her feet. He hauled himself upright, pulled up his pants and swung to face her. Blood poured from his eye and the gash on his face, saturating his shirt. He tore it off, ripped off a sleeve and tied it around the injured side of his face and head.

"I'll kill you for this, you half-breed bitch."

Cassie crouched, holding the knife out in front of her. When he lunged, she ducked to the side and he missed. She fell against the doorframe, then turned, threw herself out onto the porch and stumbled down the steps. Her lungs burned as she rushed toward the tree line surrounding the farm.

Noley followed her as far as the woods. "Run as hard as you want," he screamed. "You'll never escape me. Never."

She ran on through the dark forest, oblivious to the tree branches whipping her naked flesh. Ultimately, unable to go a step further, she collapsed into blessed unconsciousness.

The smell of smoke revived her. Fire! The house! She tried to get up, to go to her mother, but the pain in her head made it impossible to move. She touched the back of her scalp, her hair was sopping wet with blood. The next time the blackness enveloped her, the monster from her nightmares was waiting there, raising his head up out of the smoke and flames, screeching that she'd never escape him.

Now, oblivious to everything around her, Cassie clutched Lady's mane and wept. There was no more holding back. No more silent suffering. No one to hear her shrieking anger, her keening wails, as she gave vent to the agony she'd struggled so long to contain. Except for the horse, and Lady simply maintained her easy, unguided gait across the open plains.

CHAPTER FIVE

Cole turned Storm away from the wagon, enraged that Cassie had wandered off again. He'd gone there specifically to tell her how important it was to stay close to the others, only to have Brew say that she'd ridden on ahead.

What was with her? From the moment he'd met her, she'd seemed so reserved and fearful. Yet with the Indians, she'd been totally open, showing no fear. And now, she'd taken off again. Somebody needed to explain what it was like out here. Zeb and Dalton had taken a risk traveling in this country without an escort. You'd think they would have considered that before dragging a woman out here. They'd been damned lucky so far, and he intended to tell Cassie just that.

As he topped a scant rise, he saw her, stretched out across the front of the saddle, her horse clipping slowly along. He urged the buckskin into a gallop that matched his heartbeat but refused to think of what might have happened to her. He could see her back and shoulders shaking before he reined in. She must have heard him, because she suddenly jerked upright and wiped her face with both hands.

"Cassie, I need to talk to you." Damn! He hadn't meant to sound so stern. Her blotchy cheeks and red nose made her look like the thirteen-year-old he'd first thought her to be. He softened his voice and started over, annoyed that he'd let the uncomfortable situation get to him. "Is something wrong? Is there anything I can do to help?"

Cassie looked away, as if embarrassed by his concern. She sniffed, wiped her eyes again and took a deep breath. "No."

"I didn't mean to startle you. When I saw you leaning over the horse's neck, I thought maybe you were hurt or something."

Fresh tears sprang into her eyes. It unnerved Cole to watch her struggle to keep them from falling.

"I… I'm all right. What did you want to say to me?" She stared unwaveringly at him. Dark clouds eclipsed the silver in her eyes.

He could see she was far from all right, but it was obvious she wasn't going to offer an explanation. "It's about the Indians. I wanted to warn you to stay close to the wagon. I don't want you wandering off by yourself like this."

"The Indians meant me no harm," Cassie said, her gaze continuing to meet his. "I felt no threat from them."

"Yes, I know. But there could have been trouble."

"There wasn't."

"Damn it, Cassie, that's not the point." Cole shoved his hat off his forehead and took a long, steadying breath. Was she purposely trying to rile him?

"What is the point?" she prodded.

"The point is it's too dangerous for a woman like you to be out here alone."

"Aye? And what kind of woman am I?"

Hang it all! Her emotions shifted like quicksilver. He could almost see mischief dancing in those incredible eyes now. "I didn't mean it like that. I meant any woman… No woman should be roaming around out here alone."

"I didn't go far. And I repeat, the Indians meant me no harm. They were just hungry. Did Mister Barret give them a cow?"

Cole clenched his jaw before speaking. "Actually, he gave them half-a-dozen." He managed to keep his tone as light as hers when he added, "Mostly because what they really wanted was you."

"What?" Her eyes widened and her dark brows shot skyward. "What do you mean, 'wanted' me?"

He couldn't resist a satisfied smile. "I'm glad to see I'm finally getting through to you. I meant just what I said. After your little chat with Long Arrow, he decided his hunger was of a different sort. He would just take you instead. Offered to trade for you, as a matter of fact. Although he never got around to saying what he had to trade."

"Long Arrow? You know him?"

"Yes."

"What did he want me for?"

Cole couldn't believe this conversation. She had to be at least nineteen or twenty, how could she be that naive? "Just what do you think he wanted you for?"

Comprehension struck and her face flushed. "Oh," seemed to be all she could manage.

Cole struggled not to laugh. She really was inexperienced. Who was this woman and where had she come from? "You may think those over-sized duds protect you from harm, Cassie. But you need to be more careful."

"I don't wear these clothes for that kind of protection," she said defensively, coloring now with anger.

"Is that right? What kind of protection do you wear them for?"

She opened her mouth to speak, shut it again then finally muttered, "I told you, it makes things easier."

Cole decided not to push it. "Yes, you did say that. Well, even though you feel safe enough, I'd appreciate it if you'd stay close to the wagon while you're traveling with us. It'll make my job easier if I don't have to keep running after you."

"I'll stay close," she promised. "I don't want to add to your burdens."

Now Cole couldn't tell if she was teasing or not. Everything about her baffled him, which in itself irritated the hell out of him. "See that you do," he snapped and flipped the reins, spinning his horse to canter off. A moment later, he stopped, unable to resist looking back to make sure she was following.

Sunset spread over the distant mountains in expanding shades of gold, pink, red, and violet as the cowhands made their way to the chuck wagon that evening. Clouds began to assemble, capturing the brilliant hue in their billowing masses.

Cassie sat on the bank of a sandy river vibrant with reflected color. The scene reminded her of her father. Michael O'Brian had been a wonderful artist. At times like this, he would marvel at the combination of colors on nature's palette. How wonderful it would be to share this moment with him and with her mother and great-grandmother. Everything in this part of the country was so different, so untamed. Her family would love it. But then, she wouldn't be on this journey if her family were still with her. She would be at home on the porch, carving figurines while her father painted and her mother wove baskets, the three of them listening to one of Running Deer's stories.

Sorrow welled up again and filled her eyes. She brushed at the tears with the back of her hand, grateful the grief felt more manageable. Her outburst this afternoon had been medicinal. And the banter with Cole afterward brought even more relief. Somehow being able to get a rise out of the usually unflappable Mister Adams was just what she'd needed to snap her back from her painful memories.

Loud voices suddenly caught Cassie's attention. Austin's three cowhands sat with Zeb, eating their supper near the fire and provoking each other with verbal jabs. Occasionally they aimed a comment at Brew who was fussing at them to eat more and talk less. Tonight Brew had prepared 'Son-of-a-gun stew.' Apparently he was still attempting to watch his language around her because she heard the men call it, 'Son-of-a-bitch' stew. 'Two bites is all it takes to clear a person's sinuses and set fire to their throats,' Buck had said. She had agreed after only one bite.

Buck out-shouted the others as he tried to get her attention. "Nobody can ride better'n me," the lanky, cowhand bragged. "I set a record once for the most cows ever cut out of a herd and branded in a single day. Nine hundred!"

He waited for the adulation. None came.

"That ain't nothing," Dan said, pausing to run his tongue across the seam of the cigarette he'd just rolled. His thumb followed his tongue. Then he put the cigarette in his mouth and lit it, dragging on it deeply. "I can roll and light a cigarette just that smooth at the same time I'm busting a string of mustangs."

Cassie grinned and shook her head. The others howled with laughter.

"It's the truth, I tell you," Dan argued, defending his ridiculous tale with a serious face. "When the horse realizes his bucking ain't doing no good, he settles right down."

Charley waited until his comrades quieted, then puffed himself up. "Oh yeah? Well breaking mustangs is so easy for me, that I can shave my whiskers at the same time."

Raucous objections from the others didn't put him off. "It's easy. I hold a mirror in one hand, a straight razor in the other. My mug of hot water and bay rum hangs in a basket off my arm."

"Whooee, would I like a demonstration of that," Buck roared, slapping his knee.

"Me too," echoed Dan. "Especially since you only have one whisker. You show us how you do that tomorrow, Charley Boy. I can't wait to see you holding a razor against that scrawny neck of yours while a bronco has his way with you."

"Why, I would, fellas," Charley drawled. "Exceptin' we ain't got no wild mustangs, and the boss wouldn't want me taking time away from the herd."

"You boys are mighty feisty," Austin said as he and Dalton walked into camp. "Why don't a couple of you take all that get-up-and-go and use it on first watch."

Buck and Dan promptly got to their feet. They grinned and tipped their hats to Cassie as they sauntered out of camp.

Dalton walked over to sit beside her. "Good evening, Miss Cassandra. How are you feeling this fine night?"

She smiled at his use of her full name, most likely he did it to stake his own claim on her. Occasionally his possessiveness worried her. Mostly it gave her a sense of belonging to someone, something she needed badly.

"I'm much better, thank you. This makes two days in a row without a headache. That potion Brewster gave me must've contained magic."

Dalton's eyes moved over her face and hair. She had undone her braids this evening and let her hair fall loose. He reached out a tentative hand and fingered a lock. "Your hair is so thick, no one could ever tell Paps had to shave some of it off to stitch up the back of your head. How does your wound feel?"

"It's healing fine. There's only a slight discomfort now." Cassie experienced another stab of concern. If Noley ever found her, Dalton's growing affection for her could put his own life at stake. She straightened her shoulders and scooted an imperceptible distance away from him.

"You had a bad injury, Cassie. It's a miracle you weren't killed. I'd like to get my hands on that animal, I'd--"

Cassie touched a finger to his lips to stop him. When he blushed, she realized her mistake and folded her hands tightly in her lap. "You've done enough, Dalton. There is no doubt in my mind you saved my life. If you and Zeb hadn't come along... I don't know how I'll ever repay you."

"You don't owe us anything, Cassie."

"But the horse and extra tack, I have to find a way to reimburse you for Lady."

"Lady was a gift. I already told you that. Besides, I have plenty of money. My grandmother was very fond of her grandchildren. I inherit a generous sum on my twenty-first birthday in December."

"I thought.., that is..."

"You thought that since Paps wants so badly to find that lost gold, we must need the money," he finished for her.

"Aye. That isn't true?"

Dalton took off his hat and propped it on his outstretched legs, then rested back on his elbows. "Well, Paps hasn't got the kind of money my father's family has, but he has plenty. I believe it's the adventure that drove him. Mom worried about his heart, but she was afraid that his fretting about not going would be even harder on him. She decided he'd never get it out of his system if he didn't go."

"What about you, Dalton? You must have had plenty of things to keep you busy in Raleigh. Why did you come with him?"

"I thought it would be fun. I'd read books about the west and wanted to see it for myself. I had finished with two years of college and decided to put the rest off for a while. My mother encouraged me. She didn't want Paps traveling alone. When we go back, I'll finish my education. Probably go into law like my father."

Being an only child, Cassie always enjoyed Dalton's gossip about his large family. He was the baby and loved to gain her sympathy by telling her stories of the unending teasing he had endured from his oldest sibling, a brother he called Cat. Yet he readily admitted to being "spoiled rotten" by his five sisters.

Whenever he spoke of his family, his affection for them was evident in his brown eyes. He was a deeply feeling young man, and that compassion would undoubtedly mature with him and serve him well in his chosen profession. "You will make a fine lawyer, Dalton."

Cole squatted on his heels near the chuck wagon; oblivious to the biscuit he was chewing on. From the moment he'd entered camp and noticed Dalton and Cassie sitting so close together, jealousy had seized him like a vice, making it difficult to swallow. When Dalton touched Cassie's hair, Cole wanted to choke.

You're acting plum loco! He chided himself and turned to lean a shoulder against the spoke of the wheel. He watched a spider trail a tiny line in the soft ground as it rushed beneath the wagon. Dalton's laughter drew his attention back just as a gust of wind caught the ends of Cassie's hair and tossed it around her head. The waning sunlight turned the beautiful mass a burnished copper and lit her cheeks with a rosy glow. Her eyes were clear. She looked more relaxed than he'd ever seen her. The top three buttons of her baggy shirt were unfastened and part of her necklace was visible against her skin. He remembered how soft that skin looked bathed in moonlight. Her round breasts had stood out proudly, and her waist seemed so small he could have spanned it with his fingers.

A tight warning in his loins warned Cole to control his unruly thoughts. He shifted his position and swallowed a mouthful of stew. There was no point in denying it. The longer he was around Cassie the harder it was to keep his mind and his hands off of her. Her quick-changing emotions captivated him. And the pain in those large eyes made him want to hold her close until he could absorb it out of her.

Damn! He didn't want to feel anything for her at all. He stood, set his empty plate on the wagon tongue and started to return to the herd. At the last moment, he reversed his steps and stopped a foot short of stepping on Dalton. "Grab some grub, Dalton, so Brew can clean up."

Cassie flinched at his rudeness. After Dalton stomped away, she gazed up at him with a reprimanding look on her beautiful face. "You certainly have a bee in your bonnet. Did Dalton displease you today?"

"Not at all. In fact he's doing a good job. Why do you ask?"

She gave him an indulgent smile, shrugged her shoulders and shook her head. "Why don't you sit down, looking up at you from down here, hurts my neck."

"Are you suggesting I'm a pain-in-the-neck?" he returned, not at all comfortable with the easy way she could get a response out of him. Her smile made his insides feel as warm as the fire on his back.

"No, but now that you mention it..." Her words ended meaningfully, and he dropped to the ground beside her, crossing one leg over the other.

"You look like you feel better tonight."

"I am better."

"No headache? Zeb said something about you having headaches."

"No, really, I am very well." She quickly changed the subject. "Where's your dog? He's usually right by your side."

"He's out nosing around somewhere. Ring likes to find his own meals. He'll show up in a while." Cole's attention dropped to the opening of her shirt. "That's a beautiful necklace. I noticed it the other day."

Cassie's hand closed protectively over the stones. The haunted expression returned to her face. Her eyes suddenly looked as old as the hills. "It's all I have left of…"

"What is it Cassie?" he urged, when she didn't continue. "What do you mean, all you have left?"

"Please, Cole...I..."

"Cassie, what's going on? What are you afraid of? Why are you traveling out here dressed like this?"

He watched the array of emotions play across her face and struggled for something to say, something that would bring back her smile. He ached to touch her, to find words that would give her comfort. But comfort for what? He didn't even know what was wrong with her. Damn! She made it difficult to even think straight. "Tell me about the necklace. It really is beautiful. It must mean a lot to you."

For another long minute she stared over his shoulder at the fire, seemingly at war with herself. Then, in a near whisper, she finally said, "Aye, it is very special to me. It was a gift from someone very special."

Cole waited for her to continue, but she didn't offer anything else. "It looks like Indian craftsmanship," he prompted. The clouds in her eyes became murkier.

"Cassandra?" Dalton called, walking up with Charley to stand over them. "Austin just told me about your confrontation with those Indians today."

Cole tightened his jaw to keep from reacting to the ill-timed interruption.

"I don't recall using the word confrontation," Austin said, coming up behind the two younger men.

Dalton brushed the comment off with a shrug and went on, his voice elevated in alarm. "Cassie, listen to me. Buck says these Indians are bloodthirsty, heathen savages. You could have been killed today."

"They aren't bloodthirsty," Brew argued, aggressively pushing his way into the center of the group. He tilted his head back and pierced Dalton with a menacing stare. "Any hostility on their part is only a reaction to the way they've been treated."

"Back off, Brew," Austin warned, clapping the smaller man on the shoulder. "There's no point in anyone getting into an uproar about this. You both have a point. Many of the tribes are friendly, Dalton, especially the Ute's. The Cheyenne can be troublesome though, so it pays to be careful."

"I don't know, boss," Charley quipped. "Careful or not, if those red skins had wanted, they could have whisked Cassie away before any of us even knew it. Injuns are mean sons-a-bitches, more animal than human. Why, I heard tell of a family over near the Kansas border that…"

"You look tired, Charley," Brew snarled, pointedly nodding toward Cassie. "You should go get some shut-eye."

Oblivious to the hint, Charlie straightened his narrow shoulders and barked, "I ain't that tired."

Dalton bristled at all of them. "Look, I didn't mean to cause a fuss. I'm just concerned about Cassie."

"Everyone calm down." Austin held up a hand. "We all care about Cassie, but there's no point in scaring her. I'm sure she'll be more careful in the future."

Cole's attention hadn't left Cassie's face. When Dalton first walked up with his statement about the Indians, all the color had drained out of it. With each comment from the others, she seemed to shrink further away from them. Was she finally realizing the danger she'd been in today? Somehow he didn't think that was it. But whatever was wrong, he needed to do something. She looked ready to bolt.

"It's time for everyone to turn in," he announced. He rose and offered Cassie a hand up.

She cringed away from him. Dalton stepped forward to help, but she refused his help too. Instead, she quickly got to her feet and hurried into the shadows edging the camp. Several minutes passed before she returned and unrolled her blankets far away from everyone else.

Cole watched her stiff movements from his own bedroll, still smarting over her rejection. Then he remembered how upset she'd been earlier in the day, and his turmoil turned to concern. Which was even more agitating than his hurt pride.

No woman had ever rocked him this way. Not even Ramona.

The feelings Cassie roused in him were far more complex. Her dramatic beauty generated a strong physical response in him, as it probably would any man who got a good look at her. But there was also an innocent fragility about her, as if the slightest touch would leave her shattered. It made him want to keep her close and protect her at all times.

Cole shot upright. What kind of craziness had gotten hold of him lately? He'd never in his life been attracted to frail women. He pulled on his boots, buckled his gun belts around his hips, slammed on his hat, and headed for the horses. The sooner she and her two companions were on their way the better.

CHAPTER SIX

C assie struggled to escape, but her legs moved in slow motion. She chanced a glance over her shoulder and saw Noley's face looming over her. She tried to run faster, but it was too late, he was right behind her.

"I told you you'd never escape me, you half-breed bitch," he yelled in her ear as he yanked her backwards against his flabby flesh. "You'll pay for cutting me."

She tried to wrench free, but her exhaustion and throbbing head made it impossible. He raised a meaty fist to strike. All at once she was rising away from him, up into the dark sky, the stars glittering so close she could touch them. A sound like the wind roared in her ears as she rose higher. She turned into the wind and found herself face-to-face with an enormous white buffalo. Somehow she knew the great beast wanted her to mount. When she did, he carried her even higher into the heavens.

An icy wind brought tears to her eyes and tugged her hair out behind her as they soared. She had no idea where the buffalo was taking her, but she didn't care. Her head no longer hurt, and she felt light and safe and free, and soon lost all concept of time.

When they finally landed, it was beside a deep lake nestled between steep hills of pine, aspen and giant, snow-capped peaks. Cassie slid to the ground and knelt at the water's edge. Cupping her hands, she scooped a handful of clear water into her mouth. It was cold and sweet and made her breath catch when it sloshed down her chin and onto her shirt. The sun was extremely warm, but a cool breeze caressed her neck and arms. She reclined against a large rock and let the beauty and serenity of this mystical place seep into her weary soul. But too soon, the buffalo wanted to leave.

This time when she mounted, she couldn't hang on. Something evil reached through the sacred experience and dragged her off and into a dark hole. She fell faster and faster. Then a monster leaped out of the darkness, spewing fire and smoke.

The screams in her mind pulled her out of the nightmare. Her eyes flew open. The dying glow from the campfire cast a soft light through the camp, illuminating the forms of the sleeping men. Her heart banged against her rib cage so loud she was amazed no one could hear it. You're safe, she told herself, clutching her necklace. It was only a nightmare. You're safe.

A gray dawn struggled to break through the darkness the next time she opened her eyes. Feeling a warm breath on her face, she turned to see Ring's wet nose only inches from her own. "Nashoba Lusa," she whispered in her mother's language. "Black Wolf, how serious you look this morning." She stroked his head, and he inched closer. His yellow-gray eyes closed in pleasure.

The aroma of coffee wafted over the camp and urged those still asleep to wake. But Cassie couldn't bring herself to get up. She stayed curled on her side, petting Ring, waiting for the last images of the nightmare to fade. The dream was not so different from those in her past, except that the monster now had a face. Noley's face.

Flipping onto her back, she stared up at the heavy dark clouds pressing close to the earth. The bad dream wasn't the only thing on her mind. For the first time since her mother's death, she felt a spark of hope, a motivation other than fear.

What caused it? The spirit buffalo in the dream? The men's heated discussion about the Indians last night? The tears she'd shed yesterday? She wasn't sure, but this morning she felt different. Her family was gone. Nothing would bring them back. But she couldn't continue to be paralyzed by her grief and fear, or blinded by her inexperience. She couldn't continue letting other people take care of her. She would be cautious, yes, but, at the same time, she would open her eyes and learn everything she could about this new country. Learn how to take care of herself. Learn to make her own way in the world. Keep herself safe

But how?

How did a woman alone in this wild, untamed land care for herself? She would need clothes, food and shelter. She would need money. How would she get money? She'd have to go to work. Doing what? She had no skills, no experience. Her father had taught her how to carve life-like figures out of wood, but that was a hobby, something she did for her own pleasure. She couldn't support herself carving wood.

Maybe she could find gold. Dalton said gold and silver was being found all through the mountains. How did one go about finding gold? And how would she support herself in the meantime? Maybe her father was wrong in insisting she live in the white world. Maybe she would be better off with the Indians. She would have shelter, food. But would she? The Indians survival seemed as precarious as her own. And how would she fit in with their way of life? Except for stories of her Choctaw heritage, a few skills she had learned from her mother and great-grandmother and her knowledge of healing plants and herbs, she had been raised white. What did that make her? She wasn't really white. She also wasn't Indian. She didn't really fit into either world.

She thought about the fierce brave she'd met the day before. Long Arrow. She wasn't sure how she felt about him wanting to trade for her. Apparently he wanted her for a mate. She understood what went on between a man and a woman. Growing up on a small farm, her education about such matters was open and natural. Plus, a person couldn't have lived in the same home with her mother and father and not been aware of the tremendous love they had for each other, or their physical expression of that love.

She also understood what it was that Noley had meant to do to her. And the knowing made it worse. Her insides turned to ice when memories of his attack crept into her mind. Nothing in her life had prepared her for the violence, the violation she felt at his assault. Had she not used her knife… She couldn't bear to think about what would have followed.

Maybe she could marry. She knew how to cook, clean, sew, hunt, prepare hides, and do numerous other things required of a wife. As a child, she used to imagine growing up and marrying someone just like her father. But her mother said that Michael was one-of-a-kind. Would she be able to find a man that could accept her Indian blood?

An image of a tall, gun-toting, blue-eyed rogue pushed all other thoughts aside. What would Cole Adams think if he knew she was half Indian? Would he care? Would he still look at her in that way that turned her insides to mush?

"Foolish, childish thoughts," she said under her breath. "Grow up Cassandra Cathleen. You're in the real world now."

Breakfast was ready by the time Cassie joined Brew at the wagon. "Top o' the mornin', Brew," she greeted and accepted the steaming cup of coffee he handed her.

A gleaming smile replaced the sour-faced scowl he liked to wear. "How you feeling, missy? You look fit as a fiddle today."

"I feel very well, thank you. Are you sure you won't be telling me what you put in that magic potion you gave me?"

He chuckled. "Just a few things to put those roses back in your cheeks and get your blood to flowing a little faster. It makes this old man happy to see you feeling better. Now you drink your coffee real quick like, and have yourself something to eat. Looks like we got us a storm brewing."

Morning chores were done away with quickly as angry clouds rolled over-head, agitating man and beast alike. Shrill "yips" and "yahoos" whipped the protesting cattle into action and the drive got underway.

Cassie mounted Lady and followed the cook wagon onto the trail. Cole's dog trotted close by. The animal hadn't been more than three feet from her side since she'd gotten up. "What's going on, Ring? Why aren't you with your master?"

"He's apparently been given new orders for the day," Brewster answered from the wagon seat. "Cole sent him to you last night. You were making a bit of a fuss in your sleep."

His face turned pink as if telling her embarrassed him. She felt the warming of her own face, mortified at what she might have said or done in the throes of the haunting dream.

"Guess Cole thinks you need to be guarded," Zeb said. He looked stronger today and sat on the wooden seat next to Brew. "Probably because of that incident with the Indians. It's a good thing they were only hungry. Those savages could have killed you, or worse. I'll be happy when they're all on reservations where they belong."

Brew stiffened and swung his head toward Zeb. "Where they belong is roaming free over their own land. The government takes it all away, bunches 'em on little plots of ground, and expects 'em to adjust. It ain't natural. I got friends in some of these tribes. They're used to having freedom. Tradition has taught 'em that remaining in one place means death. They leave the reservations to find food because they're being starved. Fat lot of good it does though, with the 'great-white' hunters slaughtering all their game."

Zeb wasn't swayed by Brew's speech. His return was just as heated. "My brother and his group weren't out to hurt anybody, take anybody's land or food. They were just passing through the mountains on their way home from California. George was the only one to escape. He only lived six weeks after he got home. I think his death was caused as much from his mental agony over seeing and hearing the torture of his friends as it was his own physical wounds."

He pulled a handkerchief out of his back pocket, blew his nose, briskly wiped its bulbous end and stuffed it back away. "Besides, Cassie has no business roaming off by herself. Any kind of harm could fall her way."

"I'm sorry about your brother," Brewster responded, his surly tone replaced with sympathy. "It's tough to lose someone that way." He glanced at Cassie. "What I said about the Indians is true, Missy. But Zeb is right. Some of the Indians are retaliating. And there are other dangers as well. Most times a woman is safe in the west. But there's an exception to everything. It'd be best if you stayed close." He pointed to the dog. "Ole Ring there, he'll watch over you. Good idea Cole had."

Cassie refused to be frightened by their warnings. She had enough to worry about. But she did silently renew her vow to keep her Indian blood a secret. Apparently the mere mention of Indians could set off fervent reactions in everyone. Especially Zeb. She was just coming to realize the depth of his pain and resentment. It touched her own pain and gave her an odd sense of guilt. As if being half-Indian made her somewhat responsible for what happened to his brother.

The confusing thoughts were too much to handle on top of her other raw emotions, so she pushed the unwelcome feelings away and let her attention follow Brew's to the dog.

Ring was enormous. Standing next to him, his head came almost to her waist. If he stood on his hind legs, he would probably be taller than she was. "I wonder how Cole came to have such an animal," she wondered aloud.

"I'll tell you how," Brew said, shifting the leather reins to one hand and scratching his whiskers with the other. "I was with Cole the day he got that pup. We were out scouting some possible ranch land for Austin and had just ridden into this little mining community named Empire when we heard this god-awful commotion at the far end of the street. There was this big hog of a man using a litter of puppies for target practice. Six of `em was already dead. That one there," he pointed to Ring, "was laying in a pool of blood, nearly so. The bitch was tied to a tree, howling up a storm."

Cassie gasped, sickened by the grisly scene Brew had described. "Why would anyone do such a thing?"

"Didn't want 'em, I guess. He was having a good ole time showing off for the crowd. Some onlookers were shouting protests, but some of `em cheered him on. Anyhow, he started to finish off the remaining pup when Cole palmed one of his pistols and clicked back the hammer. You'll be dead before the dog, Cole told him. His voice was as quiet as death, but I don't think there was a soul on that street that didn't hear him."

Brew slapped his knee and hooted, obviously enjoying this part of his story. "Why, I'm telling you, that ole fart pissed all over his self." He suddenly caught himself, and his face turned scarlet. His brown eyes were as round as saucers when he looked over at Cassie. "Pardon me, missy, I forgot myself there for a minute."

Cassie acknowledged his apology with a curt nod. "What happened then?"

"Well, that bastar...ah, that no good varmint had the good sense to holster his piece. But Cole was too upset to let it go and lit into him with his fists. Could've killed him, he was that mad. But he didn't." Brew gestured toward Ring. "That pup was more dead than alive when Cole took him home. But he hung on. He's been Cole's sidekick for nigh onto two years now. Never leaves his side unless Cole orders him to."

Cassie could well imagine Cole's fury over the senseless killing of the puppies. She looked back down at Ring, thinking of the intelligence she'd seen in his yellow eyes, the love and loyalty she'd seen him display toward his master. "He looks like a wolf," she said.

"Yep, he does. Could have some wolf in him. Wouldn't know about that. He looks menacing though, don't he? I'd sure hate to tangle with him."

Before Cassie could respond, an earsplitting peal of thunder sent Lady into fits of minor bucking. Cassie managed to stay in the saddle as she worked to calm the excited horse. A few minutes later, another thunderous crash reverberated across the heavens, and the sky opened with a cannonade of pounding hailstones.

Pandemonium reigned. Ring barked and yelped and ran around in circles. Lady whinnied and reared, nearly unseating Cassie again. The team of horses that pulled the chuck wagon bucked and kicked, knocking Zeb the rest of the way into the back of the wagon where he'd been climbing to escape the stinging pellets.

Brew jumped down and grabbed the harness of the two horses. He nodded toward a stand of trees several yards away. "Ride for those trees," he yelled at Cassie and jerked the spooked team toward it.

When they reached the shelter of the trees, Brew ordered Zeb and Cassie to climb under the wagon. He unhitched the team and tied them next to Lady before joining them.

Cassie lay scrunched between the two men and wet dog and watched the hailstones grow to the size of quail's eggs. The sound was deafening. It didn't take much to imagine what the cowhands were going through.

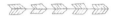

The first crack of thunder spooked the nervous herd into a frenzied stampede. Battered by egg-sized balls of ice, the men rode frantically to keep up. The lead steers veered south, and the rest followed, the drumming of their hooves adding to the clamor of the storm.

After a brief chase, Cole and Austin spurred their mounts to the front of the lead steers and reined in, slowing them to a less-frantic pace. Buck and Dan raced to the side of the point, shouting and flailing their arms, pressing the cattle into a tighter turn. Charley joined them, firing his gun. Dalton followed close behind, clinging to the saddle horn.

The cattle began to circle and mill around them, jamming together, rotating in confusion. "Watch yourself," Cole shouted to Dalton, trying to be heard above the din. "This would be a bad time to get knocked off your horse."

They were soaked to the skin. The hail continued to pound them, but there was nothing they could do but sit on their mounts and endure it. Keeping the herd bunched was the most important thing.

The onslaught ended as suddenly as it began. A light drizzle followed for a few minutes, then the clouds parted. The July sun was hot once again, a crunchy carpet of ice the only evidence remaining of the abrupt, rambunctious storm.

Cole and Austin made a quick assessment of the damage. No one was hurt other than a mass of painful welts from the hailstones. The horses were scattered, but they didn't lose any cattle. Austin sent Charley to gather up the horses, and Cole rode ahead to see how the others had weathered the storm.

Cassie, Zeb and Brew stood together, drinking steaming cups of coffee. Ring sat on the ground at Cassie's feet. Cole shook his head and grinned. "My, my, isn't this a cozy bunch. Looks like you all made it through the storm in one piece."

"Can't say the same about you," Brew answered, taking in Cole's sopping-wet clothes and sagging hat. "Get down off that horse and let me have a look at you."

Cole eased out of the saddle and tied his horse with the others, then stripped off his shirt and walked over to sit on the wagon tongue. Brew scrutinized his upper torso and shook his head. "Yep, just like I thought. We're going to have some mighty stiff and sore boys moaning around camp tonight. It's likely to take a whole bottle of liniment to stop all the whining. I'll get you a cup of coffee."

When Brew walked to the rear of the wagon, Cassie moved closer and inspected Cole's shoulders and arms in the same no-nonsense way she'd treated Zeb's gunshot wound. "You should have worn your buckskins today. Your cotton shirt and britches didn't offer much protection." She reached up and removed his wet hat. "At least your hat minimized the injury to your head."

Cole rubbed a hand over the back of his neck, way more conscious of her closeness than his soreness. "That's not how it feels."

"I have something that will help," she said, her eyes filled with commiseration. Cole thought someone should warn her not to look at a man that way. Those big, sultry, silver eyes could spark molten fire in a man. He had an intense urge to see them clouded in passion.

"Here's some coffee," Brew said. "It's strong and hot."

The interruption was like a dousing of cold water. Cole felt like a kid caught with his hand in the candy jar.

"I'll make up some salve," Cassie offered and walked away.

"What's little missy doing?"

"She's going to make something up for the welts," Cole snapped.

"You don't say." They both watched Cassie take something out of a leather bag. "How do you suppose she came to have such doctoring knowledge?"

"Who knows? There are a lot of unanswered questions where she's concerned."

Brew grinned. "That little gal has become quite a bur under your saddle. How sore you going to get before you do something about it?"

Cole gave the older man a censoring look then stood and headed for his horse. He grabbed a clean shirt out of his saddlebags and slipped it on. "I'm going back to the herd." He hoisted his aching frame into the saddle. "The others will be in soon. She can doctor them."

Later that night, Cassie lay wide-awake, gazing into an endless star-lit sky and listening to a symphony of insects. When Cole returned to camp, she watched him soundlessly make his way around the low-burning fire and sleeping forms scattered here and there. He lacked some of his normal grace and agility, so Cassie knew he must be in pain. The other men's bruising had been deep and ugly. The only reason they slept so soundly was because of the numbing quality of her herbs.

She propped her head on her hand and watched him spread his bedroll a good distance from the others. With stiff, jerky motions he unbuckled his gun belts, lowered himself to the ground and positioned the guns within easy reach. His knife came off next, then his boots. His hat was last. He laid it on its crown, beside the guns and knife. Finally, haltingly, he stretched out on his blankets.

Ring scooted closer to Cassie and she stroked his thick fur. "What do you think, boy? Should we take your master some salve? It might help him sleep better." The dog's ears pricked up. His tail brushed back and forth in the dirt.

"Okay, come on."

Cole snapped upright when Cassie and Ring approached, his left hand poised ominously over one of the guns.

"Don't shoot," she whispered and grinned as his hand eased to his lap. "I thought maybe you'd like some salve for those bruises."

Ring curled up on the ground near Cole's feet. Cole sat stock-still and stared at Cassie as she quietly continued, "The salve seemed to help the others. If you take off your shirt, I'll put some on your shoulders." Cassie knew she sounded rushed and nervous, but his continued silence made her feel awkward and self-conscious.

After a long pause, he reached up and untied the bandana from around his neck. Then he tugged his shirttail free from his pants and slipped it off over his head.

The nasty welts and bruises contrasted vividly against his skin. As did the dark mat of hair that covered his muscled chest and flat abdomen. Uncomfortable with the sensations the sight caused, Cassie pulled her attention back to his face and kneeled down in front of him. "This may hurt a little at first, but you should feel some relief soon. The herbs have a soothing affect. I treated the others this afternoon and they were already better by evening."

She bit her bottom lip to stop the nervous rambling and dipped her fingers into the balm then spread it across one of his shoulders. Her hand started to shake. Oh, bother! She thought. What was the matter with her? She hadn't had such a difficult time taking care of the other men. Biting harder on her lip, she focused on her task.

His skin was warm, as if just touched by the sun. She gently massaged the balm down his arm, feeling the solid cord of muscles underneath. Her eyes followed her hand as it moved back up to the wide expanse of his chest.

She tenderly treated each swollen, dark contusion she could see through the mat of hair.

All the while Cole sat without moving, seemingly without breathing. And Cassie found it increasingly more difficult to breathe herself. The air between them fairly crackled with tension. She was beginning to doubt the wisdom of this decision.

All of a sudden, Cole reached out and touched her face. She nearly dropped the salve. "Don't pull away," he commanded in a soft voice, stroking her cheek with the back of his fingers.

Cassie sat rigidly on her knees while he turned his hand over and slowly outlined her lips with his fingertips. Then he slid both hands into the hair at her temples. "Don't be afraid," he whispered, when she began to tremble.

Run, her mind warned. But she couldn't move. Some unfamiliar part of her wanted his touch, ached for it. Without knowing how, she found herself sitting next to him, her hip pressed tightly against his.

He held her face between his hands and looked deep into her eyes. She felt that uneasy drowning sensation. "Cole..."

"Shhh..." His gaze dropped to her parted lips.

Her body tensed at the first contact of a man's lips. The touch was light, like the slightest brushing of a butterfly wing. Slowly the kiss deepened, and her eyes closed as never-before sensations erupted throughout her body.

Cole's mouth began to move more urgently against hers. The feeling excited and frightened her at the same time. But she couldn't let go of it, or the man who gave it to her. The kiss seemed to satisfy a deep hunger she didn't even know she possessed.

After what seemed like an eternity, Cole withdrew a scant distance and drew in a ragged breath. He hesitated a moment, as if struggling with some inner demon. Then he groaned and captured her mouth again.

Cassie leaned into him and slid her hands up his arms to the back of his neck. Cole groaned again and pulled her down on the blanket next to him, deepening the kiss even more. Wave after wave of sensual bliss bombarded her fragile emotions as she savored his taste, his touch, and the feel of him.

Cole dragged his mouth from hers and began a nuzzling descent down her chin to the exposed skin of her throat and neck. As he shifted to lie more heavily against her, an alarm rang in Cassie's mind. She stiffened, and a whimper of fear escaped her lips. Hearing it, Cole froze. He mumbled something that sounded like a muffled curse and rolled onto his back.

A rush of cool air replaced his warmth, leaving Cassie chilled and feeling acutely abandoned. Her heart beat erratically as she tried to make sense of the past few minutes. What was she doing? How had she let this happen? She'd never even kissed a man before and here she was thinking of letting a man she barely knew do even more than kiss her. After her breathing quieted, she sat up. Cole lay unmoving next to her, his arm thrown over his eyes. What must he be thinking of her, behaving so wantonly one minute then freezing the next?

Hot tears threatened to fall. Her hands shook as she straightened her clothes. She got to her feet, thinking she might die from the awful embarrassment. You won't die! She silently scolded herself. You've been through worse than this.

Cole sat up and looked at her, his expression unreadable. "Cassie, I--"

"Please don't say anything." Summoning every bit of strength and dignity she could, she bent to pick up the piece of rawhide containing the mixture of herbs and handed it to him. "Here, apply the rest of this to your arms and legs. You'll be less stiff and sore in the morning."

CHAPTER SEVEN

Denver City began to emerge in the distance, tucked against the mountains like a child to its mother's breast. Cassie sat on the wagon seat between Brew and Zeb, quivering with excitement when the mirage she'd first seen finally solidified into an outline of buildings. She couldn't imagine the delights waiting in such a place.

Cairo, Illinois was the only comparison she had, and each time her father had taken her as a child, she'd been thrilled. The contrast between the quiet existence of her life on the farm to all the people and activity in the town was vast. She'd loved to watch the crowds gathered along the docks, waiting for the various barges and steamboats that navigated the junction of rivers. The sights and sounds and smells were different from anything she'd ever known. So were the people.

One time, when she was very small, she became so fixated on a Mississippi river gambler and his colorfully clad female companion, she wandered away from her father to follow them down the street. When Da finally found her, he scolded her soundly, tied a rope around her waist and led her around like a puppy the rest of the day.

She smiled inwardly at the memory, feeling the same exhilaration now.

At first, she didn't think the men would let her come. They had discussed the plans at breakfast. Zeb needed some things for their journey into the mountains, and Brew needed coffee and flour. Cassie had kept to herself, partly because she wanted so badly to go and was afraid they wouldn't let her.

And partly because she was trying to avoid Cole. She still burned with an unfamiliar heat every time she thought of the way he kissed her.

It was her first kiss, she reasoned. That must be why she'd nearly fainted in his arms. He was practically a stranger, all these men were. Yet she depended on them for her very life. Could that be part of it? Was it her dependence on Cole that made her weak when he touched her?

She used to be able to trust her feelings. But too much had happened too fast to depend on her own judgment anymore. As hard as she tried not to, and in spite of all the things she didn't understand, her thoughts continuously swept back to how much she cared for Cole. In the end, he'd been the one to sway the others into allowing her to go this morning, stating simply he would go along to keep an eye on both her and Dalton.

"We're almost there," Brew announced. "Woo wee, look how she's growing. Folks are coming in from all over the place. Can't imagine how they're all going to fit, the labor market's already glutted."

The sounds of the city reached them before they entered the bustle of the busy streets. As they rolled into the thick of it, Cassie's mouth dropped open. She didn't know which direction to look first.

An enormous, black Kansas Pacific locomotive steamed into the depot as they drove down a street named Wynkoop. A stagecoach clattered past just before they turned the corner onto Blake Street where three ox-drawn freight wagons lined up for their turn to park in front of a series of wholesale companies.

"She's something, ain't she?" Brew said, still referring to the city as if it were a favorite aunt. He pulled the team to a halt in front of a large market. "She's maturing too. You won't see the bad element hanging from the lampposts these days."

He climbed down and tied the horses to a wooden rail, then returned to help Zeb and Cassie down. "Colorado is on its way to statehood," he continued, "and Denver City is fast becoming rich. Lots of gold and silver being found up in the hills, and a great deal of it is spent here."

Cassie tucked her blue plaid shirt more snugly into the waist of her baggy, tan corduroy trousers and stepped onto the wooden walk that ran the length of the street. Turning slowly around, she tried to take it all in at once. Men of every description milled through the streets and up and down the boardwalks; businessmen, miners, teamsters, emigrants, hunters and trappers. They wore everything from denim to buckskin to finely made suits. One man sported a pair of hairy, buffalo-hide boots. Everyone wore a hat of some kind, and most were armed.

Cassie was so enthralled, she didn't notice Dalton step up beside her until he bent down to look beneath her hat and tap her under the chin to close her gaping mouth. Cole moved to her other side and took her arm. He said a few words to Brew and Zeb about meeting up after their shopping expedition, then ushered her across the street.

On the next block, Cassie saw shops of every kind, nearly every other one a saloon. There was a slight change in the citizenry too. There were more businessmen and less derelicts slouching along the edge of the walk as if they had taken up residency.

There was even an occasional woman. Cassie gazed at one passing by in a grand carriage with a jaunty hat atop her beautifully dressed hair. Cassie's hand moved to touch the slouched hat that covered her hair completely. But her self-consciousness disappeared immediately when an even more impressive woman came strolling toward her on the arm of a dapper gentleman. The woman's dress was such a startling shade of blue it would make a peacock proud. The elbow-length sleeves were trimmed in ribbons of a darker shade, and the overskirt of creamy beige had a wide blue ribbon woven around the edge. As the couple passed by, Cassie turned to see the ribbon was gathered into a bow beneath the bustle at about knee level, creating a fetching frame for her derrière.

How could a woman sit down wearing such a dress? She wondered. Her deliberation ended when she caught the toe of her moccasin on the boardwalk and fell against Cole's back. She murmured a hasty apology for not watching where she was going, and received a brusque nod for her effort. Cole had stopped walking because they were at the corner and blocked from crossing the street by a large group of Indians parading by. Cassie squeezed in front eager to see them. The men wore red face-paint and beautifully beaded buckskin shirts. Their hair hung unbound down their backs. The women rode astride on top of thick furs thrown over their saddles.

"They're Ute," Cole said, bending near so she could hear him above the noise. "There's a Ute Agency here. They come in regularly to get financial payments the government promised them in their last treaty. The merchants welcome their dollars then mock the ones who get all liquored up and stumble down the streets drunk."

Cassie glanced up him, trying to gauge whether or not he thought this horrible information was humorous, but the Indians had passed by, and Cole was tugging her along beside him once more.

On the next street, her attention was drawn by a sign in the window of a general store that boasted the sale of ANYTHING AND EVERYTHING, FROM THE TINIEST NEEDLE TO THE BIGGEST GRINDSTONE. She longed to go in and browse, but Cole and Dalton's long-legged strides moved her on by before she could form the request.

Next to the general store was a shop filled with furs of every kind, then a store that displayed a vast assortment of Indian-made goods. Cassie pulled free from Cole's arm and stopped short, determined to get a better look. But Cole took her hand and propelled her across the street.

She didn't notice the two men lounging just outside the doors of a saloon until one of them spoke.

"What's the hurry, Adams?" he yelled in a surly voice.

In one smooth motion, Cole turned, gently pushed her into Dalton's arms and released the leather thongs on his holsters. Cassie had never seen anything like it. How could anyone move that quickly with so little effort? This was a new Cole. The chilling look in his eyes changed everything about him. Two long steps ate up most of the distance separating him from the two men.

One of them was tall and thin with a filthy beard and stringy hair. His long fingers twitched nervously above his holstered pistol. The other man was average height with a stocky build and clean-shaven, pockmarked face. Both men were maybe around Cole's age and wore their guns tied down.

"I told you it was Adams," the lanky man said, his fingers jerking open and shut.

Cole's attention seemed centered more on him than the other. "Did you gentlemen want something?"

"Do we gentlemen want something? Did you hear that Marty, don't he sound all uppity?"

"That he does." The shorter man sneered, revealing a mouthful of broken and blackened teeth. He spit a brown stream of spittle that hit the boardwalk at Cole's feet. "Maybe we ought to bring him back down to earth."

Long Finger's right hand moved closer to his gun. "We heard you was fast, Adams. Think you can take us both?"

Dalton started forward. "Cole, do you…"

"Take Cassie across the street, Dalton." Cole spoke in a muted voice, his eyes never leaving the two men in front of him.

"That's right, sonny, take yer little brother and git outa here before you git hurt."

The threatening scene sparked Cassie's hated memories. She began to tremble. Her legs refused to work. Dalton had to practically drag her through the gathering crowd. When he pulled her up onto the boardwalk on the other side of the street, she jerked free and turned to watch in horrid fascination.

Cole had taken another step forward. "I think you've had too much to drink, boys," his voice carried clearly to the hushed throng of onlookers. "Why don't you go sleep it off. That way nobody will get hurt."

"Only one gonna get hurt is you, Adams. And you ain't gonna hurt much, cause yer gonna be dead."

Cole moved another step closer. "You going to shoot me, boys?" Before the words completely left his mouth, he lunged and knocked both men into the street. Long Fingers got to his feet first. He reached for his gun, and Cole smashed his face with a hard right fist. Cassie heard the crunch of shattered bones, and her stomach rolled. The man sunk to the dirt.

The shorter man dove into Cole just as he turned. Cole staggered back and then righted himself. He raised his right arm to ward off a glancing blow and leveled the man with his left fist.

It was over in seconds. Both men were out cold at Cole's feet. He bent down to retrieve his hat and dusted it off on his pant leg as he crossed the street to Cassie and Dalton. The crowd began to break up, mumbling in disappointment that there would be nothing more to the scrape.

Dalton grinned widely when Cole stepped onto the wooden walk. "I can't believe it," he said excitedly. "They were going to draw on you, weren't they, Cole? You didn't even give them a chance. I've never seen anyone move so fast. They were actually going to draw on you."

"They were drunk, Dalton," Cole said, all the tension of the past few minutes coiled tightly in his voice. He gripped Cassie's arm and propelled her down the street to a small cafe in the middle of the block. He swung the door open, escorted her to a round table with a red and white checkered table cloth and pushed her none-too gently into a spindled chair. Dalton took the chair next to her. Cole sat across the table. All three of them were subdued as a stout, middle-aged woman came up to the table with a coffee pot and three cups.

"Howdy," she said, placing a white enameled cup in front of each of them. "You folks want some coffee?"

Cole nodded, and Dalton held out a cup. Cassie couldn't seem to respond. Her fear had solidified into an almost comforting numbness.

"What about the youngster? Would he rather have milk?"

Cole gave Cassie a hard look. "No, coffee will be fine." He watched the woman fill the mugs. "Give us a few minutes, there will be two more joining us." The woman nodded and walked away.

"What would you have done if those two had drawn on you, Cole?" Dalton asked, giving voice to one of Cassie's fears. "Could you have taken them both?"

"Drop it, Dalton," Cole snapped, obviously not the least interested in fanning Dalton's fantasies about gun fighting.

"I bet you could. I've seen you draw and--"

"Look, Dalton," Cole ground out, cutting him off, "If those idiots had gone for their guns, their liquored-up bravado would have gotten them killed. And a stray bullet could have hit somebody in the crowd. So drop it."

The woman appeared again with the steaming pot of coffee and topped off the men's cups. She pointed to the untouched cup in front of Cassie. "You sure you don't want me to bring something else for the boy? How about some milk?"

Cole's eyes moved from the cup to Cassie. "Do you want something else?"

She shook her head, and the woman shrugged and walked away. "Drink the coffee, Cassie, it'll make you feel better." Cole's voice rang with impatience.

Cassie didn't respond. She was having a hard time trying to focus. Although totally unrelated, her fear for Cole had brought Noley's attack to the forefront of her mind again. Dalton finally seemed to sense what she was going through. He took her right hand between both of his and gave it a slight squeeze. "Hey, Cassie, what do you think of Denver? Have you ever seen such a wild assortment of people in all your life? How about that freight driver? I never would have believed it if I hadn't seen it with my own eyes. Imagine, a woman doing a job like that. Did you see the outfit she had on? It made your clothes look fancy."

His chatter began to work. Cassie could feel her anxiety begin to fade.

"This place is pleasant, isn't it?" he rambled on, looking around the pretty café with white curtains at the windows, bright checked table cloths and a few neatly dressed customers scattered about. "A nice change from sitting on the ground. How's the food here, Cole?"

For a moment, a dark looked streaked across Cole's face as he glanced at Cassie's hand held tightly between Dalton's. But he straightened his broad shoulders, and his normally detached facade was back in place. "I've never eaten here, but Brew claims it's the best place in town."

"And that it is." Brew said, strolling up to the table with Zeb. "Am I being talked about behind my back?"

The waitress appeared from the back room with a radiant smile on her round face. "John Brewster! Is that you?"

Brew wrapped his short arms around the woman's broad middle and squeezed her tight. "Aren't you a sight for sore eyes, Bessie? Why, you get prettier every time I see you."

The woman's cheeks turned a deeper shade of pink as she poured two more cups of coffee.

"Folks, meet Bessie Jordon," Brew said. "She's a one-woman whirlwind and the best cook this side of the Mississippi. She owns this place and does everything there is to do in it. What's the special today, Bessie girl? I'm looking forward to a meal without grit."

Color still flushed the woman's face. She tugged on a strand of gray-streaked brown hair that had fallen loose from the knot at the back of her head. "Pork chops, with mashed potatoes and gravy, corn-on-the-cob, fresh-baked rolls and hot apple dumplings."

"Sounds like a meal fit for a king bring it on." Brew took a seat on one side of Cole, and Zeb sat on the other.

When Bessie left to prepare their plates, Brew's shrewd look went from Cassie to Dalton and finally landed on Cole. "What's going on?"

"Nothing," Cole grunted.

"Oh?" The older man raised his brows. The glint in his eye said he wouldn't stop prodding till he got an answer.

When Cole still failed to respond, Dalton answered for him. "Cole almost had a shoot-out in the street. There were two of them, but he fought them with his fists."

Brew studied Cole's unmarked face. Then he glanced down at the scraped knuckles wrapped around the mug of coffee and smiled. "Looks like you won."

His abrupt laughter broke the tension hanging over the table. Cassie couldn't resist his wink at her and smiled back as the last remnants of her fear faded away. Dalton took advantage of the moment and began giving Brew and his grandfather a blow-by-blow reenactment of the fight.

Bessie returned a few minutes later, laden with food. Brew asked her to join them, and she did. The good food and relaxed camaraderie continued to have a soothing affect on Cassie. By the time they said goodbye to Bessie, she felt fully recovered from the effects of the jarring violence.

On their walk back to the wagon and horses, she purposely kept a slower pace, not wanting to leave the city yet. She paused often to look in the shop windows and enjoyed everything on display. On the third block, she stopped in front of a window to admire a beautiful red dress. She couldn't imagine wearing anything so fine and wondered what the shiny material would feel like against her skin. Suddenly, a chill of premonition ran through her, and she raised her eyes to a reflection in the window of a large man across the street behind her.

Very slowly she turned around to get a better look. Barnaby Noley. She could never mistake his thick bulk. And even from this distance, the ugly scar on his face was visible. It completely contorted his features.

The breath left her lungs in a rush. She spun and fled into a nearby alley, her heart pounding wildly. At the other end, she ran across the adjoining street, blindly knocking into people as she darted into another alley. Terror roared in her ears, but she could hear him closing in on her.

Panic exploded through her whole being as an arm of steel caught her around the waist and she was slammed back against a hard body.

CHAPTER EIGHT

Strong hands held Cassie tight as she thrashed out with fists and feet.

"Cassie! Cassie, it's me! Cassie, listen to me. It's Cole!" Cole managed to turn her so she could see him. "What is it? What happened?"

She sagged in relief against him.

Dalton ran up, breathing hard. "What's wrong? What happened, Cole?"

Cassie buried her face in Cole's chest. "He's here. He's here." Her words were little more than a whisper.

"What? Cassie, I can't hear you."

She lifted her head and looked at Dalton. "He's found me, Dalton. He's here. I saw him."

"Who's here?" Cole asked. "What the hell's going on?" He glared at Dalton, whose face had gone chalk white.

Brew and Zeb arrived to hear the end of Cassie's statement. Brew patted her arm. "He isn't going to hurt you, little missy. We won't let him. You better carry her, Cole; she's in no shape to walk."

"I don't need to be carried," Cassie said, fighting desperately to gain control over her fear. Feeling somewhat safer now that the four men surrounded her, she stepped away from Cole and folded her arms in an effort to stop trembling. "Please, can we go now?"

Cole kept his frustration under control until they got Cassie back to the wagon. He insisted she ride in the back and tucked a blanket in around her. They'd left the herd only a mile east, so it wouldn't take long to get back. Zeb promised to keep an eye on her until then.

Once Cole and Dalton mounted their horses and followed a little distance from the wagon, he turned to say, "Let's have it, Dalton. What the hell just happened back there?"

"You better ask Cassie."

"Dalton, I swear to God, if you don't explain right now, I'll pull you off that horse and beat you to a pulp." His voice shook with anger.

"All right, Cole, I'll tell you. If that man is here, Cassie is going to need all the protection she can get."

"What man?" Cole's patience was as thin as parchment.

"The man who killed Cassie's mother."

Cole fixed him with a hard stare. "Cassie's mother was killed? How? When?"

"The man's name is Barnaby Noley. We don't know him. Paps and I were on our way out here when we literally stumbled across Cassie near a road in the upper part of Kentucky. She was unconscious, curled up in a pile of leaves and dirt. At first we thought she was dead. Her clothes torn half off, and she was covered with blood. We built a fire and tended her as best we could. She had cuts and bruises all over. Paps said the injury to her head was the worst. After we cleaned her up and dressed her with some of my clothes, we waited all through that night and half the next morning before she recovered enough to talk. She told us that the man who lived on the farm next to hers raped and killed her mother."

Cole gripped the saddle horn. "And Cassie?"

"From what we could understand, he tried to rape her, too." Dalton paused, thrown off by the look on Cole's face. "He didn't succeed, Cole. Apparently Cassie always wears that knife. She managed to fight back and cut him bad enough to get away. She was in awful shape, though. It was a week before she was strong enough to sit on a horse alone."

"You couldn't find a doctor?"

"She wouldn't let us look for one. She said she could doctor herself."

"So you let her, and then you dragged her out here." The story sickened Cole. Rage burned its way up his throat and erupted in a shout. "Were you both mad?"

Dalton stopped his horse. Sweat dripped down his face as his gaze locked with Cole's. His eyes pleaded with Cole to understand. "She begged us. She was terrified that if we took her into town, he'd find her. You should have seen her, Cole. She was absolutely helpless. She couldn't even stand or walk without help. You would have done the same thing. I know you would. You've seen those haunted eyes of hers. Could you look into those eyes and tell her no?"

Cole didn't dare let himself think about the pain he'd seen in Cassie's eyes, especially now that he knew what put it there. "What about family? Didn't she have any other family?"

"She said her father had dropped dead from a stroke only a few weeks before and her great-grandmother died just a few weeks before him. Her mother was all she had left. Even her house is gone. That bastard Noley burned it to the ground after she ran away from him."

Loathsome images continued to burn like acid in Cole's mind long after Dalton finished talking. He longed to get his hands on the bastard that had hurt Cassie, and replayed over and over in his thoughts what he would do to him.

By the time they reached the herd, his rage had turned inward. Cassie had been through hell, and he'd been pawing all over her like some randy stud. He should've had more sense. Not knowing her past didn't excuse him. The fact she was inexperienced and naive should have been enough to keep him away from her.

He unsaddled Storm, rubbed him down, and turned him into the rope corral. Ring was there to greet him, but he hardly acknowledged the animal's presence. He paced the dark creek bank for over an hour before he felt calm enough to join the others.

Austin, Brew, Zeb and Dalton sat cross-legged on the ground in a tight circle when Cole finally walked into camp. A small fire burned in a clearing in the trees some distance away.

"I saved you some supper," Brew said, glancing up.

"Thanks. I'm not hungry." Cole slid to the ground, leaned against a tree and stretched his legs out in front of him.

Brew shrugged. "Nobody's got much of an appetite tonight. Cassie went straight to her bedroll with nary a word to anybody."

Austin's face was grim when he looked at Cole. "We've been discussing what happened today. Did you get a look at the man?"

"I didn't see him. I didn't even know what the hell was going on till it was too late."

"I'm not convinced Cassie actually saw him," Zeb declared. "There's no way he could have caught up with us. How would he have known where to look?"

"Cassie told me he bragged to her once about hunting run-away slaves," Dalton responded. If he was that experienced, it probably didn't take him long to determine she was heading west."

"I still don't believe it," Zeb countered. "Remember that time in Missouri, Dalton? She thought she saw him then, too."

"It wasn't him?" Austin asked.

"No." Zeb rotated his sore shoulder and scooted to a more comfortable position.

"You sure?" Brew questioned.

"I'm sure." Zeb scowled at his doubt. "We got caught in a dust storm just as we rode into a small town. Cassie's hat blew off, and this big, fat man got to it the same time she did. Cassie nearly fainted when she saw him. Later, she admitted she had mistaken him for her mother's killer. That's when she started braiding her hair. It helps keep her hat on. That hair of hers would be a dead give-away if he was looking for her. At any rate, today was probably the same as then. The man she saw probably only looked like this Barnaby Noley.

"I don't think so, Paps," Dalton argued. "She was terrified today. I believe she did see him."

Zeb wouldn't let up. "She told Brew the man was clear across the street, so how could she be sure?"

"It doesn't matter." Dalton's face turned red and his heated emotions came out strong in his voice. "Cassie is convinced she saw him. We should believe her."

Brew shook his head in amazement. "That little missy's sure got gumption, suffering through all that and riding clear out here with two strangers."

"The point is what are we going to do about it?" Austin asked, getting them back on track. "Cassie can't just keep running. This man needs to be brought before a court of law for his crimes. Maybe I can talk to someone."

Zeb flashed Dalton an I-told-you-so look. "That's what I suggested in the first place. But she wouldn't hear of it. I still think it's a good idea."

"You can't do that, Austin," Dalton exclaimed, ignoring his grandfather. "We should just go on with our plans. Cassie feels safe with us. You said the area we're going to is remote. He'll never find her there."

"It is remote," Austin conceded. But it's no place for a woman alone."

"She won't be alone. She'll be with us."

"I didn't mean it like that, Dalton. You've never been in these mountains. They're rough for anyone. Whatever shelter you come up with will be crude. And in another few months, winter will set in. You can't expect Cassie to continue living like she is now. She needs womanly comforts."

Cole listened to the discussion, his insides churning. Austin was right. Cassie needed a roof over her head, other women around her. "What about Ginny?" he asked as the idea hit him.

Austin stiffened at his wife's name and whipped his head around to Cole. "What about her?"

"We could send Cassie to Ginny. She'd be safe at your place. We can spare a man. Dan's the best with a gun. He can take her and stay until we get there. Between him and Ollie the women will be safe. If Zeb feels up to it, he and Dalton can ride along and go on up to Spirit Lake from there."

Zeb smiled broadly at the idea. "I feel plenty strong enough to ride. Can we leave in the morning?"

Dalton frowned and shook his head. "I don't like it, and Cassie won't either. No offense, Austin, but she doesn't really know you, and she doesn't know your wife."

Cole could tell from Austin's dark expression he didn't like the plan either. If everything they'd heard about Cassie was true, she was in great danger. Austin wouldn't want it anywhere near Ginny. Especially when he wasn't there to watch out for her. On the other hand, Austin still thought like a lawman. He would consider everything and everyone concerned.

"Perhaps you're right, Cole," Austin finally said, living up to Cole's confidence in him. "There's a good chance the man is moving on hunches. He couldn't possibly know Cassie is with us. Zeb's injury probably gave him time to catch up. Dalton, I know you mean well, but you and Zeb are inexperienced in situations like this. The mountains alone will present enough of a challenge. You'd never be able to handle a confrontation with a man like the one you just described. Spirit Lake is less than a day's ride from my ranch. You won't have any trouble finding it from there. Cassie can stay at the ranch."

Dalton jumped up and faced the others. "Cassie won't like being separated from us. She won't feel safe with anyone but us."

"Take it easy, Dalton," Zeb said. "She'll be fine. You heard Austin; we'll be only a day's ride away from her. You'll be able to check on her anytime you want."

Cole observed the uneasy exchange and realized Dalton was in love with Cassie. The idea didn't set well. But he had no right to his jealousy. He'd already been down that road and look where it got him. The woman he'd loved married another man the first chance she got. He wouldn't repeat the mistake. He would keep his feelings for Cassie under control. She needed protection. He would make sure she got it. But that was all.

Late in the night, Cassie woke the whole camp with hysterical screams. Cole shoved his blanket aside and was halfway up when he saw Dalton already beside her. A strange ache gripped his insides as he watched the younger man hold her in his arms and soothe away the fear of her nightmares. He finally settled back down, but sleep wouldn't return. Eventually he gave up and took an early turn at night guard.

Cassie awakened the next morning, feeling as tired as if she hadn't slept at all. Her worst fears had come true. Noley had followed her west. She lay with her eyes tightly closed, reliving the moment she'd seen him yesterday. Did he see her too? Maybe when she'd run?

No, she reasoned. If he had seen her, he would surely have tried to apprehend her.

A sudden burst of sound overhead made her heart pound. She opened her eyes to a blue sky and bright sunlight filtering through the treetops. Dozens of birds flitted back and forth, loudly scolding each other. The normalcy of their antics calmed her.

She got up to fold her bedroll then turned to take in the beautiful scene around her. They were at the threshold of the mountains near a jagged ridge that stretched north and south as far as the eye could see. Their camp was positioned in the middle of a stand of lush trees and bushes, with a shallow creek cutting through the middle. Cassie looked longingly at the water, thinking a quick dip might help wash away the remnants of fear and melancholy that clung to her like sticky cobwebs.

She found Cole and Austin by the wagon. Both men looked unusually subdued. "Morning," she said, trying to put a smile on her face.

Austin inclined his head and smiled back. Cole just watched her with those inscrutable dark blue eyes.

"Would you mind if I took a few minutes for a bath before we go?"

"No, that's fine, Cassie," Austin said. "Go ahead."

She looked up at Cole, remembering his intrusion on her bath that first morning. As if he'd read her mind, Cole assured her with, "Nobody will disturb you."

Ten minutes later, Cassie left the water feeling somewhat revived. She donned a clean shirt and pants, then pulled her heavy wet hair over one shoulder and squeezed the water out of it. When she returned to the camp, six pairs of very serious male eyes turned to stare at her, slowing her steps. Austin, Dalton, Brew and Dan stood bunched together. Zeb sat on a nearby rock. Cole leaned against a large tree trunk. Cassie's heart thudded against her chest when Austin gestured for her to come over to them.

"Cassie, we've been talking about what happened yesterday." Austin swung his arm out to include the others. "We think it would be best if you left the herd."

Cassie felt the color drain from her face. Her heart skipped a beat, and her palms began to sweat. They were sending her away? She gaped at Austin, then Cole, and then at each of the others.

Austin's face reddened as she turned back to glare at him. He cleared his throat. "As you know, I have a ranch in the mountains. Dan is going to take you…"

His speech lost its momentum when Cassie started backing away, unable to believe what she was hearing. They were sending her away – with Dan?

Her gaze flew to the cowboy in question who suddenly took great interest in his dusty boots.

Why Dan? Why wasn't she going to continue with Zeb and Dalton? The questions spun into panic. There was no control. She had no control. Once again, her life was being decided for her. She was being thrust away from the tiny scrap of safety she had been clinging to. Hot anger as fierce as her fear reared up with such force she felt she would explode. "Noooo--!" she yelled, causing all six men to flinch.

Austin recovered first and took a step toward her. She scrambled backward. He shot Cole a pleading look before turning back to her. "I'm afraid I'm bungling this, Cassie, and I apologize. Let me start over. We're worried about you and want to help. You'll be safer at the ranch with my wife."

Cassie shook her head furiously as she continued to back away. These men had been discussing her like she was nothing more than a stray animal. No one had asked her what she wanted, what she thought. They had just decided. She knew she was going to have to start taking care of herself, but not yet. Not yet. She wasn't ready. She aimed a scathing look at Dalton. "Don't you want me with you anymore, Dalton?"

Dalton separated himself from the others and moved to stand in front of her. He tried to take her hands, but she held them rigidly at her sides.

"This wasn't my idea, Cassie, it was Cole's." His voice filled with accusation as he turned to the others. "I told you she wouldn't like this."

Cassie glared at Cole. He pushed away from the tree, and his cobalt gaze imprisoned her as he advanced toward her. "Nobody's going to make you do anything you don't want to do, Cassie." His words were measured and softly spoken. He stopped close enough to easily reach out and touch her. But he wisely kept both hands in his pockets. "Think about it, you'll be much more comfortable with Austin's bride. And you'll be safer. Zeb and Dalton will ride with you. Spirit Lake isn't far from the ranch, so they'll still be close. We won't be too far behind, maybe a few days to a week."

Cassie knew it didn't matter what reasoning Cole used. She always seemed unable to resist him. And acknowledging that fact only made her feel even more helpless. She was at his mercy. At the mercy of all these men.

She hated this fear and confusion. She hated not being able to take care of herself. She felt like a feather in a storm, tossed here and there, whichever way the wind blew.

Would she ever land? Ever again feel secure? Ever again be in control of her own life?

CHAPTER NINE

The sun hovered over the tips of the western peaks when Austin's ranch came into view. The beauty of the setting made the hard, two-day ride worth it. The house backed up to a pine-covered ridge that swung around in a great irregular curve. Forests of dark green pines stood as a framework to clusters of aspen with white trunks and fluttering leaves. Lush grass and a carpet of colorful wild flowers filled the vast meadow, their sweet perfume released by the horse's feet as they trod through them.

Cassie was enchanted, just as she had been since they reached the higher elevation yesterday. For some reason, the higher they climbed into the rugged terrain the easier it became to leave her fears behind. Even though it had initially taken a few hours for her to calm down, once she did, she immediately regretted the way she'd left Cole and the others. She was sorry her panic had overridden everything else and hoped to express her apologies when she saw them again.

Dan proved to be a competent and educated guide and as led them up a narrow trail into a canyon alongside a twisting, fast-moving river called Clear Creek. The craggy canyon walls were nearly perpendicular and stripped of timber here and there by the many mining operations taking place. The walls sometimes seemed to meet overhead, and the diverse shades of the rocks took on fantastic forms against the blue-green pines.

They stopped briefly in Idaho Springs, the first mining community they'd come to. Before the gold rush, the Ute and Arapaho tribes were the only people who visited there. Each tribe had designated the area as common ground in order to use the hot mineral springs. Dan allowed them a quick soak and bath, before hurrying them on again.

They spent the night several miles further up the mountain near Empire, where Cole had gotten Ring. Empire was another mining settlement that perched on the edge of a star shaped valley at the eastern base of the mountain pass that would take them to their destination on the western side. The pass was named after Captain Edward Berthoud who had completed the first survey of this saddle in the main Divide of the country.

Riding to the top of the pass had been challenging to say the least. The trail was steep and full of switchbacks, occasionally interrupted by small waterfalls and icy streams. Dan explained that the trail was being widened to accommodate a stagecoach and other wheeled vehicles. Cassie couldn't imagine anyone wanting to take a stagecoach up that incline. When she asked Dan how the cook wagon would make it over, he'd told her Austin was bringing the herd in a different route, over the newly opened Rollins Pass toll road.

At the 11,315-foot summit, Cassie felt like she was standing on top of the world. The air was thin, making it difficult to take a deep breath and leaving the surrounding peaks bare of anything but patches of snow.

The descent from the clouds was steeper and more treacherous than the climb up. But Cassie began to breathe easier and felt she must surely be entering paradise when she saw the beautiful valley laid out below. She wondered if Austin thought that same thing when he first planned the ranch.

The newly painted, white, two-story house turned pink in the last rays of sunset. As they approached the yard, two golden puppies loudly greeted them. Ring, who'd been ordered to go with them as added protection, added his bark to the commotion. Cassie saw movement at one of the front windows, a woman's face, but just that quickly it disappeared.

A tall man with hair the color of wheat rounded the corner of the wide veranda, pointing a gun. His severe expression eased when he recognized Dan. Resting his rifle against the porch railing, he smiled broadly behind a thick, drooping moustache.

Dan stepped down from the saddle and reached out to shake the bigger man's hand. He then turned and introduced him to the others as Ollie Olsen, Austin's foreman.

"Howdy, folks," Ollie greeted. "Step on down and rest a spell."

Cassie immediately warmed to his big smile. His accent reminded her of the Swedish tinker who'd visited her family's farm and spent many a night under their roof. A moment later, the front door opened, and a small woman stepped out on the porch. Her hair was as fair as Ollie's. Her round brown eyes reminded Cassie of a wary doe. She stared grimly at each one of them, her anxiety unmistakable.

The foreman must have realized her concern because he quickly tried to reassure her. "Every t'ing is fine, Ginny. Austin sent Dan and these men here. Can they come inside?"

The woman considered this news for a moment before stepping back to wave them into the house. "Forgive my rudeness, gentlemen. If Austin sent you, you are welcome. Please come in."

Once they were inside, she gestured toward a settee and a couple of chairs. "Please sit. I was alarmed when I saw Cole's dog. I thought something might have happened to my husband. How is Austin?" She directed the question to Dan, as the rest of them took seats around the room.

"He's well, ma'am. He…ah…" Dan paused, and his face turned crimson. He aimed the rest of his words at his boots. "He, ah, sends you his love." The woman's blush rivaled that of the messenger's. She sat on the chair next to Dan and faced him. The room grew uncomfortably quiet before Dan realized she was waiting for further explanation. He jumped to his feet and twisted his hat brim. "The reason we're here, ma'am, is because Austin wanted Cassie to stay with you until he gets back. That's why Cole's dog is with us. Cole sent him along for extra protection." He stopped abruptly as if he'd run out of words.

At the mention of a woman's name, Ginny's wary gaze skimmed over the others and landed on Cassie, who suddenly wanted to disappear. Dan's brief accounting fell far short of explaining anything. And she could well imagine how she must look in her floppy hat and men's clothing. She removed her hat and forced a smile.

Zeb grumbled something under his breath, gave Dan an impatient glare, then stood and faced Austin's wife. "Let me introduce myself, Missus Barret. My name is Zeb Pettigrew. This is my grandson, Dalton Tate. And this is Miss Cassandra O'Brian. She goes by Cassie." He cleared his throat, placed his hat on the chair behind him and continued. "The three of us were on our way to Spirit Lake when we were fired upon by some desperadoes on the prairie east of Denver." He motioned to the sling supporting his shoulder and arm. "Cole Adams came to our rescue. Your husband kindly let us travel with his cattle drive for a few days. Miss O'Brian has had some trouble, and your husband thought it would be best if she stayed with you until they get here with the herd."

Ginny Barret's lips thinned into a straight line as she listened to Zeb. She looked to be close to Cassie's twenty years, maybe a little older. Her long pale hair was held behind her neck with a pink ribbon the same color as the tiny pink flowers in her cream colored dress. A sprinkling of freckles across the bridge of her slightly up tipped nose was the only flaw in her peaches-and-cream complexion.

Cassie sat stiffly next to Dalton on a small settee. A quick glance around the room left her feeling even more like the intruder she was. Austin's wife and Dan were seated on two side chairs upholstered in the same gold horsehair fabric as the settee. Zeb stood in front of a brown-leather rocker. A small writing desk graced the far wall near a squat, Rosemont parlor stove. The floor was carpeted in a subdued green and gold pattern that almost matched the pattern in the papered walls. The room reflected the calm, orderly appearance of their hostess, and Cassie hated the idea of disrupting her peaceful existence. "I can't stay here," she blurted out aiming her plea toward Zeb. "I should go on with you and Dalton to the lake."

Ginny Barret looked like she wholeheartedly supported that idea, but said instead, "If my husband sent you here, he had a good reason. There is plenty of room, so you must stay."

Cassie heard the grim resignation in the woman's voice and started to object once more, but Zeb spoke first. "Cassie appreciates your hospitality, ma'am. Now my grandson and I will be on our way."

"Nonsense." Ginny stood, smiling for the first time, transforming her face from merely pretty to quite beautiful. "As I said, I have plenty of room. You can get a good-night's sleep and leave in the morning."

Full darkness had descended by the time everything was settled. Ollie and Dan took care of the horses. Ginny showed Zeb and Dalton to two of the four upstairs bedrooms then returned to escort Cassie to a main floor bedroom just down the hall from hers and Austin's. Ginny didn't want Ring in the house, and this room would allow him to stay near Cassie by sleeping outside under her window.

Water was hauled in and heated for baths, and in spite of Cassie's reservations about staying; she looked forward to sleeping in a bed. Supper was shared around a large oval oak table in the sizable kitchen. Dan and Ollie joined them, as did another man who was introduced as Arthur Kane, the newest ranch hand.

Their hostess had obviously stretched the roast-chicken meal with additional bread, gravy, and vegetables. Everyone ate with hearty appetites. Dalton and Ollie did most of the talking. Dalton chattered about the trip west, and Ollie, who seemed pleased with the added company, entertained the group with stories about his days as Austin's deputy in Golden City.

Cassie was grateful for their cheerfulness. It helped divert her attention from Arthur Kane. Something about him reminded her of Barnaby Noley. Every time he speared another bite of food into his mouth, he glanced her way, his eyes moving over her as if he could see through her clothes.

It was nearly midnight before the house was finally quiet. Cassie was grateful to escape to the pretty bedroom she'd been given. She lowered herself onto the bed and looked around. The walls were papered in a pattern of yellow and white swirls that reminded her of cream being stirred into coffee. The woodwork was white. A candle had been mounted in a tin can and attached to the clothes-hook board by the door. A pine dresser and large trunk took up most of the opposite wall. The bedside table was covered with a delicately crocheted white doily on which rested an oil lamp. A braided rug covered the floor by the iron bed. The house smelled new, but Cassie could tell some of the furnishings were old and, probably, much loved. The feather mattress was soft and inviting.

It had been weeks since she had slept in a bed. Her bed. She shook off her troubled feelings and turned down the flame on the lamp. It sputtered for a moment then the room was thrown into darkness. She stood and removed her shirt and trousers and, having nothing else to wear, climbed naked between the crisp sheets.

Cool night air drifted through the open window, tossing the tassel on the raised roller shade as it chased out the heat of the day. Cassie closed her eyes and thought about her own room. It wasn't this pretty but she had loved it. Two of the walls had displayed an assortment of her father's sketches and paintings. The other two had been lined with shelves. Her father had lovingly chided her every time he'd needed to add another shelf in order to hold more of her carvings.

Her favorite sculpture, a large statue of Pegasus, took up nearly all the space on one shelf. Her father had carved it for her fifth birthday. The beautiful winged creature was the first thing she looked at when she opened her eyes each morning and the last thing she saw each night before going to sleep. On the nights when her nightmares came, she liked to imagine the great beast coming to life and carrying her to safety.

Hot tears formed in Cassie's throat. Pegasus was gone. She still had difficulty believing it. It was all gone. Everything that made up her life had been torched to a puff of smoke and carried away on a hot breath of air.

She squeezed her eyes against the onslaught of burning tears. There'd been no burial ceremony for her beautiful mother, neither Christian nor Choctaw. No goodbyes. Nothing. Cassie's only comfort came from believing her mother's ashes, like the rest, had been scattered by the wind across the farm she loved.

A sudden rustling sound stopped her tears. She waited and listened, heart pounding, barely breathing. She heard it again, louder this time, just outside her window. Maybe Dan or Ollie? She couldn't just lie here, waiting to find out. Slowly, she eased out of bed, grabbed her shirt, wrapped it around her and flattened herself against the wall. Once she reached the open window, she peeked around the edge.

Moonlight filtered through the pines, casting the house and yard in an eerie blue glow. She jumped when she heard the noise again, directly beneath the window. Glancing down, she saw two gleaming eyes peering back at her.

"Ring." She laughed with relief. "You scared me half to death."

Her bodyguard rose up on hind legs, rested his front paws against the windowsill and licked her hand. "Good boy." She scratched behind his ears, cooed goodnight and climbed back into bed.

How odd, she thought, that Cole would send his dog with her. But then, everything about the man was a puzzle. He managed to spark confusing emotions whether he was near or not. And it had only gotten worse since he'd kissed her.

Of course, she reasoned with herself, it was time for her to be fascinated by the mysteries between a man and woman. Her mother had been even younger when she married Cassie's father. And they'd taught her those mysteries were natural, deepening the love between a man and woman. But Cole Adams wasn't her man. They had shared a kiss, not love. And now that she knew how strongly she responded to the attentions of a man, especially to kissing, she would be careful to keep a tighter hold on her emotions.

The next morning, as Zeb and Dalton prepared to ride out, Dalton asked Cassie to walk with him a few minutes. They followed a path along the corral and into the pines. When they were out of sight of the others, Dalton turned to her and took both her hands in his. His gaze moved over her, as if trying to imprint her image in his mind. Her hair hung down her back to her waist in a single, thick braid. She wore one of his white cotton shirts, the sleeves rolled into wide cuffs at her elbows. In many towns they'd ridden through, he had tried to buy her something else to wear. But she wouldn't hear of it, finally convincing him she felt safer and more comfortable in his clothing.

"I hate leaving you." Dalton released one of her hands and touched her face.

Cassie's eyes filled with tears. "I know."

"I wish you were coming with us."

"Me too."

Dalton closed his eyes for a moment and let out a loud breath. When he looked back at Cassie, her tears threatened to spill over.

"Maybe this is the right thing to do." He sounded like he was trying to convince himself. "You probably will be better off here. Austin's wife seems nice. You'll have a roof over your head and a bed to sleep in at night. I don't think there is any way Noley will be able to find you up here."

Cassie couldn't respond. What could she say? She felt like she was losing more family. Dalton's brown eyes grew somber. His hat sat on the back of his head. She swallowed her tears and stifled the urge to push his hair off his forehead where it always seemed to hang.

"You've come to mean a lot to me, Cassandra Cathleen. This isn't good-bye. Dan says the lake isn't far. We'll see each other soon."

She finally found her voice. "Dalton, I don't know how, but someday I'm going to repay you for everything you and Zeb have done for me. You've gone far beyond kindness."

"I don't want to be repaid. I loved taking care of you."

Cassie attempted a cheerful smile. She pulled her hands free and clasped the lapels of her shirt. "You mean you won't want your clothes back? I will surely have something else to wear one of these days."

Dalton's smile matched hers. "It would be nice to see you in a dress. But I don't want the clothes back. As a matter of fact," he paused then laughed self-consciously, "I've been thinking I might get me some new clothes, maybe a buckskin outfit like Cole's."

Cassie laughed too. "Now that would be a sight to see."

Suddenly Dalton sobered and placed his hands on her shoulders. "Would you kiss me goodbye?" Not waiting for an answer, he pulled her into his arms, and his mouth covered hers in a firm kiss. When he finally let her go and took a step back, his face bloomed with color. "You take care of yourself. I'm going to miss you very much and I'll be back as soon as I can."

"I'll miss you too, Dalton. Every single day."

After Zeb and Dalton rode away, Cassie took her time returning to the house. Saying goodbye to Dalton had been wrenching, and she needed to pull herself back together. When he kissed her, it was all she could do to keep from begging him to take her along.

Wait… Dalton had kissed her! The thought stopped her short.

She had been so lost in her sadness; she hadn't really grasped what was happening. Yet, realizing how close they had grown these past weeks, kissing goodbye seemed the natural thing to do.

It was similar to the way Cole had kissed her. Similar yes, but vastly different in the way she'd responded. With Dalton's kiss there had been no fiery sensation that took her breath away and left her weak and tingly all over.

"Oh, bother!" She exclaimed out loud as she resumed her walk to the house. Her contradictory reactions made no sense at all. If only she had her mother or Running Deer to help her sort through her confusion.

Maybe she could talk to Ginny Barret, she thought. No, that would never work. First off, she wouldn't even know where to start, and second, in spite of the woman's good manners, she still barely spoke. Cassie knew she wasn't wanted here. Gazing down at herself, she could see why. She looked uncivilized. Ginny Barret was probably used to being around fine ladies.

Stepping onto the wide veranda, Cassie vowed to make sure her hostess never suspected she was half-Indian. Considering what most people thought of Indians, the poor woman would probably faint.

Throughout the rest of that day and the next few days, the two women skirted around each other. Ginny kept to herself, sewing and doing chores. Cassie preferred being outside. Dan and Ollie discouraged her from taking Lady out without an escort, or venturing too far from the ranch, so she settled for walks in the immediate area. Ring accompanied her as she chose a different direction each day. And every day she became more charmed by the beauty surrounding her.

As she returned to a favorite spot, the grassy banks of a creek behind the barn, Cassie picked a blossom off a flowering plant that grew profusely in the area. Dan had called it a columbine. She stuck it through the hair above her left ear just like her mother used to do with the wild flowers they'd find on their walks together. The memory brought tears to her eyes and made her smile. Bittersweet. She supposed the conflicting feelings would be with her the rest of her life.

The sun was intense in this thin air, so she took off her moccasins, rolled her trouser legs to above her knees and waded into the frigid stream. Anytime she was outside like this, she felt deeply connected to the earth and sky and all growing things. She supposed she had gotten that from Running Deer. The old healer seemed to be a part of any rock she sat on or tree she leaned against.

'Everything pulses with the life of Great Mystery,' Running Deer would tell her. 'And everything is connected. You must honor all parts of the earth as your teacher. Some carry special medicine. Some will call to you in your dreams. Pay attention to the messages they bring.'

Cassie remembered the words with misgiving. Maybe her grandmother could make sense of the messages she received in her dreams, but Cassie's dreams frightened her too much to even try.

Shrugging away the past, she stepped out of the water. Ring had already grown bored with splashing about and waited on the bank. She flopped down beside him. Her feet tingled as the sun brought warmth and feeling back into them. In Kentucky, the only time water got this cold was in the dead of winter.

She unbuttoned the first three buttons on her shirt and rolled up her sleeves to her shoulders. Then she reclined on a bed of grass and pine needles and closed her eyes, relishing the distinct sensations of the hot sun and cool air against her skin. She didn't realize she'd dozed off until Ring woke her with a deep growl. Alarmed, she sat up, shaded her eyes with her hand and stared in the direction of the dog's fixed look.

Arthur Kane stood on the other side of the creek. "You look mighty ah…peaceful. I hope I didn't disturb you." The lust in his eyes belied his casual remark.

It only took a moment for her to roll her trouser legs down and put her moccasins back on. "You didn't disturb me," she said with forced confidence as she stood. "I need to get back to the house. Missus Barret will want help with supper."

Kane watched her negotiate the rocks to cross the creek. When she got to his side, he moved to block her way. Instantly, Ring was between them, teeth bared, the hair on the back of his neck lifting.

"Call him off," Cane snapped. "I'm no threat to you."

"Apparently he thinks so." Cassie was determined not to show him her own fear.

"Well, he's gone berserk. Call him off."

"Why did you follow me here?"

Kane's stance was rigid, his eyes locked on Ring. The dog looked like he could easily go for his throat if he so much as moved. "I didn't follow you, I was... checking on something and happened to see you. Now call the dog off."

"Ring won't bother you if you leave."

Kane hesitated. The dog's muscles quivered. His warning snarl exposed dripping fangs.

"All right, I'm going. Just make sure he stays put."

Cassie was shaking visibly when she entered the house. She walked straight to her room and collapsed on the bed. It was like Noley all over again. She didn't believe for one minute that Austin's hired hand hadn't been following her. And she hated to think what might have happened if Ring hadn't been there. She could have cried with gratitude for Cole's insistence that Ring stay with her.

Just as she debated whether or not to say something to Austin's wife, she heard a light knock on her door. "It's Ginny, may I come in?"

Cassie stood up and wiped her eyes. "Aye, yes, come in."

Her hostess opened the door and stepped into the room, wringing her hands together. "Miss O'Brian, I...I thought...you looked upset just now. Is something wrong?"

The debate in Cassie's mind wasn't settled. Maybe her experience with Noley was making her to jump to conclusions. Austin had hired Arthur Kane. Surely he wouldn't have left the man with his wife if he weren't trustworthy. She didn't want to cause problems. "It's nothing," she lied. "I am sorry I worried you."

"In that case, I'm sorry I imposed. I'll leave you alone."

Cassie heard the upset in the woman's voice and realized how abrupt she must have sounded. She didn't want Ginny Barret to leave with hurt feelings. In fact, she didn't want her to leave at all. "Missus Barret, don't go. I didn't mean for my words to bite like that. Please stay and talk awhile."

Ginny came back into the room, her brown eyes looking everywhere but at Cassie. Several uncomfortable moments passed.

Then Cassie said, "I..."

And Ginny said, "You..." at the same moment.

Both of them smiled.

"You first," Cassie said.

"No, you, please."

"I haven't been very good company," Cassie began. "I want to apologize. I was raised on a small farm with only family for company. The most talking I've ever done with anyone else was to Zeb and Dalton and the men on the drive. Other than Dalton, that didn't amount to much."

"I'm not very good at conversation either. And you don't have to explain about talking with men. They never utter a word more than they have to. Where is your farm?"

"It's... It was in Kentucky, just across the river from Cairo, Illinois. My family is.... They're all... They recently died."

Ginny's eyes widened. She nervously smoothed her skirt and moved further into the room. "I'm so sorry. Forgive me for asking."

"You had no way of knowing. I have to face it, and learn to accept it."

"We don't have to talk about it now, though." Ginny shyly eyed Cassie up and down. "I've been thinking about your clothes. I...ah...noticed you don't really have any."

Cassie gaped at the woman, not sure how to respond. Ginny glanced down at her hands, which were tightly clasped at her waist. "Don't be put off, Cassie. I was in a similar situation when Austin and I married."

"You wore men's trousers?" Cassie asked in surprise.

"No," Ginny looked back up. "But I didn't have much to wear."

Cassie could see in the other woman's eyes there was much more to this story. Ginny Barret had secrets too, which surprisingly made Cassie feel better.

"Come with me." Ginny abruptly took her by the hand and led her down the narrow hall and into her own bedroom. She opened a large wardrobe closet and chose two simple dresses from the many hanging there. The first was periwinkle-blue, the second a checkered beige and white. She draped them over Cassie's arm, studied Cassie for another moment and then opened a drawer, picked out a chemise, two pairs of bloomers, and a petticoat. A lovely white nightgown was plucked from another drawer.

Since Cassie stood two inches taller than Ginny, they let out the hems on the dresses, getting acquainted while they worked. Ginny told Cassie about her wedding day, which was barely four months before, and listed the numerous reasons why she loved her new husband. Cassie told Ginny about traveling with the herd and agreed with her that Austin seemed like a wonderful man.

After dinner, which to Cassie's great relief, they shared alone because the men ate in the bunkhouse, Cassie changed clothes, choosing to wear the blue dress. It buttoned up the front to a prim white collar at the neck and fit snugly but comfortably over her breasts and waist, then fell in full folds to her feet. The sleeves came just to her elbow, with cuffs that matched the white collar.

Cassie had never worn anything other than the dresses of her mother's people. She looked at herself in the vanity mirror and twirled around, loving the feel of the soft under things against her skin. "I can't thank you enough, Ginny."

"It is truly my pleasure. Besides the store-bought dresses, Austin also got me several bolts of fabric. Since he's been gone, I've had lots of time to sew."

They spent the rest of the evening chatting about safe and comfortable topics, the changeable mountain weather, all the reasons why Ginny loved her new home, and Cassie's love for carving animal figurines out of wood. After they said goodnight, Cassie went to bed amazed at how quickly their friendship had blossomed. She fell asleep in a state of contentment deeper than she'd experienced in a long time.

Sometime deep in the night, Ginny's voice and a knock on the door awakened Cassie with a start. Half asleep, she stumbled out of bed and hurried to open the door.

"Get out here and close the door behind you." Kane's voice was barely above a whisper. He stood just behind Ginny in the dimly lit hall.

Stunned from heavy sleep, Cassie paused to make sense of the situation.

"I said come out here and close the door," Kane ordered again.

She stepped into the hall, and he kicked the door shut behind her. Cassie could now see that Ginny's arms hung limply in front of her; her wrists bound with rawhide. Her face was as white as her nightgown and she was trembling violently. Kane had a beefy arm wrapped around her waist. His other arm was locked over her shoulder and his hand pressed the blade of a large knife against her throat.

CHAPTER TEN

"**D**o as you're told, and nobody will get hurt. Understand me?"

Wide-awake now, Cassie began to tremble. "Aye," she gasped.

"How's that? You speak English when you talk to me." Kane had leaned forward over Ginny's shoulder, and his hot breath smelled like whiskey.

Cassie clasped her hands into tight fists to keep them from shaking. She forced herself to look into his eyes. "Yes. Yes, I understand. What do you want from us?"

"Never mind what I want. You and the missus and I are going on a little journey, that's all you need to know for now."

"You're taking us somewhere?"

"Yeah, we're going for a nice ride. Now quit stalling and do as I say."

"But we can't go off into the night dressed like this. We'll freeze to death." She motioned to their nightgowns. "You at least have to let us put on some clothes."

Kane eyed Cassie up and down, stopping at the swell of each breast not quite hidden behind the fall of hair over the front of her nightgown. He held the knife closer to Ginny's neck and ran his other hand over each of her breasts, squeezing each one so tight it had to hurt. "I like the way you're dressed just fine."

Ginny clenched her teeth as pain filled her eyes. Cassie swallowed the horror wanting to erupt from her throat. She should have followed her instincts and told someone about her confrontation with this man. "At least let us put on a coat or something."

Kane considered her request for a moment, then said, "All right, grab a couple of coats, but make it snappy."

Ginny told Cassie where to find two warm jackets. Cassie put one on and held the other out for Ginny. Kane grabbed it and threw it roughly over Ginny's shoulders, keeping the blade of the knife pressed close to her neck. "Now follow my instructions and the sheriff's wife will remain in one piece."

Cassie nodded her agreement. Ever since she'd stepped into the hallway, she'd been aware of Ring; first jumping through the window into her bedroom to lunge at the closed door, then circling the house, trying to find another way into the house.

Arthur Kane was also acutely aware. "Go back in that bedroom and shut the door behind you. Bring that dog in through the window and then close it tight. When you come back here, make sure he can't get out of that room. I'll slit her throat clean through before he can do me any harm."

Cassie tried to give her new friend a reassuring look, but Ginny had closed her eyes.

Ring jumped easily through the window when Cassie called to him. She slid it closed, then knelt next to him, wrapping her arms around his neck. "Oh Ring, what am I going to do?"

"Hurry up in there," Kane yelled through the closed door.

A harsh growl rumbled in the dog's throat. His ears pricked toward the door. "It's okay boy. You have to stay here. You stay Ring. Stay," Cassie commanded until he sat.

"Get out here." Kane raised his voice.

Ring growled again, then started barking.

"No, Ring. Quiet. Stay." She whirled to leave the room then stopped when she saw her knife and leather sheath lying on the table. She lifted her gown and strapped it around her waist. Ring continued to bark viciously as she slipped back into the hall and shut the door behind her.

Kane gave Ginny a length of rawhide and ordered her to tie Cassie's wrists behind her back. The task took a bit of maneuvering for both women since Ginny's wrists were still tightly bound. They could hear the dog lunging at the door as Kane ushered them quickly through the dark house and out into the night.

Lady and two other saddled horses waited just inside the trees behind the corral. Kane lifted Ginny and nearly tossed her into the saddle. He repeated the rough treatment to get Cassie mounted. At some point, he had replaced the knife with a gun, which he now aimed straight at Cassie's head. Where were Ollie and Dan? She wondered, praying that Kane hadn't killed them.

They rode for hours, angling diagonally along the ridge behind the ranch. By first light, they were climbing a steep slope, and the insides of Cassie's thighs were rubbed raw from the saddle. Her bare feet were numb with cold. She could only surmise Ginny was feeling the same agony. Lady trailed slightly behind the other two horses, so all she could see in the breaking dawn was Ginny's light hair as it fell down her back. By the time the sun was fully up, Cassie's bladder felt like it was going to burst. She asked Kane if they could stop for a minute. He refused, saying they were close to their destination.

An hour or so later, they were at the top of a high bluff with natural rocks protruding upward like the fingers of a huge hand. A wall made of stone and log uprights had been built around the rest of the flat area. It was like a makeshift fort and provided an unending view of the land below.

Kane climbed off his horse. "It's a favorite spot of the Ute's," he said, as if answering a question. "I accidentally found it one day and knew it would be perfect." Cassie was still in the dark about what he intended to do with them, but at the moment, her exhaustion and physical discomfort were so great they obscured all other thoughts.

After the horses were tied, Kane pulled the two women roughly to the ground. Ginny collapsed in a heap. Cassie managed to stay standing. She looked around for a private place to relieve herself.

"Don't be getting any ideas," Kane said, eyeing her closely.

"I won't leave," Cassie assured him. "I just need some privacy for a minute."

"If you need to pee, you do it right here," Kane ordered.

Ginny looked up. "You can't expect us to relieve ourselves right in front of you."

"Why not, I ain't shy." He unbuttoned his pants and urinated. Both women turned away.

When he was finished, Cassie spun to face him. "We will not take care of our personal needs with an audience."

He sneered and shrugged his shoulders. "Suit yourselves. When you have to go bad enough, you will."

"Mister Kane, you have nothing to fear by allowing us a little privacy. We are both barefoot and bound," Cassie reasoned.

Kane leered at her. She knew the leather jacket hid the top of her, but he could see the silhouette of her legs through the thin material of her gown. His eyes slowly followed their outline down to her bare feet. His small, mean eyes clearly reflected his thoughts.

"All right, go ahead over behind that rock. That side's a sheer drop off, so you can't go anywhere. But if you aren't back where I can see you in two minutes, I'm coming to get you."

Ginny struggled to her feet, and the two of them stepped carefully across the rocky ground to the other side of the large boulder. "What do you think he means to do with us?" Ginny asked in a hushed voice.

"I don't know. How are you doing? You look awfully pale."

"I don't feel very well." Ginny paused and swallowed hard. Tears gathered in her eyes. "I'm pregnant."

"Oh, Ginny."

The tears spilled over. She dried each cheek with a shoulder. "Austin doesn't know yet. Now I…"

"Are you having any pain or bleeding? Did Kane force you to…?" An image of her mother's raped and broken body swam before her eyes, and she felt like throwing up.

"No."

Cassie took a deep breath and shut the memory away. "Then try to stay calm. Maybe we can figure something out."

With their wrists bound, it was difficult for them to maneuver their gowns and squat on the ground, so they awkwardly helped each other. When they were finished, they returned to their captor.

"Sit down," he ordered. "We'll have something to eat and get acquainted while we wait for Sheriff Barret to join us."

Ginny's eyes widened. "Austin? You're waiting for Austin? He might not be back for days."

"Not according to Dan. He thinks the herd will show up today or tomorrow."

Cassie couldn't make sense out of Kane. "Do you have any idea what Austin will do to you when he finds out you've taken his wife?"

"Ha!" he snorted. "It ain't what he's going to do to me. It's what I'm going to do to him."

"What do you mean?" Ginny asked, her eyes nearly black with fear.

Kane turned and glared at her with venom. "Your husband sent my little brother to prison. When he tried to escape, the guards shot him down. Barret is going to pay for that."

"But...your brother must have had a trial," Ginny challenged. "A judge would have sentenced him, not Austin."

"Maybe so. But he wouldn't have had a trial if the sheriff hadn't tracked him down."

"Why did you drag us all the way up here if all you want to do is kill Austin?" Cassie asked. "Why didn't you just wait for him at the ranch?"

He loomed over them, a menacing expression on his face. "My brother suffered for six months in that shit-hole before he died. I intend to see that Barret suffers before he dies. His torture will begin the minute he shows up and finds out his bride has disappeared."

As Cassie listened to Kane's threats, a torrent of black fear threatened to erupt from deep inside, taking all clarity, all reason away from her. She fought to keep her wits and to understand how this could be happening again. This man was as crazy as Noley. But her concern for Ginny was even greater so she willed herself to remain calm. "Austin won't come alone. Cole Adams will be with him. You can't fight them both."

"I don't intend to fight either of them. Nobody can ride up here without being seen. I left instructions as to what I expect. If Austin comes alone, he'll see his wife alive. If I see anyone else with him, I'll kill both of you. It's that simple. I've watched Barret closely. He's like a man possessed when it comes to this little wife of his. He won't do anything to jeopardize her life. When he comes, I'll get the pleasure of having my way with her while her husband watches. When I'm through, I'll kill him. Having you along is an added bonus. You'll keep me entertained while we wait."

Ginny started to cry. Cassie's fear rose again like a giant fist, threatening to snuff the breath out of her. Then just as quick, fierce anger raged up even more commanding. This isn't going to happen, she vowed. She was through being bullied by evil men. This lunatic wasn't going hurt either one of them. She didn't know how, but she was determined to stop him.

The cowhands thought they would spend at least one more night on the trail. But once they started down the west side of Rollins Pass, and Austin could see glimpses of the luscious green valley waiting below, he pushed them hard, determined not to spend another night away from his wife. Cole was as relieved as the others to have the drive almost over. He rolled his shoulders forward, trying to stretch out some of the tiredness. Driving cattle through the mountains was definitely something he never wanted to repeat. The rough terrain and thick pines made the job of keeping the cattle moving twice as hard. And it seemed to take twice as long. The past week had worn them all to a nub.

There wasn't much relief at night, either. Especially last night; every one of them had to guard the herd after a mountain lion got one of the young steers. At one point, Cole had wished they still had Ring and Dan with them. But not for long, as tired as he was, he felt better knowing they were with Cassie, and that she was safe on the ranch.

What a strange impact she'd had on him. She was unlike anyone he'd ever met. Even before he found out she was a woman, he'd sensed there was something different about her. Learning more about her past only deepened his attraction to her. Her frailty, he knew now, was only a result of all she'd been through. Any woman who could survive what she had and keep going was anything but frail. She was courageous and intelligent, compassionate and beautiful.

And his mind couldn't let her go.

When he'd least expect it, a vision of her would drift into his thoughts. Almost always at a time when he'd be better off with his attention elsewhere.

It was late afternoon by the time the tired men settled the herd in their new pasture and rode into the ranch yard. Cole's exhaustion vanished as he anticipated seeing Cassie. Buck and Charley turned their mounts toward the barn. Brew pulled the wagon team to a halt next to Cole and Austin and jumped down.

Unsettled by the absence of activity, Austin hadn't dismounted. "What the hell's going on?" He flipped the leather thong off his firearm, and Cole, sensing his concern, did the same. They climbed down from their saddles just as the pups came running from the barn.

"I'll tend the horses," Brew said. "You two go on in the house and look around."

Silence greeted the two men when they swung the kitchen door open and walked inside. "Ginny?" Austin called out as he walked over to lay his hand on the cold stove. "She would have started supper by now."

Cole followed Austin through the parlor into the hallway. He agreed. Something was very wrong. He slipped a pistol out of the holster. Austin headed toward his and Ginny's room and Cole turned the opposite way.

When he threw open the door to the second bedroom, his insides twisted into a knot. The bed was unmade. The lamp lay on its side, most of the oil had seeped out over the top of the lace doily and down onto the floor. The window had been shattered. He stepped inside, forcing himself to stay calm. Cassie had obviously been sleeping here. Her shirt and trousers were folded on top of the trunk with her leather medicine bag next to them. Her moccasins were on the floor almost under the bed. He quickly scanned the rest of the room. When he looked behind the door he noticed that deep gouges had been scratched out of the bottom.

"Austin, come here." He walked to the window. Some of the broken shards were covered with blood and dark hair.

Austin pounded down the hall and stormed into the room. His face blanched. "My God! What's happened? Ginny's nowhere to be found!"

Cole jerked off his hat and ran a hand through his hair, fighting to maintain control so he could think straight. "I don't know. It looks like Ring was in here. I think that's his hair stuck to the glass. Let's have a look outside."

Once in the yard, they heard Buck calling to them from the barn. They followed him into the tack room where they found the other men crowded together. Ollie and Dan were sitting on the floor rubbing their wrists. Ollie's forehead was cut and swollen to the size of a goose egg; dried blood covered one whole side of his face.

Brew took in Austin and Cole's ominous expressions and stepped protectively in front of the ranch hands. "They were tied and gagged, Austin."

Austin thrust Brew aside and jerked Dan to his feet. "Where's Ginny?"

"Kane's got her, he's got both of them." The younger man's eyes flicked to Cole for a moment and then he swallowed hard and looked back at Austin. "He jumped me sometime early this morning while I was sleeping. Brought me in here and tied me up. He'd already cold-cocked Ollie and dragged him in here." His expression filled with remorse. "He had his gun to my head, Austin. Told me he already had the women and if I made a move he'd kill them. I'm sorrier than hell I let you down." His voice cracked with his last words.

Austin dropped his hands and clenched them at his sides. His entire body shook with fury and fear. His voice rang loud in the small room. "Did he say anything? Tell you anything?"

"He's going to the Ute fort. Said he wants you to follow him. You alone." Dan glanced pointedly at Cole. "If anyone comes with you he'll kill the women."

"What does he want?" Austin ground out. "Get on with it, man."

"Apparently you arrested his brother some time back. He was sent to prison and died trying to escape. Kane blames you."

Austin shook his head slowly back and forth. "What an idiot I was to trust that son-of-a-bitch. If he hurts Ginny, I'll never forgive myself."

"It's my fault," Ollie interrupted. He tried to stand but couldn't make it. "You left Ginny in my care."

Cole helped Ollie to his feet, his calm manner defying the rage and fear ripping through his insides. "You better go on into the bunk house and lie down for awhile, Ollie." He turned to Dan. "You say they left this morning?"

"Yeah, a few hours before dawn. But funny thing, Cole, I thought I heard a window break quite a while later."

"I think it was Ring. He must have been locked in Cassie's room and broke through the window to get out."

"I'm getting a fresh horse," Austin said and pushed past the others, his long strides already taking him out of the room.

Cole followed. "You're not going alone."

Austin kept walking. "He said he'd kill Ginny if I didn't."

"Don't be a fool, Austin. He may kill her anyway."

Austin snarled and spun around. He grabbed the front of Cole's shirt with both hands. Cole threw up his arms to break Austin's grip and shoved him backwards. "Get a hold of yourself. You know better than to race off half-cocked like this. He doesn't have to know I'm along. I'll hang back when we get up there."

Austin answered with a savage look before he rushed off to saddle a horse.

Cassie could feel sweat trickling down her back and underneath her arms. The sun was penetrating in the high altitude, even in the later hours of the day. With no trees, there wasn't any relief from the heat and glare. She longed to take off the coat, but her wrists were bound too tightly to even consider it. Besides, the brilliant light made the gown practically transparent, and she didn't want to give Kane any more encouragement.

She looked over at Ginny who was leaning against a rock, eyes closed, obviously spent from worrying. Her cheeks and nose were turning bright red with sunburn, and Cassie could tell from the way her own face felt that it probably looked the same.

Kane was out of sight. He frequently disappeared behind the large rocks, pacing from one lookout to another to watch for Austin. But he was never gone for long. Cassie was debating whether or not she should try and grab her knife when she heard his booted steps. He stopped directly in front of her. She glanced up, and her heart raced at the look in his eyes.

"Stand up," he ordered.

Ginny's eyes flew open. Cassie's limbs failed to move. Kane grabbed the front of her coat and jerked her to her feet. He put both arms around her and held her close while he untied her hands. Cassie was repulsed by his smell of filth and fetid alcohol. Her wrists stung as he worked the knots loose. When the rawhide fell free, he yanked her coat off and threw it aside. She stumbled from his rough treatment, but quickly righted herself, trying to massage the feeling back into her hands and wrists. Fear swelled in her throat. Her mind scrambled for some way out of this ordeal.

Kane's leering gaze moved down the length of her. "Take off the nightgown."

"Don't do this, Kane. You'll be sorry if you do." Cassie used every ounce of control she had left to keep fear out of her voice.

Ginny lurched to her feet. "Leave her alone. If you have to do this, take me."

Cassie couldn't believe Ginny's foolish reaction. She thought of the new life growing inside her friend's womb and moved to stand protectively in front of her. "No, don't listen to her. I'll do it."

Kane bent over with laughter. "This is rich. You two gonna fight over me?" He looked at Ginny and hissed, "Yer time's coming, just as soon as the sheriff shows up."

He grabbed Cassie's arm. She jerked free, ripping the sleeve of her gown to expose a shoulder and the upper part of her breast. Kane grunted an obscene remark and attacked her again. When his big hands fastened on her shoulders, Cassie's mind snapped. Suddenly it was Noley's face that sneered at her, Noley's laughter ringing in her ears. A white-hot hysteria exploded from her throat, "NO!" She screamed at the top of her lungs and pounded at his face and chest. Kane threw her to the ground and fell on top of her, forcing the air from her lungs.

Cassie gasped for breath and savagely clawed at his eyes. He cuffed the side of her head and locked both her wrists in his left hand. As he reached for the hem of her gown, a dark shadow streaked over them. Cassie twisted her head in time to see Ring land against Kane, knocking him off of her. Before Kane could react, the massive dog flattened him to the ground and tore at his face and neck with his fangs.

Cassie scooted away and groped under her gown for her knife. Both women's hands shook as she cut through the rawhide around Ginny's wrists. Then they held each other and watched the horrible thrashing of man and beast.

Kane swung at the dog with a fist, but missed. Ring's vicious attack had caught the man off guard, weakening him. Still, he managed to get his gun out of the holster. Cassie held her breath as Kane fumbled his hold, and the gun slipped out of his bloody hands. She ran over and picked up the gun as Ring continued his assault. This time Kane got a foot under his belly and kicked. The dog yelped and fell away. Kane clambered to his feet. He turned to kick the stunned animal again.

"Don't move." Cassie's words swung him around. Blood flowed from deep slashes on his face and neck. The top of his shirt was shredded. He started toward her.

"Don't take another step." Her voice shook, but her words were firm. "I know how to shoot, and I won't hesitate to do so."

"Fucking bitch," he muttered and leapt for the gun. The bullet hit him square in the chest. He staggered forward. The next bullet shattered his face.

Cassie's legs folded and she sank to the ground. Ginny ran over and held her close. They sat on the ground, rocking and crying until Ring limped over and prodded Cassie's face with a wet nose. She couldn't even raise her hand to pet him.

Ginny noticed her lack of response. "Come on, Cassie, let's get out of here," she prodded, standing to shrug off her coat and then wrapped the gun in it.

Cassie continued to sit in a heap while Ginny tied their coats behind their saddles. Finally, with gentle urging, Cassie was able to climb into the saddle by herself. Ginny sighed in relief once she was on her own horse. Her friend would be all right with rest, she reasoned. And in a near panic to get home, she headed both horses down the trail.

CHAPTER ELEVEN

Cole followed behind Austin. Daylight was gone, so they trusted the horses footing on the mountainside. He'd only been to the Ute Fort one time and was grateful his friend seemed to know the way, even in the dark. Both of them were obsessed with what the two women might be facing. Cole knew better than to even bring the subject up, so he kept his thoughts and his fears to himself and concentrated on keeping his senses alert.

Time dragged by, marked by the moon's slow ascent across the sky. Cole figured it must be after midnight when a sound in the trees up ahead put him on full alert. Austin heard it too and motioned Cole to stop. They strained to see through the darkness, heard another sound and finally glimpsed movement.

Ring burst out of the darkness and barked an enthusiastic greeting when he saw them. The horses carrying the two women appeared soon after. Austin kicked his horse forward, swept Ginny off her horse and onto his lap, then buried his face in her hair. "Oh, my God, you're safe. You're safe."

Ginny clung to him and sobbed deliriously. "It was aw…awful. He tied us up… wouldn't let us dress. He…was going to kill you after he…. He t… tried to…to…rape Cassie. She k…killed him, Austin. Ring came. He…was going to make you watch… Oh, Austin."

"Hush, baby, it's over now. I've got you."

Cole tried to make sense out of Ginny's hysteria as Ring ran in circles around him, continuing to bark. Cole signaled him to stop and leaned down

114

to scratch his ears. He could feel blood matted in the dog's hair. "Good boy, Ring. Good boy,"

He straightened and urged his horse closer to Cassie's. She looked small and forlorn. He ached to hold her, to feel her in his arms. Instead he asked, "Are you all right?"

She didn't answer. Even in the darkness, Cole could see her face was sunburned and streaked with dirt, and she didn't seem to be aware that her gown was ripped, revealing a considerable amount of shoulder and breast. "Where's Kane?"

Ginny heard the question and looked over at Cole. "He's back at the rocks, Cole. He's dead. Cassie shot him." She turned back to her husband. "I don't know what's wrong with her, Austin. She hasn't spoken since..." Her voice broke again with fresh sobs.

Cassie looked like she might fall off the horse any minute. Cole couldn't stand it. He reached for her, and she fell into his arms. He lifted her onto his lap, and she collapsed against him. He saw the leather jacket behind her saddle, untied it with one hand, and wrapped it around her. When he nestled her back against him, he felt the bulge of her knife beneath the thin gown. *My God, what had they been through?*

Austin signaled him to start back, and they turned their horses down the trail, knowing the other horses would follow. Cassie continued to tremble, and Cole tightened his hold on her, wishing he could say or do something to help. Her feet were bare and probably freezing, but there wasn't anything he could do about them right now.

He thought again about what Ginny had told them. Cassie had killed Kane. That made twice, now, she had been forced to fight off a madman. "A man ought to think real hard before he messes with you, little warrior," he whispered to the top of her head.

It was nearly dawn when they reached the ranch. Dan was waiting for them, pacing back and forth with a lantern. His worried expression turned to one of immense relief when he realized the women were safe.

Austin apologized for his earlier rough treatment and assured his young friend that he wasn't to blame. He related to him the little he knew about Kane's death, and asked him to leave at first light to get the body and take it to the sheriff at Hot Sulphur Springs. Then he dismounted and carried Ginny to their room.

Cole carried Cassie into the yellow bedroom and sat her gently on the edge of the bed. Someone had cleaned up the glass and the rest of the mess, and the lamp had been replaced. Cole struck a match and lit it, then kneeled on the floor in front of her. Just then, Austin looked in on them and shot Cole a questioning glance.

"I think she's in shock." Cole said.

"They've had a rough time. Will you take care of her, Cole? Ginny's already asleep, passed out the second she laid down. I'm going to clean up and go to bed myself."

"Before you do, would you mind staying with Cassie long enough for me to clean up?"

"Yeah, go ahead."

After a quick wash, Cole returned with a pan of warm water. Austin said goodnight and left them alone. Cassie sat on the edge of the bed unmoving. Cole rinsed the dirt off her face with a cloth. She showed no signs of awareness that he was even in the room. He rinsed the cloth out and then wiped it over her neck and shoulder, purposely avoiding the half-exposed breast. Next, he washed her hands. Fury tightened his jaw when he saw the raw flesh around her wrists. He wished Cassie hadn't killed the bastard; he would've liked the pleasure of taking him apart with his bare hands.

He reflected on all she'd been through and marveled at her ability to endure it all. When he bathed the soles of her feet, he moved the cloth tenderly around the cuts and bruises, wondering if she'd be able to walk in the morning. Throughout his gentle care, Cassie showed no response. Finally, he set the dirty water aside, returned to the bed and kneeled in front of her. "Cassie, you're worn out. Why don't you lay down now and try to get some sleep." He noticed the torn gown had slipped farther down. When he grasped the torn sleeve to tug it up, she jerked violently away from him.

"It's okay. I won't hurt you. You're safe."

She focused on him for several heartbeats before she seemed to understand who he was. Then she muttered in a whisper he could barely hear, "He found me, Cole. Noley found me. He took us to the Ute fort. He's going' to kill Austin."

Cole's stomach clenched. "Cassie, listen to me," he spoke as gently as he could. Noley's not here. It was Kane. Arthur Kane took you and Ginny. But he won't hurt you anymore. He's dead, remember?"

She was trembling again. "He's dead?"

"Yes."

She sagged back against the wall, her expression ravaged. "They're all dead. Da, Mum, Running Deer. Ring too. Noley killed Ring. Everyone's gone. Burned up. There's nothing left. No one left." She rambled now, under her breath.

She was scaring him. "Cassie, you're exhausted. Lay down now and get some sleep. We can talk in the morning. Ring isn't dead. I'll bring him in and let him sleep by your bed. You'll be okay with Ring here."

Her eyes filled with terror. She grabbed at his shirt. "Don't leave. Please, don't leave me."

"All right, I won't leave." He drew her to her feet, turned down the blankets, and eased her back down. Then he kicked off his boots, stretched out beside her on the narrow bed and pulled the blankets over them both. When he reached to turn down the lamp, she stopped him.

"Please, leave it on."

He did as she asked. She curled up on her side, facing away from him, nestling her small rump against him. A perfect fit, he thought, and encircled her with his arms.

Very little time passed before Cole heard her soft breathing and was grateful she'd gone to sleep. He held her close and rested his cheek against her hair, wrestling with the sensations that besieged him whenever this woman was near.

She wasn't asleep. He felt hot tears on his hand. A few minutes later, her quiet sniffles erupted into soul-wrenching sobs. He held her tight, not moving, not saying a word, and feeling completely helpless. He couldn't believe anyone could cry that hard or that long. But when the last fragments of horror were cried out, she surrendered to sleep.

His own sleep eluded him until much later.

When Cassie awakened, she felt as if she'd been trampled by a herd of cattle. Everything hurt. Her face burned, her back ached, her wrists stung, and the insides of her thighs were on fire. But she needed to get up and use the chamber pot.

She groaned when her feet hit the floor, it felt like she was standing on hot coals. A glance down at the torn gown brought back images of the previous day. From the time she was old enough to understand, she had been taught to honor life. But a man was dead by her hands. The horror of it made her sick inside. She had blown his face off with a gun.

Ginny stood in front of the stove stirring something in a big iron pot when Cassie entered the kitchen wearing the beige and white checked dress. "Hello." Her voice sounded as weak as she felt.

Ginny set the spoon down, placed a lid on the simmering pot, and wrapped her arms around Cassie. "I've been so worried. Are you all right? How are you feeling?"

"Better. Sore. What time is it?"

"Late afternoon actually. I've only been up a couple of hours myself. Sit down and I'll get us some coffee."

"Thank you." Cassie sat on one of the ladder back chairs at the far side of the table. "I've applied ointment to just about every part of my body. I brought you some. How are you? How's the baby?"

Ginny took the concoction of herbs and set it aside. "Thank you. I'll use it in a bit. I'm very sore, and a little tired, but otherwise fine." She handed Cassie a cup of coffee and took a chair across from her. She placed a hand over her belly. "The baby's fine too. I've been concerned about you, though. You seemed really confused last night. I'm so relieved you're better."

Cassie stared at her cup. She took a deep breath and slowly let it out. "I killed him, Ginny. I killed Kane."

"Yes."

"It was horrible."

"Yes, it was. But Cassie, Arthur Kane was crazy. You had to do it. You saved not only our lives, but the baby's too, and probably Austin's."

"Perhaps, but it just keeps haunting me. His face. When I shot him... Did you see his face?" She looked up at Ginny, remembering Noley's face too, after she cut through his eye with her knife.

Ginny swallowed hard and glanced away for a second. "Yes, I saw it. You had to do it Cassie. Don't you see that?"

"I do, Ginny. It's just that..." How could she explain her feelings when she didn't understand them herself? Twice now she had been forced to protect herself from ruthless men. She had scarred one for life and killed the other one. Her spirit felt sickened by the brutality of it. When would all this violence end?

Ginny placed a hand over Cassie's. "Don't think about it anymore. What's done is done. We just need a little time and we can put it all behind us. Tomorrow it won't look so bad. And the next day will be even better."

Ginny still held one hand protectively over her belly. Cassie forced a smile for her friend. "Have you told Austin? About the baby, I mean?"

Ginny smiled back and nodded. "Just a little while ago."

"And?"

"I think he was pleased. His response was a little reserved."

"I'm sure he was delighted. He needs some time too. He was probably scared to death when he arrived home and found you gone."

"He was. He blames himself. I tried to convince him that he had no way of knowing about Kane, but he wouldn't listen. He insists he was a lawman for years and should have known better. It's this responsibility thing he has for me. Ever since we met, he has taken on the role of my rescuer and protector."

"Rescuer?"

Ginny's face turned a darker shade of red beneath her sunburn. "Cassie… I…ah." She took a deep breath and looked away for a minute as if carefully measuring her next words. "When Austin and I met, I… worked in a brothel."

This hesitant confession was the last thing Cassie had expected to hear. She carefully kept her expression bland. It had obviously taken a great deal of courage for Ginny to say those words, and she didn't want to put her off.

Ginny stared down at the table where she was drawing circles with a spoon. "Five years ago, a man found me wandering the streets of St. Louis. I was 16, homeless, starving, and wearing rags. He…um…used me for his own pleasure, and then he sold me to a woman who owned a brothel. I was so destitute in every way that I didn't care. I had no place else to go. There were three other girls there. The woman, Sadie, she treated us badly. She also cheated the men who…um.... visited us. Eventually the law ran us out of town. We ended up here in Colorado Territory, in Golden City, where Austin was the sheriff." She paused for a moment and her hand stilled. Then a modest smile took the pain from her eyes. "Austin said he fell in love with me at first sight."

Cassie was sick at heart for her friend, but couldn't resist smiling back at the shy way Ginny spoke of her husband's love.

"Right from the beginning," Ginny continued, more animated now, "Austin set out to protect me and get me away from Sadie's grasp. The easiest way was for him to buy me. He didn't have a lot of money, but he paid Sadie every month to keep other men away from me. A year later we were married."

She stopped talking so abruptly it took a moment for Cassie to realize she was finished with her tale. She seemed to wait with dread for Cassie's reaction. "Thank heavens Austin was so persistent."

Ginny laughed with relief. "I must say, that certainly wasn't the response I'd imagined. Hoped for, maybe, but…"

"What do you mean?"

"Oh, Cassie, you don't know how good it's been for me to have you here. I've never had a friend before. My father died when I was small. My mother remarried right away. I was five. My stepfather was…. he was…" Her hands tightened on the cup and she stared down at them." My stepfather was very cruel. He felt it was his right to…use me, you know, in that way, whenever he wanted. My mom turned her back on the situation. I pretty much kept to myself in school and finally ran away from home when I was fifteen. I didn't make friends with the others who worked for Sadie. I don't know why. I just couldn't seem to trust anyone. Even after Austin and I married, I had no friends. The nice ladies in town wouldn't accept me, even though Austin was respected. Or maybe it was me who couldn't accept me. I don't know. But when Austin decided to leave his job, move up here and build the ranch, I was elated."

She got up and went to the stove, then topped off their cups with coffee. "I think it was Cole who suggested it. He would come by now and then to check on me. I guess he could tell I was having a tough time. He's been a good friend." She smiled again at Cassie. "But you're the first woman friend I've ever had."

Cassie felt honored by her statement and her trust. "You're my first friend, too. My mother and great-grandmother were like friends. We were so close. But I've never been around other women. I'm sorry about what you went through as a little girl. My childhood was so different. I was sheltered and protected and loved. Too much so, perhaps. I lived an isolated existence, but never once felt deprived. We had so many books, and my father taught me more than I could have ever learned in school. Still I feel totally unprepared now that I'm on my own. You did what you had to in order to survive, Ginny. I could never judge you for that. If it wasn't for Zeb and Dalton, and all of you, who knows where I'd be right now."

"Your survival instincts are pretty strong too, Cassie. You proved that yesterday."

"Aye. But that was yesterday. I don't know where I'm going or what I'm going to do tomorrow or the tomorrows to come. Is it as difficult as it seems for a woman to make it alone?"

"Yes. It is very hard, especially out here. That's why there are so few of us. Even in a city that's growing as fast as Denver, women are given few choices. Their wages are less than six dollars a week, barely half what men make. And even if they're lucky enough to find work as a servant, or something related, their days are ten to fifteen hours long. That kind of toil wears a woman down real fast."

Cassie was beginning to feel even more doubtful about her future. Ginny's words painted a bleak picture. "I guess it's easy for prostitution to move to the top of the list when you're starving."

Ginny nodded, solemnly. "For some women it's the only answer. There was a woman named Emily who came to work for Sadie shortly after we moved out here. She was forced into prostitution after her husband divorced her. She tried to find other work, but there wasn't anything. Men control the world, Cassie. Women need men in order to survive, so that means men control women as well. And there are always men around to offer prostitution to a woman alone. Many of those men are even considered respectable citizens." Her voice grew quiet. "Cassie, some of the girls they use are as young as ten." The horror on Cassie's face brought her up short. She lightened her next words. "But you don't have to worry about any of that. You have a home with us for as long as you want."

"I heard that," Austin said, coming into the kitchen. He stepped behind his wife's chair and placed his hands on her shoulders. "And I second my wife's invitation. We want you to stay, Cassie, forever if you want. Besides, we're going to need you come February. He smiled at Ginny's upturned face then he looked back at Cassie. "I know how good you are with gun-shot wounds and hail bruising, how are you at birthing a baby?"

Cassie grinned at the two of them, seeing the same passion and love between them that her parents shared. "I would be most happy to help with the baby. Thank you for making me feel so welcome, but..." her words trailed off as she struggled to find the words she wanted to say.

"But what?" Austin prompted.

Cassie took a deep breath and let it out with a sigh. "I don't think it's a good idea for me to stay here."

"Why not?" Ginny asked.

Cassie stared intently at Austin, willing him to understand, yet afraid he wouldn't. "Because of the danger following me. Austin you don't want that kind of trouble around Ginny and the baby."

"We need to talk about that, Cassie." He pulled out the chair next to his wife, sat down and propped his elbows on the crocheted tablecloth. "I think we should go to the law with this. I've got people I can talk to. That man needs to be hunted down and brought to trial for his crimes."

Cassie set her cup down and dropped her suddenly clammy hands to her lap. Her voice was scarcely audible when she said, "Please don't do that, Austin."

"But why?" Austin seemed genuinely baffled by her resistance to seek legal help. "Did he or did he not kill your mother?"

"Austin!" Ginny exclaimed, "Why are you being so harsh?" She turned to Cassie, her eyes filled with tears. "Oh, Cassie. No one told me your mother had been killed. I'm so sorry."

Before Cassie could respond, the screen door swung open, and the three people at the table turned as one to stare at Cole as he stepped into the room. "What's going on?" he asked, his eyes narrowing.

"Sit down," Austin said. "You might as well be in on this."

"In on what?"

Austin waited for Cole to take a chair at the end of the table. "We were just talking about Cassie's situation. I was repeating my feelings about asking for help from the law."

Cole looked deep into Cassie's eyes as if he were searching for something. His scrutiny moved lower for a moment before returning to her face. She realized he had never seen her in a dress before. "Is that what you want, Cassie?" he asked, his voice gentle. "Do you want to go to the law?"

"I can't get any help from the law." Cassie chewed on her bottom lip, knowing what was coming and wondering how to handle it.

Austin leaned forward in frustration. "There's more to this than we know isn't there? What aren't you telling us, Cassie?"

"Austin, please," Ginny pleaded. "It sounds like you're interrogating her."

"Honey, you don't understand. Cassie claims her mother was murdered and she was nearly killed herself. I'm just trying to get some answers."

"What do you mean, `she claims' her mother was killed?" Cole bristled. "Are you implying you don't you believe her?"

"Of course, I believe her. That's not it at all. Look, the man has already tracked her as far as Denver. If we're going to help her, we need to know everything we can."

All eyes turned toward Cassie. She felt like a rabbit trapped in a cage. She knew she had to tell them something. But what?

She was so tired of the deceit.

Maybe her father was right, she thought. Maybe the white world couldn't accept the Indian race. But according to what Ginny had told her a few minutes ago, life wasn't easy for any woman, Indian or white. And what difference did it make anyway? Life as she knew it had been destroyed several weeks ago. She didn't have a home anymore. No clothes. No belongings. Nothing. She was totally dependent on others for her very existence. And she was worn down from it. These people had befriended her. Surely they wouldn't cast her out just because of her Indian blood. Besides, Ginny had trusted Cassie enough to confide her past.

She straightened in her chair, folded her hands on top of the table, took a deep breath, and began. "My father was an artist and a writer. He was from Ireland, traveling through this country documenting his adventures with pen and ink as well as paint on canvas. When he met my mother, he fell deeply in love. After they married, he bought a small farm in Kentucky near the Mississippi river. My mother loved him too, and was happy to go anywhere with him. She was a beautiful, gentle woman. She was also a native of the Choctaw Nation."

No one moved a muscle or said a word. They simply stared at her expectantly. So she found the courage to resume.

"Barnaby Noley lived on the neighboring farm. He never bothered us until my father had a stroke. After he died, his lust for my mother grew out of control. He raped and killed her when she refused to submit to him. I ran in just after it happened. When he attacked me, I cut him very badly and got away. He wants revenge and won't stop until he gets it. Since I am considered a half-breed, no white court of law would take my word over a white man's. I'm sorry, Austin, but I will not expose my whereabouts to him by going to the law."

The stony silence continued around the table for another few moments.

Ginny found her voice first. "Oh, Cassie, I'm so sorry. How dreadful for you." She looked imploringly at her husband. "Austin, don't you see? Cassie's right. She can't go to the law. We'll watch out for her ourselves."

Cassie glanced briefly at Austin, who remained thoughtful, then confronted Cole's piercing-blue scrutiny. As usual, his face gave nothing away of what he was thinking.

With great effort, she dragged her attention away from the men and turned to meet Ginny's soft brown eyes, shimmering with tears of concern. Cassie's filled with tears of gratitude. "Thank you for understanding, Ginny. And I appreciate your offer to stay here, but it would put you in too much danger."

"You aren't leaving because of me," Ginny flatly stated, with the slap of her hand on the table for emphasis. "I'm not afraid. Besides, that man will never be able to find you up here."

"She's not going anywhere," Austin assured his wife. He turned to Cassie. "I understand now, Cassie, and I agree. Unfortunately, our courts can be prejudiced. And I'm sorry about that. This is definitely a time I'd like to see justice served. Ginny's idea is best. You'll be safer here than anywhere else. I learned a hard lesson with Kane, I'll make sure nothing like that ever happens again."

Ginny stood and pushed her chair under the table. "Good, then everything's settled. You men go and wash up for supper, it's just about ready. Cassie, you can set the table."

Cassie didn't feel like anything was settled. But she was hugely relieved to have everything out in the open, grateful there were no more secrets.

Suppertime was pleasant. Cassie still had no idea what Cole was thinking, because some of the other men joined them and the conversation was kept light and companionable. No one mentioned Dan, but Ginny had told her earlier that Austin sent him to retrieve Kane's body and take it to the sheriff.

After supper, Buck and Charley retired to the bunkhouse, taking along a plate of food for Ollie who was still nursing a headache. Austin, Brew and Cole sat in the living room, smoking cigars and talking about the coming winter and how it would affect the ranch. Cassie and Ginny put the kitchen in order. When the last dish was dried and put away, Ginny said she was going to join the men. Cassie excused herself and walked outside into the black night.

Ring and the two pups greeted her with wagging tails. They followed close behind as she walked to the corral and leaned a shoulder against a pine rail.

Clouds moved overhead, occasionally parting to reveal the light of the moon. Cassie marveled, for what seemed like the thousandth time, at how close the sky felt in this high country. She took a deep breath of the crisp, sweet-smelling air, loving the contrast of the hot days and chilly nights. In fact, there wasn't much she didn't like about these mountains.

She had made that statement at supper, and Brew had responded that she would feel different after she spent a winter in them. Then he'd gone on to relate stories of the people he'd met who'd been enticed by the beauty of the mountains, only to desperately move back out of them as soon as the snow piled up several feet high and the temperature plummeted to freeze man and beast alike.

But his dire predictions didn't discourage her one bit. In fact, winter could prove to be her ally. If she could keep Noley from finding her until winter, maybe he'd give up and go back home. A chill moved through her as she recalled his vow to track her down. She had scarred his face horribly. And even though she couldn't go to the law, she was still a threat to him. What if he never gave up?

Her heart skipped a beat as she sensed someone behind her. She whirled around to see Cole step up and rest a booted foot on the bottom rail of the fence.

"It's dark out here, tonight."

"You move like a cat. I didn't hear you coming."

"I spent some time with an old mountain man. He trained me well."

She turned back around and stared into the night beyond the corral, waiting for her heart to settle back down. But Cole shifted closer, causing it to kick up even more erratically. Even though he wasn't touching her, she could feel him against the entire length of her back.

"A mountain man, huh. When was that?" she asked.

"A few years back." With each word, his breath teased the top of her hair.

Cassie had never been more aware of the unseen power of another human being. "He taught you to sneak up on people?"

"He taught me a lot of things. Sneaking up on people was only one of them. Moving without being heard is necessary when you are hunting... or hiding from Indians."

His tone was teasing, but she was still unsure of his feelings about her earlier declaration. She turned to face him. "Are you afraid of Indians?"

"I respect them. There's a difference."

"Aye." A big difference, she thought, and began to relax a little.

"You've been afraid of us, Cassie."

"I've been afraid of everyone and everything since I left Kentucky. I haven't been sure who to trust or how much I could say. My father taught me to hide my Indian heritage."

"You speak with a hint of the Irish."

"You noticed that, did you?"

"Yes." He was standing close, but dark clouds blocked most of the light, making it difficult to see the details of each other's faces.

"My father never lost his strong brogue. I guess I picked up a bit of it."

"What is your name? Your full name, I mean."

"Cassandra Cathleen O'Brian. I was named after my paternal grandmother. I supposedly look like her too."

"She must have been a lovely woman."

Cassie was grateful for the darkness. She felt like her entire body was blooming with color. "What a lovely thing to say."

Cole skipped quickly back to her heritage, making her feel as if she'd misinterpreted the compliment. "Why did your father want you to deny your Indian blood?"

"By the time he met my mother, he'd already begun to understand the tragedy the Indians were experiencing as the white population and the government demanded more and more of their land. She had no family left except for her grandmother because most of her people were forced to relocate. Word got back of the horror and suffering they experienced along that journey. My father believed that the Indian race was doomed. That the white's crusade to control and own all the land in this great country would leave the Indians with nothing. He did everything he could to protect my mother from the outside world. After I was born, his protection included me. He educated me himself, so I wouldn't have to leave the farm to go to school."

"He kept you a prisoner."

Cassie's spine stiffened. She drew herself up to her full five-feet-four-inches. "I was not a prisoner. My father was the most kind, loving, generous, supportive man who--"

"Who would have been wiser to prepare you for the real world. Looking white didn't keep you from being nearly raped and killed by two different men."

Cassie was shocked into speechlessness by his heated statement. She stared at him, her mouth open, trying to gauge where he was coming from. Was he upset with her or for her?

Before she could think of a response, he said, "I apologize. I had no business saying that."

Cassie was surprised by the abrupt turnaround. He sounded as if he meant it, and she had a feeling apologies didn't come easy for him.

When she didn't say anything, he veered another direction. "Do Zeb and Dalton know your mother was an Indian?"

"No. I was afraid they wouldn't take me with them if they knew, so I didn't tell them everything."

"Have you told us everything?"

"Aye," she said, "I'm grateful to have all the secrets out in the open, at least with you, Ginny and Austin. She still wasn't sure how Cole felt about her mixed blood, but at least Ginny and Austin seemed to accept her for who she was. Which made one less burden to carry.

Cole sensed her hesitation. "What's wrong? Is there more?"

"No." She lifted her eyes to him. "I can't quit thinking about Kane. I shot him in the face, Cole. You can't imagine what it looked like. It reminded me of the way Noley looked that day in Denver. His scars are hideous." She shuddered and folded her arms protectively over her chest. "I hadn't realized how severely I wounded him. One side of his face is a mass of scars, and the eye is gone." She shuddered again and dropped her gaze.

Cole placed his hands on her upper arms. "It's over now, Cassie. You did what you had to do."

"Maybe it's over with Kane, but not with Noley. He said he would find me. And he will, Cole, I know he will."

"Look at me, Cassie." Cole gently squeezed her arms, and she looked up. "It would be very difficult for him to find you up here. You have friends now that will do everything possible to keep you safe.

"I appreciate your good intentions, Cole. But you can't spend every waking moment with me."

Cole ran his hands up her arms to her shoulders and lowered his face in order to see her better in the darkness. "Maybe not, little warrior, but I'd sure like to try."

Cassie experienced the familiar drowning sensation and looked away, resisting the overwhelming urge to touch him back. Her emotions were too fragile right now. If she didn't take care, her feelings for Cole would consume her. Unconsciously, she reached for the necklace tucked inside the top of her dress.

Cole had obviously observed the gesture before. "Who was Running Deer, Cassie?"

Her gaze flew back to his. "How do you know that name?"

"You said it last night. You said Running Deer was dead."

"She is." Cassie tried to look away again, but Cole caught her chin and turned her back. The sincerity in his face prompted her to tell him. "Running Deer was my great-grandmother. She was a wise and wonderful old Choctaw healer."

"She taught you."

"Aye." Tears stung her eyes and the back of her throat as memories flooded in. Their long walks in the woods. The stories and legends. The hours and days spent tending the deep gash in the neck of a very pregnant doe then helping deliver her fawn. The badger with the broken front leg. Birds with broken wings, even an occasional baby bird or animal, abandoned for one reason or another by their mother. Running Deer had used anything and everything to pass on her healing skills and to teach Cassie about life.

"She also taught me that all living things are connected, and that the connection must be respected. In the short time I've been out in the world, I've come to understand why my father was so protective. The white world thinks differently. They seek only to conquer and control, whether it be rivers, land, animals, or other people. They abhor anyone and anything different from them."

"Not everyone is like that, Cassie."

His quiet statement made her sorry for the sudden, impassioned outburst. "No. There are exceptions. My father was one. And Ginny and Austin." She wanted to include him, but still wasn't sure if she could. "My great-grandmother didn't approve of my father's decree to suppress my Choctaw heritage.

She always told me I should be true to myself. But I'm not sure who or what I am anymore."

"You've been through enough to confuse anyone, Cassie. You need some time to mend. You're safe here, but if you don't want to stay here, you can come with me to Georgetown."

The impulsive statement seemed to shock them both. Cassie snapped out of it first and laughed at the look on his face. "And what would you be doin' with me in Georgetown?"

Cole looked flustered, as if he wasn't sure himself what he'd do with her. She didn't know much about him, but Ginny had told her that he was a gambler, and that he lived in a hotel room over a saloon owned by a woman friend. "Stuck for an answer, are you?" she teased.

"No, I--"

"Aye, you are." Her voice reflected her sudden burst of loneliness. It was past time to end this conversation. "You see, Cole? You can't keep me with you every minute. None of you can. You all have your own lives to live, and I have to find a way to get on with mine." She stepped out of his grasp and turned to walk back to the house.

Cole refused to let her go. He reached out and pulled her back. "Don't go in yet." He turned her in his arms and looked down at her. "Stay and talk for a while. It's still early, we can…"

She looked up at him, waiting for him to continue. But there were no more words. He gazed into her eyes for what could have been eons or only a moment. Then his mouth closed the scant distance between them to touch hers.

Cassie couldn't resist the sweet taste of him. He deepened the pressure against her lips, and she opened to experience more.

The kiss drugged them both. When he finally released her mouth and trailed his lips across her cheek to seize her ear, Cassie felt a coil of delicious tension spiral through her body to pool in her most private parts. She forgot her pledge to keep a tight hold on her feelings. She wanted to run her fingers through his hair, the same way his moved through hers, but her hands were trapped between them, just as she was trapped by the passion he aroused in her.

Cole loosened his hold and trailed soft kisses across both her eyes and the tip of her nose before moving to nuzzle her other earlobe. Cassie's hands were free now, and she locked them in the thick hair at the nape of his neck, straining herself closer against him.

His mouth burned like fire as he captured her mouth once again, forcing her back against the corral railing.

Instant pain shot through her, causing her to yelp and wrench away.

Confused, Cole dropped his hands to his sides.

Cassie rubbed her lower back, breathing heavy, still dizzy from the passion they had shared. "It's my back. It's bruised from being thrown on the ground. When we... When you... The fence... I...I'm sorry..." Her voice lagged in embarrassment.

Cole pulled her back into his arms. He put his large, hand under her chin and tipped her head up. "I'd like to kill that animal all over again for hurting you."

Cassie forgot about the pain when Cole's soothing caress re-ignited her passion along with her uncertainty. "Cole, I ought to go in, Ginny will be wondering where I am."

"No, she won't," he said, his voice had taken on a lighter note. "She and Austin already went to bed."

"They did?"

"Yes, they did."

"Oh...."

He threw his head back and laughed.

"Are you laughing at me?"

"No!" He chuckled again. "Well actually I guess I am." He was teasing her, and she liked it. She liked it too much. It was as clear as a mountain stream that the physical attraction between them was mutual. Which made it even more dangerous. She pushed against him. "Let me go now."

He tightened his hold. "Why? I like having you here."

"Cole."

"Yes?"

This man took all her good sense away. She gazed up at him and knew it was a mistake. He dipped his head toward her.

She leaned back. "Please don't kiss me anymore."

"I kind of thought you liked it."

"I do.... that is...." She lightly pushed at his chest when he chuckled at her again. "Cole, I can't think straight when you kiss me. I'm not used to being kissed."

"You're not used to it?"

"No, and I think it would be better if we didn't do it."

"Didn't do it?"

"Quit repeating everything I say. You know what I mean." A sudden gust of frigid air blew around them and Cassie shivered. "Cole, my life has been turned upside down in the past several weeks. And whenever you... whenever anyone gets too close, I...get all befuddled. I have trouble making sense out of anything."

"You're right." Cole dropped his arms and stepped back, his voice as cool as the wind. "We better get you inside before you freeze."

Cassie didn't feel the relief she'd expected when Cole walked her back to the house. Cold night air rushed around her, and she shivered again. Even though he'd only done as she asked, she felt rejected, and didn't look forward to the isolation of her room. They made it to the porch just as a loud peal of thunder rumbled across the night sky.

"That's a welcome sound," Cole said, as he opened the screen door and ushered her in. "It looks like the dry spell up here might be ending."

In the kitchen light, she could see his mask of indifference was back in place. Cassie was amazed by how quickly he could slip it on. He escorted her to her room, and then turned to leave. She touched his arm to stop him. "I hope I didn't… offend you just now. Outside, I mean."

His hands were shoved deep in the pockets of his pants. His back was rigid. But the mask slipped for a brief moment as he bent to kiss the tip of her nose. "No, little warrior, you didn't offend me. You're just taking care of you, which is exactly what you should be doing."

CHAPTER TWELVE

C ole left the house early the next morning and spent most of the day with Brew and Austin, checking the cattle and looking over the rest of the ranch. Austin hadn't said anymore about the incident with Kane, but he understandably needed to assure himself that everything else remained as he'd left it during his absence.

They inspected the ranch boundaries first then crisscrossed the interior. Everything in sight glistened from the rain Cole had heard in the early morning hours. Billowy white clouds skittered across the otherwise blue sky, creating a constantly changing patchwork of color on the face of the surrounding mountains. The snow on the highest peaks shone brightly each time the sun made its appearance. The pine forests below went from green to various shades of grey and purple, then back to green again. On the valley floor, wildflowers bloomed in every color of the rainbow.

On and on it went, and Cole was struck anew with the grandeur. He'd been the one to find this land for Austin, and he'd worked side by side with his friend during every minute of the ranch's construction. He'd helped plant the hay that waved gently in the morning breeze. He'd hauled supplies, hammered and sawed and dug holes until every muscle screamed.

He couldn't remember a time before when he'd felt such a sense of accomplishment. He almost envied Austin's new life. Almost. Austin's responsibilities were huge now. He was married, had a ranch to take care of and was heading toward fatherhood.

Complicated, Cole thought. And he liked things simple. He'd worked hard to achieve that end. He had plenty of money in the bank from his interest in several gold mines. Daily games of poker and faro kept him entertained and his mind sharp. And he had any number of willing females when he sought amusement of a different kind.

That thought brought a nagging stab of guilt into his pleasant reverie. He hadn't meant to start anything with Cassie when he followed her out to the corral last night. But she'd bewitched him as usual. The moment he touched her, he was doomed. The single kiss he'd allowed himself promptly soared out of control. He couldn't get enough of her. She affected him the same way as alcohol. One taste and he had to have more. Which is precisely why he'd quit drinking anything stronger than coffee. It hadn't taken more than one night in jail for him to finally admit to himself that every time he'd let himself get suckered into a gunfight, he'd been drinking.

He shifted his weight in the saddle, still aching with desire. It had been a strange but pleasant pleasure to lay with Cassie two nights before, simply holding her while she slept. And he enjoyed talking with her, too. Hell, he figured he'd like doing just about every damned thing there was to do with her. But he knew beyond all doubt now, if he let himself get close enough to talk to her he'd want to touch her. And touching would lead to kissing which would get him in too deep.

A bald-faced, rust-colored cow raised her head and stared at Cole with soft brown eyes. She chewed rhythmically on a mouthful of grass, her eyes watching him as if knowing the thoughts circling through his mind.

Brew must have sensed them too. He picked that precise moment to say, "Hey, Cole, I thought you'd had enough of this herd. But you don't seem in much of a rush to get back to Georgetown."

Cole stiffened with irritation and tugged his hat more firmly into place. He felt as if his mind had been wide open the past few minutes, giving everyone a view. "Mind your own business, old man."

Brew chuckled, not at all put off by the ominous tone. "You seem much more interested in holding a lariat these days than of a deck of cards. You better be careful or you'll find yourself roped and branded just like Austin."

"A man could get his skinny nose bit off sticking it into corners where it doesn't belong," Cole warned.

"Could happen. But I've managed to keep my facial features intact for a good many years now." Brew turned to Austin. "You better watch out. Our friend here seems to find the scenery here in Middle Park much improved since a certain young woman arrived. He might never get his carcass off your ranch."

Austin couldn't resist a jab of his own. "That's okay by me. I appreciate the extra muscle." He pointed his thumb toward Cole. "The work's been good for him. He's even lost his barroom pallor. He almost looks like he belongs here."

Brew's laughter increased. "Then you might just as well keep him on as a hired hand. He's probably forgotten how to play cards by now, anyway. Course, I don't think he'd be any too happy about moving his bedroll out of that comfortable house of yours and sharing the bunkhouse with Ollie. He wouldn't want that much distance between him and that pretty skirt in the room just below him."

Cole shook his head and grinned. "Aren't you getting tired, old man? Shouldn't you be getting your old bones off that horse and back to the house?"

"As a matter of fact, I am a little tired. I think I'll mosey on back and get me a little pampering from those two charming females. And get me a piece of rhubarb pie while I'm at it." Brew nudged his brown filly into a trot. "See you boys later."

Cole shook his head again, not the least bit pleased with the ribbing. It rattled him to think his friends could read him so easily. Constant thoughts of Cassie wafted through him like a strong perfume. Ever since she'd come into his life, nothing had been the same. During the last days of the drive he'd been anxious to get back to the ranch just to look at her again, prove to himself she wasn't a mirage. And now that he was here, he wanted more.

But more of what? In spite of his fantasies, he no longer had it in him to settle down with one woman. His experience with Ramona had driven that point home. He also knew he couldn't pursue Cassie with any other end in mind. She wasn't some saloon maid, eager for a quick roll behind the barn. Like she said last night, her whole world had been shattered. She was confused about her very identity. He had no business confusing her anymore than she already was. But could he be around her and not touch her? No. Impossible.

That evening as he and Austin rode toward the ranch house, Cole announced his plans to return to Georgetown. "Why do you look so damned surprised?" he asked, when Austin stared open-mouthed at him. "Everything is running smoothly here."

"I know. But I thought you'd stick around for awhile."

"What for? You don't need me anymore. There isn't anything left to do that you and Ollie and Dan can't handle."

"Maybe not, but…"

Cole slanted him a piercing look. "But what?"

"You know damn well what I was going to say. I'm not any blinder than Brewster. It's damned obvious that you're getting mighty attached to Cassie."

"Well, I'm fixing to get unattached."

"Why?"

Cole bristled. "That's none of your business."

Austin looked offended. "Don't throw that shit at me. Who do you think you're talking to? I know you better than anyone. Cassie means something to you. Why would you be so quick to walk away from her?"

Cole took off his hat and ran his fingers through his hair, struggling for words that wouldn't come. How could he explain the insanity of his feelings to Austin when he couldn't make sense out of them himself?

It was Austin's turn to shake his head. He took in his friend's troubled expression and said, "Ever since the day we met, I've found you more than willing to face down any challenge. Yet..."

"I'll never forget that day," Cole interrupted. "Your timing was perfect. You came through the door of that saloon just as I drew my piece. We had a couple of tense seconds there, didn't we? Till I figured out the drunk with the broken whiskey bottle wasn't coming at me. And you figured out I wasn't going to shoot anybody."

"Quit trying to change the subject. I..."

"You've got to admit it was an interesting way to begin a friendship. Gave the good citizens of Golden City something to poke fun at us with; their sheriff and the gun slick having a showdown over a drunk with a broken bottle."

Austin grinned and eased back in his saddle. "I know what you're doing, but you're going to hear me out."

Cole gave up. He slammed his hat back on his head and glared.

Austin sobered and continued. "I've never seen you afraid of any man or any situation. Yet your feelings for Cassie have you running away with your tail between your legs. You won't let yourself connect with anything or anyone other than your horse and that dog. I can only hope something happens one day to make you see the folly of your ways."

Cole refused to be goaded into an argument, so he kept his remark light. "That's quite a speech, Austin."

"Maybe so, but you'd be doing yourself a favor if you'd pay attention to it."

"Look. Just because you've found marital bliss, doesn't mean every other man will. Right now, Georgetown is calling, and I've got an itch to play some faro. Like Brew said, I've been away too long." He also needed to find a soft female to take away the ache he'd been afflicted with ever since meeting Cassie. But he kept that remark to himself. It would only bring another lecture.

"He didn't say goodbye." Cassie's voice sounded small to her own ears. It seemed a ridiculous, childish thing to say, but she was terribly disappointed that Cole had left so suddenly.

"He rode out at dawn," Ginny said. "All Austin told me is that Cole was in a hurry to get to Georgetown. He took Ring with him."

Cassie stopped kneading the bread dough and stared at her friend. "He did?"

Ginny stopped kneading her dough as well, and their eyes met over the kitchen table. "Yes. He said he felt confident that you'd be safe enough here on the ranch with Austin. I told Austin you'd be upset."

She was upset, hurt by his abrupt departure. Why didn't he tell her he was going? She searched her mind, trying to find an explanation. But nothing came. He'd hardly said a word to her since their time alone two nights before. He and Austin hadn't returned to the house until after dark, last night. She and Ginny had kept the men's supper warm and sat at the table with them while they ate, telling them about their visit from the sheriff when he came to ask questions about Kane. Austin assured them it was routine.

Cole had avoided Cassie's eyes every time she looked at him. He was reserved and spoke only when he was asked a direct question. She longed to get him alone and find out what was bothering him, but he excused himself and retired early.

Now he was gone. She punched the dough, trying to think of what she might have said or done to offend him. She punched it again. Then again, harder. Maybe it had nothing to do with her, she argued with herself. Maybe he just felt it was time to leave. She'd always known his stay on the ranch was temporary. He had his own life to live. She'd been the one to point that out. She had no right to be hurt when he took off to do just that.

She folded the butter-colored lump over on itself then squeezed it through her fingers. It was probably for the best. Hearing him say goodbye and watching him ride away would only have hurt worse.

The next thought immobilized her hands and brought along a cold, bleak feeling. Maybe it was because of her mixed blood. Maybe he'd thought about it and decided he wanted nothing to do with a half-breed.

No. She refused to believe that was the reason. Because if it was, she didn't think she could bear it. Still, whatever his reason, he was gone, and his departure increased the size of the hole inside her heart. And for some reason, his taking Ring with him made the feeling worse.

Self-pity threatened to dissolve her to tears, so she took her pain and frustration out on the bread dough, pounding it with a vengeance. Ginny eyed her knowingly, but said nothing.

Brew, Buck and Charlie left the next day. And the rest of the week passed quickly for those left behind as they established a comfortable routine. Austin and Dan stayed gone much of each day working on various parts of the ranch. Ollie felt better, but stayed close to the house, tending to less-strenuous tasks and keeping a watchful eye on the two women. Cassie helped Ginny with the cooking, baking, cleaning, and other endless chores.

Friday was washday, and Cassie insisted she would tend to that job by herself, freeing Ginny to sew baby clothes. She was hanging a basket of freshly laundered linens on the line when the pups started barking. She peered over the top of a sheet and noticed a rider galloping hard into the yard. Zeb. She dropped the clothespins back into the basket and hurried over to greet him.

His face was contorted with what looked like panic. Cassie's heart started to pound. "What is it? Where's Dalton? What's happened?"

Zeb stepped down from the stirrup, his entire body shaking. "He's been hurt."

"Hurt? What happened? Where is he?"

Ginny came out on the porch and heard the exchange. "Come in Zeb, let me get you a cup of coffee."

"There's no time, but I'd take a drink of something stronger if you've got it."

Cassie followed him into the house, ringing her hands. "Zeb, where is Dalton? How did he get hurt?"

"Indians," he spat. "They shot my grandson full of arrows..." His voice broke. He took a hanky out of his pocket and blew his nose. Ginny handed him a shot of whiskey. He downed the amber liquid, cleared his throat and continued. "He's hurt bad, Cassie. I didn't know what else to do, where to go for help. You've got to come."

"Of course I'll come. Where is he?"

"He's in a shack up by the lake. We haven't been able to find the gold. Early this morning we decided to look higher up and ran into the Indians. They acted drunk, yelling and gesturing for us to get out. Dalton tried to talk to them, but it only made them worse. We took off as fast as we could, but Dalton took two arrows in the back before I got enough shots off to scare them away. I managed to get him back to the shack, but I had to leave him alone to come for you."

His voice broke again and he burst into sobs. "I don't know if they followed us. I...don't even.... know...if he's still alive."

Ginny poured Zeb another drink and tried to console him while Cassie ran to her room. She changed out of her dress into a pair of Dalton's pants and a shirt. She tied her knife back around her waist, packed her bag of herbs and supplies then grabbed her hat and a jacket on her way out the door.

"Austin isn't going to like you riding off like this, Cassie." Ginny stood by wringing her hands while Cassie saddled Lady.

"I know, but there's no time to wait for him." Lady let out a noisy chuff of air when Cassie pulled the cinch tight around her middle. She finished knotting the leather strap, then lowered the stirrup and turned to her friend. "I'll be all right, don't worry."

Zeb was already cantering out of the yard by the time she pulled herself into the saddle. Lady easily caught up with him, and they raced across the meadow toward the hills on the other side.

They pushed on for hours, stopping only to rest their mounts a few minutes at a time. Their pace slowed when the terrain became rough. By then the light was low over the western peaks, and Cassie was exhausted. Zeb told her the cabin was at the other end of the lake, which was just a short distance ahead.

When the lake finally came into view, the sight was breathtaking. Tree studded hills stood in silhouette behind a lake that looked like a large, oval jewel. A crescent moon floated on the mirrored surface already brilliant from the reflection of sunset in shades of gold, magenta and deep purple. Although the details were cloaked with the growing darkness, Cassie had a strange sensation she'd been here before.

The memory came in a flash. She had seen this before, in a dream. A white buffalo had carried her to this very spot. Her stomach did a quick flip. Had it been a sign? Had Great Spirit been telling her she would come to this splendid place? She remembered the peace she'd felt in the dream, the sense of safety. She also remembered feeling as if the buffalo wanted to take her someplace else, or to tell her something, but she couldn't recall what happened after that.

When Zeb stopped his horse in front of a small log cabin, Cassie climbed down from the saddle, her legs nearly numb from the long ride. She steadied herself a moment by holding onto the stirrup. Both horses were lathered and the air was cold. She hated to leave Lady in that condition, but she had to check on Dalton first.

The interior of the cabin was so dark she couldn't see anything. She heard the strike of a match and knew Zeb was lighting a lamp. Soon there was enough light to see. The cabin consisted of only one small room. Zeb carried the lamp to the back wall, and Cassie followed. She gasped when she saw the inert figure lying on his stomach on a cot in a pool of blood. Two arrows protruded from his back.

She hurled a shocked look at Zeb, who stood rigid next to the bed. Then she bent to touch Dalton's neck. "He's still alive." They both exhaled in relief. "We'll need a fire. And water, lots of water."

"I'll see to it." Zeb flew into action.

"I'll need help with the arrows, Zeb."

"I'll do anything you want." He threw some kindling into the rustic fireplace and set a match to it before coming to kneel beside Cassie. "I was afraid to take them out myself. Afraid I'd kill him for sure. And I didn't dare move him anymore. I was taking a chance just bringing him back here."

"You did the right thing," she said, trying to calm them both. She felt completely overwhelmed. "Now get some water. And would you please wipe the horses down while the water heats? We rode them awfully hard."

Zeb hurried to do her bidding. Cassie looked around the room, trying to clear her mind. The floor was hard-packed earth, but it had been swept clean. The cabin walls were sound, so the room would warm up fast when the fire was going. There was only one window and it was over Dalton's cot. The pane of glass had been wiped clean in the middle. A crude set of bunked beds stood against the adjacent wall. Three wooden pegs protruded from the wall next to the door, holding various articles of the men's clothing. Three wooden crates turned on their sides and stacked on top of each other served as shelves. A small, awkwardly built table with a three-legged stool leaned against the wall to her right. She carried the stool over next to the cot and sat down.

She touched Dalton's neck again and ran her hand over the side of his face and brow. He burned with fever. Removing the arrows without killing him seemed insurmountable. One protruded from beneath the right shoulder blade. The other was imbedded in his lower back. How could he possibly survive their removal? Yet he stood no chance at all if she didn't try. She could only pray that Running Deer's teachings would come forth. She threw her head back and took a deep breath. "Great-Grandmother, I need your guidance. I don't think I can do this without you." Her hand went to the stones hanging around her neck, and she softly chanted one of the healing prayers Running Deer always used.

By the time the cabin radiated with the fire's warmth, Cassie had Dalton's back bathed clean. She dropped the cloth she'd used into the pale of water and turned to Zeb. He stood by the fireplace, his face twisted in agony. "I need your help now," she told him in a voice much stronger than she was feeling.

He hurried to her side. "What do you want me to do?"

"I need you to hold him down while I remove the arrows."

"Oh God, the pain will kill him."

"No it won't. He won't be feeling a thing. And if he does become conscious, I have something we can give him. Hurry now, hold him down."

Zeb's hands shook as he placed a hand on each of Dalton's shoulders. He hesitated only a moment before abruptly applying weight.

Cassie scooted the stool closer and sat down. Placing her shaking hands between her knees, she closed her eyes and quieted her mind. She silently called on Great Spirit to guide her. A moment later, she found the peaceful place she sought and visualized healing power flowing through her to Dalton. When she opened her eyes, she was ready.

Her knife felt awkward as she held the tip to Dalton's back, but she maintained her prayerful state of mind and sliced through skin and muscle. Gratefully, the first incision brought back her training, and she continued with instinct and knowing. Dalton didn't so much as flinch, so she instructed Zeb to let go of one shoulder and help mop up the blood that had begun flowing again.

After the first arrow was removed, she cleaned out the wound and packed it with healing herbs. Then she repeated the procedure with the other arrow, which was much more difficult.

Dalton still hadn't moved. Time passed slowly as Cassie worked, but she was unaware of anything but the deep wounds. When she finished, she straightened and sat unmoving on the stool.

Zeb touched her shoulder, and she looked up at him. Tears ran down his face. "Is he still alive?"

Only half of Dalton's face could be seen as he lay on his stomach with his head turned to the side. Cassie bent close to his nose. "Aye, he's still breathing." Barely, she noted to herself.

"Here, have some coffee," he said, handing her a steaming cup he'd just poured. "You look all in."

She accepted the tin cup and took a sip.

"Will he live?"

She shrugged her shoulders. "I don't know. He's lost a lot of blood."

"Nobody could have done a finer job, Cassie. I'm beholden to you."

"No, you aren't, Zeb. You and Dalton saved my life too."

Cassie looked at the maimed figure on the cot. "He might not make it Zeb. The first arrow didn't do too much harm, but I'm not sure about the other. It was in a bad spot. It could've damaged something vital." She turned tired eyes up to Zeb. "If you're a praying man, you better say all the prayers you can."

Dalton lived through the rest of the night. Cassie and Zeb never left his side. They took turns bathing him with cool water and made sure he swallowed small amounts.

Ollie arrived the second afternoon bearing messages from Austin and Ginny. Ginny sent her love and prayers. Austin demanded that Cassie return to the ranch immediately. Ollie was to escort her, and Zeb and Dalton, too.

Of course they couldn't leave. She explained the situation to Ollie and asked him to assure the Barrett's that she was fine. She would stay at the lake as long as necessary.

The third morning, Dalton became fitful. He tossed and pitched so violently they had to tie him down. He continued to burn with fever, and Cassie felt helpless. By then, Zeb was so exhausted from worry he stretched out on the lower bunk bed and slept for hours. Cassie sat on the stool, napping periodically with her head next to Dalton's, and leaving him only long enough to take care of her personal needs.

The next few days brought more of the same. Keeping Dalton and his bed clean was a difficult task, but with Zeb's help, she managed. And they succeeded in getting a bit a more water into him along with some thin broth.

Cassie prayed silently when Zeb was close by, and chanted aloud whenever he left the cabin. She asked for help from the white man's God the way her Christian father taught her, and from Great Spirit, in the way of her mother and Running Deer's people. She believed both deities were one and the same, but she wasn't going to take any chances.

By the third day, Zeb was afraid Cassie would collapse. "You've got to rest," he told her. "You can't help my grandson if you get sick."

"I don't want to leave him."

"You won't be leaving him. Just lie down for a while. I'll wake you if anything changes."

Cassie was so tired she couldn't move, so Zeb helped her to the lower bunk and covered her with a blanket. She fell asleep immediately.

Zeb placed his hand on the back of his grandson's feverish head. With chin on chest, he imagined returning to Raleigh without the boy. How could he tell his only daughter that her youngest child was dead?

His thoughts drifted back to the beginning of their journey west. He had never really gotten to know any of his grandchildren very well. His focus in life had been on building his business. Dalton was the youngest and had always driven him nearly mad with his non-stop chatter. But on their journey, they had become more acquainted. Pretty soon, Zeb began to enjoy the lad's sunny disposition, his optimistic outlook, his exuberant yammering, and found he was grateful to have his company.

Dalton was the youngest of seven children. At home, he'd always sort of faded into the woodwork. Zeb decided that was probably the reason he talked incessantly when he was away from home. With one older brother and five older sisters, he probably never got a word in edgewise.

And now this grandson that he'd grown to love so much was fighting for his life.Cassie whimpered in her sleep and Zeb turned her way. She looked small under the quilt, almost like a child. And he was depending on her to be a god, to create a miracle and save his grandson's life. He looked at one petite, moccasin-clad foot sticking out the end of the quilt, then at the long dark hair spilling over the edge of the mattress. Her face looked dusky in the shadows of the upper bunk, giving her the appearance of an Indian.

The idea stiffened his spine, and he scolded himself for the thought. But the thought persisted, and he continued to wonder. The moccasins, the knife, her knowledge of plants and herbs, it all added up. By her own account, she had even cut up a man's face with that knife.

His mind was churning now, boiling over from the stress, and fed from past hurts and resentments. She must be an Indian, he thought. But she couldn't be. The very idea revolted him. She's as white-skinned as I am. And she's educated. And her hair is as much red as it is black. Yet, something about her…

All of a sudden a choking knot of disgust formed in his belly. The walls of the small cabin began to press in on him. He hurried to the door, threw it open, and stumbled outside. What if she was Indian? It was Indians that killed George, Indians that shot their hideous arrows into Dalton's back.

He leaned against the trunk of a nearby aspen, feeling weak and dizzy. He and Dalton had taken care of her like she was one of their own. Fed her, nursed her back to health, and offered her their protection. Had she been deceiving them the whole time?

"Zeb?" He jumped and spun around. Cassie stood in the doorway, her face heavy from sleep, her brow knotted in bewilderment. "I heard the door. Is anything wrong?"

He glared at her. "Are you an Indian?"

The question seemed to hit her like a physical blow. She had a hard time responding.

"Answer me." Zeb screamed, his face contorted with fury, his lips pursed and white. He felt like he would fall over if he let go of the tree.

"Zeb, I...."

"Answer me!" he yelled, again.

Cassie opened her mouth to speak, but before she could utter a sound, Zeb grabbed his chest and slumped to the ground. She realized it must be his heart and ran back inside for something to give him. When she returned, Zeb was still clutching his chest. His face was void of color and wet with sweat. Cassie dropped in the dirt near him and pulled his head and shoulders onto her lap.

"Here, drink this." She held the cup of water mixed with extract of may-pop-flower to his lips. He took a long drink and then pushed it away.

"It's your heart, isn't it?" She smoothed his thick white hair from his face. He was breathing easier now, and the pain was receding from his eyes. "You should feel better in a few minutes, but you have to stay calm."

He wouldn't look at her.

"I'll answer your question now. I am half-Indian. My mother was Choctaw, my father was Irish. My great-grandmother was a Choctaw medicine woman, an alikchi, a healer. She taught me a lot of her skills before she died." She continued to smooth his brow, hoping it would help his acceptance of her words. Her body shaded his face from the sun. The rays warmed her back, helping to ease the chill that ran through her blood.

"That is the reason I couldn't go to the law after my mother was killed. Nobody would take the word of a half-breed over a white man. I didn't tell you and Dalton for fear you wouldn't take me with you. And I would have died for sure if you had left me."

Cassie didn't know if Zeb heard what she was saying, but her voice seemed to quiet him if nothing else. Soon his eyes became heavy. Before long, he slept.

Since some of the herbs she gave him would make him sleep, and he was too heavy for Cassie to lift, she covered him with a blanket and used the stool and another blanket to create some shade. Then she returned to Dalton. He didn't seem so hot. She sat on the floor next to his bed. Her head throbbed. She was hungry and couldn't even remember when she had last eaten. This latest event with Zeb had drained her completely. Her instincts had been right. He'd been horrified to find out she was an Indian.

How did he figure it out? She wondered, knowing it didn't make any difference anyway. He knew now, and she had no idea what he would do when he woke up. Or if he'd wake up. Or what shape he'd be in if he did. Finally, her fatigue made her too numb to care. Her surroundings slowly began to fade and she stretched out on the floor in a depleted sleep.

The distant sound of wolves woke her. The room was dark and cold. It took a minute for her groggy mind to clear. Then she sat up quickly and placed her hand on Dalton's face. He felt even cooler. The howling continued. She hurried outside and found that Zeb was still sleeping. "Zeb, wake up. You've got to come inside, and I can't lift you."

She helped him to his feet and staggered under his weight. When she got him inside and onto the lower bunk, she covered him. Within seconds he drifted back to sleep.

The hot coals in the fireplace leapt to life when she tossed in a handful of kindling. She added more wood until it crackled loudly and began to warm the room. She stepped back out to the dark yard only long enough to relieve her full bladder.

When she returned to the cabin, she put some coffee on and poked through the crates and saddlebags till she produced some potatoes, onions and dried beef. Chewing on the beef, she poured water into a cast iron pot, peeled and cut the potatoes and added an onion. Then she lugged the heavy pot to the fireplace and hung it from the iron bar next to the coffee pot. While her late-night meal bubbled away, she heated another pan of water. Once she'd cleaned up and braided her hair, she felt better.

An hour later, she sat on the earthen floor in front of the fire and listened to Zeb's snores. She prayed he would recover. Dalton seemed better. His breathing was even and his temperature remained cool. She would check his wounds in the morning but finally felt confident they would continue to heal.

The wolves now sounded like they were right outside the cabin. She was certain they couldn't get through the door or the window, but the howling had a forsaken, eerie quality that increased her loneliness.

Her mind wandered to Ginny and Austin and how things might be going at the ranch. She tried to imagine what Cole was doing. But nothing came to mind. They'd never had enough time to really get to know each other. Ginny had told her he was a gambler and that he had gone to Georgetown where he had a room in a friend's hotel and saloon. The friend was a woman named Ruby.

Cassie was surprised at the strange sadness she felt when she thought of Cole with another woman. Even as inexperienced as she was, she was quite sure what kind of relationship a man like Cole Adams would have with a woman friend. He was undoubtedly very skilled in lovemaking. Her brief moments in his arms had proven that. She didn't want to think of him holding another woman the way he had held her, or looking at another woman the way he looked at her.

Is that why he'd ridden away so abruptly? Was it because he missed his woman? She wished she had asked Ginny. But it was too late now. She didn't know when she would see Ginny, or if she would ever again see Cole.

And right now, they all seemed very far away.

Her aloneness became even more acute. Yet she had lived with the feeling for so long she was growing accustomed to it. Grief and loneliness seemed to be the only constancy in her life now. So instead of retreating from the pain, this time she embraced it, settled into it like the arms of an ever-present companion.

CHAPTER THIRTEEN

Cassie must have slept, for the room was light when she managed to open one eye. She rubbed sleep out of both eyes and then forced them open to see sunlight spilling through the window in dust-filled rays. For a minute she watched a pine bough scrape back and forth across the pane of glass until an ache in her back urged her to move. She stretched her stiff limbs and rolled to her side. There her gaze collided with a wide-awake stare from Dalton.

She sat up and scooted the scant distance to sit next to him. "Welcome back," she whispered, laying her palm on his cheek. It was cool. He tried to move and groaned with the effort. "Stay still, Dalton. You've been hurt very badly. You have to stay on your stomach."

"What...happened? His words came out in a hoarse whisper. "How did you get here?"

"Zeb brought me here after you were injured. Let me get you some water." Cassie got up to get the canteen and noticed that Zeb's bunk was empty. Returning to the cot, she placed a cloth beneath Dalton's chin and tipped the canteen to the side of his mouth so he could drink.

"Do you remember being hurt? You took two arrows in the back from a group of Indians." When Dalton finished drinking, she set the canteen down and wiped his mouth. "You've been real sick. I wasn't sure you were going to make it."

"I'm glad to...see you." He gave her a half smile, then his eyes closed and he slept again.

The door swung open behind her and Zeb came in. His face was as gray as the pail of water he carried. His white hair hung limp against his forehead and over his ears. He set the pail down and moved slowly to the bottom bunk and eased himself down.

Cassie walked over and stood before him. "You shouldn't be up and around yet, Zeb. I can manage the chores."

He nodded his head and turned away from her.

"I'll fix something to eat," she told him. "We could all use some food."

At her emphasis on the word all, he swung his gaze to Dalton's cot.

"Aye, he's better. He was awake for a few minutes. When he wakes again, I'll feed him a bit. He should be all right now, Zeb. It will take a while for him to fully recover, but recover he will."

The old man's eyes filled with tears and he turned away from her again. Cassie suspected he was grateful to her for taking care of Dalton. But his bitterness and resentment was long standing and weighed heavy on his heart. She covered him with the quilt and went to stir up the coals in the fireplace.

Over the next few days she stayed busy caring for both her patients. The men slept most of the time, so the cabin stayed relatively quiet. When they were awake, Zeb spoke only when necessary, and Dalton was still too weak to say much of anything.

With meat in short supply, Cassie took Dalton's rifle and managed to kill a rabbit. After that initial hunt, she followed with two more rabbits. The following week, she killed an elk, and used Dalton's horse, Blue, to drag it back to the cabin.

Sitting on a stump several yards from the cabin, she worked on the carcass, proud and grateful at the same time. Salted, the meat would last for quite some time, and she could use some of the hide to make herself another pair of moccasins. Hers were nearly worn through. She would also make a knee-high pair and some gloves for winter, and line them rabbit fur.

Using a large butcher knife she'd found in the cabin, she drew the blade along the edge of the hoof, cutting just deep enough to separate the skin. She did the same with the other hooves and continued on the inside of each leg all the way to the belly until the skin on each leg was peeled back. Then, after a bit of a struggle, she managed to turn the carcass on its side and disemboweled it. She cut out the animal's heart and held it to the east, thanking Great Spirit for the accuracy of her shot, and thanking the spirit of the elk for giving up his life.

All of a sudden, she felt a prickly sensation and spun around to see Zeb standing in the doorway. "You're looking better," she said, relieved that he did, and sent off another quick prayer of gratitude. "How about an elk steak for supper tonight?"

Zeb stepped into the sunlight and focused his eyes on the squirrel sitting on a branch above Cassie's head. "That sounds fine. You want me to do anything?"

Cassie was so pleased with his lack of animosity, she could have cried. "Aye, you can see to Dalton for a bit, if you would. You can help him sit up for awhile. His wounds are healing nicely, so it shouldn't hurt too much."

Zeb nodded his head and walked back inside.

Throughout the next week, the tension between Zeb and Cassie lessened even more. He remained polite and kept his resentment to himself.

When Dalton could spend more of each day out of bed, Cassie accompanied him on short walks. She measured his returning strength by the distance they were able to walk from the cabin.

One afternoon they made it to the edge of the lake. Dalton eased himself onto a large rock that rested near the water's edge. "What are you grinning at, Cassie? Are you poking fun at the way I move?"

Cassie's eyes moved from the top of his blonde hair to his shoulders and on down his long legs. She and Dalton were nearly the same age, but she felt years older. His recent weight loss made him look thin and frail and even younger. "No. It just feels good to see you getting stronger. You came awful close to dying on me, Dalton. I'm very grateful you didn't. I feel like part of my family has been returned."

"Golly, Cassie, I didn't think you cared so much," he mocked, giving her a teasing grin.

She swatted his boot with a stick. "Don't be so ornery. You're perfectly aware of how much you mean to me."

Dalton visibly basked in the warm words. "You mean a lot to me too, Cassie. And I owe you my life."

"Well, that makes us even then, doesn't it?"

Dalton leaned back on his elbows and stretched his legs out in the warm autumn sun. "It does feel good to be alive."

"Aye, that it does." She sat cross-legged on the ground and looked across the lake to the emerald hills and blue sky mirrored on its placid surface. It had been a long time since she'd felt so peaceful.

"What are you looking at, Cassie?"

"Nothing. Everything. Isn't it beautiful here, Dalton? I think I'd like to stay here forever."

"You'd probably feel different if it was cold and the snow was knee deep." He saw her tense. "What's wrong?"

She slowly shook her head back and forth. "It's not what I see, but what I don't see. Every now and then I feel like somebody's watching us." She turned to face him. "Do you feel it?"

"I don't feel anything, Cassie." He shaded his eyes and scrutinized the surrounding area. "You have to quit thinking about Noley. He'll never find you up here."

Cassie turned her attention back to the lake. Maybe he was right. Maybe the eerie feeling of watchful eyes was just a hangover from the fear Noley had instilled in her.

In the days that followed, there was a distinct change in the air. The sun still warmed the days but the breeze that blew down from the higher peaks was colder. Nights became frigid. The aspen captured the sun in their quivering leaves and turned to gold. Large flocks of geese flew overhead, their loud resonant cries signaling a farewell to summer as they headed to warmer climes.

As Dalton improved, Cassie had more free time, so she started to carve again, using pine she'd chopped for the fireplace. The return to her favorite pastime brought poignant memories. But the memories were kinder now, less brutal in their assault.

Because her recovering patients tended to sleep late, morning was one of her favorite times of day. This morning she decided to seize a few minutes of solitude to sit in the sun and work on a replica of the sleek mountain lion she and Dalton had spotted on one of their walks. When she opened the door, she stepped into a winter wonderland. Last night's drizzle of snow and rain, along with the frigid temperature, had frosted everything with glittering silver and white jewels. The sun turned the frosted ground into a carpet of diamonds.

Cassie sat on a log and leaned against the cabin wall, reveling in the glorious sight. She loved this rugged land. In the past few weeks, the peace of the hills had seeped into her soul. The darkest aspects of the grief and fear were beginning to dissipate. She was beginning to feel whole again, free and safe.

As the sun melted the splendor of the frost, her knife appeared to have a mind of its own. It wasn't long before the head and shoulders of the mountain lion sprang forth as if ready to pounce. She could hear her Da say, 'Hold it gently, lass. See with your fingers how you want the form to materialize.' She smiled at the memory and another few nicks revealed a hint of a muscled leg yet to come.

"What are you doing?"

She jerked around and almost dropped the knife. "Dalton, you nearly scared me out of my wits."

Dalton held onto the top of the doorframe with both hands and stretched the tender muscles in his back. "I slept the morning away. Why didn't you wake me?"

"You need the rest and you better get it while you can. When you're mended, I'll work you good."

Cassie stood and brushed the chips of wood off her pants. "Are you hungry? There's some porridge on the stove."

"Yes, I'm ravenous." He grabbed her hand as she walked past. "What have you got there?"

Cassie handed him the carving. He turned it over and over, examining every detail. "It's remarkable," he said, then gazed deep into her eyes. "And so are you."

His words were heavy with unsaid meaning. She wasn't sure how to respond, so she scurried past him into the cabin. "How about some breakfast?"

Zeb woke up and ate with them. Dalton returned to his easy-going self and Cassie relaxed, thinking she must have imagined the intimacy behind his words. They talked easily about several things, including the weather, tossing out speculations as to when winter would set in for sure and what that would be like.

Zeb said nothing. He didn't even look up from his bowl.

Dalton studied his grandfather. "You feeling all right Paps?"

The old man swallowed another bite. "I feel fine."

"Then what's bothering you? You've barely spoken to me since I've been up and getting around. Are still upset about what happened to me? Because I don't..."

"Nothing's bothering me. I told you, I'm fine."

Dalton wasn't buying it. "Are you anxious to start hunting for Uncle George's gold again? I'm strong enough now, and Cassie can help too."

"The gold can stay where it is."

"What?" Dalton stared at his grandfather, his spoon poised midway to his mouth. "What are you saying?"

Zeb's eyes rose to meet his grandson's. "Just what I said. I'm not looking any longer. In fact, we're going home."

"Home? Why? I'm sure there's still plenty of time before snow will be a problem. Besides, I thought you wanted to spend a year out here. If you're worried about over-doing it, Cassie and I can search. You can stay in the cabin and rest."

"I don't need to rest." He cast a quick glance at Cassie before looking back at his grandson. "I just don't have it in me to search anymore. That gold has caused enough heartache. Let it lie where it is."

"But Paps..."

"There's nothing to discuss, Dalton. My mind's made up." Zeb stood and walked to the door.

Cassie knew what was bothering him. "Zeb, I can leave now. You and Dalton are both strong enough to get along without me."

Dalton was obviously growing more confused by the minute. "What are you saying, Cassie? We don't want you to leave, do we Paps?"

Zeb looked at them with listless eyes. "She can do as she pleases. We're going home. We'll ride as far as Denver and take the train."

He walked outside and the sound of his footsteps faded away from the cabin.

Dalton sat in stunned silence. After a few minutes he looked at Cassie and wondered aloud, "I don't understand what's gotten into him. Do you think he feels worse than he's letting on?"

"No. I think he's recovering okay."

"Then what is it? Why would he just give up like that?"

Cassie didn't know what to say. She was sure Zeb hadn't said anything to Dalton about her being a half-breed, and she wasn't sure if she should tell him either. "Maybe, with you getting hurt so bad, he just realized that the gold wasn't worth it."

"He had to know there would be risks coming all the way out here, especially since he chose to come on horseback. In fact, I believe it was the risks that made the journey attractive to him. He always envied his brother's spirit of adventure."

"Maybe, but dreaming about taking chances and watching someone you love nearly die because of it is two different things. You didn't see him like I did. He was nearly consumed by his worry for you."

"I realize that, but he's been through it before. He watched his brother die from wounds he got from the Indians."

"Which is precisely my point. You nearly died as well, the same way. It's probably too much for him, and…" She caught herself before blurting out the additional reason for Zeb's stress. She wasn't sure what he'd do. What if he recoiled from her the way Zeb did? She didn't think she could stand it.

"And what? There's more isn't there. Something else happened didn't it?"

"Aye."

"Well, what is it? Tell me, Cassie."

She gazed across the wobbly table at the young man that had come to mean so much to her. "Your grandfather discovered something about me he doesn't like."

"What are you talking about?"

Steeling herself for his response, she looked him square in the eye and said, "I have Indian blood."

"Indian?" He stared at her uncomprehendingly. I don't understand. What are you saying? You don't look… You can't… Your name is O'Brian, isn't it?"

His struggle made her face burn. She wrung her hands together on the table in front of her. "Aye. My father was Irish, but my mother was from the Choctaw nation."

Dalton's jaw dropped. His brown eyes grew round with surprise then narrowed as he took it all in.

"I didn't tell you before because I was afraid."

Dalton continued to gape at her, so she rushed on. "I'm not ashamed of my mixed blood, Dalton. On the contrary, I'm proud to be half-Choctaw. They are a fine, illustrious people. I never told you because I was afraid you and Zeb wouldn't be as quick to offer help if you knew. Unfortunately, my fears were justified, at least where Zeb is concerned. Your grandfather's pain over his brother's death hardened his heart to anyone who is Indian. His weeks of worry over you only made it worse."

"But you're only half-Indian," he finally managed. "Besides, it wasn't your people who killed Paps' brother. And it was a renegade bunch that jumped us. They'd been drinking or they probably wouldn't have bothered us at all. We've seen others since arriving up here, and they just ignored us."

Cassie gave him a sad smile. "That doesn't matter to Zeb. Maybe in time he'll be able to unravel the bitterness in his heart, but for now, you must accept his feelings and respect his wishes."

"I can't just ride away and leave you, Cassie." He reached across the table and took her hands in his. "I love you. It doesn't matter whether you're Irish, Indian, or anything else. I want you to go home with me, to meet my family. They'll love you as much as I do. I know they will. I want you to marry me."

Now it was Cassie's turn to be stunned. Never even for a moment did she imagine Dalton felt that way about her. She felt incapable of responding.

"Please say yes, Cassie. Please say you'll go home with me and become my wife."

Zeb stood in the open doorway looking just as shocked as Cassie felt. He finally entered the cabin, walked to his bunk, sat down and dropped his head into his hands.

Cassie was so unsettled she could barely breathe. "I don't know what to say, Dalton." She pulled her hands from his grasp and stood. "I need some time to think. I'll be back in a little while."

As she turned to leave, Dalton got up and moved to stand in front of her. He placed his hands on her shoulders and bent to kiss her soundly on the mouth. "All right, you take a few minutes, but remember what I said. I'm not leaving without you."

Cassie pulled away from him and fled out the door. She hiked quickly away from the cabin with no destination in mind, reeling from Dalton's declaration. A proposal of marriage was the last thing she'd expected to hear from him. And she was numbed by Zeb's decision to leave. How could she say goodbye? And if she didn't, would Zeb let her go with them?

Her hike eventually took her up a steep incline. The smell from the pines was pungent. Chipmunks and squirrels skittered through the trees, intent on their busy collection of food-stores for the winter. Birds chirped back and forth. A light breeze whistled through the pines, aspen and willow shrubs, merging with the sound of rushing water up ahead.

Just when her legs began to resist, she came to the top. Across a deep chasm flowed a fast running creek that split into three roaring waterfalls, one plunging into the other. Her heart pounded a beat faster as she edged her moccasins to the lip of the drop-off and looked down. Numerous large boulders blocked her view of the water below. Seized with a wild curiosity, she looked for a way down.

A short search brought her to a spot where descent appeared reasonable. She carefully eased herself over the side and managed to go from one outcropping of rock to another as she slowing crawled down the side of the cliff. When she neared the bottom, she vaulted the last few feet and landed on a cushion of grass and layer upon layer of pine needles and leaves.

Pines and aspens filled the small glen, along with willow and other plants and trees. They grew close together here and there and their boughs created a dense canopy overhead. On her right was a concave wall of stone, worn away by wind and water to create a natural shelter. The back was smoke-blackened, and she wondered if this magical place was a campsite of the Ute's or other native tribes.

She walked along the springy turf to the sandy banks of a crystal-clear creek. On the other side, an enormous flat-topped boulder looked like it would provide a clear view of the bottom of the falls, so she strolled along the water's edge, looking for a way to cross. Circling around a stand of trees, she saw a fallen log that bridged a narrow bend. Holding her arms out for balance, she traversed to the other side and walked back along that side of the creek to climb onto the boulder.

The rock was as large and flat as the floor of Ginny's house and, as hoped, provided a perfect view of the falls. She sat down and wrapped her arms around her knees, completely absorbed in the sight before her. The roar of the rushing water drowned out every other sound. Mist billowed up, drenching the face of the surrounding stone cliffs, turning them green with moss. Grayish-green tendrils of moss hung like spider webs from the trees above. At her feet, a rock-rimmed basin captured the last cascade and formed it into a deep, crystal pool before it surged on to become another fast-moving current.

She suddenly remembered something her great-grandmother had told her. She was young at the time, and Running Deer had taken her to a favorite spot where the Mississippi River turned a bend. The water was deep and wide as it curved next to a tree-covered glen, much like this one. *'Wherever we are, wherever we go, we each must find a special place to connect with the earth, a place where she can give us solace. When you find your place, you will know.'*

The sun warmed Cassie from head to toe as she reclined on her back, pillowed her head in her hands and closed her eyes. "This is my special place."

After a few minutes, she allowed Dalton's words to flow once more through her mind. He wanted to marry her. He was offering her a way to mend her broken life, a solution to the unending questions about how she would survive. He loved her. And she loved him too. Never mind that her feelings were more like she'd have for a brother. She loved him and that was all that mattered.

Wasn't it?

She had no idea how long she laid there letting thoughts appear then fade away. When she finally opened her eyes, she gazed in wonder at the pines touching the blue sky, the aspens trembling gold in the breeze. These mountains had come to mean so much to her. How could she abide leaving them? She threw an arm over her eyes. Her thoughts raced again. How could she stay? She had no money to buy supplies. How would she survive the winter all by herself? Her only hope was with Dalton.

But what about Zeb, would he approve her admittance into the family? She didn't want to cause him any more heartache. Is it possible that in time he'd soften and come to realize the futility of the kind of resentment he carried?

Even if he didn't, he couldn't prevent their marriage. Could he? Dalton was old enough to make his own choices, she reasoned. And maybe the rest of his family wouldn't care about her mixed blood. She could learn to fit in, learn how to be a proper wife for him.

But what about school? Dalton had put off his education for a year, but he still planned to go. How could he attend college if he was married? And what would his family think when they realized she'd never even been to school, that her education had come from her father? And how would the two of them live? It would be nearly a year before Dalton inherited the money his grandmother had left him. What would they do until then? Where would they live? Would he want to stay in Raleigh? Living in a city would be a big adjustment, but she could do it. Couldn't she?

"No." The answer was exhaled on a long sigh, delivering tears and truthful reality along with it. She opened her eyes again and looked around at the trees, the water, and the sky. She would feel smothered in a crowded city. For as long as she could remember she had spent more time outside than in. She needed the earth and the sky the same way she needed food and air. How would she ever find a place like this in a city?

Like a dog chasing its tail, the debate in her mind continued, each question and thought taking her to the next until she'd end up back at the beginning. She wanted to scream.

Once more, Running Deer's words filled her mind: '*You need courage to enter the Opening where Future lives. Only you can decide which path is best for you. Listen to the Stone People. They are the record holders of the earth. Their whispers will ring in your heart and tell you all you need to know.*'

She squeezed her eyes tightly shut against the tears threatening to fall. She sniffed a couple of times and willed her mind to still, determined to follow her great-grandmother's advice. Eventually her frantic thoughts began to subside. The roar of the falls blocked out every other sound as she retreated to a quiet place within and sought the direction of her heart.

Time no longer existed. Even the sound of the falls disappeared. She went deeper and deeper still, seeking solace, seeking answers.

Her peace was short lived.

Someone was watching her. The sudden awareness brought her back to full consciousness and tied her stomach in knots. Gooseflesh broke out on her arms and the back of her neck as she forced herself to sit up and open her eyes.

He stood at the edge of the rock looking at her with pinprick dark eyes; a wiry little man with a scraggly white beard at least six inches long. His faded grey felt hat nearly covered his white hair and looked as old as he did. The wide brim was flattened across the front, giving the sun complete access to his beak of a nose. This, along with his forehead and cheeks, was deeply tanned. His stooped shoulders, skinny chest, and long arms were clothed in red long johns. Suspenders held up a pair of black trousers on his scarecrow frame. Pencil-thin fingers held the barrel of a gun nearly as long as he was tall, the butt rested on the ground next to his nearly colorless boots.

"The lady rests there on the rock, listening to voices only she can hear. Good manners tell me I should stop; to go much closer is to interfere. Do I listen? I do not. But I tread lightly as I near."

The singsong words rang loud enough to be heard over the thunder of the falls. He smiled a broken-toothed grin at Cassie. "I must apologize for the intrusion, but I'm afraid I just couldn't resist any more. I've been looking at your loveliness from afar for much too long."

"Who are you?" She finally managed, matching his volume in order to be heard. "Where did you come from?"

"Thought you had these hills to yourself, did ye?

"No. Well, pretty much, I guess."

"You never saw my cabin?" A bony finger pointed behind him. "On the opposite end of the lake from yours, facing Round Mountain. I guess it's not easily seen unless you are close by."

"You live here?"

"I sure do. Been here since sixty nine."

"You've been watching me for some time." Her mind was finally working again.

"Yes. You and your two men."

A great sigh of relief rushed out of her, taking with it the fear that it was Noley who had been watching her. "I could feel someone was near. I thought it was someone else."

"You are happy it is me."

"Aye, very happy."

He stepped onto the rock and edged close enough to lower the volume of his words. "Your voice has a touch o' the Irish, but not entirely. Let me see." He paused, rubbing the end of his beard between his thumb and forefinger. He looked her up and down, taking in the shiny red glints in the dark hair, the baggy shirt and trousers, and the moccasins. "If I were to hazard a guess, I'd say you're from the south. And I bet you've a bit of Indian in you, too."

She couldn't believe he'd figured that out so easily. "How did you know?"

"Observation, my dear. It always pays to be observant. I have lived all over this great land and I remember what I see and hear. Where are you from?"

Cassie warmed to him fast. His resonant, well-educated voice belied his neglectful appearance, and the contradiction amused her. "I am from Kentucky, across the river from Cairo. My father was from Ireland. My mother's people are from Mississippi, she was raised there."

"Your mother's people would be Choctaw, would they not?"

"Aye," she answered with no small amount of awe.

"I didn't know there were any Choctaw left in Mississippi. They were one of the first tribes pushed west."

Cassie grinned at his knowledge. "Some stayed. At the signing of the final treaty, they were told they could keep their land if they registered as citizens. However, things didn't work out that way. They eventually lost everything and had to become sharecroppers to remain on the land they loved. A small part of the tribe still lives there."

"Well, I'll be. I didn't know that." He slid his bony hand up under his hat to scratch his head as if surprised that there could actually be a piece of information he was unaware of.

Cassie scrambled up and stood next to her neighbor. He was only an inch or so taller. "My name is Cassandra O'Brian, but please call me Cassie."

He swept his hat off and bowed. "I am very pleased to make your acquaintance, Miss Cassie. I am Josiah Westfield. And I am pleased to have your company. Most of my visitors are hunters and fishermen. Just a few now and then. And of course the Ute's and Arapaho. The lake has some of the biggest trout you ever did see. And word is getting out. Pretty soon, they'll be coming in droves." He placed his hat back on his head. "Will you and your gentlemen be staying long?"

"I... don't know. That's the very question I was asking myself when you--"

"When I invaded your privacy," he finished for her. "I must apologize again. And I offer my ear. I can be a very good listener." One eye closed in a teasing wink and he flashed her a crooked grin. "There are times when the wise thing to do is sit alone and look within. But other times it's helpful to rise from your musings and speak with a friend." He offered his arm, and Cassie let him lead her off the rock to a shady spot under the trees.

Evening shadows were turning to dusk before she made it back to the cabin, anxious about the decision she'd made.

CHAPTER FOURTEEN

C ole paced back and forth, trying to calm the restless energy that chewed at him constantly these days.

Ruby sat on the edge of her ornate brass bed and watched him. "Trying to talk to you these days takes more energy than it's worth. Sit down before you wear a path in my new rug."

Ring curled up in the corner out of the way when Ruby's voice increased in volume. "What's the matter with you? You're as jumpy as a toad on a hot skillet. You can't even concentrate when you're at the tables. How much have you lost in the past week?"

"I don't know. Doesn't matter." Cole shrugged and began to pace the room again. He was well aware that he was losing large sums. It should bother him a lot. But he didn't need her or anyone else reminding him of it.

"Cole, sit down." She patted the mattress next to her.

The springs creaked beneath his weight.

"Take off your hat. You look like you're going to leave any moment." She reached over to remove his hat, and he jerked his head out of her reach, instantly regretting his action when he saw the hurt in her hazel eyes. Next to Austin and Ginny, Ruby was his closest friend. When they first met, they tried to make it more, but their effort didn't pan out on either side. After a few weeks, they finally gave up and accepted the friendship for what it was. Through the years the two of them had grown as close as brother and sister. He wouldn't consciously hurt her for the world.

"What happened while you were gone?" she persisted, her tone softer. You haven't said three words about it since you got back."

"Nothing happened," he said, making a conscious effort to calm down. "I helped Austin do some building and drive some cattle."

Ruby studied her well-manicured fingertips. "Maybe that lifestyle fits you better than this one now."

"What's that supposed to mean?"

She laid her head against his shoulder. "Something's changed you. You leave here a few months ago, your cool, intrepid self. You return seething like a caged lion. The boys tell me you aren't even a fun challenge at the tables any more. They can read every thought in your head. I'm worried about you. You need to get ahold of yourself before somebody tries to beat you at something more dangerous than cards."

"I can take care of myself. I was away too long, that's all. I just need a little time to re-establish myself." He gave her a lopsided grin. "Maybe I need a little female persuasion."

"Hah." Ruby bounded off the bed and turned to face him. "Who do you think you're kidding? I hear things, you know. You haven't touched a woman since you got back. I want to know what's going on."

Cole heaved himself off the bed. Close friend or not, the interrogation was over. He snatched up his jacket and hat and yanked open the door.

"Isn't that just like a man," Ruby said, flouncing past him into the hallway. "The conversation is over when the subject gets a little too close for comfort."

Head high, bright red curls bouncing, she hurried toward the stairs to the main bar room. Cole turned the other direction. Ring followed close on his heels as he pounded past his own room, down the back stairs and through the door that led outside.

Standing on the wooden walk that ran the length of the saloon, he put on his hat and shrugged into his jacket. Anywhere else, the sun would already be lighting and warming the morning. But in the deep hollow where Georgetown nestled, it wouldn't show its face for another three or four hours.

He pulled a cheroot from his pocket and let his eyes scan the dim shadows as he lit it and took a deep drag. The silver-mining town never slept, but it was quieter this time of day than any other.

Lights glimmered in some of the windows of the unpainted, gable-ended houses perched here and there on the steep terrain. Fresh cut pines shored up the sides of each one to keep the wind that often blasted through the gorge from blowing them away.

Down the street, a mongrel dog lifted its leg and urinated in the run-off from the peaks. Ring eyed the animal, disinterestedly.

Cole took another drag off the cigar then clamped it between his teeth with rigid tension. Ruby's concern and accusations irked him. He knew perfectly well what his problem was, but he didn't want to face it. And he certainly didn't want to admit it to anyone. He'd been convinced that once he returned to town, his old diversions would remove the hunger Cassie had roused in him. But nothing had worked. Neither the women nor the gambling.

He'd tried Sally Jane first. All the way to Georgetown he made himself focus on the pretty brunette. But the minute he was alone with her, he found himself comparing her to Cassie. And lost all interest.

Next he'd tried Mandy. Mandy's bountiful gifts would please any man. But the same thing happened with her. He hadn't even gotten his shirt off before Cassie hovered between them as real as if her spirit had flown into the room.

He had finally given up and turned to the gaming tables. But Ruby was right. He hadn't been able to concentrate. All he could think about was Cassie.

She reminded him of a small-injured bird that had fallen from the nest prematurely. She needed protection and care. She needed someone to watch over her, which is the precise reason his attraction to her was so damned hard to understand. He usually went for the self-assured type, like Ruby.

Or Ramona. But Ramona didn't count. She was a long time ago. A time when he was young and foolish. And in the six years since he'd last seen Ramona, he'd made a friend of time and he'd grown up. Indeed, one of the things maturity had taught him was that he didn't have to love a woman in order to enjoy her company. Women made fun playmates and good friends.

He focused again on Ruby. They'd been attracted to each other the moment he walked into her failing saloon in Denver a few years before. In no time they'd become good friends, and when he suggested that her business would do better in one of the front range mining towns, she agreed and chose Georgetown. The move proved to be prosperous. There wasn't a man in town that would dare cross her, not unless he wanted to be ousted from the best gambling house in town. She ran her saloon and brothel like the pro she was. She treated her girls fairly, allowing them to keep the biggest share of the money they brought in. On his advice, she had invested in a few mines and, at 28, was a very successful woman; smart, independent, proud and strong. Her business always came first, and she needed no one. Which made it easy to be her friend.

Cassie was different. She needed someone to take care of her. And the only way to do that would be marriage. Just thinking about marriage brought a painful reminder of love gone sour. It brought bleak images of his haggard mother and his over worked father. It brought back the miserable pain of losing everyone he ever loved. It gave him the same claustrophobic feeling he'd had at 14 years old when he stowed away in a cramped little hole in the belly of the ship that brought him to this country.

Somewhere a rooster crowed. Cole stamped out the cheroot and headed for the cafe. Maybe a strong cup of coffee would help dispel his bad mood.

After a big breakfast of steak and eggs, he saddled Storm and rode through the hills for a couple of hours. The fresh air helped clear his mind. Upon his return, he joined a poker game that was underway in the Ruby Slipper.

Though night was hours away, the sun had already receded behind the western peaks, casting Georgetown into shadow. Lamps blazed in the crowded saloon. Cigar and cigarette smoke hung in the air.

Cole sat at a table with four other men, watching a reed-thin man deal a hand of five-card draw. The gaunt man was the only one at the table Cole wasn't familiar with. His black garb made him look like an undertaker. Every time he slapped a card on the table, he stared down his long nose pointed on the end like a quill. His slatted eyes never opened wide enough for Cole to determine their color. He had introduced himself as Frenchy, and that was all Cole knew about him. That and the fact he wore his gun belt tied down.

A quick glance at his cards told Cole he had absolutely nothing. His instincts told him to let this hand go. When the play came to him, he stacked the five cards on the table and extracted his length from the wooden chair. "I'm going to let this hand go, boys. I need a break."

"Where do you think you're going, Adams?" The thin man demanded. "You can't rake in most of the winnings for the past hour, then just get up and leave."

Cole spared him an impassive look, then carried his coffee cup the few steps to the bar and asked McGraw, Ruby's bartender, for a refill.

The others continued the hand without him. Thomas Brown, a successful miner whose luck often deserted him at the gaming tables, ignored the temperamental newcomer. "I'll open," he said, and threw a five-dollar chip in the middle of the table. His delight with the cards he held beamed like a beacon on his chubby, whiskered face.

The fourth player was Rusty O'Fallon, a very inebriated Irishman. Also a miner, he was down on his luck and fast losing the money he'd come west with. His sharply defined cheeks were almost as ruddy as the mop of hair that brushed across his bushy red brows. He took a long swig of his beer, wiped the froth off his thick, drooping moustache and followed Brown's lead, tossing out two chips. "I'll see your five and raise you five more."

August Mathews, the fifth player, studied his cards as Cole returned to the table and sipped his coffee. August, nicknamed Gusty, was from the assay office. He'd always enjoyed playing with this group, but today he seemed nervous. He cast a tense look at the new man and folded. Laying his cards on the table, he gathered up his drink and his money and moved to stand by the bar.

Rusty swallowed another mouthful of beer and called after him. "You don't want to be quitin' lad, the afternoon's still young."

"Let him go," Thomas quipped, "There's plenty of butts around to fill his chair."

Thomas won that hand and the next three. Cole won a hand, then a few more. Even Rusty won a couple. Throughout the afternoon, the surly newcomer became more agitated with each hand he lost, harassing Cole particularly. Inside, Cole seethed, wanting nothing more than to ram a fist into the man's tightly pinched face.

By evening, a small crowd had gathered around the table. The atmosphere was tense as Thomas placed a good-sized bet and turned to Cole, beaming his excitement over his cards. Cole studied his own cards and contemplated whether to call or raise.

"You're sure taking your sweet time, Adams," Frenchy charged. "This ain't no Sunday-school picnic, you know. Some of us are here to play cards."

Cole kept a tight lid on his temper and called the bet.

In spite of Thomas's optimistic assumption, Cole won. The thin man's loss was exceptional. He threw his cards down and yelled, "Where'd you get that fourth jack?"

Cole's hands stilled from raking in his winnings. "You best be careful with talk like that." The now-silenced crowd could barely hear his soft reply.

Rusty tried to slide his chair away from the table, fell off of it, and was pulled to his feet by a couple of onlookers. Thomas eased himself into the crowd.

Cole proceeded to pull the pile of winnings to his side of the table, purposely avoiding his adversary's cold eyes.

"Take your sore-loser attitude and disappear, mister," said a voice from the crowd.

"I don't like cheaters," Frenchy responded, his tone challenging.

"Cole don't cheat," yelled another voice.

Frenchy's hand disappeared. The movement was lightning-quick. But before his gun could clear the table, the barrel of Cole's .44 was pressed tight against the end of his nose.

Cole was standing now, bent slightly at the waist as he leaned across the table. "Drop it," he ground out through a rigid jaw. He held the pistol in his left hand. His right was clenched rock-hard on the table.

The man hesitated.

Cole rammed the barrel even harder against the end of his opponent's reddening nose. "Give me an excuse."

Finally, carefully, the thin man set his gun on the table and raised his hands in the air. But Cole couldn't bring himself to withdraw. The confrontation had unraveled weeks of frustration that now blasted through his system looking for release.

Ruby had been watching the scene from behind the bar. She came up beside Cole and touched his arm. "It's all over, Cole. Let him leave."

The intrusion only served to further inflame Cole's fury. "Butt out, Ruby. This little pip-squeak has been asking for this all day." He grabbed the back of Frenchy's head with his right hand and ground the gun barrel even harder against the man's nose.

The crowd seemed to take a collective breath. Ruby realized her mistake and backed away.

The skinny Frenchy began to visibly quake. Blood trickled from a cut encircling his nose. It dripped down his lips and chin and fell in bright red drops onto the collar of his white shirt. The sight snapped Cole out of his rage as effectively as a gunshot. His mind filled with a vision of Cassie and how upset she'd been over his brawl in Denver. He withdrew the pistol, holstered it and strode through the crowd into the night.

Ruby found him later in his room. He had changed into his buckskins and was shoving things into his saddlebags. Ring lay on the floor near the end of the bed. His muzzle rested on his front paws. His watchful eyes followed Cole as he moved around the small room.

Ruby's eyes did the same. "Where are you going?"

"Away for awhile." He grabbed a box of cartridges and put them in his bags.

"Away? That's all you're going to say?"

"I've got to get away from here, Ruby. You've been nagging me for weeks about something being wrong. And you're right. There is. I'm not doing myself or anybody else any good like this."

She walked up behind him and slid her arms around his waist. "You don't have to leave now. It's late. Wait till morning."

"I'm going now." Cole turned, set her away from him and resumed his packing.

"Where?"

"I'm not sure. Probably back up to Austin's."

"That's what I figured," she scoffed.

He turned to look at her, his frustration still close to the surface. "Meaning?"

"Meaning what I said before. Something happened to you up there. If that wasn't such a god-forsaken wilderness, I'd think this is about a woman."

Realization struck the moment she said the words. The look that came over Cole's face confirmed it. He swung away, picked up his saddlebags and slung them over his shoulder.

"Don't turn your back on me. Our relationship may not mean much to you, but it means a lot to me. You at least owe me an explanation."

Her words drained part of his anger. Cole dropped the bags back on the bed and turned to face her. "You mean a lot to me, and you know it. But I can't explain something I don't understand myself."

He turned away again and shifted restlessly around the room. "I need to get way from here so I can think."

She softened her voice. "I told you that other lifestyle might have become more attractive."

One side of his mouth curved slightly. "Maybe. Maybe not. All I know is I have to get out of here." Cole bent to place a chaste kiss on her mouth, then turned at a sharp rap on the door. He walked the few steps to the door and swung it open.

A slender, middle aged man in a wrinkled blue suit stood in the hall. "I'm looking for a man named Adams," he said, twisting his bowler hat in his gloved hands. "Coleman Bernard Adams. The man downstairs behind the bar said I could find him here."

"I'm Adams," Cole said, his interest piqued. It had been a long time since anyone had used his full name. He glanced at Ruby. She arched an auburn brow at him and exaggeratedly mouthed his middle name.

Cole glared at her then turned back to the stranger. A look of prudent hope shown on the man's face. "Are you the Coleman Adams who was employed by Roman Brown of St. Louis?"

Cole stiffened at the name. "I am. Who are you? What do you want?"

The man's face was beaming now. He stuck out his hand. "I am Archibald Morrison and I am pleased to finally meet you. You are a hard man to catch up with, Mister Adams. The firm I work for has been searching for you for some time now."

Cole ignored the man's outstretched hand. "What firm? Why have you been looking for me?"

The man dropped his hand to his side. "I work for Blake, Blake and Brownell, a St. Louis law firm." He cocked his head to glance appreciatively at Ruby. "Is there someplace we can talk? And maybe have some refreshments? I've had a long ride and I'm quite parched."

Ruby swept past the two men and turned to look at them over her shoulder. "You can use my rooms, Coleman Bernard. They're more comfortable." She grinned at Cole, plainly amused by the situation. "I'll get some drinks. What would you like, Mister Morrison?"

"A glass of red wine will do nicely." He gawked at the fetching shape of her bustled backend as she sashayed away from them.

Cole led the way to Ruby's apartment. The attorney hurried to keep up with his long strides. When they stepped into the large drawing room, Morrison turned round and round, taking in the color that always stopped everyone in their tracks. The walls were papered in a pink and grey pattern. The oriental carpet was four shades of pink, the palest pale to nearly red. Soft rosy sheers draped the room's one large window. Each of the three ornate settees was covered in light green silk with an assortment of tiny pink roses.

As if the temperature had suddenly increased several degrees, Archibald Morrison ran the tip of an index finger around the inside of his stiff shirt collar. "She certainly likes pink."

Cole gave him a censoring look and indicated for him to sit on a nearby chair, also pink. Cole sat on the closest settee. "What's this all about, Morrison? What do you want with me?"

The anxious man brushed at any possible dust clinging to his trousers and perched on the edge of the chair. He reached inside his coat and extracted a sealed envelope. "Roman Brown is a client of ours. Several months ago he asked us to find you. We hired a detective agency. Four weeks ago they reported that you were in the Denver area. The firm sent me with this letter for you."

Cole accepted the envelope, suddenly flooded with memories, good and bad. He'd met Roman Brown after his first eighteen months in this country.

He was sixteen and had just survived his second long, brutal winter, living on the streets of New York City. He'd been wondering if he'd ever again get through an entire day without his stomach feeling like it was eating itself, when he heard that a family moving to St. Louis was looking for a strong lad to take with them who would work for room and board.

It was the chance he'd been hoping for and he'd wasted no time. He stole a set of freshly washed clothes, scrubbed his face and hands till they stung, and slicked his curly hair flat with water. Roman Brown must have been impressed by his size and determination if nothing else, because he hired him on the spot and took him home to meet the rest of his family.

Cole had fallen in love with Ramona the moment he laid eyes on her. She was Cole's age and the eldest of the Browns' four children. Her statuesque, blonde sophistication stole his heart. And to Cole's utter amazement, Ramona had fallen for him just as fast.

Over the next few years, Cole worked hard, determined to learn his job and impress Roman. He also educated himself by reading the many books in Roman's library. By Cole's 21st birthday, he and Romona were talking marriage. The only thing that stood in their way was money. His lack of it. As much as Roman liked Cole, there was no way he'd allow the two of them to marry. Any man given that privilege would need to produce the kind of income that would give his beloved daughter the comfortable life she was used to.

The newspapers of the day had been filled with news of gold and silver strikes in the west, and Cole was sure his name was written on some of it. Roman loaned him the money for his journey. And in less than a year, Cole returned with enough money to secure a good life for his daughter. But Ramona hadn't waited. He never even got to see her. Roman met him at the door and told him his daughter had married into a prominent St. Louis family. She was pregnant with her first child, and he didn't want Cole to disrupt her new life. Roman seemed genuinely sympathetic and tried to refuse Cole's repayment of the loan, but the reality of the situation was glaring. Cole was good enough to work for the Browns, but not good enough to become their son-in-law. Ramona enjoyed his attention and promises of love, but she hadn't cared enough to wait for him.

His young heart had been crushed, and he'd mentally kicked himself all the way back to Colorado Territory for being so gullible, for being fool enough to think he could have love, have a family, have a girl like Ramona. It took over a year for the pain to subside to a dull ache. And that's when he realized that Ramona would never have been happy away from the excitement of the city, and he would have decayed if he had stayed there. He finally accepted the situation as a hard lesson and vowed it would never happen again.

Now, staring at the envelope in his hands, his pain felt as fresh as the first day. "I haven't seen Roman Brown in nearly six years," Cole finally said. "What does he want with me?"

"You might open the letter. It is quite urgent and very important."

Cole tore open the envelope and removed the short note.

Dear Cole;

I hope this letter finds you in time. I will be arriving in Denver on September 5. It is urgent that I speak with you. I realize our last meeting was unfortunate and hope that time has healed any ill feelings you may have had. I will be staying at the American House hotel, but will return to St. Louis by rail on the 10th.

Please come. My reason for seeing you is extremely important.

Sincerely,

Roman Brown.

Ruby returned with a tray of drinks. She handed Morrison his wine and poured Cole a cup of coffee. When he failed to take it, she softly asked, "Is it bad news?"

Cole shot to his feet. "What's today?"

"Wednesday, why?"

"No, I mean the date. What's the date today?"

181

"It's the ninth, I think."

Cole turned to address the attorney. "Do you know anything about this?"

"Only that Mister Brown has been frantic to find you. When I arrived in Denver, my office wired me that he would be arriving to speak with you. I was instructed to get word to you as soon as possible."

"This note says he'll be leaving tomorrow. He's been here since the fifth."

Archibald Morrison rose indignantly. "Mister Adams, the detective agency told us you would be in Denver. It took time to trace you to this.... this.... god-forsaken place. And it's not an easy place to get to. I had to hire a man to show me the way. And, I might add, I am not accustomed to riding a horse in such terrain. Nevertheless, I have done my duty. You have been notified."

Cole wasn't the least effected by his little speech. "Do you know what time Roman is planning to leave tomorrow?"

"Yes, I do. I am returning on the same train. We depart Denver at four p.m. As you see, there is little time for chitchat. No matter what you decide to do, I must return to Denver at once."

CHAPTER FIFTEEN

Cole barely noticed the comings and goings of Denver's populace. He wanted to get his meeting with Roman over with so he could get up to Austin's. Once he'd made up his mind to confront his feelings for Cassie, his impatience drove him hard.

He and Archibald Morrison had ridden most of last night, stopping only for a couple hours sleep around dawn. The annoying little mouse-of-an-attorney had complained incessantly about the hardships of this assignment, emphasizing that he couldn't wait to get back to "the civilized world." Cole had silently acknowledged his own haste to see the man return to where he'd come from.

They had arrived in Denver an hour earlier and, to Cole's relief, parted company. After a quick bath and change of clothes at the boarding house where Brew stayed when in Denver, Cole asked his old friend to watch over Ring, and then hurried to the hotel. But he was too late, Roman had already checked out. His only hope now was to find him at the train station.

He rode down Twenty-Second Street and turned at Wynkoop, cursing his bad timing. He pulled his watch from his pocket. It was 3:20. The train was scheduled to pull out in forty minutes.

The station bustled with activity. Cole tied Storm out of the way and hurried through the front doors. He waited a minute for his eyes to adjust to the dim interior before hurrying around the vast, noisy room, scanning the many people passing by. None of them had Roman's tall, angular build, his receding, pale-blond hair, or his handsome, almost feminine, features.

The noise followed him as he exited the doors facing the tracks. He shielded his eyes from the brilliant sunlight. In front of him a massive black locomotive hissed restlessly at the head of it's accompanying cars. A throng of travelers in all shapes and sizes streamed between him and the waiting train. Laughter and loud voices rose above the steady hum of activity. Children chased each other under their parent's watchful eyes. Somewhere a baby cried. Luggage was being hastily loaded and, further back, horses and other livestock.

Before he could move, he heard his name called. He turned to see a man walking briskly toward him. It was Roman. He had aged considerably. The hair showing beneath his tall hat had faded to silver. Thin lines fanned the sides of his handsome eyes. He offered his hand and a tentative smile. "You're looking well, Cole."

Cole accepted his gloved handshake. "Roman."

"I'm very happy you came."

"I would've come sooner, but I didn't get your letter until last night. How's Mary?" he asked, remembering Roman's wife with fondness.

"She's...not well, Cole."

"I'm sorry to hear that."

Roman glanced around. "There isn't much time, let's find a place we can talk." He spotted an empty bench near the end of the building and directed Cole toward it.

Once they were seated, Roman glanced briefly at Cole and then nervously aimed his words at the hills northwest of the tracks. "As I said in my note, I realize that our last meeting was difficult. We parted under unfortunate circumstances." His eyes found their way back to Cole's steady gaze. "Mary and I were fond of you and didn't like seeing you hurt."

"Look, Roman, that's all in the past, I..."

The older man touched Cole's sleeve to stop him. "Please, let me finish. There is very little time and I have a lot to say."

Cole forced down his impatience and leaned back against the wooden slats of the bench. Roman resumed. "Everything I said to you at that time was factual. Ramona had indeed married while you were gone. If you remember, I told you she was going to have a baby."

Cole inclined his head, not anxious to hear this again.

"She was very ill during her pregnancy. The baby, a girl, was born healthy, but it took Ramona many months before she was able to leave her bed. It took years for her to fully recover. The doctor warned her that she would be putting her life in grave danger if she were to conceive again. She ignored the warning. That is, her husband ignored the warning. He insisted she have another child." His voice broke and tears filled his eyes. He reached into a hip pocket for a handkerchief.

Cole ground his teeth together, growing more uncomfortable with each word.

Roman wiped at his eyes. "Harold got his child. He was born eight months ago, but my daughter…" He paused again to wipe his eyes. "Ramona died during his birth."

Cole's gut tightened. He'd feared from the outset that Roman might be leading up to this. He remembered Ramona's fragile beauty, her zest for living, and her love of children. What a tragic story. For a moment his anger toward Roman was renewed. Why had he let her marry such a bastard? Then it shifted to the bastard. What kind of man would knowingly put a woman's life in danger that way?

He clenched his jaw to gain some control. Ramona had been lost to him a long time ago when she decided she didn't love him enough to wait. He'd done his grieving. It had taken some time to let go of her, but it was over. "I'm sorry, Roman, it must have been a terrible blow for all of you."

"Thank you, Cole. I thought you might want to know, but that isn't the reason I'm here." He straightened his shoulders, placed his hanky back in his pocket, and glanced at his pocket watch before his eyes once again met Cole's.

"Now then, I must get to the point of my mission. I think the best way to proceed is to just to say it right out…"

Roman's declaration ran out of steam, and Cole grew uncomfortable watching him struggle for words. Finally, he continued. "Cole, Harold insisted that Ramona get pregnant the second time, because the first baby wasn't his."

Cole stared at him, wondering what he was getting at.

"Ramona was pregnant with your child when she married Harold."

"What?" Cole shot to his feet and glared down him. "My child?"

"Yes. She was pregnant when you left."

Cole turned away as the possibility swept over him. It was their last night together. He and Ramona had been cleaning the store. Cole's plans to leave for the west the next morning had heightened their desire. They made love in the aisle between dishtowels and tablecloths. It was the first time for both of them. Afterward they clung to each other, talking and laughing and relishing what they had discovered. He vowed his undying love. She made him promise to hurry back so they could be married.

"I know this is a shock, Cole. But there's more I have to say." He waited until Cole turned his dazed attention back toward him. "When Ramona told us she was pregnant, I was furious. I had grown quite fond of you and felt that you had betrayed my trust. Also, we had no idea when you were coming back. So I forced her to marry Harold. I don't know if you remember him. He is my banker's son."

"I remember him," Cole managed to say. He remembered how sick he'd been when he thought that Ramona had actually chosen such a pantywaist moron over him.

"Then you remember that Harold was always quite taken with Ramona. With you gone, he jumped in quickly to snare her. His family has money. I thought he'd make a good husband. I didn't know for some time that he was cruel to her. By then, it was too late to change anything."

Cole removed his hat and dragged his fingers through his hair. "What do you mean he was cruel?"

Roman's eyes looked haunted. "He wouldn't let us see her very much. Once in awhile she'd sneak out. She never said anything, but there were bruises. He resented the baby from the moment she was born. He didn't mistreat her, Ramona wouldn't let him. But he ignored her, treated her as if she didn't exist. When Ramona died, he refused to keep the child. Our other children love their niece, but their own lives made it impossible to take her in. Mary and I have done our best to give her the love she needs, but we can't keep her any longer. Mary isn't well. Harold rarely lets us see our grandson, and Ramona's death hit her hard. She is grief stricken and confined to her bed, heavily medicated. It was her idea to find you. I had my doubts. I kept remembering the semi-wild, intense teenager who first came to work for me and couldn't imagine placing my granddaughter into his care. Seeing you now, I realize how wrong I've been, on every count. The child needs care and love that we can't give her. She needs a parent. She needs you."

Cole's mind reeled. He fought for composure. "How can you be so sure the child is mine?"

"She was born six months after Ramona and Harold married."

Roman's eyes misted again. His lips twisted into a sad smile. "From the moment she was born, there was no doubt in anyone's mind, especially Harold's. If you remember, Harold is as fair as Ramona was. His eyes are brown. Victoria's hair is nearly black, her eyes are a very deep blue."

"Victoria?" Cole's throat constricted as he repeated the name. He felt the earth tip.

"Yes, Ramona named her after your baby sister. You talked so much about her those early years with us. My daughter never stopped loving you, Cole." Roman cleared his throat and continued. "I made a terrible mistake, a terrible choice. Living with that knowledge is my punishment. To say I am sorry to you isn't enough. Mere words never could be."

The bench seemed to reach up and grab Cole. He landed with a thud, bent over and rested his elbows on his knees. He was blind to everything but the pictures flashing through his mind. Ramona had been pregnant when he left. She hadn't chosen someone else over him. Her marriage had been forced.

If only he'd known. Things would have been so different. She never would have suffered like she did. Neither one of them would have suffered.

The locomotive hissed and belched unending smoke-plumes that rose on the breeze and disappeared into the clouds. Men, women, and children milled around, saying last goodbyes and hastening to board the rail cars that would take them eastward.

Roman glanced at Cole's bent head. He pulled his watch out of his pocket and frowned at it. This wasn't happening the way he'd planned. This rush was only going to increase the pain and confusion for everyone. Especially Victoria.

His eyes sought the little girl's standing several yards away, holding tightly to her nanny's hand. She stared back at him, pale with fright.

Roman glanced at the steaming engine, then again at his watch. Placing the gold timepiece back into his vest pocket, he observed his granddaughter with concern. He couldn't remember the last time he'd seen her smile, certainly not since her mother had died, and not a whole lot before. Whatever she'd been through in that house had built a wall around her heart, keeping out any love but her mother's and grandmother's. When Mary first told Victoria that they were going to try to find her real father, she had begged her grandmother not to send her away. But after she realized they wouldn't change their minds, she accepted her fate with her normal detached reserve. Exactly as she responded to everything else in her short life.

That was the argument Mary had used to finally convince Roman to do this. She was afraid that Harold's attitude and Ramona's death had crushed the child's spirit, and that Victoria's only chance for a normal life was to send her to a completely different environment -- preferably one where she'd find love and acceptance. Roman had finally given in, only to be confronted with the fear that sending Victoria away might ultimately kill his wife.

His own heart felt like it was being torn out of him as he thought of leaving the little girl behind. He had done everything he could to prepare her, explaining over and over again about her real father, and how much her mother had loved him. There was nothing more he could do. They were out of time.

He waved at the woman in charge of his granddaughter and placed a slender hand on Cole's shoulder. "Cole, this is Victoria, your daughter."

The words came at Cole as if from a great distance. He raised his eyes. She was here? His daughter was here? He ignored the middle-aged woman being introduced to him and fixed his attention on the small girl standing next to her, clinging to her nanny with one hand and clutching a yellow-haired doll with the other. A powder-blue velvet hat framed her delicate, heart-shaped face. Her cobalt eyes were enormous with fear in spite of her obvious attempt to look brave. She had a mass of near-black ringlets hanging all the way down her back to the middle of her blue coat. Her white-stockings covered legs as long as a colt's.

Tears burned the back of Cole's throat. His baby sister would have looked just like her if she had lived to turn five.

Victoria and Cole continued to stare at each other, frozen statues in the midst of the surrounding din, until the locomotive let out a great bellowing sound, breathing a slight breath back into them.

Cole stood and acknowledged the nanny. At first she looked at him as if she wanted to jam her parasol into his ribs. But her attitude softened when it became apparent that the starch had already been knocked out of him. She gave him a slight nod.

A shrill whistle pierced the air again, and all activity accelerated. Roman turned to shake hands with Cole, assuring him that he'd be in touch and asking him to send word if there was anything he or Victoria needed. Tears streaked down the nanny's face as she tried to wrench her hand free from the little girl's.

Roman knelt next to his granddaughter. She was visibly trembling when he took her hands in his. He nodded to Miss Waverly, and the woman hurried to the train, a hanky held to her mouth. "Victoria, Granddad has to hurry or the train will leave without him. Please try to understand. Even though Grandma and I can't be with you, we'll be loving you. And we'll write you letters, okay?"

"I can't read, Granddad," she answered in a tiny voice.

Roman swiped at the moisture in his eyes. "No, not yet. But you'll learn. And until you do, your daddy will read the letters to you." He glanced up at Cole. Victoria's frightened eyes followed her grandfather's and locked on the matching eyes of the huge stranger.

Cole nodded.

The engine chuffed and the wheels clanged as they began to turn. Roman gently prodded the immobile child toward Cole. "I have to say goodbye now. Go to your father." He backed away, choking on a sob. The train began to pick up speed; Roman bolted for it and swung on board.

The forlorn child stood rigidly as she watched the train fade to a black dot in the distance, its smoke a thin trail in the heavens. Only then did she allow her hand to be touched by the scary man who was supposed to be her father.

Cole clasped her tiny hand in his, and when she turned her large dark blue eyes to look into his, he knew his eyes held the exact same look of fear and confusion.

As Cole rode into Austin's yard, the travel-worn child perched in front of him on the saddle, anxiety tromped through his belly like soldiers marching toward a dreaded foe. Was it only three days ago that his biggest concern was to see Cassie? It seemed more like three years. In a frozen instant in time, his whole life had been turned upside down.

He'd been trying to clear his mind and regain some self-control since leaving Denver, but it was futile. Right from the beginning, he'd gotten off on the wrong foot with his daughter. He kept going over it in his mind. They had stood outside the station staring at each other for what seemed like an eternity. He had no idea what to do or say. Or where to go. Georgetown was definitely out of the equation. His sparse room above Ruby's saloon was no place for a child. But it was the only home he had. The only home he'd needed. Until now.

The best choice he could come up with was to seek help from Austin and Ginny and Cassie. Holding that idea like a talisman, he'd asked the little girl if she had anything warmer or more comfortable in her bags than the light coat and frilly dress, knowing she couldn't wear outfits like that into the high country. Victoria had just stared at him, her eyes wide. He had shaken his head at the quandary he was in, and reached out to touch her dark curls. But his sudden movement had startled her so badly; she jerked and cringed away from him.

The overreaction had rocked him. He'd knelt down beside her and quietly said, "Victoria, look at me." She refused, so he softened his voice to a near whisper and gently turned her face toward his. "Please look at me. I only want to ask you a question."

She stiffened her back and thrust out a quivering chin.

"Why did you jump just then? Did you think I was going to hit you?" There was a slight nod. "Why? Did your other father hit you?" Another nod.

Fury had blazed through Cole, white-hot. Roman had explicitly said that the bastard hadn't mistreated her. From that moment on, Cole had done his best to assure the child that she never ever had to fear that kind of thing from him, but she couldn't seem to hear him.

When he stopped at the boarding house, there had been a slight softening of the child's features when Brew brought the dog outside, and Ring bounded up to them. But it didn't last. Her remote stance was back in place throughout that evening, the shopping expedition for new clothes the next morning, and the entire ride over the pass to the ranch.

She'd hardly spoken in three days. His insistence that she wear boy's pants and boots didn't help either. But he'd wanted her to be warm and more comfortable riding on Storm.

Their first night on the trail produced another major problem. She had never been away from the finest comforts, including indoor plumbing. So when he explained that she would have to relieve her bladder behind a rock or a tree, she was appalled. It had embarrassed them both.

One of the few things she did say, before she quit talking altogether, was that she had never ridden a horse before. Since he hadn't wanted to push her too hard, they had been forced to spend two nights outside. She had never slept on the ground, either. Ring was the only one she'd let close enough to offer comfort and warmth. Nobody got much sleep. He had no idea how to handle this new turn-of-events in his life and held out a thin thread of hope that Ginny or Cassie would help him find some answers.

His control was as fragile as it had ever been in his life as he reined Storm in by Austin's front porch. The rambunctious collies came charging from the back of the house with noisy greetings. Ring joined in their exuberance, and the loud barking stretched Cole's tension to near breaking. He commanded Ring to be quiet and sit. His sharp voice cowed the collies too. They dropped to the ground beside Ring.

Victoria's eyes grew large with fright. Cole silently cursed himself, dismounted, lifted her to the ground and untied the assorted bags from the back of the saddle. He was unsaddling Storm when the kitchen door squeaked open and Austin stomped toward him, his face set in a grim line.

"Where the hell have you been? Austin demanded, coming around Storm's rump to stand next to Cole. "It's been weeks since I've heard anything from you."

"Nice greeting, Austin." Cole shot back. He had no idea why Austin was so surly, but he was in no mood for it.

"Yeah? Well yours isn't so great either. What took you so damn long to get back?"

"Since when have you been so concerned about my whereabouts?"

"Since a certain troublesome woman entered our lives, that's when."

Cole spun around and glared at him. "Cassie? Has something happened?"

"Yes. Something's happened."

Victoria leaned against the bags, which toppled them over and drew the men's attention. Austin hadn't noticed her until now. He stared at the child in astonishment. His voice lost its edge. "It looks like you've got something to tell me, too."

Cole wouldn't be diverted. "What's going on with Cassie?"

"It can wait."

Cole gave his friend a disgusted shake of his head and turned back to Storm's needs.

"Leave the horse, Cole. Ollie will take care of him. That tyke looks all in. Let's get her into the house."

Cole followed Austin's gaze back to his daughter. She was nearly horizontal now. Her face was dirty and her eyes half-closed. He cursed himself again. He should have thought about how exhausted she must be. He'd practically tossed her on the ground like another piece of baggage.

Ollie appeared from the barn and greeted Cole. His eyes strayed to the little girl and he smiled. Austin asked him to take care of the horse, then picked up the bags and headed for the house. Cole bent down and picked up Victoria. She went limp in his arms, and her fatigue increased his sense of remorse.

As they entered the kitchen Ginny welcomed Cole by pulling him down for a kiss on the cheek. Her brown eyes glimmered with curiosity when she looked at Victoria, but Cole's attention was riveted on Zeb and Dalton who were seated at the table behind her.

She motioned him to a chair. "Supper's ready, Cole. Pot roast. You two look like you could use a hot meal." She hurried to heap two plates full of food, and poured a large glass of milk for the little girl.

Cole took the seat opposite Dalton, continuing to hold Victoria on his lap. Austin sat at the end next to him. Everyone stared at the new arrivals. No one uttered a word.

Cassie's absence dominated Cole's thoughts. The anxiety at the table was palpable. "Where's Cassie?" He fired the question directly at Dalton.

Dalton's eyes moved from the child on Cole's lap to Cole's face. "She's up at Spirit Lake."

Cole pinned both him and Zeb with a penetrating stare. "Alone?"

"Yes," Dalton answered. His voice cracked with emotion. "You've got to go get her, Cole. You've got to talk some sense into her. She refused to come back with us."

"What the hell is she doing up there?" He bellowed. Victoria jumped and looked at him in terror.

Ginny marched over to Cole and held out her arms. "Give that child to me, Cole Adams," she ordered in a no-nonsense voice."

Victoria went willingly into Ginny's embrace. Ginny glared a scathing look at Cole, and reached for the glass of milk. "Austin, please bring me the child's plate." She turned with a huff and left the kitchen.

Ginny's chastisement set hard on Cole. He didn't need to be reminded that he had a lot to learn about taking care of a little girl. He started to follow

Ginny, but Austin put a hand on his shoulder. "You stay. I've had my fill of this situation." He grabbed the plate of food and followed after his wife.

Before he was even out of the room, Zeb picked up the conversation, beginning by relating the Indian attack. He talked about his ride to get Cassie. He expounded on her boundless energy and skilled treatment of his grandson's wounds, and related his own problems and recovery. Cole got the distinct impression Zeb was stepping around certain things, but was prevented from expressing any questions when Dalton interrupted with his version of the story. He told about waking to find himself face down on a cot in the cabin they'd found. He said that Cassie worked endlessly to take care of him and his grandfather, even hunting for meat so they could eat.

Cole was still plagued with the feeling they were giving a watered down version of their recent weeks. The tension between them hung over the table like a guillotine ax ready to fall. "That doesn't explain why she isn't with you now."

Zeb angled a sharp look at his grandson. Dalton frowned back at his grandfather. "Don't give me that look, Paps. This whole thing is your fault."

"My fault?" Zeb shouted. "I've done nothing to harm that girl. I've been generous with her from the moment we found her."

"And she's repaid us, many times over. We'd probably both be dead if it wasn't for her." Dalton was shouting now too. "How could you behave so condescendingly after all she's done for us?"

"I haven't forgotten what she's done," Zeb's hand hit the table with a resounding whack. "But you've got to get rid of that hare-brained idea about marrying her, she's not our kind. And it's obvious she knows it."

Dalton stood and faced his grandfather, fists clenched, his body ramrod straight. "What a ridiculous, bigoted thing to say. She is as fine a woman as anyone could ever hope to meet and you know it. You're just too pigheaded to admit it."

Cole listened in dismay. Zeb apparently had found out about Cassie's Indian heritage. But that wasn't what caused his gut to churn. It was the fact that young Dalton wanted to marry her.

Austin returned and tried to diffuse the situation by pouring fresh coffee.

Zeb took a sip of his then looked at Cole. "You might as well know if you don't already that she's half-Indian. She took off out of that cabin like a shot after Dalton asked her to marry him. The idea was ludicrous, and she knew it. When she came back, she told him her answer was no, and she refused to leave with us. She'll be fine. She's probably half-wild anyway. Think about how she sliced up that man who killed her mother."

Cole rose from his chair, cold fury flashing through him. Dalton lunged at his grandfather. Austin threw himself in front of Zeb and gave Cole a threatening look. "All right, everybody, calm down. There won't be any fighting in here."

Cole sat back down and held the arms of the chair in a grip of steel, knowing if he let go he would smash the old man's face to a bloody pulp. "Sit down, Dalton," he ground out. "Let's get to the end of this."

Dalton struggled to keep his voice steady. "I accepted her refusal to marry me, Cole, even though I love her. But I couldn't understand why she wanted to stay up there alone. I'm worried sick about her. She seemed different when she came back from her walk that day. With everything she's been through, I don't think she knows her own mind. And certainly not the danger she's in up there all alone. We argued about it for days, but she refused to budge." He shot a resentful look at his grandfather. "Paps was no help. He encouraged her by letting her keep his gun and ammunition and most of the food supplies."

"She wanted to stay, Cole," Zeb defended himself. "I'm not without feelings. I'm grateful for what Cassie's done for us. I wasn't going to leave her up there without something to defend herself with."

Cole wasn't listening anymore. His thoughts were locked solely on the fact that Cassie was alone in a desolate area. It wasn't only Indians that worried him. There was any number of wild animals she could fall prey to. Smokey, the old mountain man who'd befriended him when he came west, had been far better equipped to take care of himself than Cassie, and he'd been mauled to death by a grizzly. Cole would never forget the horror of returning to the cabin he shared with the old mountain man and finding him ripped to shreds. How he'd managed to kill the bear and drag himself back inside, Cole would never know. But the agony of losing his friend in such a gruesome way would stay with him forever.

Austin straddled the chair next to him. "What do you think we should do, Cole?"

Cole ran a hand over his face and through his hair. He took a deep breath and let it out with a rush. What a mess. He couldn't just take off and leave Victoria, but he couldn't leave Cassie up there alone either. "I'll leave in the morning," he said with grim resignation.

"You can leave the child here," Austin said.

"I don't know. She's had a rough few days. She's not even used to me yet. I better think about it." He forked a bite of food into his mouth. He wasn't hungry, but he'd learned a long time ago to eat when he got the chance.

An hour later he stood in the doorway of the yellow bedroom. Victoria slept soundly, her yellow-haired doll clutched tight under her chin. Ginny sat on the edge of the bed watching her. Her hands rested on her small rounded belly, and Cole wondered if she was thinking about the child she carried.

As soon as he stepped into the room, Ginny stood and turned down the lamp. Cole met her at the end of the bed. "She's exhausted," he whispered.

Ginny barred his way, not yet ready to forgive him for his earlier disregard of the little girl. "She's your daughter."

"How did you know?" He had told no one but Smokey about his association with Ramona.

"Cole, it's obvious. She looks just like you. Do you want to tell me about it?"

"Yes, but not now." He gently, but firmly, moved her aside.

Moonlight filtered in beneath the window shade and fell across Victoria's face, illuminating the tears she cried in her sleep. Cole moved silently to the edge of the bed. He tenderly dabbed at her damp cheeks with the edge of the sheet and bent to kiss her brow. You are so young, little one, he said with his heart, to lose your mother and be dumped out here with a man who doesn't know the first thing about taking care of a child. What a load for such a tiny thing to carry. Well, I'm scared too, sweetheart. Crossing an ocean alone at fourteen wasn't near as scary as the responsibility of taking care of you. I don't know how we're going to make it. But I promise, I'm not going to give up till I figure it out.

CHAPTER SIXTEEN

Acool breeze rippled the lake's surface and chased clouds across the sky. Now and then a cloud captured the sun's heat and raised goose flesh on Cassie's arms. Minutes later the eclipse would end, and she'd warm back up.

She sat cross-legged on the bank of the lake, anticipating a strong tug from the trout nosing around the worm at the other end of the fishing line. She'd had several false tugs on the bait, but she didn't care. At this moment in time, this enchanting place was like a lovely dream. Could she really be sitting here fishing in this beautiful lake? Was this really her new home?

Home. She loved the sound of it. The way it tasted. The way it felt. It conjured many images, happy, horrid and extremely sad. For a little while she let the feelings wash over her, adjusting to the extremes, and accepting the fact that the memories, all of them, would always be a part of her.

The line gave a slight twitch. She waited for a harder jerk, but it didn't come. "You're still teasing me," she said to the fish. "Some of your sisters and brothers will be, and I send them my thanks. The sacrifice of their lives will make it possible for me to live through the winter."

Josiah had loaned her the fishing pole and line shortly after Zeb and Dalton rode away. He told her where to find his favorite fishing spots around the lake and explained that she could make money by selling the enormous Browns in Georgetown. Added to the money Zeb had stuffed into her hand before leaving, she felt certain she'd be able to buy enough supplies to make it through the cold and snowy months.

She was grateful for all their help. She knew full well that she could never have stayed without it. Josiah had spoken with Cassie a long time that day at the falls, preparing her for the workload she faced if she planned to stay. But when she returned to the cabin and informed Dalton she wouldn't be leaving, she had purposely elected not to mention her new friend. Dalton would have had an even bigger fit if he had known there was a man living right across the lake. She didn't want to cause him any more pain. Saying goodbye was difficult enough.

So far, she'd had only one moment of doubt over her decision. It came shortly after the two men rode away. She had wrapped herself in feigned bravado and waved until they were out of sight. But the minute she returned to the cabin, the glaring emptiness overwhelmed her. Even though she couldn't return Dalton's feelings, she loved him as deeply as she would a brother, and the realization that she might never see him again increased her ongoing heartache.

She had immediately rushed back outside, thinking to saddle Lady and chase after him. But it was too late, and she didn't really want to leave anyway. She didn't cry long. The time for tears was over. And she wasn't sure she had any tears left anyway.

In no time at all the splendor of the surrounding hills replaced her loneliness and filled her instead with happy expectancy. She had taken off at a dead run around the lake in the direction of Josiah's cabin, feeling like a child again as she raced through the trees.

As if anticipating her arrival, Josiah had met her partway, carrying two fishing poles. They spent the rest of that day fishing and making plans for winter. He asked about her supply of wood, telling her she'd need a couple of piles as big as the cabin to carry her through. Then they discussed her other needs and planned a shopping trip to Georgetown.

Thinking of Josiah aroused Cassie from her musings. Where was he? She glanced at the sun to see the morning was growing late. He was supposed to arrive before noon to escort her to his cabin for lunch.

As if on cue, he came walking up, whistling a jaunty rendition of "Wearing of the Green."

Cassie jumped to her feet and began winding in the line. "I was beginning to think you might have forgotten our plans."

"Josiah Westfield would never forget an appointment with a beautiful lady." He gave her a courtly bow. "Are you ready my dear? My humble abode awaits our return."

Cassie laughed and curtsied the way her father had taught her when they'd pretended to be at a ball. Her squire took her fishing pole, picked up the stringer of fish she'd caught, then led the way to his cabin.

Their walk took nearly thirty minutes, and Cassie was surprised when she finally moved through a tight stand of pines and found herself standing outside the door of a sturdy, two-room log cabin. It blended so well with it's setting, she would have missed it if Josiah hadn't led her right to it. She twirled around and looked back across the lake. Zeb and Dalton must have ridden near it a dozen times and still not seen it.

"It's hidden quite nicely, isn't it?" Josiah stood at the door, waiting for her to enter.

"Aye, it is that." She stepped through the doorway, pausing for a moment to let her eyes adjust to the dim light. When she could see again, her gaze swept over a clean and orderly room with a hard-packed dirt floor. A big rock fireplace took up most of one wall, providing heat and a place to cook. At least a dozen army muskets along with an assortment of swords, bayonets, and pistols hung on either side. An open door on the other side of the room led to what she surmised was a bedroom. Delicious smells emanated from the large Dutch oven sitting next to the fireplace and made her mouth water.

Her host gave his broken-toothed grin. "Have a seat, my dear. I will pour us some tea."

She sat on one of the two chairs at either end of a pine-plank table and watched Josiah retrieve a blackened kettle from the iron supports in the fireplace. He poured steaming dark liquid into two canning jars as ceremoniously as if they were the finest china.

He kept the chipped one for himself and handed her the other. She hid her smile and held the tea to her nose. "This smells wonderful, Josiah. I haven't had tea since... It was my father's favorite drink."

Josiah disregarded her hesitation. "As it is my own." He carefully avoided the broken edge on his jar and took a sip, then grinned at her. "One must make do with what one has."

Cassie smiled and sipped her own tea, agreeing that it was delicious no matter how it was served.

Josiah jumped then, as if some signal had gone off in his head. He moved quickly to the Dutch oven and extracted a cake. "We will dine on sourdough and trout, with sweet cake for desert. How does that sound?"

"Like a feast." Cassie stated, her mouth watering again from the smells. "I haven't given much thought to food for some time." She looked down at herself. "My clothes seem to be growing. Not to mention becoming threadbare."

The old man tossed her a look over his shoulder. "They are looking a mite shabby. But I am not aware of any fancy parties coming up real soon, so I imagine you'll get by."

Before Cassie could ask for another cup of tea, Josiah had the trout on the table, along with slices of fresh-baked sourdough bread. He refilled their empty jars and sat across from her.

"Eat up my dear, before it grows cold." He took a bite of the succulent trout, pulled a bone out of his mouth, and then continued talking as they ate. "My life is simple here, but I prefer it that way. I turn my plate over and wipe it out after every meal and wash it on Sundays. Sunday is also the day I sweep my floor and wash my clothes."

He paused for a moment, chewing and contemplating some thought in his head. When he continued, he looked contrite. "I am careful to imbibe whiskey only once in a great while, as it has a tendency to make me a little...

unbalanced. But you are not to worry, I seek only my own company during those times."

"I won't worry, just see to it you don't fall in the lake and drown. I would hate to face the winter without you."

"No chance of that happening. I have the utmost respect for that body of water. She'll make a believer out of you real fast. I witnessed a man's drowning just last year."

Cassie lowered the bite of bread she had been about to eat. "A drowning?"

Josiah nodded and stuffed another bite of trout in his mouth. He washed it down with a long swig of tea. "Two men, brothers I believe, came to the lake from Denver to fish. We are getting an increasing amount of tourists and fishermen these days. But I digress. The two men built a small raft and paddled out to the middle. Shortly thereafter, the wind kicked up and blew the lake into a rolling froth. It tossed their raft around like it was made of twigs. I watched from shore as one of the men fell off. He disappeared from sight very fast. His body never did surface."

Cassie shuddered. "And the other one?"

"The other one eventually made it to shore and returned to his home alone."

"How dreadful."

"Yes. After you live here awhile, you learn never to take the lake's placid moments for granted. She's deep. Very deep. Formed by a glacier long ago. The middle stays frigid year round. The Grand River flows through this side and never freezes over, even in the dead of winter. And the wind can erupt like a tempest on the calmest day. You've never seen anything like it."

"I'll remember."

Josiah was enjoying himself immensely. His visitors were few and far between. It had been quite a spell since he'd had anyone to entertain with his stories. "The Indians honor her, too," he continued. "It was the Arapaho that named her Batan-Naache, meaning Spirit or Holy Lake."

Cassie remembered hearing Cole use the name Spirit Lake.

"Legend has it that one year the lake began to freeze over early. The nights were bitterly cold. Except for a spot in the very center, the ice was soon thick enough to hold up many buffalo. A fresh snowfall left the surface blanketed in gleaming white. When a band of Arapaho arrived, they noticed the tracks of many buffalo around the shoreline. One very large set of tracks came from the open water in the middle of the lake, and also returned there. The Arapahos believe it is a spirit buffalo, and that he makes his home in the lake."

Cassie stopped chewing and gaped at Josiah.

"Is something wrong?" He asked.

"No I..." It was too incomprehensible to explain. In her dream, a Spirit Buffalo had carried her to the shore of this very lake. She lowered her gaze and changed the subject. "Josiah, I haven't seen any Indians around the place, but Zeb said Dalton was shot by Ute's. Do they come here much?"

"According to an old brave I met back in '66, this was once a favorite spot for the Ute. But they never come close to the lake anymore. Didn't you tell me your friends were attacked farther away?"

Her interest was piqued again. "Aye. Zeb said a mile or so. Why don't they come near the lake?"

"Ah, 'tis a sad reason." He placed his fork on his plate and leaned back in his chair. "I was told that one day about eighty men, women and children were camped along the shores when a large bunch of Cheyenne and Arapaho swarmed down on them. A fierce battle ensued. The Utes were vastly out-numbered. As the battle raged on, the women and children fled to the middle of the lake on logs and rafts."

He reached behind him and picked up the pot, refilled their cups and put it back over the fire. "One brave, the same man who told me the story, ran to seek help from a neighboring camp of Ute some distance away. As he climbed a nearby hill, he looked back in time to see a giant wave swamp the rafts and carry all the women and children to the bottom. When he reached the other

Ute camp and told his gruesome tale, the chief and his band returned with him. They managed to kill most of the attackers. But there was no glory, because they lost many in the battle and the lake."

"What a tragic story," Cassie said. She wrapped both hands around the jar of hot tea, feeling suddenly chilled from the inside out. "No wonder they stay away."

"Yes. The Ute believe the spirits of the drowned women and children continue to haunt the lake. On cold winter nights, their ghostly forms have been seen rising in the mist."

Cassie looked into his dark eyes, trying to decide if he was serious. "You've seen them?"

"No, can't say as I have. But sometimes the wind carries the eeriest sounds as it gusts across the lake. Almost like wailing children."

Josiah must have realized that Cassie didn't want to hear any more sad tales because, to her relief, he changed the subject to narratives of his life as a wanderer.

The afternoon grew late. They said goodbye as the sun hung low over the western peaks. On her walk back to her cabin, the legend of the spirit buffalo preoccupied her mind. She could almost feel Running Deer walking on the path next to her, nudging her to take the dream seriously.

It frightened her to think of her dreams as prophetic. She didn't have her great grandmother's wisdom to make sense out of them. Maybe in time she'd be able to find hidden meanings or guidance she was meant to follow. But right now, the fact that she was beginning to acknowledge this particular dream as a foretelling vision was already enough to make her very uncomfortable.

By the time her cabin came into view, just as she had dismissed all thoughts of dreams and visions, a sudden movement ahead made her think she must be dreaming for sure. An animal bounded toward her at break-neck speed, and she realized almost too late that the illusion might flatten her. She raised her hand and yelled, "Sit!"

Ring skidded to a halt at her feet and landed on his haunches. His entire body quivered with excitement. His bushy tale lashed rapidly back and forth in the dirt. She dropped the fishing pole and squatted down to hug him. "Where did you come from, Nashoba Lusa?" He tried to give her face a bath with his tongue, she laughed and dodged away.

"Where have you been?" The booming voice came out of nowhere and startled her so bad she fell onto her backside with a jolt.

She turned around and dropped her mouth open. "Cole." She couldn't believe he was here, real flesh and blood, standing near the door of her cabin. She had thought of him so often, wishing she could turn her imaginings into the real thing.

She clambered to her feet and started toward him, but his sharp words stopped her cold.

"What kind of stunt do you think you're pulling?"

The angry words stung. She was so glad to see him she'd nearly run into his arms. It was obvious he wasn't feeling the same. "Stunt?"

He bore down on her, looking very much like he wanted to throttle her. "Why didn't you return to the ranch with Zeb and Dalton?"

She crossed one arm over the other and stiffened her spine to match his stance. "I'm going to live here now. This is my home."

He swept out his arm at the dilapidated cabin. "This? This is a shack, Cassie, not a home."

She closed the distance between them and stood toe-to-toe glaring up at him. "This may look like a shack to you, Cole Adams, but it is my home. And I'll thank you to remember that piece of information from now on."

"I'll remember it. And that's what you'll be doing too, remembering it from afar. Because you're leaving here, first thing in the morning."

"What are you talking about?" She stepped back.

"I'm taking you to Austin's."

Cassie refused to be drawn in by his magnetic gaze. Angry or otherwise, it always had a strong effect on her. She dug in her heels. "I am not goin' anywhere with you. I told you, this is my home now. You can't just ride up here and…" A scuffling sound behind Cole caught her attention. She tilted her head to look around him and saw a little girl sitting just outside the cabin door with a riot of long, dark curls and a pair of eyes identical to the ones playing havoc with Cassie's senses. But the child's were wide with fright.

Cassie hurried forward and knelt beside the child. "Hello there. And who might you be?"

The little girl stared at her for another long moment. "Victoria," she finally answered in a small voice.

"What a pretty name for such a pretty lass." She reached out and stroked the child's cheek, happy to see the fear dissipating a little. "How nice of you to come and visit me. My name is Cassie."

The child continued to stare, then caught Cassie off-guard with, "Your house is very ugly."

Cassie laughed, a spontaneous, musical sound that lifted on the breeze and brought an even more relaxed look to the little girl's somber features. "Aye, that it is. I doubt that it will ever be a handsome house, but it is sturdy and warm and all I have, so it will have to do. I have some wonderful cake in my pocket, full of currants and molasses. Why don't we go in and have some."

Cole looked dumbstruck as his daughter slipped her hand into Cassie's as natural as if she'd known her a lifetime. He followed them inside, ducking under the doorjamb to keep from hitting his head. "Our discussion isn't over, Cassie."

"Aye it is, Cole." She cut the sweet cake Josiah had sent home with her. After handing a piece to Victoria, she held one out to him. "I told you, this is my home now."

He accepted the cake and looked around, obviously wondering where she'd gotten it. He had probably already discovered there wasn't a single ingredient to bake anything like it, nor anything to bake it in. He looked even more amazed when she reached into a pocket and extracted a large chunk of the fragrant bread Josiah had baked.

"This is for supper," she said to the little girl, while taking great pleasure in Cole's annoyance. "We also have some venison steaks." She pulled a couple of potatoes out of another pocket. "I only have two of these, but you and I can split one, can't we?"

Victoria had a mouth full of cake, and could only nod. Cassie laughed again. "You better have a drink of water to wash that down." She strolled past Cole, refusing to look at him, and scooped a ladle of water out of the bucket near the door.

When the little girl was finished, Cassie said, "How would you like to go outside and play with Ring while I fix some supper?"

Victoria nodded shyly, then said, "Ring is my friend."

Cassie tousled her black curls and smiled. "I'm sure he is. He's my friend, too."

"He is?"

"Indeed."

"I had a dog at home." She looked down at the toes of her new boots. "He wasn't really mine. He belonged to Harold." After a long pause, she looked back up and continued as if she were telling a great secret. "His name's Ivor. He's a mastiff. Harold told me I could never touch him cause he'd tear my arm off. But Ivor would never hurt me. We played when Harold went to the bank. Ivor liked to chase sticks."

Cassie didn't know who Harold was, but she hated him for telling this child such a thing. "Well, Ring will never hurt you, either. In fact, he will protect you. Why don't you take him outside and see if he wants to chase a stick."

When Cassie and Cole were alone, she folded her arms and gave him a questioning look.

"She's my daughter."

"I thought she must be. She looks just like you. Who is Harold?"

Cole took off his hat and hung it on a peg near the door. When he turned back around, Cassie realized for the first time how tired he looked. "Harold is her stepfather," he said. "It's a long story, Cassie."

"Are you wanting to tell it?"

He sunk down on the cot. "I'm not sure where to start."

"Try the beginning."

Cassie listened quietly while he unraveled the shocking events of his past several days. As he talked, she busied herself with supper preparations, peering constantly through the door or window at the little girl outside. She shared Cole's anger when he explained how he'd discovered that the stepfather had mistreated his daughter. As she made coffee and waited for it to brew, he continued, telling her about his relationship with the child's mother and how touched he'd been to find out Ramona had named their daughter after his baby sister.

Cassie wondered if he was aware of the emotion in his eyes and voice. She poured him a cup of coffee, all the while remaining silent, not wanting to disrupt his willingness to confide in her.

"My baby sister was two years old when my mother and father and three brothers took turns dying from cholera," Cole said, refocusing the story to his childhood. "In one month, the epidemic took the lives of twenty-one people in our village. Stoke Gabriel wasn't that large, so the loss was devastating. Victoria and I got sick, but we didn't seem to get it as bad as the others. I finally recovered and thought the baby would too. But she took a turn for the worse. He turned away. "Did I tell you I was born in England?"

Cassie said, "No," but knew he wasn't really expecting an answer. His eyes seemed focused on the past, and she had a feeling this was the first time he'd said these things to anyone. "Our village was nestled between rolling green hills on the river Dart. The sea was just a short distance down the river. We lived in a little stone cottage big enough for maybe four people. There were seven of us. My father was a fisherman. He never made much money. My mother was sickly, but whenever she was well enough, she supplemented his income by making quilts and clothing for others."

His mouth curved ruefully with the next memory. "My brothers and I helped too, although the older two seemed more intent on leading my younger brother and me into trouble. Our cottage wasn't far from the church, and we were always and forever getting chased out of the churchyard. Our favorite place to play was under a giant Yew tree. It was over a thousand years old and the branches snaked out so far they covered the church and the graveyard. We used to pretend the tree was a giant sea monster." His smile disappeared. "My family's buried under that tree."

He stood and began to slowly pace the few feet in the center of the small room. His face and voice lost all emotion as he told of sailing his father's boat down the river to Dartmouth after his baby sister was placed in the ground. It wasn't long before he managed to beg a ride on a small vessel heading to Plymouth. From there he stowed away on the first ship to anywhere away from the death and devastation.

Cassie could barely conceal her horror as she listened to his memories of hiding for weeks below the deck, fighting the rats for bits of garbage. He was only fourteen, so young for such a harrowing experience. His story continued for an hour as he related his experiences in New York, living on the streets, back alleys, any place that offered protection from the elements, many times stealing in order to survive. The gang he'd joined for protection fought regularly with rival gangs. Finally he ended with the way he'd met the Brown's and how much they'd meant to him.

He stopped abruptly, shook his head and gave Cassie a look of chagrin. "I shouldn't have gone on so long. You make it too easy for a man to talk."

Those words warmed her all the way to her toes.

He stepped to the door and looked out. "My daughter's scared to death of me. You're the first person she's responded to since Roman left her."

Cassie walked over to stand next to him. She watched Victoria throw a stick through the trees. Ring returned it, dropping it wet and dirty at her feet. When the five-year-old bent to pick it up and toss it again, there was no little-girl joy in the game. Cassie understood only too well. All her joy had been robbed by the harshness of life. "Maybe she recognizes a kindred soul in me."

"Maybe you're right. You would certainly know what she's feeling."

"And you too, it seems."

He was quiet for a moment, his face once again expressing no feeling at all. "My losses were a long time ago. Time heals all wounds, isn't that the way the saying goes?"

Cassie's heart went out to him. He was obviously reeling from the impact of the recent happenings. And she wasn't convinced that he'd healed from his past hurts. Sounds from outside took her attention back to the little girl. "She's a darling, Cole. With time, she'll adjust."

"I hope you're right. I've got a lot to learn about being a father. So far I've botched the job real good."

"It mostly takes a lot of love, and I'm sure you've got plenty of that." Just being near him could inflame feelings of love in her, she thought. He had adored his family, especially his baby sister. It shouldn't take long for him to win over his daughter's heart.

But as they ate their meal, Cassie had second thoughts. Cole's frustration over her refusal to leave was uppermost in his mind once again, making him surly and caustic and uncomfortable to be around.

Victoria sat on the three-legged stool and picked at her food, shooting fearful glances at her father whose very size dominated the small cabin. He was perched precariously on the upright end of a log he'd brought in to use as a stool. Cassie sat on another log, determined to enjoy the delicious meal in spite of his snide comments about the rough furnishings of her home. But the more she ignored him the more irritated he became, and the more exaggerated his efforts became to draw her into his bad mood with him.

When he reached for a piece of bread and nearly toppled off his unstable seat, she choked back a giggle. Cole righted himself and glared at her. "And you call this preposterous place a home. How can you even imagine living like this?"

"I wasn't expecting company. If you'll be visiting often, I'll see to it you have a chair to sit on."

His eyes narrowed. "Cassie, don't start that again. We're leaving in the morning, and you're going with us."

"I'm not starting anything. The discussion is closed." She kept her voice pleasant, in spite of his goading tone. Her eyes skipped again to the little girl and noticed the untouched food. "What's the matter darling, don't you like your steak?"

Cole's gaze followed and took in his daughter's pale face and luminous eyes. "Is something wrong, Victoria?"

Cassie watched in complete fascination, as the child's forlorn look disappeared, and a mask of stoic indifference took its place. An expression equal to the one her father liked to use. She hid a smile as she watched Victoria pick up her fork and begin eating as if nothing at all was bothering her.

CHAPTER SEVENTEEN

The rest of the meal was eaten in silence. Cole didn't want to upset his daughter, and Cassie didn't want any more arguments.

Later in the evening, the two of them tucked Victoria into a pile of blankets on the bottom bunk. She fell asleep almost instantly, her doll clutched in her left hand, her right dangled over the side to rest on Ring's head where he slept on the floor. The dog hadn't left the little girl's side since she'd come into his world.

Cassie finished cleaning up the supper dishes, sloshed the dirty water into the yard, and hung the rag near the fireplace. Cole pulled a carpetbag from under his coat near the door and placed it on the cot. "Cassie, come here, I have something for you."

"What is it?" She came up beside him and gazed curiously at the large satchel.

"I don't know, Ginny sent it."

"Ginny?" She rubbed her hands on her thighs, suddenly as excited as a child at Christmas.

"Yes, and since Storm's legs nearly gave out carrying it to you, I think you should open it and find out." His teasing tone was back, and it felt good to see his smile, even though it only partially lifted one side of his mouth.

Feeling like she was unwrapping a special present, she unhooked the clasp and pulled it open. Folded on top were the two dresses Ginny had given

213

her. She pulled the blue one out, held it in front of her and twirled around. "Would you look at this? She sent me the dresses."

Cole caught her enthusiasm. He leaned against the plank wall and nodded toward the bag. "What else is in there?"

Digging deeper, she found the soft undergarments. She quickly folded them beneath the dresses. Next she found some food items: a loaf of bread, a jar of raspberry preserves, a container of butter, a bag of beans, several potatoes, packages of flour, sugar, and other baking essentials, some much-needed salt, and a jar of milk. Under it all were two warm blankets, a large bath sheet, and two delicately embroidered dishtowels.

She picked up one of the towels and ran a fingertip along a grapevine, considering the hours that went into the tiny green stitches and the thoughtfulness of her new friend to send her something that represented home, fragrant kitchens, family.

All at once the shabbiness of the cabin glared in contrast to the pretty, white cloth. Her eyes darted around the small interior, taking in the rock fireplace, the one grimy lamp, the dirt floor, the table tilting to one side, the two upside down crates that served as shelves, the dented dish pan, the few tin plates and cups.

It wasn't much to make a home out of. But how could she leave? There was no place else to go, not if she wanted a home of her own. Surely Great Spirit wouldn't have led her here unless there was a reason. In time she could make it better, turn it into a real home. Already she had a start on a good number of fish to sell. The woodpile was growing each day. She could hunt. She could trap. In fact she had a lot of skills. Plus Josiah was close by. She could make it work, couldn't she?

Cole must have sensed her uncertainty. "Cassie, Ginny said to tell you she misses you and wants you to hurry back. I hope you're starting to realize that you can't stay up here."

She laid the towel aside and turned toward him. "I can't leave."

He struggled to hold his anger in check and find a way to convince her. "I don't think you realize how hard winter can be up here."

Her eyes met his. "I have a very clear picture of what I'm facing. I've already got a good start on the wood I'll need. The cabin is sound. As you've seen, it warms up fast."

A muscle in his jaw tightened. "Warm is fine. But the snow will pile up several feet high. And you'll need supplies. What you have here won't last you long."

"I realize that," she said lightly, beginning to enjoy his ire. "I'm going to Georgetown to get more."

His eyes narrowed to mere slits. "And just how do you propose to buy more supplies?"

"By selling the fish I've been catching."

Her nonchalance goaded him, and he began to stalk the small confines of the room. He glanced at the fishing pole leaning against the wall. She could tell he wanted to argue about the number of fish it would take to make even the smallest improvements on the run-down shack, let alone buy food and other necessities. She had already spent hours thinking about it, and was prepared to argue that she could get by with less than most people. But he let it go and tried another tack. "That still doesn't solve the matter of safety. You can't stay up here alone, and that's that."

Cassie was no longer amused. Her mind was made up. She'd already lost one home, never again would someone force her to leave another. She arched her brow. "That's that, is it? And just who are you to come ridin' up here to tell me what I can and c'not do?"

The brogue she'd picked up from her father always thickened when she was upset. Nevertheless, Cole pushed harder. "I'll tell you who; A man who's spent enough time in these hills to know what's smart and what isn't. A man who has enough sense to make sane and logical decisions when necessary."

"Sense, is it? And logic?" A muffled sound took her attention to the bunk beds, and she lowered her voice. "Whose logic? Yours?" Her face felt scorched from the anger she fought to control. "My logic tells me I will do just fine up here. I've got good sense, and I'm capable and strong."

A muscular arm shot out and enclosed her in what felt like a band of iron. "Just how strong are you, Cassie?" Cole growled. "Strong enough to fight off a man? How about a determined bear? My friend Smokey was very strong, but even he couldn't survive a fight with a grizzly."

She wriggled and pushed at his chest. Her heart pounded, but not from exertion. Her insides always did flip-flops when this man got this close. Her breasts, stomach and private parts tingled from every inch of his hardness pressed against her. And her resistance only served to increase the intense sensation. Besides, it was futile to try to break his hold. He was right in this instance, she could never match a man's strength or a bear or any other large animal. She rested her hands on his forearms, her eyes level with the fringe on his shirt. "Let me go, Cole. Please."

"Have I made my point?" He continued to hold her tight.

"Aye. You have. I'll be very careful when I encounter a bear."

"Cassie." He released her, placed his hands on her shoulders and gave them a gentle shake. "This isn't funny. I'm not leaving you up here alone. Anything could happen. If you got sick or…"

"I won't be alone, Cole." She looked up at him.

His eyes narrowed. "What do you mean?"

"Just what I said. I won't be alone. I have a neighbor, a man who lives on the other side of the lake."

Her statement, meant to reassure him, had the complete opposite effect.

"Who?" He hurled the word like a lance.

"He's a mountain man, of sorts. But not really. He's been living in the hills a long time, but he's well-educated."

Cole looked at her with eyes gone wide and brows arching high. "You mean to tell me Zeb and Dalton left you up here with a complete stranger?"

"They didn't know about Josiah. I didn't tell them." She tried to wrench away from him, but his grip on her shoulders tightened.

He lowered his voice, talking to her as if her mind would completely snap at any moment and she'd need to be taken to an asylum. "Cassie, what's gotten into you? You're not making any sense at all. I think Dalton's right. You've been through too much. In the morning…"

"Cole, why can't you understand?" She interrupted, beseeching him with her eyes. "I know this cabin isn't much. But it's better than nothing. It belongs to Josiah, the land too. He and I are working out an arrangement so I can buy it from him. In the meantime, he doesn't care if I live in it. I want a home. I have no place else to go."

"You have a home with Ginny and Austin."

"Aye, they kindly offered to let me stay with them. But that is their home. I want my own." Her passion gave emphasis to her reason. "I love this wild place. It's helping me feel whole and alive again. I thought Noley had killed off that part of me as surely as he killed my mother. But he didn't. He didn't. Don't you see? I feel self-sufficient again. And I want a home of my own. I want to put down roots, attach myself again to the earth."

Her words must have hit some chord deep inside him, because his anger seemed to drain out of him. His eyes took on the same faraway stare she'd seen earlier when he was describing his childhood home to her. She tugged on his sleeves with her hands. "Are you listenin' to me, Cole? Can you hear what I'm sayin'?"

His attention swung back. He looked deep into her eyes and something shifted between them. "I hear you, Cassie."

His cobalt gaze tunneled through her, creating an opening for his hunger and loneliness to enter and meet with hers. His touch felt like hot embers as he pulled her against him again. This time she came willingly and met his hungry mouth with her own.

The kiss was fevered. They devoured each other like starving souls. Cassie clung to the back of his leather shirt and gave herself up to the volcanic force roaring through her body, setting her on fire. Cole's mouth moved on hers as if he wanted to absorb her, as if she were nectar and he wanted to drink her in like a man lost on the desert too long.

When he pushed her away a few moments later, she was stunned. She reached a hand out to the wall to steady herself, trying to make sense of his rapid shift. One second, he acted like he couldn't get enough of her, the next, he seemed repulsed. She watched him run a shaking hand through his dark curls then step away from her, struggling with some inner demon, just as he'd done the night he kissed her on the prairie. She searched his eyes, seeking some sort of explanation for his constant mixed reactions. But the blue-black orbs were unreadable. Still, before she could move or speak, he groaned and pulled her back into his embrace. His hand moved to her chin and tilted her mouth toward his. His lips slanted over hers again, gentle now, silky, a searching kiss, one that longed for answers, or permission. Yes, her heart sang. Yes!

She locked her hands in the hair behind his neck and the kiss became hot again, raging. Just when she thought she might faint from her elation, he softened it once more. She sighed from the sweetness, from the aching happiness of being held and being loved by him. She pulled herself even closer.

Her action seemed to startle Cole. He abruptly ended the kiss and simply held her tight against him. Cassie rested her head against his chest. She could feel his body shudder; hear his ragged breathing and the erratic pounding of his heart. Her heart answered with a drumming of its own. She sensed his battle but had no idea what caused it. Her hands began to move on his back with soft, nurturing strokes. But the tenderness only seemed to frustrate him more. His mouth moved to her ear. "I can't do this," he breathed into it.

Cassie froze at his words. Her heart pounded so loud she thought the sound must surely fill the cabin. She didn't understand his rejection. It was obvious that she affected him the same way he did her. Yet he fought it. Fought her. Maybe she was doing it wrong. Maybe there was an order to kissing and loving she was unaware of. Something more than just following her body's dictates.

His breath was warm on top of her head. She felt snug and secure in his arms. But she couldn't allow this to happen any more. Every time he touched her then pulled away, she felt wounded in some way. She didn't need any more pain. She didn't need him to come riding into her life and tear open her freshly healed scars.

She stepped back, stealing herself against the rush of abandonment she'd feel when she left his arms. "I don't want you to touch me anymore, Cole."

Her straightforward remark unnerved him. "What the hell is that supposed to mean? You didn't seem to mind my touching you a minute ago."

She wanted to hit him. He had just told her essentially the same thing. Now he suddenly acted as contrary as a wounded bear. She turned away before her impulse to scratch his eyes out got the better of her. "Oh bother. Never mind."

He spun her back. "Why are you acting like this all of a sudden?"

Her anger exploded like cannon fire. "Take your hands off me. I just told you I d'not want you touchin' me."

The intensity of her rage stopped him. His hands fell from her shoulders. "Cassie, we need to talk about this. We need…"

"We need to get some sleep." She turned away and began cleaning off the cot." You and Victoria have a long ride tomorrow, and I have work to do."

He held his tongue, but she knew it cost him to do so. And the knowing soothed her injured heart and pride. "You will sleep on the cot," she instructed. "I'll take the bunk above Victoria."

The next morning, Cassie and Victoria woke at precisely the same moment, just as dawn was stirring the birds to song. Cassie peered over the side of the bunk. "Good morning," she whispered.

The little girl studied Cassie for a minute, her little mouth displaying its usual rigid line, her eyes sad. Then, all at once, her expression softened, and she pulled a small hand out from under the heavy quilt and bent her fingers a couple of times in a slight wave.

Cassie climbed down from the bunk, held a finger to her lips, and nodded toward Cole. He slept soundly on the little cot, though how he managed, she couldn't fathom. One arm hung to the ground. Both legs stuck off the end clear up to his calves. The blanket only covered him from chest to knees, leaving only his long johns and socks to keep his lower legs and feet warm.

She helped Victoria into her coat, and the two of them tiptoed out of the cabin and into the trees for some privacy. The little girl seemed uncomfortable with the situation, and moved behind a large boulder. When she came back, her face was bright pink.

"This is all new to you, isn't it lass?"

"Yes," Victoria answered in a shy voice. "We had a room in the house for... to do this." She tugged her britches up with a scowl.

Cassie imagined the little girl was used to wearing fine dresses. "You'll be happy for the britches as soon as you get used to them. You'll like the freedom they give you. Boys are the lucky ones, you know. They don't have to be confined by all the skirts and petticoats and frills ladies have to wear. Nor bustles, either." She winked at Victoria's upturned face. "Now that's a fine piece of fashion. I've always wondered how ladies manage to sit with those things fastened to their derrieres."

The five-year-old didn't seem to appreciate Cassie's humor. "Will he always expect me to wear these?" She plucked at the wool pant legs.

"Oh no, I'm sure not. In fact, Ginny sent me a couple of dresses, so we'll clean up and change into something more lady-like this morning. Would you like that?"

A somber nod was the only response.

"Cheer up, love. There will be times when your da will want you to wear the prettiest dresses you have."

Victoria gave her a quizzical look. "Why do you call him my da? That sounds funny, like baby talk."

Cassie grinned at her. "I guess it does. My father was Irish. That was the name he taught me to use."

"What's Irish?"

"Irish is what you call people born in Ireland. That's where my da was from."

"Where's Ireland?"

"A long way from here, miss Vicky, across the Atlantic Ocean. It's close to England, where your daddy is from."

"I know about the ocean. My grandmother told me about it." Victoria bent and picked up a stick and began dragging it through the dirt. Ring followed, sniffing at the pointed end. "You talk funny."

"I grew up hearing a mixture of words, expressions and speech. I guess I must sound very strange to others."

Victoria looked quizzically at Cassie. "No one ever called me Vicky before."

"No?"

"It's all right if you do, though." She dragged the stick over the ground again, then paused and rested her hand on the dog's back. "Is Ring a wolf?"

Cassie smiled at the pair standing side by side in front of her. The dog's head was level with the little girl's. "I don't know. Maybe. Why don't you ask your da? I mean, your daddy."

The little girl's gaze dropped to the tip of the stick. "I want you to ask him for me."

Her voice was small again, and Cassie hoped the child's heartless stepfather hadn't generated a fear too great for Cole to overcome. "Perhaps we could both ask him."

Victoria seemed pleased with that suggestion. She tossed the stick to Ring and sat down beside Cassie. Cassie wrapped an arm around the little girl's shoulders. "Your father is glad you came to live with him. Do you know that? He was feeling very lonely and hoping a pretty little girl like you would come and keep him company."

Cassie received an I-don't-believe-you look.

"It's true. Did you know that your father once had a baby sister named Victoria?"

"Like my name?" Her dark blue eyes widened in wonder.

"Aye, yes. Just like yours. In fact, you were named after her."

"My Grandma told me Victoria is the name of a queen. Where does she live?"

"Who?"

"My fath... his little sister."

"Well, she died, a long time ago."

The cobalt eyes became somber. "My mommy died."

"I know. That must have been very sad for you."

The child's chin jutted out. Her shoulders stiffened. "Was my... father... was he sad when his baby sister died?"

Cassie watched the little girl fight her grief and wondered how to stop the painful discussion. Nothing came to mind, so she continued on. "Aye, he was very sad. He loved her very much. Having you come to live with him makes him feel better."

"My other father, Harold, didn't want me. He never liked me." A large tear spilled down her face. She swiped at it with the back of her hand and sniffed. "I didn't want my mommy to die."

"I know." Cassie drew up her knees, tightened her hold on Victoria's shoulders and stared at the thick morning mist hanging over the lake. "My mother just died too."

Victoria looked up at Cassie with astonishment. "She did?"

"Yes. And my father and my great-grandmother as well. I've been lonely and sad and very angry."

"You've been mad at them?"

"Yes."

"Why?" Victoria leaned an elbow on Cassie's knee, now fully absorbed in the conversation.

"Because they all went away and left me alone. I miss them very much."

Victoria pursed her mouth and squeezed her lips tight. Cassie was afraid she'd gone too far in sharing her own pain with such a little tyke. But then Victoria lifted her face to look at Cassie and whispered, "I've been angry too." Then she hiccupped a sob.

Cassie watched her battle to hold in the tears. "It's okay to be mad, you know. The anger, the sadness, it's all a part of saying goodbye." She tilted her head toward Victoria's. "I imagine you feel pretty homesick right now."

The tiny shoulders started to tremble. Cassie lowered her knees, drew the child onto her lap and rocked her back and forth, crooning soft words of comfort, wondering how long it had been since the little tyke had cried for the mother she'd lost. Or if she'd even been able to cry at all.

Cole stood inside the doorway, acutely conscious of his daughter's pain and his own inability to help her. In hardly any time at all, Cassie had penetrated the child's defenses and embraced her with compassion and understanding. Yet his daughter was still a stranger to him. He didn't have any idea how to reach her.

He felt the same helplessness when dealing with the woman comforting her. He closed his eyes for a minute and ran his fingers roughly through his hair. He was still smarting from their disturbing separation the night before, and still chastising himself for starting something he knew he couldn't finish. What was the matter with him? He'd been ready to throw her down on the dirt floor and ravish her. And with Victoria sleeping in the same room, glaring proof of what that kind of heedless behavior could bring. Somehow he had to find a way to keep his hands off of Cassie so he could concentrate on what he was going to do about his daughter.

His daughter. He was still shaken by those words. Things were moving too fast. In one brief moment his simple life had take a sudden sharp turn. Now everything was terribly complicated. He couldn't think straight any more. The control he could always count on for his very survival was slipping. And watching his little girl cry her eyes out on Cassie's chest nearly tore him to pieces.

When Victoria sagged against Cassie, her tears depleted, Cassie kept one arm tightly around her shoulders and said, "Tis a wonderful thing to give your tears to the earth. Your tears are filled with all the hurt in your heart. Every time you cry, more of that hurt is healed by the light." She tipped up the little girl's chin and wiped away the dampness clinging to her face.

Cole wondered if Victoria was too young to comprehend what Cassie was telling her. But as she continued talking, he could see the harsh line between those sad little eyes begin to fade.

"Your mommy's not gone from you. Not really. She's just finished with her earth-walk and has traveled on to another place."

"Heaven?" Victoria's eyes lifted to the sky. "Grandma says she is living in heaven."

"Aye, some call it that. But whatever name you give it, she's not far away. Her spirit lives on in you and all around you. She is as near as your thoughts or your memories. Sometimes you'll feel her presence when the breeze touches your cheek, or when the sun smiles down on you."

Victoria shook her head. "I don't like to think about her. It hurts too much."

"I know it hurts. But if you go ahead and think about her anyway, and cry when you need to, you'll begin to feel her love, and that love will help you feel better. It takes time, but pretty soon the hurt will ease a little and you'll just feel the love."

Cole watched the play of emotion displayed on his daughter's face and was thankful to Cassie for sensing how to reach her.

"After awhile," Cassie went on, "you'll feel that love and comfort from your daddy too. He loves you very much. I'm sure your mommy is very pleased that you've come to be with him."

"Do you think she knows?" Cole could see Victoria's clashing emotions in her luminous eyes. Even at this distance, their piercing blue depths cut a path through his heart.

"I'm sure she knows. There was a time when your daddy made your mommy very happy, and I think she hopes that you'll learn to be happy with him too." Cassie bent to kiss the tip of Victoria's nose.

Cole had to turn away. Cassie's words blasted through him with a force that nearly knocked him over. He stepped back into the cabin and leaned against the rough frame of the bunk beds. Not once since the day his baby sister's lifeless body had been pulled from his arms had he felt such pain. Not during the immediate days after or all the years since.

He'd mistakenly thought his grief was gone. Instead, all the sorrow continued to lurk beneath his struggle to forget that day, that life, put it behind him and simply survive. But his grief had jabbed him when he held Cassie in his arms the day she fainted. He'd received another jolt when he told her about his past. The same thing was happening now. Cassie's comforting words to his daughter managed to find his own pain. The knot of heartache he thought he'd buried so long ago was beginning to unravel and he felt powerless to stop it.

How could this woman continue to reach inside him and touch things he didn't want touched? Why couldn't he just get on his horse and ride away from her?

"Well, what do we have here?"

Cole spun toward the new voice coming from outside, his hand on his pistol. Through the open door, he could see a skinny little man who looked as old as Moses, leaning on the stock of an old rifle.

"Another pretty female. Not quite as old. But just as lovely to behold." The bearded oldster bent over at the waist in a comical-looking bow.

It was a moment before Cole realized that this old coot must be the man Cassie was talking about. *She can't seriously expect me to ride off and leave her with the likes of that old geezer. He looks like he can barely take care of himself.*

Cassie jumped to her feet. "Josiah, meet Victoria. She and her father came to visit me. Vicky, this is Josiah Westfield, my neighbor."

The old man touched the brim of his hat. "How do you do?" Victoria gaped at him. He turned to Cassie, beaming an amused grin. "More visitors, how nice."

"Aye. And you're just in time for breakfast. You will stay won't you?"

"I'd be happy to have a spot of tea. But no breakfast, I've already partaken."

"Will coffee do? I'm afraid I don't have any tea."

"You do now." He handed her a cloth bundle.

Cole moved to the doorway and watched her untie the knot. Her eyes lit up when she uncovered five eggs, each protectively wrapped in individual pieces of cloth. She opened another one and found a generous amount of black tea leaves. She flashed him a broad smile, then kissed his cheek. "Josiah, you are so kind to me. Thank you."

As they turned to enter the cabin, Cole blocked the way.

Cassie took one look at his menacing expression and unconsciously moved a step closer to Josiah. Victoria moved a step closer to Cassie. Josiah noticed both actions and stared at the man who'd caused them.

Cole planted his feet, crossed his arms over his chest. The width of him filled the doorway. The top of his head rose inches over the frame. The message was clear; no one was entering until he gave way.

Instead of being intimidated, the old man coughed behind his hand in order to hide his smile. Cole wanted to smash a fist into his skinny face.

"And this must be Victoria's father," the old man said, thrusting out a hand in greeting. "How do you do, sir? My name is Josiah Westfield."

Cole stared at the bony hand for a long moment before accepting it in his own, conscious of the fact he could crush it with little effort. After a quick shake, he crossed his arms again.

Cassie frowned at Cole's rudeness. "This is Mister Adams, Josiah. Cole Adams," she ground out.

"I don't need you to speak for me, Cassie," Cole said, flashing her a threatening glare. Cassie mirrored his scowl right back to him. Sparks flew back and forth between them. Then Cole fixed his assessing stare back on the old man. His lips curled into a sardonic smile. "This is the...ah...gentleman who will be your protector?"

Cassie was appalled. Her eyes hurled silver daggers at Cole.

"Protector?" Josiah intervened, obviously growing more amused by the moment. "Is there someone here who needs protecting?"

Cassie moved between the two men, hands on hips, and faced Cole. "I'd like a word with you, alone, please."

Cole thought her challenging stance laughable, and shot back a look of long-suffering tolerance. But he followed her around to the back of the cabin.

She spun to face him. "If you are tryin' to embarrass me, you are doin' a fine job. Didn't your mother teach you any manners?"

"My mother and my manners have nothing to do with this. You can't seriously expect me to ride away and leave you here with that old codger."

"I would like to know where you ever got the idea that you are my keeper. Yes, you've put yourself out to help me more than once. And I am very grateful. But that does not mean you have to take me on for a lifetime. I d'not need a protector. I need friends, which is what Josiah is. Now I am goin' to fix some breakfast. You are welcome to have some… before you leave," she emphasized. "But you better behave yourself."

Cole wasn't swayed, not even a little. He didn't know where this new stubbornness in Cassie came from, but he could be stubborn too. There was no way he was leaving without her. How could he make any decisions concerning his daughter if he spent all his time worrying about Cassie? He stepped forward till he was close enough to smell the sun in her hair. He narrowed his eyes and glowered down at her, speaking slowly and precisely as if addressing an errant child. "You go right ahead and fix breakfast. And when you're finished, you will get on your horse and ride out of here with us even if I have to hogtie you and throw you over the saddle."

Cassie looked like she wanted to slap his face. Hers turned red. "I'm stayin' here, she said through gritted teeth."

"Cassie, so help me, if…"

"I'm staying with Cassie," said a small voice behind them. They both whirled around to see Victoria standing a short distance away, one hand on the cabin wall, the other on Ring. Neither Cole nor Cassie could speak for a moment.

The little girl held herself straight as an arrow, chin thrust forward, as she walked up and slipped her hand into Cassie's. Then, leaning into Cassie for support, she addressed her father. "You don't have to take care of me anymore. I'm going to live with Cassie now."

Cole opened his mouth, and then quickly closed it. He looked at his daughter's determined face and Cassie's look of surprise. He had a sudden image of trying to force both females, kicking and screaming, back down the mountain. What a fine way that would be to win his daughter's love and trust.

He couldn't think of a damned thing to say.

His deliberation lasted a few more seconds before relishing the shocked look on Cassie's face when he threw up his hands and announced, "All right, you win. We're all staying."

Victoria gave a relieved sigh. Cassie's jaw dropped. "You're staying?"

"That's what I said. We're all staying," he repeated. "Did you say something about breakfast? I'm starved." He turned on his heal and disappeared behind the cabin wall.

CHAPTER EIGHTEEN

B y the time Cassie collected her wits and led Victoria back inside, Josiah and Cole were drinking tea and conversing like old friends. Josiah stood to pour some tea into a tin mug for her. "I took the liberty of making myself at home and preparing our tea. I hope you don't mind," he said, his eyes twinkling at her.

Cassie accepted the mug and took a sip, then focused her concentration on preparing breakfast. Her determination to appear unruffled amused Cole.

"Actually, part of the structure was here when I arrived," Josiah said in answer to a question Cole had asked before Cassie came in. "It was sort of a lean-to. I finished the walls, built the fire place, furnished it, such as it is." He scanned the interior of the shack with a harsh eye. "It still needs a bit of work. I left it as it is when I moved to Shangri-La."

Cassie stopped whipping the eggs. "Shangri-La?"

"Shangri-La. That's what I call that wonderful spot surrounding my cabin. I prefer it to any other area around the lake. Didn't you notice the nice view of Round Mountain from my front door? Nothing else compares to it."

Cole leaned back on the cot, only half listening to the old man's rambling. Instead he was acutely aware of his daughter sitting on the earthen floor a short distance away, stroking Ring's head and gazing at the old man with rapt attention. The tired look around her eyes was gone. She looked more at ease than he'd ever seen her.

Cassie moved past him, and his gaze switched to follow her as she poured an egg mixture into the iron skillet and propped it over the fire. Her trousers seemed baggier than ever. The shirt hung looser. She had obviously been working too hard and not eating enough. That would be one of the first things he put to right, now that he was staying. No woman in his care would waste away like his mother did.

A slow smile spread through his insides. When he'd committed to staying, it was out of defense. He'd felt like Cassie and Victoria had him backed into a corner with no way out. But now that he thought it over, he liked the idea. It would give him some time. Time to decide what he wanted to do. Time to get closer to his daughter. And time to keep an eye on Cassie. He shied away from looking at any reason other than Cassie's safety as his motivation. His feelings for her would have to be put on the back burner until he helped his daughter become more comfortable with him.

Of course he'd have to do something about this place. It wasn't even tolerable in its present condition. Especially since they were well into September now. The weather was unpredictable. It could continue to stay warm and relatively dry for another month or so, or it could snow any time.

"What do you think, Mister Adams?"

Cole looked at Josiah, who had obviously been directing some remark to him. "Think about what?"

"Cassie and I planned to ride to Georgetown soon for some supplies. Since you've decided to stay on, maybe you could take her, and I'll keep an eye on things around here."

"Sure... I'll take her," he drawled, slanting Cassie a droll look. "We'll make a list tonight."

It was obvious that Cassie didn't like the plan at all. Her back became stiff as an oak. Her beautiful chin jutted out. "You don't have to go, Cole. Besides, I don't think I have enough fish yet."

Cole choked on his swallow of tea, but managed not to laugh. He couldn't believe she actually thought she could get enough money for the kinds of things this place needed by selling fish. "I'll pay for the supplies this time. We'll work out some sort of arrangement for you to repay me."

He enjoyed the increase of color that rose in her sculpted cheeks over that statement. She turned her back on him and filled three tin plates with scrambled eggs and spread globs of butter and raspberry preserves onto thick slices of bread.

"The weather can be unpredictable from here on out," Cole went on speaking to her back." So the sooner we get going and get back the better."

Josiah gave him a wry grin, downed the last of his tea and stood. "I've got a list of my own to make, so I'd best be on my way. Thank you for making that ride for me. These days I much prefer staying on the ground to sitting on a horse. This cooler weather settles in my joints like glue. You folks enjoy your meal."

A distinct sound of muffled chuckles drifted back on the morning breeze as Josiah meandered away from the cabin.

The three he left behind ate their meal in silence. Victoria licked the jam off her bread and spooned eggs into her mouth, now and then slipping a small bite to Ring who rested his head in her lap. Cole looked around the cabin's interior, mentally assessing all he would need and need to do to make it more habitable. Whenever he glanced Cassie's way, she refused to meet his eyes.

After breakfast, Cole went outside and strolled around the area, looking at it with new eyes. The shack set several yards back from the lake in a wide expanse of towering pines that climbed all the way to the top of the mountain behind. Scattered stands of aspen crowded in on three sides, sprinkling the emerald hills with flashes of white and gold. The rocky hill behind the cabin was steep, but the land in front sloped gently as it met the shore. He was grateful to see there was enough flat area on either side to expand the walls.

A short distance away, the Grand River rushed from its source to join the glacial depths of the lake. It amazed him to think that such a narrow stream at this point could travel on with enough force to carve its way to the Pacific Ocean hundreds of miles away.

It had been a while since he'd stood still long enough to really take in the peace of the hills. Years before, when he roamed through the mountains with Smokey, he'd felt there could be no better way to exist. A sudden happy anticipation surged up for this new turn in his life.

At one point, he saddled Storm and scouted a broader region. When he returned, it was nearly dark. The door to the cabin stood open, and as he bent to step over the threshold, he was met with such a homey scene it brought him up short.

The radiance of the fire blazing in the rock fireplace muted the room's unpleasantness. The orange and yellow flames illumined Cassie and Victoria in soft amber light as they sat on a blanket in front of it, playing a game with a piece of string.

Cassie wore the blue dress Ginny had sent her. It softly hugged her narrow shoulders and trim arms, molded snugly over her high breasts and narrow waist, then billowed out around her. Her hair hung loose down her back and over one shoulder. The fire's red glow turned it a dark, burnished copper. His daughter wore one of the frilly dresses the Browns had sent with her; a pink frock with layers of ribbon and lace. She looked like a delicate figurine on top of a music box.

A rush of tenderness pierced his heart. He stood suspended for a moment, not wanting to lose it. Cassie had the strand of string wound through her fingers and urged Victoria to take hold of the two long sides extending between her hands. When the five-year-old took the pieces between her thumbs and forefingers, Cassie let the excess slip through her hands till both of them held two ends. Then she seesawed the string back and forth. Enchanting giggles filled the room.

Cole closed the door, and the sound stopped the game. Cassie pulled the string off her fingers and hastily got to her feet. A sweet, tentative smile lit her face. He hoped it meant she had accepted his decision to stay.

"We've already eaten," she stated. "But we saved you some stew. I've kept it hot. There's sourdough bread left from this morning. Plus there's some of Ginny's loaf. If you want to wash up, I'll get you some."

Her words sounded like nervous babbling. Cole finally spoke, putting her out of her misery. "Either bread will do, Cassie. I'm hungry." He stood his rifle against the cabin wall, unbuckled his gun belts, and hung them over a peg. He secured his hat next to them. "I washed up in the river before I came in." He held his hands out as proof.

His daughter's eyes took in his every movement. He smiled as he dropped to sit next to her and Ring. "Have you ladies had a nice day?" She eyed him warily and nodded her head. "And how about you, Ring? You were so preoccupied today you didn't even bother to accompany me on my ride." He covertly watched his daughter watching him, and continued to address the dog as if expecting an answer. "Did you figure you'd have more fun with Victoria?"

"We went fishing." The little girl finally rewarded him with a reply. "Not Ring. He took a nap. I caught the biggest fish. Cassie helped me."

Cole smiled inwardly. She was actually conversing with him. He pressed for more. "And what did you do with your fish? Did you have it for supper?"

"No, silly. I had stew." Her normally distrustful look softened even more. "Would you like to see the fish? It's a trout."

"I'd very much like to see it."

"Come with me then." Victoria stood and motioned for him to follow. "Cassie keeps them in a barrel of water out back." She started to reach for his hand, but decided against it. As they went out the door, she said, "We have to keep boards over the barrel, so the bears and other animals can't get our fish."

Cole managed to say all the right things as he looked into the dark barrel. Victoria continued to relate her experiences with catching fish. When they walked back into the cabin, Cassie set his meal on the table and urged Cole to sit on the stool to eat. He gave the stool a dubious look and carried his tin plate over to sit on the edge of the cot instead. Victoria perched on the stool and played with the string while he ate. The moment he was finished, she set out to teach him how to play the game Cassie had taught her.

After several failed attempts, Victoria tossed the string aside. "Your hands are too big," she stated matter-of-factly, and immediately launched into another subject. "Is Ring a wolf?"

Her rapid change in interest fascinated Cole. That and the wonder of having her talk to him at all. "I don't know. His mother wasn't. But I suspect his father was."

"Where did you get him?"

He hesitated for a moment, remembering the unpleasant circumstances and wondering how much he should tell a five-year-old. "I...sort of found him."

"Did he have brothers and sisters?"

"Yes."

"Where are they?"

"They.... aren't... living anymore." Do all children ask so many questions, or just this one?

"Why?"

"Well..." He seemed to have dug himself into a hole, and had no idea how to get out of it. "They...ah, died."

Victoria's eyes rounded. "They died? How?"

Cole searched for a way to not explain the gruesome event. Damn! He didn't know how to talk to a child. His daughter was finally warming to him a little, and he didn't want to scare her away.

"Your daddy rescued Ring." Cassie said, coming to Cole's rescue. "He rode into a town one day and found a man shooting a whole litter of puppies with his gun. Your daddy was too late to save the others, but he managed to save Ring. Ring was just a little baby then. He was hurt bad, so your daddy took him home and doctored him until he got well."

The little girl's delicate brows arched to fine points above blue eyes streaked first with outrage and then tears. She looked at her father as if seeing him for the first time. Her gaze shifted to the huge sleeping animal next to her. "Poor Ring." She caressed his head. Once more she pinned Cole with a penetrating stare. "That man was bad. I hope you beat him up."

Cole blinked in surprise. The story hadn't upset her at all. On the contrary, it appeared to have given him a step up. He gave Cassie a puzzled look then told his daughter, "As a matter of fact, I did beat him up."

Victoria looked pleased. She bent over and laid her head on top of Ring's. The dog opened one eye then contentedly closed it again. Cole smiled at Cassie, so pleased with the evening he couldn't contain it. She returned his smile, clearly as delighted, and scooted from the back of the cot where she'd been observing to kneel next to Victoria. "We better get you in bed, little lass, before you fall asleep on top of Ring."

Cole stood and turned down the blankets on the bottom bunk while Cassie took Victoria outside. After they returned, Cole went out. When he came back, he saw that Victoria was dressed in a long, flannel nightgown. Cassie had deliberately delayed tucking her in so he could do it. With nervous self-consciousness, he knelt down, pulled the quilts up to Victoria's chin, and tucked the sides under the straw mattress. He brushed her hair off her face, wanting to drop a kiss on her brow, but was afraid of pushing too far, too fast. So he settled for a hasty, "Good night, sleep tight."

Cassie was fussing with his bedroll on the cot when he stood back up. She straightened when she felt him at her back. "Thank you," he whispered close to her ear.

"You're welcome," she whispered in return.

The fresh-air and lilac scent that was only Cassie's wafted over Cole as he leaned near her, close enough to touch his lips to her dark red hair. The velvety contact sent fire coursing through him. He reached out to grasp her shoulders. But she spun away from him and glanced at the bunk, certain that Victoria was still awake. But the little girl had fallen asleep fast. So she thrust a hand at Cole in a keep-back gesture. Passion seemed to war with reason in her silver eyes. Reason won. Her expression became as rigid as an old-maid school teacher's, letting him know in no uncertain terms that she planned to stick to her resolve from the night before.

Skirting around him, she climbed to the top bunk and clambered under the covers. A hushed "goodnight" was her final word.

Cole thought she was being a little theatrical. All he'd done was tell her thank you. He pulled off his boots and stripped off his shirt and pants. He kept his long johns on and climbed into his bedroll. His legs shot off the end of the cot, instantly elevating his irritation. No way was he going to spend one more night on this stupid cot.

He got up, threw his blankets onto the floor, and piled into them. Damn! He thought. Who was he trying to kid? Cassie's swift rebuff had prevented him from taking her into his arms, and they both knew it. And they both knew where it would lead. She was just smarter, that's all.

Cassie's slight movements were just visible in the dying firelight. He watched her discreetly slip an arm out from under the blankets and hang her dress over the end of the bunk. His breathing became shallow as she repeated the action with her petticoat. She wriggled around for a minute and out came another soft garment. Finally she snuggled deeper into her blankets curled onto her side and faced the wall.

He wondered what, if anything, she still had on.

Morning brought low clouds and a threat of rain. The lake was shrouded in fog, and thunder rumbled off the mountaintops.

Cole had both horses saddled and the packs filled and secured by the time he woke Cassie and Victoria. He pushed warm mugs of tea and strips of dried beef into their hands and explained that they had exactly 15 minutes before they left for Georgetown.

Cassie argued that she wasn't ready. She had more fish to catch. He assured her she was ready. They weren't waiting another day, the weather was too risky, and they had too much to do before winter set in. The argument continued for several minutes until he convinced her this wasn't some trick, that he truly would bring her back. They stopped at Josiah's and got his list and best wishes for a safe journey. Then they were on their way.

A cold mist fell all day, making the journey miserable. Cole pushed them hard, stopping only for short breaks. They arrived at the Barret Ranch in the late afternoon and spent a warm and cozy evening with Ginny and Austin.

The next morning brought even worse weather. The wind was colder, the rain harder. Lady to shied at every shadow. Cassie cooed soothing words and patted the mare's neck, but the horse refused to be comforted. With every bolt of lightning and resulting crack of thunder, Lady would throw her head and trot sideways. Which set off Cassie's nerves since, in many places, the trail narrowed and dropped away for hundreds of feet.

Storm seemed undisturbed by the commotion. Cole rode with Victoria perched on the saddle in front of him, and they gained quite a bit of distance while Cassie used all her energy to keep Lady under control. "You've become soft with nothing to do but graze and loll in the sun, Lady girl."

The rain became a grey curtain that concealed all but the undergrowth of nearby dwarf spruce and shrubs. Cassie didn't think things could get any worse when a sudden snorting and crashing in the dense timber caused Lady to shy and rear up. A brown bear crashed through the brush and rose up on hind legs. Lady snorted and plunged forward so violently Cassie was thrown off and landed with a thud on her rump. The startled bear darted back into the trees.

Thunder covered Cassie's painful yelp. So Cole had no idea what was happening as a rider-less Lady galloped past him, throwing her heels high.

He spun Storm around to see Cassie, limping along, rubbing her backside. "What happened?" he yelled.

"I'll tell you later." She waved at him. "You better catch Lady, I don't feel much like hiking, right now."

Cole set Victoria on the ground, instructed her to stay with Cassie, and then ordered Ring to stay with them both.

It was nearly twenty minutes before he returned. "Damn mare, I didn't think she'd ever let me catch her. What happened?"

Cassie and Victoria sat on a rock huddled together under their rain gear at the side of the trail. Ring lay curled at their feet. "A bear came out of the trees and nearly scared us out of our skin," Cassie answered.

"A bear?" Cole lurched out of the saddle. "And you let me ride off and leave the two of you? Are you crazy? You don't even have a gun."

"Calm down, Cole. The bear was as scared as we were. He ran away as fast as he could.

"Ring wouldn't let him hurt us," Victoria defended Cassie. "He's not scared of bears."

"You're right," Cole said, relaxing his tone. He gave Cassie a look of exasperation, and knelt down to pet the dog. "Ring's not afraid of bears, but we don't want him to have to fight one, do we?"

Another flash of light and peal of thunder brought an abrupt end to the exchange. "We better keep moving," Cole said. He hoisted Victoria onto Storm and tucked her raincoat more tightly around her. Then he walked over to Cassie, pulled her hood further over her face and buttoned the top button. "Can you ride?" he asked.

"Aye, my vanity's more bruised than I am." But when she threw her leg over Lady's back and settled into the saddle, she found that statement not-quite true. Her tailbone throbbed. She had to lean on one butt cheek in order to find some relief.

Lady's excitability persisted throughout the rest of the day, and Cassie grew weary. But Cole refused to spend the night on the trail, so they kept going long after sunset. By the time they rode into Georgetown, Cassie was spent. In spite of her outer protection, she was wet to the skin and nearly frozen to the saddle.

The frigid rain didn't seem to bother the ragged looking inhabitants of Georgetown. Men filled the saloons or crowded together in boisterous groups under the overhangs of the buildings. Several miners and other men called out greetings to Cole and curiously eyed the pair with him.

Cole stopped the horses at a hitching post in front of a well-lit hotel. The two-story Barton House sat atop a raised plot of ground in the center of town. Cole deposited Victoria inside the doorway and returned to sweep Cassie off of Lady and carry her in as well. After another trip outside for their bags, he ushered them both further inside the warm interior.

The desk clerk eyed the dripping group through a pair of wire-framed lenses resting on the end of his nose. His myopic scrutiny landed for a scant second on the large, wet dog. Cassie had noticed the dogs-not-allowed sign, but apparently the man wasn't going to be the one to tell Cole Adams his wasn't welcome. He forced a big smile behind his trim moustache and said, "Evening Cole. You all look done in."

"Hello, Mike. I need a couple of rooms, adjoining if possible." If he noticed the clerk's raised eyebrows, he didn't show it.

"Sure, Cole. The street-side rooms at the top of the stairs are available." The clerk handed the keys to Cole and turned the registry around. "Just sign here, please."

"Thanks. Would you get someone from the livery to take care of the horses?"

"Right away."

The only thing that was keeping Cassie on her feet was the thought of getting into some dry clothes and eating a hot meal. She silently urged Cole to hurry. Just then the door burst open and a woman raced in, robbing her of all thought. The beautiful redhead crossed the room in a hurry, followed by every eye in the place. She stopped in front of Cole and threw her arms around his neck.

"Rusty said you were back." The woman's voice was deep and husky. "What are you doing here? Your room at my place is clean and waiting."

The hotel's warmth had diminished Cassie's shivers, but she felt them start again. Victoria pressed against her leg, shaking just as badly. She bent and picked her up, then cuddled her close as she watched the stunning stranger remove a black, full-length cape and slip her arm through Cole's.

Cassie had never seen anyone so beautiful. The woman's brilliant auburn hair was piled on top of her head in a cluster of large curls. Tighter corkscrew curls surrounded her hairline. Her cheeks and lips were rouged just enough to entice, and her hazel eyes were outlined with something that enhanced the color. She wore a cardinal-red velvet dress trimmed in pink. It hugged every curve, of which she had plenty. Her bosom was lush and threatened to spill out the top of the low-cut gown. There was no bustle to hide the very feminine posterior, just folds of material that cupped slightly before falling gracefully to the floor.

No wonder Cole was so anxious to get back to Georgetown, Cassie thought, angry with herself for caring so much. The woman turned curious eyes toward Cassie and the dripping wet bundle she had propped on her hip. Victoria pushed her hood back, and the woman's expression darkened with alarm.

Cole placed a large hand on the woman's shoulder as he introduced them. "Cassie and Victoria, meet Ruby, a very good friend of mine. Ruby, this is Cassie O'Brian and Victoria, my daughter."

Cassie offered a small smile and wondered exactly what Cole meant by the term very good friend. Cole didn't seem the least bit concerned at the woman's shocked look as she continued to stare at his little girl. He raked his eyes over Cassie and Victoria. "Let's get you two upstairs and out of those wet clothes." To the desk clerk, he said, "How about sending up a tub and some hot water, Mike."

"Yes sir. Right away."

He gave Ruby a small grin. "Why don't you bring some coffee and join me upstairs? We can talk after I've cleaned up."

"You bet," Ruby answered, coming out of her stupor. "I wouldn't miss this for the world."

Two hours later, Cassie and Victoria were warm and clean. Cassie had donned the blue dress. Her hair hung to her waist in loose curls, almost dry from brushing it near the stove. She began to fasten the tiny row of buttons up the back of Vicky's darker blue dress. "Are you as hungry as I am?" she asked her small charge.

"Yes."

"I wonder what's keeping your daddy?" Her eyes strayed to the door separating the two rooms. Other than bringing her a hot cup of coffee and Victoria a cup of hot chocolate, she hadn't seen any sign of him.

Throughout her bath, there'd been no sounds from the next room. But when Vicky started bathing, and for the past forty-five minutes, she'd heard Cole's muffled voice, along with Ruby's, coming from the other side of the door.

Finished with the tiny buttons, she turned Vicky around to face her. "Feel better?"

Vicky nodded her head.

"Warm?"

Another nod.

"But hungry, right?"

Another nod.

"I'll let your daddy know we're ready for our supper." She moved to the door and started to knock when she caught a fraction of the muted conversation on the other side.

".... Don't know how long I'll be up there. But it will be good for Victoria."

"Cole, even if your daughter feels safe with her, you said she's nothing but a half-breed. What can you possibly…" Ruby's voice stopped abruptly. But it didn't matter. Cassie had heard enough.

CHAPTER NINETEEN

Cassie was unaware that the fairer sex was few in numbers in mining towns like Georgetown, especially the unpainted variety. And since she didn't think of herself as a normal white woman, let alone an attractive white woman, she could never imagine drawing attention from anyone. Nevertheless, quick as a forest fire, word spread that an unusually lovely woman with dramatic silver eyes was heading to Max's place with a pretty little girl in tow.

From the minute she and Victoria ordered their meals, the hated term – half-breed – burned into her mind. Cole had obviously told Ruby about her heritage, and his betrayal hurt in a way she'd never felt before. That's the reason he pulls away from me, she thought. He doesn't think about my mixed blood until he gets too close, and then his mind overrules his passion. Well, I'll make sure he never has to endure the battle again. We'll have an even exchange. He can help me with the cabin. I will help him with his daughter.

She glanced at Vicky. The little girl's back was rigid, her blue eyes downcast. One hand rested demurely on the napkin in her lap. With the other she forked lady-like bites of potatoes into her mouth. Cassie smiled. My part will be easy. This child has already wound herself around my heart. "You look tired, lass, do you feel all right?"

Vicky nodded, her expression somber.

Everything will be fine Cassie wanted to tell her. Someday you'll find life worth smiling about. Her own smile faded as she noticed at least a dozen men gawking at her over the top of Victoria's head. She glanced quickly around, self-consciousness escalating with each heartbeat. The small restaurant was filled to the brim with men. They overflowed the tables and chairs, crowded along the walls and packed the doorway. The two front windows were plastered with faces pressed against the glass from outside. Some stared, openmouthed. Some leered. Some looked at her as if they were in love. Cassie became light headed as blood rushed to her face.

As she clung to the table, trying to decide what to do, two men separated themselves from the crowd and stood next to her.

"Where'd you come from, honey? Yer perty enough to've descended from the heavens." The man who spoke wore filthy overalls and a plaid flannel shirt so grimy there was no distinctive color. He looked more like a lumberjack than a miner. He reached out a calloused and dirty hand to grip a lock of hair hanging over the front of her dress.

"Such beauty deserves to be petted," said the other one, just as tall, but not nearly as big around. He touched her face with an index finger that wasn't much more than a stub.

Both men reeked of alcohol and unwashed flesh. Cassie's stomach convulsed. Only her concern for Vicky kept her composed. What a fool she'd been traipsing off without even a thought to their safety.

Before she could react, a bald man came out of the back room. He wore a white apron and carried a ladle. "Leave the lady alone, she doesn't appear to want any company," he said.

"Mind your own business, Max," said the thinner one. He drew his gun and pointed it at the aproned man. "The lady likes our company just fine, don't you honey?"

Cassie jerked her head, trying to pull her hair free, but the big man held it tight in his fist. She cast a frightened look at the spectators. No one seemed willing to challenge the gun.

A sudden commotion in the doorway drew everyone's attention. Relief flooded over Cassie when she saw Cole push his way in, Ring right behind him. The men inside the restaurant moved as one to press together behind Cole, setting off a bigger uproar as they blocked the view of those still outside.

Cole's eyes flashed with rage as he propelled himself across the room. "Take your hands off of her and get out."

The smaller man now leveled his pistol at Cole's waist. "You get out, mister. This ain't any of yer concern."

"The hell it isn't." The words reached the gunman's ears at the same moment Cole's fist landed in his face. The blow snapped the man's head back and sent him and his gun to the floor with a crash. "Guard," he commanded, and Ring crouched over the prostrate man, fangs exposed.

Cassie watched the violence unfold helpless to do anything else. The larger man released his hold on her hair and launched himself into Cole, gripping his chest in a powerful bear hug. Cole's head fell back and jerked forward, smashing the offender's nose and breaking his grasp. Blood poured from his nose.

Cole turned to assure himself that Cassie and Victoria were all right. Cassie had pulled the child onto her lap; her scream swung Cole back around, but not in time to prevent a slicing gash to his midriff from a large knife. In less than a heartbeat, Cole drew his pistol and fired. The man howled as the bullet splintered his right hand and sent the knife flying.

"Get the sheriff," Max called to the crowd, a shotgun now replacing the ladle in his hands. "Cole, take those two females out of here. I'll tell the sheriff you'll be in to see him tomorrow."

Cole holstered his .44, picked up his daughter, wrapped his other arm around Cassie, and headed for the hotel.

Once in their rooms, Cassie waited for the lecture she deserved. Her guilt for endangering Victoria was almost more than she could bear. The look on her face must have said as much to Cole. He merely scowled at her and carried Victoria over to the bed.

Cassie walked woodenly to sit down next to her and pulled the little girl into her arms. "I'm so sorry about all of that, sweet girl. We're all fine. You're safe." She glanced up at Cole and saw the anger waiting behind the concern in his eyes. He removed his jacket, and her eyes dropped to his shirt. It was red with blood.

Not wanting to scare Victoria any worse than she already was, Cassie lifted her further onto the bed, laid her down, and looked around for the doll. When she spotted it on the chair by the washstand, she gestured for Cole to get it.

He handed it to her. She tucked it into the little girl's arms and pulled a blanket over her. "You lie here and rest for a minute, all right?"

She was relieved when Vicky nodded. "Here Ring." Cassie patted the bed and the dog leapt up and curled himself against the little girl. "Your daddy and I will be right there in the other room. I'll leave the door open."

When Vicky shifted onto her side and cuddled up to the dog, Cassie motioned Cole into the adjoining room and pushed him onto the chair near the bed.

Cole removed his shirt to reveal a cut that ran diagonally from the middle of his breastbone to a spot near the top of his pelvic bone. Blood oozed steadily along the entire length. Cassie wadded up his shirt and pressed it against the wound. "Hold this tight," she ordered and ran back into the other room.

After checking on Victoria, who seemed to be asleep, she grabbed her medicine bag and knife and sailed out the door and down the steps. Mike looked up with concern when she demanded a bottle of whiskey and more towels, but obeyed with little fuss.

When she burst back into his room, she found that Cole hadn't moved. She ushered him over to the bed. "Lie down. It'll have to be stitched."

She assembled the needed items and sat next to him. "This is gonna hurt somethin' awful. I've got whiskey, you better drink some before I begin."

Cole shook his head. "I don't want anything. Just get it over with."

Cassie tossed the blood-soaked shirt on the floor. The gash continued to bleed. With a bar of soap, she lathered the entire area and used Cole's razor to remove a swath of dark hair from either side of the cut. Cole hissed a quick intake of breath as she doused whiskey over the wound. "Are you ready?" she asked, picking up a needle threaded with catgut.

"Get on with it," Cole ground out.

She winced with him as the needle pierced his skin. "The wound bled a lot," she said, pushing the needle through the other side of the cut. "That's good. It'll heal better." She pulled the catgut tight. "Vicky's asleep," she rambled on, penetrating the painful flesh again.

She cast a quick glance at Cole's face. He stared at the ceiling, a clenched jaw the only sign of his agony. "I know I was wrong tonight. I wasn't thinking." The painful stitching continued. "We were hungry, and you...you hadn't come back. I want you to know that I will never again put Victoria in harms way like that. I promise."

Each time the needle pierced Cole's skin, his stomach muscles flinched. It seemed to take forever and Cassie marveled at his control. Perspiration formed on her brow, under her arms, and on her palms. More than once she had to pause and wipe her hands on her dress. Dalton's wounds had been much worse, but he had been unconscious when she'd worked on him. This was much harder.

When she finished tying off the end of the catgut, she packed herbs around the wound and wrapped it with clean bandages. She glanced again at his face. His lips were white. His face and chest were slick with sweat.

She poured clean water from the pitcher into the bowl. His eyes closed as she drew the wet cloth across his brow. His jaw muscles eased as the cloth gently moved down each side of his face. When she wiped it across his lips, she was pleased to see color filling them again.

She bathed every inch of his face with the cool water, releasing more tension with every stroke. She moved the cloth on down over his neck and chest, his arms and stomach, touching every part of him with her eyes and heart as well. There was no point in denying that she adored everything about him. His expressive brows and slightly imperfect straight nose. His chiseled mouth and stubborn square jaw. She loved the way his curly black hair refused to stay tamed. She loved his strength as well as the vulnerability he tried so hard to hide.

But as much as she loved him, she was just as determined to never let him know. She may not have a clear picture yet of where she fit into the world, but she knew distinctly where she didn't. She'd never be completely comfortable in the white world and was prepared to accept herself that way. What she wasn't prepared to accept was any more pain from losing those she loved. She resolved then and there to guard her heart well.

Cole's chest rose and fell in an even rhythm, and she knew that the herbs were lessening the pain and allowing him to sleep. Still she couldn't bring herself to leave him. Not yet. Not while it was safe to be this close to him without the struggle to keep her feelings inside.

Moments before the roosters began to crow, Cole woke up, feeling much like the old days when he'd been drinking too much. Then he remembered the energy it had taken to block the stabbing agony of the needle when Cassie stitched his wound.

He tried to sit up but the pain across his midriff and a weight on his left arm stopped him. The room was nearly as black as pitch but he didn't need sight to know his arm was pinned beneath Cassie. Her lilac scent filled his senses. He relaxed back onto the mattress and relished the awareness that her left knee rested on his thigh; her left arm lay over his chest.

As sure as the dawning day, she's not aware of the situation she's in. He smiled with contentment and amusement. He had no explanation for how she came to be in his bed but it didn't matter. Moment's like this should never be questioned; only enjoyed. His eyes drifted shut, and he let his free hand make a discreet journey over her hair, down her shoulder and arm, and across her waist and hip. He could reach no further without jarring her, so he reversed the exploration. She felt firm, yet supple. The fabric of her dress was soft. He turned his hand and slid his fingers through her hair. It felt like rich satin. He loved the weight of it, and had a moment of curious contemplation about how burdensome the weight must feel to her.

He played with a burgundy strand for a minute, then let his hand drift back over her shoulder to her waist. In her sleep, Cassie reacted to his touch by emitting a soft sigh and snuggling closer against him. Cole nuzzled the top of her head with his mouth and nose, desire making him want much more. There was no use fighting it, she belonged in his arms. He tightened his hold, drawing her higher, within reach for his mouth to close over hers.

Consciousness spread through Cassie slowly. Once she realized where she was and what she was doing, she jerked her mouth free. "Cole...stop."

"Oh god," he groaned. "Don't keep pulling away from me."

"Me?" She hurried off the bed. "Me pull away?"

The gray light of day dimly lit the room. Cassie was shivering. Cole got up slowly, pressing a hand to his middle. He made it to his feet and reached for her. "You're cold, come here."

She stepped away from him, her breathing rapid, as if she'd just run up a flight of stairs. "I told you not to touch me anymore." She realized how ridiculous the statement was the minute it was out of her mouth.

Cole echoed her thought. "You were in my bed."

She nervously smoothed the front of her dress, then tried to finger-comb her hair into order. She felt heavy with sleep, passion and confusion.

"What were you doing in my bed?" he asked.

"I...must have fallen asleep...after I..." She couldn't seem to go on.

"Treated my wound," he finished for her.

"Aye." She slanted him a brief look. "How do you feel?"

"You tell me."

Her face burned. "You know what I mean. How does the wound feel?"

"Sore, but I've been hurt worse. Maybe you should take another look at it."

"No!" She gathered up her medicine makings and walked to the door of the adjoining room. "I mean...not right now. I'm sure it's fine. I'll... check it later. Just keep it dry."

Ring's ears pricked up as Cassie entered the adjoining room. His tail thumped the bed. She hurried to him and pressed his tail still. "No boy," she whispered, her nose close to his. "You'll wake Vicky." The dog immediately stopped moving, and Cassie marveled at how much he always seemed to understand.

She hurried through her morning toilette, focusing on the frigid water to keep her mind off of Cole and the keen impression of waking in his arms. But a glance in the mirror when she smoothed down the beige checked dress revealed it all. Her eyes gleamed. The high curves of her cheeks were tinged a deep rose. Her lips looked fuller and felt tingly.

Only hours after she vowed to keep him at a distance, she was in his arms again. What was she going to do? How would she ever manage to keep her feelings locked down day after day in the small confines of the cabin?

Vicky stirred and interrupted her thoughts. Ring jumped to the floor. He stretched his fore legs, shook himself all over, dropped to his haunches, and vigorously scratched an ear with a hind foot.

Cassie laughed at him and addressed the waking child. "Hello, little one. How'd you sleep?" She prayed her absence from the bed last night had escaped Vicky's notice.

"Ring slept with me," was the drowsy reply. "Where were you?"

Cassie laughed again, mostly at herself. Both father and child were able to echo her thoughts today. She held her arms out to Vicky. "I slept somewhere else. Come here and let's get you dressed."

She helped Vicky use the chamber pot, and picked out a chocolate-brown dress for her to wear. "Are you feeling okay?" she placed her hand across the little girl's brow. "You seem a little flushed."

Victoria pushed her hand away. "My Grandma used to do that."

"She did, huh?"

"Yes. I don't like it."

"Well, I'll try to remember that." Cassie slipped the dress over Victoria's head and discreetly checked her for fever again. She felt warm, but not really feverish.

"Did you have bad dreams last night?" she asked, turning Victoria around to look into her eyes.

"No."

"Are you still upset about all that fuss?"

"No."

Cassie buttoned the little girls dress, and brushed the tangles out of her long curls. She separated the dark tresses into two halves and tied each side close to her scalp with ribbons. Once again she turned Victoria to face her and was happy to see that the two tails gave Vicky's somber features a softer look. "Do you want to talk about last night?"

There was a slight hesitation. "Was he hurt bad?"

"Your daddy?"

Victoria nodded. "He was bleeding."

"You saw that, did you? Aye, he was cut pretty bad, but we doctored him all up. He'll be fine."

"He kept those men from hurting you."

"That he did. Your daddy is very brave."

"And strong."

"Aye. Strong too."

The discussion came to an end as Victoria's attention turned to Ring. She slipped to the floor and hugged the dog.

Cassie stepped to the adjoining door, half-afraid to knock. Images of her previous day's eavesdropping loomed dark and painful. But the door swung open immediately at her loud rap and she was face to face with Cole.

He was wearing a light-blue cotton shirt and a pair of black ribbed pants tucked into calf-high black boots. His two gun belts and pistols were in place, as was the large knife he wore just above his left boot. His hair curled haphazardly off his face and down the back of his neck, defying an obvious recent combing with water.

Cassie peered nervously around him. Cole arched a thick brow. "Looking for someone?"

"No." Her eyes dropped in chagrin. When she raised them again she took in his wry grin. "I'm ready to do whatever we're going to do today."

Cole cocked his head to one side and gazed down at his daughter. "You ready too?"

Victoria nodded.

"What would you ladies like to do first?"

"Eat," they said in unison.

Their return to Max's was not uneventful, but it was a much more pleasant experience. The men in the street gawked at Cassie with appreciation and called out or whistled, but kept their distance. The sky was cloudless and though the air was cold, the day promised to warm up.

Throughout a pleasant breakfast of flapjacks and eggs, they shared ideas for what they'd need at the cabin. The shopping expedition began as soon as they left the café. The sun appeared from behind the canyon's peaks around eleven, and brought wonderful warmth to the day. As the size of their purchases began to stack up, Cassie became worried about transporting them back over the pass. Cole told her he was hiring some help. He also took care of sending a wire to Denver for the items Georgetown couldn't provide.

At one point he surprised Cassie by pressing a wad of money into her hand, telling her it was from the sale of her trout. She thought it seemed a bit much for the amount of fish she'd caught, but she didn't question him. She just stuffed it into her leather bag, relishing how independent and self-sufficient it made her feel.

Late afternoon found Cassie and Victoria back in their hotel room, tired and ready to sit down. Cole had other things to attend to and made them promise not to leave the room until he returned. Which, he assured them, would be in time for supper.

Vicky sat on the floor under the window playing with a new wooden toy her father had purchased for her. It was a clown that danced up and down on a wooden platform when she tapped it on her knee. Ring lay beside her. Cassie opened some of the packages, inventoried their contents, separated hers from Josiah's, and then packed everything back up. All the while, she tried to keep her thoughts off of Cole. He hadn't told her where he was going or what he was doing, and she wondered if he had gone to see Ruby.

Jealousy was a new awareness for her. It felt dark and evil; a shadow-side of herself she didn't like. But its ugliness refused to be pushed away. Like a demented shrew, it taunted her with memories of Ruby's beauty, her allure, and her overpowering presence as she'd swept into Cole's arms. It echoed 'half-breed,' over and over until she wanted to scream.

She fell back on the bed and closed her eyes. Her mother and Running Deer would be appalled if they knew the shame the hated label evoked in her. They'd always been proud of their heritage. Proud to be Choctaw.

She had been raised to believe that each person was the same beneath their skin. And because they were the same, each life was as precious as the next. *A person must honor their own life and everyone else's too,* she could hear Running Deer say. Much easier said than done, Grandmother. She still doubted that she'd ever fit in anywhere, especially in Cole Adams' world.

CHAPTER TWENTY

"Is the coffee hot, McGraw?" Cole called out as he stepped up to the bar in the Ruby Slipper.

"It's hot. You know Ruby always keeps a big pot on the stove. Though why I don't know. Nobody but you and her drinks it." The bartender disappeared through a door and returned with a steaming mug.

"Damn." Scalding dark liquid sloshed onto the highly polished bar as Cole jerked the cup away from his mouth.

"Told you it's hot." Phil McGraw shook his baldhead and swiped up the spill with a stained rag. He was as protective of the Ruby Slipper as he was of its owner and wasn't happy when anyone made a mess on his prized oak counter top.

Cole remembered how excited Ruby had been when the 16-foot-long cabinet and matching back bar and mirror was installed. She hadn't expected anything so fine. He had ordered them for her from a manufacturer in Chicago and loaned her the money to pay for them. It had taken every dime she'd had just to have the building constructed and purchase the rest of the furnishings.

Six months after opening, she paid back every cent he'd loaned her, as well as the banknote for the corner lot she so prized.

Strains of music rose above the hum of conversation and laughter. Cole rested a boot on the foot rail and turned toward the piano and the group of people gathered around it. Frank Branson, Ruby's piano player and relief bartender, belted out a rendition of, "My own love Maggie dear, sitting by my side." Two barmaids and three miners joined in.

The song was one of Ruby's favorites. Cole didn't know why the ballad always brought tears to her eyes, because she was very close-mouthed when it came to her past. But he did know that her real name was Margaret, and he suspected that her intense feelings over the popular war song were tied to the reasons she left home and trekked west after the south fell in defeat to the north.

He was proud of her. She was a good friend. That's why he hated the rift between them. But her vicious remarks about Cassie still disturbed him. It wasn't like Ruby to be judgmental and cruel. For the first time since knowing her, he'd been sorry for confiding in her. He'd thought that Ruby's own dealings with prejudice would give her empathy for Cassie and her mixed blood. But it hadn't. And he wished he'd never said anything about it.

He finished off the coffee and McGraw refilled his cup. Idly he noticed how small the pot looked in the bartender's large hands, even bigger than his own. He was tall and brawny and the one man in town Cole would shy away from in a fistfight. In spite of the fact there was an occasional glimmer of gentleness in the man's brown eyes, his face bore evidence of his years in the boxing ring. His thick moustache and full beard still couldn't hide some of the scarring.

Cole had always felt confident in Ruby's safety knowing McGraw was so devoted to her. She'd encountered him on the streets in Denver, past his prime, washed up and alone. When she learned about his past, she hired him immediately. In return, he'd attached himself to her like a shadow. A man would have to be either very drunk or very crazy to ever think about hurting Ruby while her loyal bodyguard was around. And if his brawn alone didn't stop you, the shotgun he kept under the bar most definitely would.

The bartender busied himself at the other end of the bar, and Cole turned his thoughts to the mental list of things he'd been working on. He'd talked to the sheriff. Both the men he'd tangled with last night had been patched up by the doc and were cooling their heels in jail. He'd made arrangements for pack-mules to carry their supplies back to the lake. He'd jotted down several more items he needed from Denver. All he had left to do was send off another wire. They should be able to leave first thing in the morning.

A niggle of enthusiasm moved through him at the thought of returning to the lake. Who would've believed that Cole Adams could be standing in a saloon and gaming house without even a thought for faro or poker or anything else? Even more humorous was the fact that he was actually looking forward to isolating himself in a cabin with a child who could barely tolerate him and a woman whose very presence could almost drive him mad.

"What's the goofy grin for?"

Cole spun around. "Brewster...!" He clamped a hand on Brew's shoulder. "It's good to see you. What are you doing here?"

"Came looking for you."

"Well you found me. What are you drinking?"

"Bourbon."

"Hey, McGraw, pour a bourbon. This old character looks like he needs a pick-me-up. Actually, you look like you had to shoot your horse or something. What's wrong?"

"You seen Cassie?"

Cole's mood shifted instantly at the ominous tone in his friend's voice. "I've seen her."

Brew picked up the shot glass the bartender set before him and threw its contents down in one swallow. He choked, cleared his throat and asked, "Is she alright?"

"She's fine," Cole said, growing impatient. "Why? What's going on?"

"I'll have another," Brew called to McGraw, then turned back to Cole. "Is she still at Austin's?"

"No. Get to the point, man."

"That guy who's tracking her is still around. He may be closing in." Brew downed another drink. "I had breakfast at Bessie's yesterday. Apparently the guy showed up at her place, asking a bunch of questions. She told him she'd seen Cassie with me."

Cole's fist came down on the bar. "Why in the hell did she do that?" Several men quieted and turned their way. They resumed their own business when they realized there was nothing exciting to gawk at.

John Brewster shrugged. "She didn't know any better. Nobody ever explained anything about Cassie to her."

With effort, Cole lowered his voice. "How do you know it was him?"

"She said that a large man with a badly scarred face came in with a story about his daughter running away with two men. He told Bessie that the girl's mama was sick and needed her at home. Bessie remembered how upset Cassie looked that day. When she took her hat off to eat lunch, Bessie got a good look at her and her hair. Cassie fit the man's description perfectly. Bessie felt sorry for him and told him everything she could remember, including how to find me.

"Have you seen him?"

"No. I hightailed it out of Denver as soon as she told me. Apparently he and I just missed each other. She said he left just before I came in. That's the reason I know about it at all. Otherwise she probably would've never thought to mention it. At least not in time for me to do anything about it."

"Good. If he can't find you, he won't know how to find Cassie."

"Cole, Bessie told him about all of us. He may try to find me first, since she told him where I live. After that, he may try to find you. He knows all our names now. It won't take him long to start checking out all your hangouts. At some point, he'll head up here. Eventually he's bound to show up at Austin's."

Cole ran a hand over his face. He had to get Cassie back up to the lake.

Brew's voice softened in concern. "Where is she, Cole?"

"Here, in Georgetown with me."

"You got your little girl with you?"

"Yeah. Damn! What a mess. I don't want that murdering bastard anywhere near either of them."

"How's it going with your daughter? You two getting to know each other?"

"It's going slow. Sometimes I think she's warming up to me. Mostly she's still scared. But you should see her with Cassie. She latched onto her like a drowning man grabbing for a life raft." He gave his older friend a twisted grin. "I have to admit the whole thing scares me. I honestly don't know what I'd do without Cassie. She's more or less taken over Victoria's care. You know, doing all those little things I wouldn't know how to do."

The softening in Cole's features when he talked about Cassie and his daughter gave Brew a clear picture of his feelings. "Are you staying in Georgetown?"

"No. In fact, we're leaving in the morning. Cassie's been staying in a cabin up at spirit Lake. We rode in here yesterday for supplies."

"You're staying up there with her?"

"Yeah, I plan to."

Brew gave him an I-told-you-so smirk, but said, "Well, I'll sleep a little better knowing you're with her. Are you going to tell her about Noley?"

"Yeah, but I hate to. You wouldn't know her, Brew. She's changed. That always-watchful demeanor is gone. And she's beginning to recover from the worst part of her grief." His voice hardened. "Damn that bastard to hell. I hope we do run into each other. I look forward to damaging much more than his face."

Late that night Cole was even more agitated. He paced back and forth in his room, frustrated that he hadn't had a chance to get Cassie alone all day. After his discussion with Brew, he'd run into Ruby who apologized profusely for her attitude and hurtful remarks about Cassie the night before. She'd been so contrite, he invited her to join them for dinner. And from the moment they'd all sat down, Cole knew it was a mistake.

259

Throughout the entire meal, she'd made it difficult for him to give his daughter the attention he wanted to, and impossible to say a word to Cassie. Every time he tried, Ruby touched his sleeve or asked a question that demanded an answer. Any other time, he'd have found her possessiveness laughable, but not tonight. Tonight it irritated the hell out of him. Even Brew couldn't hold Ruby's attention. And Cassie seemed ill at ease. Cole was relieved when the meal finally ended.

They had gone as a group back to the hotel, where Brew retired to his room, and Cole made sure Cassie and Victoria were safely locked in theirs, before he escorted Ruby back to the Ruby Slipper.

He'd returned later than he intended and found that Cassie had already retired. Now his agitation made it impossible to go to bed. He paced and smoked; annoyed that Cassie hadn't waited up for him. Besides wanting to tell her about Noley, he'd looked forward to spending a few minutes alone with her. If for no other reason than to assure she was all right.

Her need for independence made it difficult to get close to her. She resisted every bit of help and protection he offered. Victoria's presence added its own complication. He had to take care of her as well and hope that somewhere along the way, he could establish some kind of relationship with her. And in between, turn that god-forsaken cabin into some kind of decent living quarters. What a challenge. The days ahead should prove interesting.

At that point, Cole heard a soft rap on the adjoining door and moved quickly to open it. Cassie stood on the other side, illumined by the moonlight spilling in from the window behind her. A prim white gown and robe covered her from neck to fingertips and toes. Her hair cascaded down over one shoulder to her waist where she clutched her leather bag. "I heard you pacing around in here and thought maybe your injury was bothering you."

"Come in," he answered, matching her whisper. He knew the cut was healing fine, but wouldn't have stopped her from looking at it for anything. He closed the door behind her and lit the lamp. "I'm sorry I didn't get back in time to help tuck Victoria in. Did you have any problems?"

Cassie smiled ruefully. "We did have one small battle."

"A battle?" He leaned against the door and watched her.

"Aye. Since we allowed Ring to sleep with her last night, she couldn't understand why I said no tonight."

"That's right..." He couldn't hide his amusement. "Ring had your spot, didn't he?"

She turned a darker shade of red and pointed to the bed. "Lie down."

His grin widened. "That sounds good."

"So I can check your wound."

"Ah yes, my wound."

He stripped off his jacket and shirt and eased himself down on the bed. The slash across his belly rebelled against the backward motion, but once down, he relaxed and linked his fingers behind his head. He gazed up at her as she leaned over him. But decided he'd better look elsewhere before another part of his anatomy announced her affect on him.

He studied the wormholes in the wood ceiling as he felt the bandage being moved and the soft probing of Cassie's fingers. Her hands were cold.

"Does that hurt?" She asked.

"No."

"How about here?"

"It's tender, but not the kind of pain you're looking for."

"There's no redness. It seems to be healing fine."

Cole kept his focus on the ceiling the entire time she re-bandaged the wound, but when her fingers paused, he glanced down. His breath caught in his throat as he watched her lightly, almost imperceptibly, caress the springy curls on his chest. He exhaled with pleasure when her silver gaze roamed slowly down his torso. When her attention moved higher again, she saw that he was no longer looking at the ceiling. Her hand halted and her cheeks filled with color but she didn't look away.

The moment lengthened to two and then three, before Cole felt compelled to move. He reached out and wound a strand of her hair around his hand. He held it up and watched the lamplight bring out the wine-color. He brought it to his face. Ah how he loved the smell of her.

A myriad of thoughts flashed through Cassie's eyes. But none of them said no, so he tightened his hold on her hair and drew her down until her lips touched his. His other hand captured the back of her head. But it wasn't necessary. She completely rocked him when she was the first to deepen the kiss.

Softly, sensually, she brushed her mouth back and forth against his, seeming to revel in the pleasure, not asking for anything in return. The tip of her tongue delicately flicked back and forth between his lips, torching the blaze that had been smoldering in his groin. But he held it in check, waiting for her next move, loving her assertiveness and not wanting to risk its cessation.

The effort was worth it. Her tongue became bolder, her lips more forceful. Soon it took every ounce of strength he had to placidly let her take the lead with their passion. His body screamed at him to bury himself inside her. But he resisted, wanting to see how far she'd go.

Her fingers glided over his face, his eyes, the corners of his mouth, where her own mouth continued the kiss. When her fingers moved down his throat to slide through the hair on his upper chest, fiery sensations shot through every part of his body. His swollen organ raged and pulsed for release.

Through her gown, he could feel her heat, and it increased his own. He had wanted her for so long, but the wanting had never been like this nearly out-of-control pain.

He groaned as she released his mouth and left a wet trail to his ear. One glorious sensation after another lifted his hips from the bed as she nipped and licked his earlobe then used the tip of her tongue to outline the inner crevices of his ear. His hands curled into tight fists to keep from grabbing her, tearing her gown off, and plunging between her legs.

Her bold exploration dropped to his neck, where she kissed and licked and sucked with abandon. Then her ardor moved to his shoulder and across the top of his chest. She kneaded his taut muscles with her fingers and kissed each spot she touched. But she couldn't seem to venture any further. Cole sensed her hesitation. In spite of her desire, her inexperience would only let her go so far. It was the signal he'd been waiting for.

Ignoring the pain in his midriff, he shifted her onto her back beside him and took his time savoring every inch of her. The luxurious mass of red-tinged sable hair fanned out across the pillow and over his arm like a silken sheet. Her eyes turned a smokey grey as they met his gaze. Her expressive mouth was swollen from its assault on him. Her nipples were stiff with desire, jutting up against the soft flannel gown with each erratic breath she took.

Once more her nerve fled and she closed her eyes. Cole bent his head and kissed each eyelid. "Open your eyes and look at me, Cassie."

The thick lashes lifted to show her uncertainty.

"Do you have any idea how beautiful your eyes are? They change color, did you know that?"

Her face flushed. She tried to turn away. "Cole…"

He placed a finger against her lips and began to outline each sensuous detail. "Your eyes are silver when you're happy or excited." His eyes dipped to follow his finger's slow exploration, then returned to hers. "When you feel scared or angry, they fill with dark clouds."

He altered the direction of his finger to a back and forth motion between her lips. "Right now the silver in your eyes is ablaze with passion and rimmed with the darkest charcoal."

He used two fingers now, while Cassie stared hypnotically up at him. His fingers opened her lips wider, then slipped into her mouth to touch her teeth, her tongue. He let his mouth take their place. His tongue dipped inside, and Cassie moaned. She locked her hands in his hair and pulled his mouth harder against hers, meeting each dart of his tongue with her own.

Her uninhibited response nearly set off the inferno that raged inside him. He counted to fifty in an attempt to gain some control. But Cassie wouldn't let him relent. Her mouth moved over his with complete abandon.

Without another thought, he grasped the hem of the gown, tugged it over her head and tossed it aside. Her body arched, as he fell on her breast and encircled the rigid nipple with his tongue. Alternately he ravished each breast, gently biting and then sucking each nipple into his mouth, until Cassie was in a near frenzy. Her heat sparked more of his own. Like molten steel it scorched a trail that gathered and expanded in his swollen member until he thought he'd burst.

But he wasn't ready to end this glorious torture. He cupped her breasts, rubbing their hard buds between his thumbs and forefingers while he buried his face in her soft stomach and sucked at her navel. When Cassie moaned, his descent continued. He traced the outline of her body, with his hands, skimming down her rib cage, her waist, around the contour of her hips to her thighs. He gently pried them apart and slid one hand up to the velvet softness at their apex.

Cassie gasped and grabbed his hand.

"It's all right," he said, his voice raspy from tightly controlled passion.

She sunk back onto the pillow, eyes wide. He watched her while he sought her opening, needing her trust. Once inside, he probed gently, moving his finger in and out until he felt her soften. Then his fingers shifted, found the tiny nub of her passion and brushed back and forth against it in a subtle rhythm. Her eyes closed and she sighed in pleasure. He moved between her legs to kiss the sensitive spot.

"Cole..." Her head jerked up, and she pushed at him.

"Cassie, it's okay. It's beautiful. Let me show you. Let me teach you."

She wasn't sure and tried to shift away. "I'll stop if you don't like it, I promise."

Once more she let him have his way. He focused anew on the source of her heat, using his mouth, his teeth, his tongue as her head thrashed back and forth on the pillow. Her pleasure sent white-hot waves of heat through his loins, and he thought he couldn't last another second.

She began to shudder and then arched in exquisite surrender, giving him what he wanted. He couldn't wait any longer, and quickly began to unbutton his pants. She whimpered. "Cole, don't stop. Please..."

He smiled at the change in her objections. "We're not stopping, Cassie. I promise." He rolled off the bed, stifling a groan as his wound made itself known. He yanked off his boots and socks and stripped out of his pants and long johns. Her eyes followed his every movement, begging him to hurry.

His muscles quivered as he poised over her. Pain seared through his abdomen, but he willed it away. His need for release would wait no longer. He parted her legs and settled between them. Her body opened for him, as if admitting that this was what she was meant for, who she was meant for. Her hands moved to his hips, and she guided him in.

He reveled in that first sensation of his flesh inside her hot core. He slid further in, pulsating with need. They both felt the resistance, and Cole pulled back. "God, I don't want to hurt you."

"I'm not afraid of the pain." She shifted her legs higher and urged him further in. He withdrew slightly, then pushed deeper. Again the resistance. He held himself back, rocking slowly in and out, creating a delicious demand in them both. Until Cassie dug her nails into his buttocks and lifted to meet his thrust, and Cole plunged through the membrane for complete penetration.

Cassie gasped, and he held himself rigid while she adjusted to his size. A minute later, she arched higher, letting his fullness completely fill her.

At first he moved slowly, measuring each thrust with caution. But each time he sheathed himself completely, her muscles clutched him so sweetly he lost a little more control. She had haunted his days and nights for so long he thought he'd go mad with want. Now his body desperately sought completion. Cassie seemed to need the same thing. She raked her nails down his back and curved into him. His control snapped, and he rammed into her with the entire force of his need. Over and over he pounded into her, feeling the wall of her womb with each lunge. Thankfully, mindlessly, he gave into the frantic need to conquer her spell, and free himself from the torture of wanting her so much.

Cassie matched his intensity. Her legs tightened around him as the pressure built inside. Their combined heat became a towering wave that launched them ever higher, and they found soul-wrenching deliverance together.

Cassie drifted back into consciousness a little at a time. As she did, the glorious sensations Cole had given her dissipated one after the other. A voice from deep inside her mind wanted to know what she planned to do now that she had bound this man to her heart and soul without any hope that he loved her.

It doesn't matter, she argued back. His desire is enough. Is it? The voice asked. No, she thought, it isn't. She pushed at Cole's shoulders and turned her head away from him. When he moved off of her, she pulled out of his arms and stood up.

"Wait a minute. Where you going?" He reached out, grabbed her hand and pulled her back to the bed. His breathing was still not completely normal. "Don't go away, come back by me."

Cassie could feel the tension that ran through his body and suspected it wasn't all from passion. In spite of the heated look in his eyes, his brow creased as if he were also in pain. Glancing down, she saw that the bandage around his middle was saturated with fresh blood. A thin, red line of it trailed onto the white sheets.

All other thoughts vanished. She pulled her hand free and searched for something to press against the growing spot of blood.

Cole grabbed her hand again. "Take it easy, Cassie. It's not that big a deal."

"How can you say that?" She jerked away from him. "What were you thinking? What was I thinking? We shouldn't have been…"

Cole grinned at her befuddled state. He swung his legs over the bed and started to sit up. "Been what?"

"Been wrestling around on the bed. Now lay back down. You've probably ripped the stitches."

He slid his hands around her back and pulled her against him. "Mmmm…. you feel good. Come back to bed. I want more."

She backed away from him and held her hand out to stop him from following. "Cole Adams, look at you. You are bleedin' all over yourself, me, and the whole darn bed."

She put a stern look on her face and forced her eyes away from his mocking grin. "This isn't funny. I… should never have let you make love to me like that."

"You made love to me too."

Her entire body flushed with embarrassment as well as building desire. "Aye. I did. But never mind. Lie down and let me look at you."

He didn't lie down, but scooted back against the metal bed frame instead.

She untied the bandage and lifted it off. Just as she suspected, several stitches had ripped open. "Oh, Cole." She envisioned a repeat of the painful stitching.

He brushed her concerns aside. "Don't worry about it, Cassie. Just bandage me tighter. It'll heal okay. Just leave a bigger scar, is all."

"I don't know."

"I do. Clean it up and put some more of your magic herbs on it. It's not infected. It'll be fine."

Thinking he was probably right, and to save further argument, she did as he suggested. Once again, her touch and the herbs had a relaxing effect. Cole eased himself to a flat position on the bed. Before long, his eyes closed.

Cassie finished wrapping the bandage and stood. Her eyes gazed lovingly at the way his face softened when he slept. She bent and kissed his parted lips. In his sleep, he reached for her, but she slipped away and proceeded to straighten up the mess.

Cole's jacket was on the floor. The minute she picked it up, she was assaulted by the overpowering smell of Ruby's perfume. Further evidence that Cole didn't belong to her, not in the way she wanted. She clutched the jacket against her breast and remembered the miserable supper she'd suffered through earlier in the evening. Ruby had looked more beautiful than ever. Cassie didn't know if it was her stunning blue gown, the creamy color of her skin, her bright red hair, or maybe just the way she carried herself. In comparison, Cassie felt like a little brown mouse.

Throughout the uncomfortable meal, she had done her level best not to think about the woman across the table. Her opinion of Cassie was more than obvious. Every time Ruby's hazel eyes had skimmed over her, she'd felt branded. Even now, she thought, as she hung the jacket on the back of the chair, she could still feel the intensity of the other woman's scorn.

A nagging voice tried to make her feel guilty for giving herself completely to a man who didn't love her. But she refused to listen. Making love with Cole with something she'd never regret. Whether he knew it or not, she'd just given him her heart. The fact he only wanted her body was his problem. She would cherish this memory for the rest of her life.

By the time the room was in order, Cassie had ordered her thoughts. She knew what she had to do. Taking one last look at the man she loved, she turned down the light and walked out of the room.

CHAPTER TWENTY ONE

"What the hell?" Brew muttered as he roused himself from sleep.

The pounding on his hotel room door grew louder. He jerked up, threw his feet over the bed, and limped to the door. As he turned the key, the door burst open, nearly knocking him over.

"You sleep like the damned dead," Cole growled as he stormed into the room.

Brew made his way back to the bed, yawning and scratching his chest through his bright-red long-handles. "Hey, settle down and tell me what's going on."

Cole's long strides brought him to a halt in front of the bed. "She's gone! That's what's going on!"

Brew yawned again. He rubbed his bony knuckles over the white bristles on his jaw. "Who's gone?"

"Cassie...! Dammit, Brew, wake up and listen to me! She's gone. That damn woman. I can't believe she's pulled that stunt again."

The frantic tone in Cole's voice finally penetrated Brew's sleep-fogged mind and he sat up straighter. "Cassie's gone? Gone where?"

"Back to the lake."

"Alone?"

"Yes, alone, and with that lunatic stalking her."

Brew struggled to understand. "Why? What happened?"

"Nothing happened... I don't know what happened. I just woke up and found her gone." He shoved a piece of paper at Brew. "She left this."

Brew didn't believe for one minute that nothing happened, or that Cole was unaware of whatever did happen. He pushed the paper away. "What's it say? You know I can't read."

"It says goodbye, give Vicky my love. She doesn't want me to follow her. She appreciates all my intentions to help, but she can make it on her own. The money she received from the sale of the fish got her most of the things she needed. She'll do without the rest."

Cole wadded up the note and threw it on the floor with a disgusting grunt. "The money she got from the fish," he grumbled. "Can you believe that? She thinks all that money I gave her came from those few measly trout she caught. She doesn't have a clue what she's doing or what the real world is all about."

He paced some more, stopping by the narrow dresser across from the bed. He slammed his fist down on the top. "She says I should return everything I purchased and get my money back."

"Did you tell her about Noley?"

"No, I didn't have a chance."

"You're going after her."

Cole dropped onto the chair next to the bed and ran a hand over his face. "I can't. That's why I came for you. Victoria is sick."

Brew got to his feet. He shuffled around and found his pants and put them on. Cole's naked feelings made him uncomfortable, like he was seeing private things he shouldn't be seeing. "What's wrong with the little tyke?"

"I don't know." Cole leaned against the back of the chair and glanced up. "Her skin is hot and dry. She's barely responding when I talk to her. She must have a fever." He stood and walked to the door. "I've got to get back to her."

"You want me to go after Cassie?"

"No…Yeah. Hell, I don't know what to do. I can't let you get involved in this. You'd be no match for the kind of maniac that's following her. I just need you to get the doctor."

Brew wasn't offended by the remark. He knew his own abilities. Even in his prime, he was never a fighter. "I'll get the doctor, then I'll ride up to Austin's and fill him in. Maybe if we tell Cassie what's going on, she'll stay at the ranch with Austin and Ginny."

"Yeah, maybe." Cole sounded like he didn't believe that at all.

And Brew realized he was right. Cassie would avoid anything that endangered Ginny. What a mess. He needed to get up there.

Cole watched Brew cross the room to grab his shirt. "What's wrong with you?"

"Nothing."

"What do you mean nothing? You're limping."

Brew jerked his shirt on, pissed at his age and his body's aches and pains. "It's just my rheumatism acting up. My old bones ain't what they used to be."

"You can't ride in that condition."

Brew hobbled across the room and stuck his face up close to Cole's. "The hell I can't. I haven't seen the day yet that I can't set a horse, and I'm not about to see it today." He backed off and began buttoning his shirt. "I can make it to Austin's just fine. Now git on out of here so I can finish dressing."

When Brew entered Victoria's room, Cole nodded at him but continued wiping cold water over his daughter's flushed face. Victoria opened her eyes when Brew approached the bed. He smiled down at her and winked. "Hi there, little miss. You feeling poorly?"

She nodded her head then turned toward Cole. "Why did Cassie leave me?"

"I'll find the doctor," Brew said, and the two men shared a worried glance. "Then I'll head on up to Austin's."

"Thanks," Cole said, nodding to his friend as he shut the door behind him.

"Victoria, Cassie didn't leave you." Cole's explanation about Cassie's sudden departure had been going badly. How did you tell a five-year-old that the one person in the world she felt secure with snuck off in the middle of the night without a word of goodbye? He took her little hand in his. "She... was just in a hurry to get back to the lake and knew you wouldn't feel up to riding today."

"But I do, I want to go now."

"We can't just yet. We have to see what's wrong with you first. Storm won't want you to ride on him if you don't feel good." Cole's heart constricted when she pulled her hand away. He could see the doubt in her eyes, the mistrust. How would he ever win her confidence if these kinds of things kept happening? He touched her hand again. "Victoria, I promise if you hurry and get well, we'll head straight up to the lake. All right?" He searched her eyes as she searched his face. "All right?" he urged once more.

Her dark blue scrutiny softened a little. "All right."

It was enough to ease Cole's distress a little.

Come hell or high water, he'd keep his promise. And it wouldn't be just for his daughter. He'd never felt as crazy as when he woke to find Cassie gone. It made him feel disjointed split into a dozen painful pieces. And the only way he'd feel whole again was with Cassie beside him for the rest of his life. Acknowledging that truth rocked him to his toes. Because he feared she was feeling the exact opposite. Why else would she have run away?

Fear burned in his gut like a shot of bad whiskey. She was alone, and her mother's killer could be anywhere. What if she encountered Noley on the trail? Cole's hands shook as he wrung the water out of the cloth and smoothed it over Victoria's arms. All he could do was hope Cassie made it to the cabin and stayed there. Surely, Noley would have no way of knowing she was there, and Austin would stop him if he came by the ranch.

He turned his mind back to his daughter. Her eyes were closed. The shape of her lips formed a perfect heart. Her mother's mouth. A bittersweet ache wrenched through him. Look what our love created, Ramona. Our daughter is beautiful. Loving you wasn't wrong, it was very right.

And loving Cassie isn't wrong either, he decided. It's probably one of the most genuinely right things he'd ever done.

All he had to do now was get up to that damned lake and convince her of that fact.

"God, keep her safe," he found himself praying. "And keep this child safe. I don't want to live if anything happens to either of them." The impulsive words brought with them a memory from long ago. When his baby sister died in his arms, he'd turned his back on God, as surely as God had turned from him.

At this moment, he felt just that young, just that vulnerable, just that powerless. Every muscle in his body screamed to go into action, exert some control over this damnable situation. But there was no way he could leave his daughter. She was sick, and he didn't know what was wrong. Didn't know how to help her.

What could he do?

Trust. The word jumped out at him. He was asking his child to blindly put her faith in him. How could he do any less? He dropped the cloth, folded his hands and continued to pray, hoping beyond hope that God was listening this time.

Cassie opened the last bag and began removing its contents. She had already put the food away. It gave her a good feeling to see it stacked on the few crude shelves she'd managed to put together.

The .32 caliber, rimfire revolver Austin had given her was the next thing she unwrapped. She held it in her hands and remembered how grim Austin had looked when he handed it to her. She had resisted taking it, saying she had the rifle that Zeb left her and plenty of ammunition. But he wouldn't take no for an answer, insisting there might be a time she would need them both.

Austin had been furious with her when she showed up at the ranch without Cole. Ginny had intervened and calmed him down when he started ranting and raving about Cassie traipsing through the mountains alone. She apologized for any upset she had caused her new friends, but nothing or no one could divert her from her goal. She wanted a home of her own and was determined to do anything necessary to bring that about.

The next thing she unpacked was a hand mirror with a delicate brass handle. Ginny had given it to her, as well as the pretty, mint green gingham curtains it was wrapped in. They had been alone in the yellow bedroom when Ginny presented her with the gifts. And then she'd quickly confronted Cassie about her feelings for Cole. "There's no point denying it. I can see that you love him. Your feelings shine like a beacon out of those sad eyes," Ginny had said, and then gently scolded Cassie for running away.

But after Cassie explained about meeting Ruby, and admitted to over-hearing her hurtful words, Ginny had understood. That's when she handed Cassie the mirror, making her look into it and telling her she was just as pretty as a dozen Ruby's. Cassie had pushed the mirror away, arguing that no matter what the mirror reflected, she wasn't fully white. Then she'd foolishly stated that Ginny couldn't know what it was like to feel such ridicule. The frank look of disbelief that transformed her friend's face had shamed her. Of course Ginny knew. No one could know better what it felt like to be shunned.

The two women had sat wordless for a moment, then they'd fallen into each other's arms, each of them knowing exactly how the other felt, and grateful to have such a cherished friend to share their feelings with.

The memory made Cassie smile as she spread one of Ginny's embroidered towels over the top of a crate, transforming it into a bedside table. She arranged it so that the embroidered grapes and leaves were displayed at the front and laid the mirror on top of it. She shook her head as she compared the makeshift table with the rest of the room; grateful that Ginny couldn't see the primitive state she was living in.

After the contents of the last bag were put away, the room looked less empty. When she'd first walked in, Cole and Vicky's absence was all she could see. Now the sharp pain she'd been coping with for two days had ebbed to a dull ache. She would survive their loss, just as she had her parents, Running Deer, Zeb and Dalton. Better now than later, she thought. Cole had never given her any hope that she meant anything more to him than someone to warm his bed or help with his daughter. The longer she lived with the two of them, the harder it would be to let them go.

A stab of guilt hit her when she imagined Vicky waking up to find her gone. Stop it, she assured herself. That little one needs time with her father. He's the one she needs to lean on, not me.

By the next afternoon, her feelings reversed again. She missed Cole and Vicky so much she doubted the pain would ever go away. Deciding that hard work was the only solution, she took on the duty of chopping more wood. The axe that Josiah had loaned her was sharp and heavy, requiring her every bit of effort and concentration to wield it. But with each swing, she grunted out some of her misery.

Whack! That was for the agony she'd felt when she found one of Cole's socks under the cot that morning.

Whack! That was for the discovery of Vicky's blue hair ribbon peeking out from under the pillow on the lower bunk.

Whack! That was for the cheroot that must have fallen out of Cole's pocket when he walked out to the woodpile before they left. She wanted to wail in misery. Instead, she chopped. For hours, she slammed the axe blade into the pine until her hands could no longer hold the handle and her arms refused to raise the weight over her head. Then she spent another hour adding the pieces to the growing mountain of firewood. By moonlight, she cleaned up the area around the cabin and added a mound of small branches and twigs to the kindling next to the fireplace. At midnight she collapsed on the bed and fell asleep the moment her head hit the pillow.

Cole studied the cards in his hands; a three, a pair of sixes, and a pair of jacks. "I call your bet." He threw down his coin and looked across the table. "Well, what have you got?" he prompted.

"Three queens." His opponent fanned the cards on the table.

"Three queens?" Cole roared in outrage. "How'd you manage to get three queens?"

His opponent stared him down. There was not so much as a twitch in the stoic face. "You dealt."

"Yes, I did," he said in resignation. His large hands began gathering up the cards while the tiny pair across from him raked in the winnings. "I should never have taught you how to play. You're too good."

A small, delicately winged brow arched at him. "I know. Give me the cards. It's my deal."

Cole couldn't resist smiling. His daughter was a delight. The more time they spent together, the more convinced he became that no brighter or prettier child ever lived. She became stronger with each passing day, and her eyes were losing their despondency. In spite of that, and the fact that Doc Sievers assured him there was nothing seriously wrong with her, that she was just run down and needed some rest, Cole couldn't stop worrying. Old fears were hard to shed. They continued to haunt him every time he looked at the delicate face that reminded him so much of his baby sister's.

The doctor had been there that morning, just as he had the past three mornings, and twice each afternoon. This time, after he finished examining Victoria, he pulled Cole into the hall, stuck his chubby finger into Cole's chest and notified him that, "Your child is recuperating just fine. I have other patients in this town, and more important things to do than run up these dang hotel stairs every time she so much as sneezes." Cole had felt properly chastised and promised not to bother the doctor again.

Victoria finished dealing the cards and Cole quickly arranged his in his hands. Victoria left hers on the table. She stared at them as if she could see through them. Cole cocked his head to one side and asked, "What's up, peanut? Don't you want to play anymore?"

She lifted her eyes to meet his. "When can we go see Cassie?"

It was the same question Cole had asked Sievers just two hours ago. "Well, Doc says we can leave whenever you feel up to it."

"I feel up to it now." Her eyes became hopeful.

"Are you sure you feel strong enough?"

"I'm sure." She climbed down off the chair and came to stand beside him. "Please, can we go back to the lake now?"

He placed the cards on the table. He yearned to reach out and lift her onto his lap. But he didn't dare. Not yet. They had made great strides the last few days, but she still resisted any affection he tried to give her. "We'll go first thing in the morning."

It was a contest of who was more thrilled at the decision. Victoria's eyes sparkled with enthusiasm, and she came closer to smiling at him than she ever had. Cole felt like a huge weight had been rolled off of him. He sucked in a deep breath and released it. Finally, they could be on their way.

"I'll make a bargain with you," he said. "You climb back into bed and take a good nap, and I'll ask Miss Johnson to sit with you while I get things ready to go. When I get back, we'll have supper. Deal?" He offered his hand.

"Deal." She placed her small hand in his, and they sealed their agreement with a shake.

First he met with the man he'd hired to haul all his new purchases over the pass. The easy-going muleskinner had come highly recommended. He didn't have a last name, and was one of those people who defied description by age. Burl could be fifteen or fifty. There was just no telling. His slight stature was also deceiving. He hefted heavy bundles onto the mules' backs as easily as if they contained feathers. Burl assured him everything would be loaded and ready to go by dawn.

Cole's next stop was the Ruby Slipper. Because of his close association with Ruby, he wanted to warn McGraw that Noley might come there looking for him. When he was certain the bartender understood the seriousness of the situation, he went looking for Ruby.

He found her in her office. A bright smile lit her face when he stepped through the doorway. "I've missed you," she said in her sultry voice.

He didn't back away when she approached, neither did he touch her. "I came to say goodbye."

Her smile vanished. "You're leaving today?"

"In the morning."

"But...I thought your little girl was doing poorly."

"She was. She's better now. She wants... we want to get back to the lake."

"Am I supposed to read some sort of meaning into that?"

"Yeah, I guess you are," Cole drawled.

"I heard that Cassie left." She took a deep breath and released it with a sigh. "I hope you know what you're doing."

"I do." He finally touched her hand. "Ruby, this doesn't have to change anything between us. We can still be friends."

"No we can't." Her voice shook with emotion. She turned her back and leaned a hip against her desk. "Not like we have been. Who knows when I'll see you again? How will I get along without you?"

He smiled at her feigned frailty. "You don't need me. You're just used to having me around. I'm not going back to England, you know. I'll be back now and then." He turned her to face him. "Now will you stop whining and listen?"

Ruby stiffened her spine and stepped away from him. "What?"

"The man who killed Cassie's mother has trailed her to me. He may come here looking for us."

She shot him a wounded look. "You can't believe I would tell him anything."

"That's not what I'm worried about. This guy is crazy with revenge. He could do anything. I've warned McGraw to keep an eye out. Now I'm telling you. No matter what, I don't want you alone with him."

His concern touched her. "I'll be careful, Cole." She paused and looked deep in his eyes. "You've got it bad for her, don't you?"

He smiled and nodded slowly. "Yeah. Real bad."

She reached up, pulled his head down, and kissed him soundly on the mouth. "Then get going. Don't worry about me. I'll ask McGraw to hire a couple of extra men for awhile."

The following morning dawned crystal clear and cold. The ground was frozen, causing Storm's steps to echo through the canyon, along with those of the slow moving pack mules that followed behind.

Cole breathed deeply, relieved to finally be on his way. Victoria sat bundled in front of him, snuggled in warm layers of a fur-lined coat and hat and wool blanket. Only her nose and eyes could be seen as she peered down to make sure Ring was close by and leaned forward to pat Storm's neck. Things are looking up, Cole thought. She likes Cassie and the animals, and tolerates me. A little more time and maybe she'll afford me that same affection.

As usual, once Cassie invaded his thoughts, he couldn't get her out. How could such a slip of a woman maneuver him into giving up the comforts of an easier life? How could she continue to control his every waking thought and his dreams? He actually looked forward to the difficult existence offered by that wilderness.

She had become his dream. He didn't know how this venture would work out. But he could no longer imagine a life without her. The worst part of it, the part that kept his guts churning, was that he didn't know for sure how she felt. How could she respond to him the way she did and then just walk away?

He could hardly wait to have her in his arms. First he'd shake some sense into her for scaring him half to death. Then he'd make her promise to never leave him again.

CHAPTER TWENTY TWO

Barnaby Noley slowed his mount to watch the horsemen and string of mules creep slowly up the mountain to his right. He'd seen other such processions since arriving in the west. Prospectors determined to strike it rich and other such fortune hunters. Hell, maybe he'd have a go at it, after he finished his business.

He was getting close. He could feel it. After weeks and weeks of anticipation, he was finally going to claim his prize. He wanted to shout it from the mountaintops, but that would come later.

He glanced back over his shoulder, wondering when his two companions would catch up. The pair he'd met in Golden City asked if they could join him, claiming they had their own axe to grind with Cole Adams. He didn't care one way or the other. He wasn't interested in them or the man named Adams. The woman was all he cared about, and he'd told them so, making it clear they were to leave their hands off of her.

His mouth salivated at the thought of what he planned to do to her. He'd start where he left off the first time. He'd hurt her so bad, she'd beg him to have his way with her. He vibrated with need to sexually own that tight little body. Afterward he'd cut her up good. And he'd use her own goddamn knife to do it. The same knife that had left him looking like a freak.

He'd save that fine-looking face till last. When he was through, it would match his. And he'd make sure she was alive to see it. Then she'd die.

With that satisfying thought he urged his horse on up the street until he saw the sign for the town doctor. It seemed nearly every man in town knew about Adams and his little girl being sick. And they'd had no problem singing their praises of the woman Adams had with him. There was no doubt she was the half-breed.

He'd hoped to make quick work of questioning the doctor, but when he went inside, he found the man bent over a patient.

"Open a little wider... Say ahhh..."

"Ahhh," the male patient croaked and broke into a spasm of coughing. "Dang it, Doc. You nearly drove that stick down my throat."

"Quit being a baby," scolded the robust woman standing next to him. Her height and girth dwarfed both the doctor and her scrawny husband, and she had no reservations about using her formidable size to try and dominate the situation.

The doctor looked like he couldn't wait to get rid of her. He gave his head a slight shake as he split the stick in two and tossed it into the box of trash behind him.

Barnaby Noley stood inside the doorway silently watching and listening. It hadn't taken long to find out the doctor had been treating Cole Adams' daughter. Everything was falling into place so quickly now he could hardly contain his excitement.

"Well, what is it, Doctor?" The woman stepped forward. "What's wrong with him?"

"He's got a sore throat."

The woman's plump, work-roughened hands went to her stout hips. She gave the doctor a scathing look from beneath the wide brim of her sunbonnet. "I know he's got a sore throat. It's kept him out of the mine for three days. I want to know what's wrong with him."

The doctor shook his head again and reached behind him. Then he addressed his patient. "There's nothing seriously wrong. Gargle with salt water morning and night. Suck on one of these whenever the pain gets too bad. And lay off those cigars for awhile."

The miner avoided his wife's I-told-you-so scowl as he accepted the small package from the doctor and climbed off the examining table. "Thanks doc."

As soon as they scooted around him and out the door, Barnaby asked, "Are you Doctor Sievers?"

"Yes." The doctor flinched when he saw Barnaby's mangled face, but quickly composed himself. "What can I do for you?"

"I'm looking for a man named Cole Adams. I've been told you know him. That you've been taking care of his little girl."

"That's right."

"I need to find him. I've been asking around and was told he left town this morning. I was hoping you could tell me where he's gone."

The doctor hesitated, looking as if he wasn't sure he should answer. "What business do you have with Cole?"

Barnaby struggled to hide his flash of hostility. He softened his voice with a hint of self-pity and introduced himself as Mister Bernard from Kentucky. Then he proceeded to explain about his high-strung daughter who'd run away and his ailing wife who grieved for her. He described Cassie then said, "You see, Doctor Sievers, there's been a terrible misunderstanding between us and our daughter. I've got to find her so I can make amends and take her back to her mother before it's too late. I have reason to believe she may be with Mister Adams."

His sad story did the trick. The doctor was much more relaxed when he stated, "I heard about the exotic-looking young woman with Cole. In fact, the whole town has been buzzing about her. Apparently, within days of speaking to her, three different miners discovered good-sized veins of silver and now credit their luck to the 'Angel with the silver eyes.' I never saw your daughter, but she could have been the young woman with Cole. Cole's little girl told me that she left a few days ago, heading for Spirit Lake. Though why

283

she'd want to go up there alone is beyond me. From what I hear the area is remote and used only by Indians and occasional hunters and fishermen."

Barnaby's feeling of triumph had him soaring. He reached out and clasped the doctor's right hand between both of his and pumped it up and down. "Thank you, doctor. You've been most helpful. More than you'll ever know."

He turned to leave, but the doctor stopped him with, "You know, Austin Barret's ranch is supposed to be located just on the other side of the pass. The sheriff is a good friend of Cole's. I would imagine they'd stop there for the night."

"Sheriff?" Barnaby's hand froze on the door handle.

"Yes." The doctor answered. "Well, actually ex-sheriff. He used to be the sheriff of Golden City. But since Cole just left this morning, you might be able to catch him at the Barret ranch."

"I appreciate the tip, Doctor. Thank you, again." Barnaby hurried out the door already feeling the success of his hunt.

CHAPTER TWENTY THREE

Cassie scanned the checker board and realized she was trapped. Any move she made would end in a loss. "You're too good."

Josiah laughed at her look of defeat. "Give up?"

"Aye that I do. What choice have you left me, you rascal?" She yawned loudly. "I've got to get home. The nights are too short for me."

"We shouldn't have played that last game. You're done in."

"I'm glad we did, I needed the diversion. But you're right. I'm worn out. I'm taking myself home."

Josiah helped her into her coat and grabbed his own. "I'll walk with you."

"That's not necessary, Josiah."

"It most certainly is. Josiah Westfield would never let a lady walk home alone after dark. What would people think? I've a reputation to uphold around here."

Cassie laughed and followed him out the door. The temperature had dropped considerably from the warm afternoon. "It's a good thing you brought your lamp. There isn't much moonlight. When did those heavy clouds move in?"

"Early this evening. They came in fast from the north."

"Do you think it will snow?"

"I doubt it, at least not enough to stick around very long. This seems to be one of those years winter plans to come late. Could start in earnest by the end of the month, but even then, we probably won't get the worst of it until the middle of October or even November."

An owl hooted overhead, letting them know they weren't alone on this black night. Josiah lifted the lamp higher. Cassie appreciated his company and his solid hold on her arm as they wove their way through the dark pines. She'd been fighting an uncomfortable sense of foreboding most of the day and wasn't looking forward to the lonely cabin that waited for her.

All of a sudden she stumbled, catching herself just before she landed on a knee.

Josiah pulled her upright. "Cassie, you've been working too hard. You're nearly out on your feet. Why don't we go fishing tomorrow? Your wood pile has grown sufficiently for now."

Cassie thought the idea sounded like heaven. Every muscle in her body burned from swinging the heavy axe and doing the dozens of other burdensome tasks in preparation for winter. Sitting at the edge of the lake all day is just what she needed. "That sounds wonderful, Josiah. What time would you like to meet?"

"Let's see. I have to gather some bait. We could meet at the outlet about an hour past dawn. I'll bring some extra poles, and we can each work six or seven. What do you think?"

"I think my arms and back thank you."

"I'm beginning to worry about you. You looked ready to collapse when you walked in this evening. Are you getting any sleep?"

"Aye, I'm sleeping." Somewhat, she finished to herself. In spite of her exhaustion, she'd been having a tough time staying asleep the past few of nights. And when she did, her dreams wore her out. The old nightmare continued to haunt her. But she dreamed about Cole too. And, in a way, those dreams were even worse, leaving her so sick at heart she could hardly function.

This is not the time to torture yourself with thoughts of Cole and Victoria, she scolded herself. Not when you're fast approaching a dark, cold cabin and another long, lonely night. She forced a brighter note in her voice. "There's a lot to do yet in order to get that place ready for snow. You advised me yourself, Josiah. Don't forget that. And don't you be worrying about me. I'm young and strong. I can rest up later."

They walked the rest of the way in silence. When they got to the cabin, Josiah waited until Cassie had her lamp lit, then left her alone. The room was terribly cold, but since it was late, she didn't bother with a fire. Instead, she pulled a flannel gown over her full-length underwear and heavy wool socks and buried herself inside the heavy blankets on the cot.

As she lay shivering, her longing for Cole returned with a vengeance. The nights would be so different if he were wrapped around her, keeping her warm. She turned on her side and hugged her knees, wishing she'd never written that note, never ridden away from him and Vicky. Why couldn't she stop behaving so recklessly and foolish? So what if he didn't love her? So what if he did eventually leave? She could have had him with her for a little while. At least as long as Vicky needed her.

But she'd told him in the note she didn't want him to follow. He must have taken her request seriously, it had been days since she'd left and he hadn't shown up. So why continue all this mental torment? She wondered. It always proved to be a vicious circle that led nowhere.

Sleep finally took her over and with it, the nightmare. *She stood outside a burning cabin. The fire's roar deafened her and leapt closer with scorching fingers of blistering heat. She screamed and ran into its midst, frantic to find her mother. Heavy black smoke tore the breath from her lungs and left her panting, but she sucked in searing pain instead of air. Sparks flew everywhere. They caught in her hair. She whirled around, beating at her hair with her hands, and realized she had to find the mirror Ginny had given her.*

The mirror held all the secrets. It would stop the choking smoke. It would put out the fire. It would take away the shame and confusion about her heritage. Cole would love her if he saw her in the mirror. Her fingers burned as she frantically snatched at one flaming object after another. Then she saw it, encircled by the flames. But before she could reach it, she was grabbed from behind. She thrashed painfully, trying to get away. A blazing timber fell next to her, illuminating the grotesque face. Her scream was deafening. It went on and on and on as the fire ate everything around her. Finally, even the scream was consumed.

The next morning, Cassie held a cup of hot tea and watched her breath mingle with the steam rising from the cup. She'd already dressed and was ready to meet Josiah for their day of fishing. The small fire she'd built to make the tea had done nothing to warm the room. Still, with each breath and every sip, she felt better, more clear-headed and more removed from her miserable night.

She opened the door to a gray fog. Tendrils of heavy mist separated here and there and looked almost alive as each fragment moved eerily across the surface of the lake. The gloomy scene threatened to send Cassie's mood plummeting. She grabbed her coat, stepped out and shut the door behind her. The cold fog along with the frightening nightmare reinforced yesterday's feeling of foreboding. Was the dream a recurrence of her old nightmare or was it an omen she should heed? Could Noley find her up here? Was he still tracking her? Had she let the isolation of this place lull her into a false sense of security? Whatever is going on, she reasoned, I can't let it immobilize me. Josiah is waiting.

With one last look at the cabin, she picked up the bundle of food she'd prepared for lunch and walked toward the path.

Lady whinnied from her new pen. Cassie glanced at her as she passed by. Her first morning back, she'd built the small corral by weaving small branches and ropes in and out of the existing trees and rocks. She'd even extended it to include access to the river, so Lady could drink whenever she wanted. Each repair or task she completed in and around her cabin heightened her self-confidence. "I'll be back later, girl," she called, smiling at the horse. "You have food and have plenty of water. Behave yourself and we'll go for a ride later."

The eerie feel to the lake continued as Cassie walked along the bank. It reminded her of Josiah's warning to never take the lake for granted. The fog hung thicker in some places than others. She couldn't see more than a few feet in front of her. The pines still dripped with moisture from last night's rain. Cassie dipped her head and picked her way carefully to keep from being doused by a wet bough.

After one such near-encounter, she straightened, only to have a sudden chill ice down her spine. Directly in front of her, a slender coil of mist began to increase in substance until it took the form of a woman -- an Indian woman.

Cassie's mind became deathly hushed as the apparition glided toward her, extending a vague arm and hand with the palm pressed forward - as if in warning. Cassie took a step back, trying to contain her fright by repeating over and over in her mind that she was merely imagining things. But the wraith drifted closer, the hand lengthening. Cassie stepped back again and caught hold of a wet branch to keep from falling. The form continued to advance.

Behind her, the ground rose steeply, and Cassie struggled to maintain her balance as she scrambled backwards up the rocky hill. Abruptly her heel caught on a half-buried root, and she landed sideways along a fallen tree. The apparition hovered over her for a moment longer, the hand still extended, before being absorbed into the fog.

Cassie lay on the wet ground, trying to control her erratic breathing when a sound reached her from the shore. She raised her head to see a horse and rider appear through the mist. Her heart skipped a beat. She recognized the bulky shape and the way he sat a horse. Noley! He'd found her.

She didn't move. Didn't breathe. Terror rang in her ears. Her mouth was so dry she couldn't have uttered a sound if she'd wanted to. Before she could formulate a clear thought, another rider appeared, followed closely by another. The horses' feet thudded dully in the dense air. Cassie felt each impression as if they'd landed on her back. She waited, frozen to the bone, until the steady hoof beats diminished and ended before she allowed herself to suck in great gulps of air. But she still didn't move. All the while, her mind scrambled for answers. Who were the other two men? They were heading in the direction of her cabin. Would Noley know the cabin belonged to her? If she stayed out of sight, would he leave?

Her hand went to her hip. The knife was there, but this time it wouldn't be enough. She needed a gun. Austin had told her to keep the pistol close by at all times. But she never remembered to carry it. Carefully, slowly, she raised her head to make sure they were gone. She would have to go on to Josiah's. He had weapons.

The door to Josiah's cabin was wide open when she arrived. She rushed inside and shut it behind her. Spinning around, she saw that the table was turned over. Josiah was lying on the floor beside it with a bloody gash on his head. His eye was red and swollen shut. "Oh, no! Josiah?" She bent down and pressed her trembling fingers against his neck. His pulse beat strong.

She righted the table and got some water. After she cleaned him up, she wrapped a bandage around his head. It would have to do until she had more time.

As she stood, he moaned and opened his eyes. "Cassie?"

She kneeled back down beside him. "Hush, Josiah. Don't try to talk. You've taken a hard blow to the head."

"Three men... They asked...about...you."

"I know, I know. Don't talk, just rest."

"One...ugly...scar. He's...the one?"

"Yes, Josiah, he's found me." Nausea rose in her throat. "I'm so sorry they hurt you. I need a gun. Both of mine are in the cabin."

He tried to sit up. The effort brought a moan. He fell back and closed his eyes.

"Don't move, please. You were hit hard. You have to lie still. Just tell me where."

"The holster...hanging by...the...door. It's loaded. The Winchester too.... there, by...the fireplace." He pointed without opening his eyes.

Cassie grabbed a pillow and blanket off his bed to make him more comfortable. She grabbed both guns and put the pistol in his hand. "I'll take the rifle, you keep this one in case they come back here."

"Be careful."

"I will, I promise."

She eased back out the door. Her legs shook so hard she could barely make them work. Her breath came in shallow gasps. There was no plan. She was too scared to think of one. But it would do no good to hide. She'd foolishly told Cole she didn't want him with her. And he'd done as she'd asked. Now, once again, she'd have to face Noley alone.

By the time she made it half way to her cabin, the sun had dissolved all remnants of the fog. Cassie climbed away from the shore in order to come out above her cabin so she could stay hidden but see what was going on. Her body vibrated with fear but she kept moving, staying deep within cover of the trees.

As she neared a small clearing, she smelled smoke. Finally she could see the cabin. It was engulfed in flames. No! Her mind screamed. Not again. She couldn't lose it all again. She dropped to her knees and rocked back and forth. Silent, racking sobs tore from her chest. All her supplies, the pretty things Ginny had given her...

A loud whinny pulled her mind back. She leapt to her feet and strained to see Lady's corral, but it was on the other side of the cabin. The horse screamed again, and Cassie began running down the mountain. The smoke grew thicker. It poured out the cabin's door and window.

The corral came into sight. Two men were inside it, struggling to get control of Lady. One of them carried a rope as he limped toward the horse. The other one tried to grab her mane. The mare's ears were pressed flat against her head, her eyes were wild and her nostrils flared as she whinnied again and reared up. The bearded man ducked and dove to one side to avoid her thrashing hoofs. The man with the limp spun around and swung the rope. The knotted end slashed across Lady's neck.

Cassie raised the rifle butt to her shoulder and tried to keep from shaking as she aimed through the notched sight. Just then Lady reared again and lunged forward. Both men darted to the side of the corral and threw themselves under the bottom branches. The horse ran wildly in a tight circle, kicking her hind legs high in the air. Then, with one easy leap, she cleared the makeshift fence and galloped off.

Cassie sunk back to her knees in relief. "Run, Lady, run," she muttered under her breath.

Flames feasted on the roof now, and hot sparks darted into the sky. Cassie prayed that the heavy moisture clinging to the trees would keep them from catching fire. She stood and made her way closer. The two men were nowhere in sight. Neither was Noley. She could see their horses tied by the shore. Where were they?

She inched closer until she stood in the trees just behind the blaze. Smoke filled her lungs. She pressed herself against the white trunk of an aspen.

A few seconds later, the man with the limp stepped into view. He turned to say something to someone she couldn't see. She sighted down the rifle. As if knowing she was there, he turned and looked right at her. She fired. The bullet hit his left shoulder, spinning him and knocking him to the ground.

Too high, she thought, remembering her father's instructions that all guns were different and that you had to learn how to sight in each one. The other man appeared briefly in her view, but before she could aim, he darted back into the trees.

Where's Noley?

The roar of the fire absorbed all sound, so she didn't realize that anyone was shooting at her until a bullet lodged in the tree next to her, sending bark flying. She pulled a splinter from her cheek and scrutinized the area. A brown-coated shoulder was just visible from behind a boulder. She aimed. Her shot went wild as she was yanked backwards by her hair. Pain burned a path from her head to her tailbone as she landed hard on a rock. Stunned, she struggled to focus.

"I knew that fire would draw you out," Noley crowed in triumph. Sweat beaded his face and trailed down the scarred empty socket that used to be his eye. I told you you'd never escape me. Your ma got off easy compared to what I'm going to do to you."

He jerked Cassie's coat off of her, then slammed her back down again with his booted foot, knocking the breath out of her. She reached for her knife.

"Not this time." He yanked the knife out of her hand and, holding her down with a knee, slowly cut each button off her shirt.

Cassie felt her shirt fall open, and as he used her knife to slice through her necklace, all the fear and heartache and physical exhaustion became a burden too great to bear. Reality tilted into a strange altered motion. She drifted up away from her body and watched the event from above. She saw Noley's lips move, but couldn't hear what he said. She was vaguely aware that the other two men loomed over her body and thought that was strange since she clearly remembered shooting one. But it didn't matter. She felt nothing as she observed Noley grab a fistful of her hair and drag her to a nearby tree and tie her to it with her hands behind her.

Smoke and flames surrounded them. The men's mouths moved. Their eyes leered. But all Cassie heard was the thunder of hooves. In an instant, she was mounted behind the white spirit buffalo's great hump. He pawed the air with his front hooves and then leaped forward to carry her away from the hurtful hands, the terror and heartache. He soared into the blue sky and the warm sun, and she was truly free at last.

CHAPTER TWENTY FOUR

The buckskin's mane and tail blew out in the wind as Cole raced toward the lake. He'd pushed the horse hard since leaving the ranch, running him dead out, then slowing as long as he dared to let him get his wind. Like always, Storm gave him all he had, but Cole didn't want to run him into the ground, so he tempered his anxiety as much as he could.

When they finally drew close, he eased back. The horse slowed to a trot and then a walk. His sides heaved. His breath clouded the cool air. Cole patted his foamy neck. "Good boy, good boy. Take it easy for bit."

When he straightened in the saddle, he saw a heavy black line of smoke rising above the trees. His heart slammed against his ribs. It was much more than chimney smoke. Oh, God. No. Cassie, please be okay. He nudged his heels into the horse's sides. "Don't give out on me yet, boy."

Storm broke into a canter just as another horse came galloping toward them.

Lady.

Cole reined Storm to a slow walk, untied his lariat, shook out a loop and tossed it over the mare's head as she drew near. Her eyes were wild, but as he pulled her to him, she smelled Storm and began to settle. Just then, gunfire echoed through the hills sending Cole's heart into his throat. He kicked Storm and both horses lunged forward.

The cabin was nearly burned to the ground. He dismounted a good distance from the smoldering remains, left the buckskin ground tied and knotted the end of Lady's rope around a pine. A movement up ahead drew him stealthily through the trees.

There were three men standing side by side, facing away from him. Where was Cassie? Two of the men shifted, and he saw her. Her body slumped limply forward, held to a tree by a rope. Her shirt hung open in the front. Cole couldn't tell if she was alive or dead and his fear nearly paralyzed him. One of the men ran his hands over Cassie's breasts, and Cole's fear turned to fury and then to icy calm as years of self-discipline kicked in. He needed to get closer.

As he made his way through the trees, he could see the repulsive scarring on the largest of the three men. That would be Barnaby Noley. The other two were younger. They seemed familiar. A full beard covered the face of the shorter one. The other had a baby face. His left shoulder was wet with blood.

The injured man limped a short distance away, picked something up off the ground, and returned to stand next to the other two. The memory came swiftly. The rustlers. The two that he'd let ride off. Somehow they had teamed up with the maniac tracking Cassie. Cole's left hand went for his pistol.

The man with the beard started to touch Cassie again, but backed off when Noley waved a knife at him. "I told you to stay away from her," he shouted. "I thought I made that clear. No one is to touch her till I'm through with her."

Noley held the knife in front of Cassie's face. Her eyes were open, but she didn't respond. "Wake up you bitch. I want you begging for mercy." He touched the tip of the blade to her neck. Just as it began to draw blood, Cole's gunshot shattered his hand and sent the knife flying.

The other two men jerked around and raised their guns, but Cole shot both of them in the center of their chests before they could fire.

Noley watched them crumple to the ground. Holding his injured hand close to his belly, he reached his other hand around his wide girth for his pistol.

"You're a dead man, Noley." Cole stepped out of the trees, a revolver in each hand.

A crazed look flashed in Noley's eyes. "She has to pay. I'm going to make her pay."

"You're the one who's going to pay." Cole stopped a short distance in front of him, wanting a good look at the man he was about to kill.

Noley howled with rage and lunged at Cole. The guns bucked. Two holes appearing as one opened the fat man's chest.

Cassie's eyes stared vacantly as Cole cut her free. Her skin felt cold and clammy, but she was alive, she was breathing, he reminded himself as he lowered her gently to the ground. "Cassie," he called and rubbed her hands briskly between his.

There was no response. Not even a blink.

"Oh, God, what's happened to her?" He quickly checked her for injuries. Dark bruising was beginning to show on her face and arms. A small amount of blood seeped from the wound on her neck. But from what he could see, her physical injuries weren't enough to cause the state she was in. Which only increased his fear. She was way worse than after Kane's attack. Cole had never seen anything like this and had no idea how to deal with it.

"Cassie," he shouted hoarsely, and shook her shoulders. "Cassie! Dammit it, talk to me." He pulled her stiffly into his arms and cradled her head to his chest. "Cassie, don't do this. Come back to me. Please talk to me."

He rocked back and forth for a minute, unable to think clearly. His eyes skimmed over the bodies littered around him, the cabin's smoldering remains, the horses tied in the trees. His gaze came to rest on the mountain of wood a few yards away. He shook his head in misery when he realized how hard she'd been working the past several days. "Why did you run away, little warrior? Why do you keep trying to handle everything alone?"

After a few minutes, reason returned. She had to have shelter and warmth. He scanned the area again. The woodpile and the corral were all that was left. He'd have to take her to Josiah's.

As he neared the front of Josiah's cabin, his arms ready to give out from carrying her so far, the door opened slowly, and Cole faced the business end of a shotgun. A wobbly Josiah, his head wrapped in a large bandage, one eye red and swollen shut, appeared next. He lowered the gun when he saw who it was. "Holy saints, I was afraid of this. What happened?"

"I don't know. She won't respond to me in any way. They had her tied to a tree when I got there. They burned the cabin to the ground. What little she had is gone."

"Take her in the bedroom." Josiah pointed toward the other room.

Cole swept past him and laid Cassie on the bed. He covered her with the wool blankets folded at the foot. Josiah stood next to him. They both stared down at her ashen face, made even paler by the empty gray eyes and dark hair fanned out against the dingy pillow.

"She doesn't appear to be hurt that bad physically", Cole said. "But she's been like this since I found her. I can't reach her, Josiah. She won't respond to anything."

Josiah leaned against the bed-frame for support. "I've seen this sort of thing before, during the war. I don't think her life is in danger, unless it takes her too long to come out of it. I don't know what the condition is called. The Indians would say her spirit is hiding."

Cole tossed his hat onto the chair across the room and raked a hand through his hair. "What should we do?"

"I'm not sure... Keep her warm... Make her feel safe. I really don't know. Am I correct in assuming those men are no longer around?"

"They won't bother anyone again." Cole squeezed out.

Josiah touched his shoulder in encouragement. "Let me make some tea. We both could use some."

They drank their tea sitting on wooden chairs next to Cassie's bed. After they emptied the pot, Josiah returned to the main room. Cole slid over to sit on the edge of the bed so he could be closer. He held one of her hands and gently stroked her fingers. Dear Lord, had he lost her for good? What would he do if she never came out of this strange condition?

The day crawled sluggishly by while he waited for some hopeful sign from the motionless figure with the empty eyes. Images of the past floated through his mind: His first impression of Cassie as an ailing, teenage boy. His surprise when she appeared like a goddess in the middle of the river. His constant confusion and frustration over her quicksilver mood changes and his fascination over the way those changes expressed themselves so clearly in her eyes. He thought about the gentle sensitivity she expressed with Victoria, always knowing the right thing to say and do to make his daughter feel more secure. He recalled in vivid detail the fury and agony he'd felt when he discovered the reason she had fled Kentucky and all the violence she'd been subjected to.

He'd wasted so much precious time trying to run from the feelings she stirred in him. But not anymore. And he wouldn't let her run from him anymore either. She needed him, whether she knew it or not. And he needed her. He couldn't understand why, what sorcery she had used. But it didn't matter. She was stuck with him.

Late that afternoon, Burl showed up at Josiah's cabin with heavily packed mules and word that Victoria was doing fine with the Barrets. Cole conversed only long enough to direct him to the shack on the other side of the lake, then returned to Cassie's bedside.

After supper, Josiah stretched out on an old army cot he'd set up in the main room. Cole stayed with Cassie. Throughout the night, he kept the lamp on low so he could see her slightest movement. Around midnight, a whisper of breath expelled from her lips and her eyes closed. Cole caught her to him in alarm and groaned so loud it brought Josiah through the door.

The old man had to pry her out of Cole's arms in order to determine what had happened. "I think she's asleep. It's a good sign. I think she'll be just fine if she just gets some rest."

He raked his eyes over Cole, taking in the dark shadow of beard, the dirty, sweat-stained buckskins, and the red-rimmed eyes. "We could all use some rest. Lie down, get some sleep. Everything will seem better in the morning." He turned and left the room.

Reassured by the old man's words, Cole turned off the lamp. It sputtered for a few seconds then went out, leaving a pungent smell of kerosene in the room. Cole stripped to the bottoms of his long johns. Then he pulled the blankets off of Cassie and removed her coat. There was hardly anything left of her shirt. Cole removed it too and gritted his teeth against the image of her limp body tied to a tree. She still didn't move, even when he eased down beside her, pulled her into his arms, and drew the blankets over them both. Finally he rested his chin on the top of her head, closed his eyes and allowed himself to relax. "Please God, keep your hand on this woman. Help her heal and bring her back to me."

She felt so right in his arms, like she'd been made for him. Cole reminded himself of how wrong he'd been when he compared her to a small, injured sparrow, forced out of the nest too soon. She was more like a dauntless, mystical raven. Some of the Indian cultures believed the raven to be the carrier of powerful medicine. Cassie is like that, he thought. She has an inner strength that radiates out to everyone and everything she touches. "Come back to me, little warrior," he whispered against her hair.

The next morning, Josiah looked stronger. He told Cole his headache was gone and he managed to cook up some beans and bacon for breakfast. Cassie slept on. Cole ate quickly and then prowled back and forth between the two rooms, feeling like a deranged bear. He'd never been able to stand idly by and wait for anything. After contending with more than an hour of the irritating behavior, Josiah begged him to find something to do till suppertime.

After extracting a promise from the old man that he'd come and get him if Cassie woke up, Cole returned to the burned-out cabin and the work awaiting him there. When he rode into the clearing, he was pleased to see a well-set-up camp. The horses were enclosed in a new, larger corral. The mules were staked in a grassy area several yards away. Sheets of canvas covered most of the lumber and boxes of supplies he'd purchased in Georgetown.

Burl emerged from the pines on the side of the hill. Bright yellow suspenders contrasted vividly against his blue flannel shirt and brown woolen britches. The sun turned his ash-blonde hair to silver.

Cole eyed the shovel he carried over his shoulder. "You been digging this morning?"

"Yup. Found the nasty remains of some fellas. Dragged 'em up the hill last night. Buried what was left of 'em this morning. By the way, I found a couple of things you might want." He dropped Cassie's turquoise and coral necklace into Cole's palm. "And this too." He handed Cole her knife.

Cole muttered a quick "thanks." His feelings of rage and fear returned with force and he almost gave into his impulse to return to Josiah's immediately. What if he hadn't gotten here when he did? What if Josiah was wrong? What if Cassie never came out of the strange condition she was in? What if he lost her forever?

He stared up at the treetops and willed his mind to clear. Cassie will come out of it. She will. He looked back down at the broken necklace before dropping it into his shirt pocket. The knife fit easily next to his larger one sheathed inside his boot. Nodding to Burl, he reached into a pant pocket for a wad of money. He peeled off several bills and handed them to him. "Here's the rest of what I owe you. You're probably anxious to get on back. Thanks for unloading the supplies and... everything else. I'm sorry I wasn't here to help."

Burl looked at the ground as he pocketed the money. Obviously he'd already put two and two together about everything that had been going on up here. Some of the information had probably come from Austin. And Cole knew from their conversations in Georgetown that, like everyone else who'd seen Cassie, he'd become smitten. "If it's all the same to you, Cole, I thought I'd stick around awhile. I ain't ever been up here before, and I got nothing dragging me back right away. Figured you could use some help."

Cole was more than pleased with the offer. "As a matter of fact, I can use all the help I can get. There's a lot to do before the weather turns." He glanced at the shovel nosed into the dirt at Burl's feet and grinned. "Since you seem to have a hankering to dig, how about digging a hole for a privy?"

Burl returned Cole's grin with a gap-toothed one of his own. "Where you want it?"

The next bit of time was spent discussing the best place for the outhouse, the layout of the new cabin and pacing off measurements. When the dimensions were firmly fixed, Burl bent to the task of digging, and Cole started sifting through the charred remains of the cabin. It didn't take him long to decide there was nothing left to salvage. He could well imagine the agony Cassie had felt when she watched her second home burn to the ground.

By nightfall, the burned area had been cleaned up and a hole dug for the outhouse. The two men returned to Josiah's filled with the satisfaction of doing a good day's work. They were both hungry, and Cole was riddled with anxiety over how he'd find Cassie.

He found her still in the position she'd been in that morning, flat on her back in bed. Cole couldn't imagine anyone sleeping so deeply for such a long time. Once more, Josiah had to assure him that she would be fine. She needed the rest because, along with the horror she'd experienced, she had also been working from sun up till dark as hard as any man.

Throughout supper, Josiah and Burl carried on a steady conversation. Cole concentrated on his food. When he finished eating, he checked again on Cassie before he stepped outside to be alone with his thoughts. The night was dark and still, with only the sounds of insects and owls to break the silence. Cole walked the shoreline for hours, trying to expel his uneasiness about Cassie. But the only thing he accomplished was to further wear himself out. Burl had already gone back to the building site to sleep when Cole returned to the cabin. Josiah was asleep on the cot in the main room.

Cole took the lamp from the table and went into the bedroom, where he lit another lamp. Then he returned the original and put it out. Cassie had rolled to her side, which he took as a good sign. He undressed quickly and eased into the narrow bed next to her. He settled on his side, his left arm around her waist, his knees tucked against the back of hers, his groin pressed against her round bottom. He could feel her warmth through his underwear. It awakened his need for her. He snuggled closer against her, hoping to arouse some response. But there was nothing. A sharp jab of fear threatened to keep him awake, but his exhaustion paid off, and he fell into a deep sleep.

Cassie tried to open her eyes, but her eyelids felt too heavy. She tried to formulate a thought, but the scant impressions that floated by wouldn't come together. She tried again a few minutes later and managed to force her eyes open and looked around. Light streamed in through a small window above her. She could hear birds chatting loudly outside and the hum of voices from beyond the closed door. She was in a small room with knotty-pine walls. Nothing looked familiar. Her eyes closed again.

She felt weak and disoriented, as tired as if she'd just returned from a long journey. Her thoughts drifted. Had she been away? Georgetown. No, she'd returned from Georgetown. She'd been cutting wood... No, fishing... No, she was supposed to go fishing with Josiah.

Her heart started to pound. She hadn't reached Josiah... A spirit from the lake stopped her... Noley. He'd found her. Her hand flew to her neck. The necklace was gone. "Noooo..."

Cole was by her side before the wail faded. He dropped on his knees beside the bed and took her hand in his. "Cassie, open your eyes. You're safe. Look at me."

Her heart pounded so loudly she could hardly hear. Her eyes opened, and he filled her vision. "Cole?"

"Yes, I'm here, Cassie. And Josiah's here." He nodded toward the open doorway. She looked over and saw Josiah smiling at her.

"You're in Josiah's cabin," Cole continued, "in his bed to be exact."

"Where's Noley?" Her hoarse voice sounded like it belonged to somebody else.

"He's dead, Cassie. You don't ever have to worry about him again."

She pulled her hand from Cole's and touched her neck. "My necklace is gone."

He tugged it out of his pocket and dangled it in front of her. "No, it isn't. It just needs some repair work." He reached into his boot. "Here's your knife too."

She clasped them to her, squeezing her eyes against a sudden rush of tears.

Josiah stepped into the room. "Cassie, you've been asleep a long time. You need to drink some water."

Cole helped her sit up, and Josiah held the jar of water while she took several sips. Awash with embarrassment over how weak she felt, she offered a quiet, "Thank you," then turned her head away from the two men and lay back down.

Cole seemed to struggle with his words before finally saying, "You rest some more, Cassie. We'll be in the other room."

She heard the door shut and turned her head to make sure she'd been left alone. Swiftly and silently the tears came, wetting her face, her hair, and the pillow. It was over. She could hardly believe it. Noley was dead. Cole had sounded adamant when he'd said that. Her mother's killer was dead. It seemed like a lifetime ago that she'd found him standing over her mother's body. Had it only been four months? Four months of running, grieving, trying to say goodbye, trying to let go, trying to figure out how to live without her family.

Never again would she have to look over her shoulder in fear. She was free.

Her chest heaved with hushed, jerking sobs. She turned on her side and clutched the knife and necklace to her breast. She could get on with her life now. But how? Everything was gone. The cabin. All her supplies. She would have to start over with even less than she'd had before. How would she ever do it? At that moment, it seemed impossible. She was too tired. The tears continued to spill until her exhaustion left her empty, and she fell into another deep sleep.

The next morning, Cassie felt like a new person. Except, she needed very much to relieve herself. Finding nothing left of her shirt, she wrapped herself in a scratchy dull-green blanket from off of Josiah's bed and hurried out of the bedroom. She was startled to see Cole, Josiah and another man sitting at the table. As one, they stood and smiled.

Cole looked her up and down with a fierce expression on his face. He pulled another chair up to the table. "Sit down before you fall down. You haven't eaten in days."

"I need to.... go outside first." She forced her eyes off of Cole and smiled at Josiah. She wondered about the stranger as she clutched the blanket tighter around her and headed for the door.

Cole caught her before she could step outside. "I'll walk with you, you're probably weak."

The idea of him escorting her to Josiah's outhouse brought a fresh surge of embarrassment. "No, I...I'll make it fine."

The short walk actually did her good. By the time she was back inside and seated at the table, she was eager for a cup of tea. Josiah had a cup waiting. He hovered over her while she drank it. His eye was an unpleasant yellow rimmed by circles of purple. "I'm sorry about your eye, Josiah. Does it hurt?"

"Like the devil. But I do believe my pride is hurt worse. I can't believe I let myself be attacked like that. I'm usually more prepared." His statement ended abruptly, as if he wasn't sure she should be reminded of the event.

Cole and the other man sat on either side of the table, both of them intent on her every move. Cassie still felt somewhat bewildered, like the world was moving on without her. She blew into the steaming mug and took another sip. The dark liquid burned all the way down, helping her feel more connected.

The men's silent watchfulness made her uncomfortable. She wished they would go on about their business or at least say something. Her eyes flitted from one to the other. She was overwhelmed with gladness that Cole was there, but the intensity of her feelings made it impossible for her to look at him. So she focused on the stranger across the table. "Who are you?" she asked.

He beamed as if suddenly granted favor from a queen. "My name is Burl, Miss Cassie. I'm pleased to meet you."

Cole explained, "Burl owns the mules that hauled our supplies up here."

Cassie managed to meet Cole's eyes for a moment, wishing she could find a way to express her gratitude to him. No doubt he had come to her rescue again. "He...brought supplies?"

"Yes, much of what we need."

"You still plan to stay?"

"Yes."

She dropped her eyes and swallowed another sip of tea. "Where's Vicky?"

"At Austin's. She'll join us soon."

"Oh." Cassie studied the back of her hand where it clasped the blanket together in front of her. Several different feelings bombarded her at once; excitement, gratitude, grief, all together sending her into overwhelm. "The cabin's gone. There's no place to stay."

Cole ignored the forlorn note in her voice. "The cabin was too small anyway. We've got a new one started. Got the floor measured and laid out today."

She glanced up in time to see him and Burl exchange gratified nods. "The floor?"

"Yes, the floor."

"You've already started to build?" The happy surprise made her smile.

"Yep," Cole and Burl answered at the same time, satisfaction over her pleasure beamed on their faces.

Josiah slid a plate of eggs and buttered bread in front of her and aimed his words at the other men. "You two are wasting daylight. Get on with your building and let Cassie eat."

Cole and Burl nodded their agreement and made their way to the door.

"Cole?" Cassie spoke so softly she wasn't sure he could hear her.

But he turned, seeming to struggle with himself to keep from walking back to the table. "Yes?"

"My clothes are.... I don't have anything to wear."

His scrutiny moved from her face to the green blanket and back to her face. "Never before in my life have I ever met a woman who has such a problem with clothes." He smiled in satisfaction when the corners of her mouth lifted ruefully. "I'll see what I can come up with."

After Cole and Burl left, Josiah loaned Cassie a blue plaid flannel shirt and a pair of wool pants. They were the oldest and smallest clothes he owned. Cassie was pleased because they fit better than Dalton's. As she bathed and scrubbed her hair in Josiah's washtub, she couldn't keep from thinking about all the new clothes she had just purchased, plus everything else she'd lost in the fire; the dresses Ginny had given her, the beautiful towels Ginny had lovingly embroidered, and the delicate brass mirror.

They could never be replaced. Their value lay in what they represented. They had symbolized her new life, a starting over, and a new self-reliance. Here she was again, dependent on others for clothes, food, and a roof over her head. She wondered if she could come up with the energy or the will to begin again.

Later that morning, following Josiah's advice to take it easy, she followed him to a pretty spot by the outlet of the Grand River and spent the rest of the day stretched out on the bank with a fishing pole in her hand. The sun was warm. The air held the crisp feel of fall. Glorious colors of the changing season dappled the surrounding mountains. The earth smelled of crumpled golden leaves and tangy pine needles. Her tired spirit soaked it in and she began to feel reconnected to the earth, the sky, the plants and trees.

By late afternoon, Cassie and Josiah had each caught several good-sized browns. A few were set aside for supper, the rest were stored in baskets suspended in the lake. After preparing a sturdy meal, Cassie and Josiah headed around the other side of the lake to fetch Cole and Burl.

As they strolled leisurely along, Cassie's mind whirled with questions of the previous days' events. She remembered nothing past looking up and seeing Noley. She asked Josiah if he knew what had happened, and he explained as much as he'd been told; confirming what she'd guessed -- Cole had killed all three men. Her gratitude knew no bounds, but she was sorry he'd been forced to kill for her. She shivered with the thought.

"You're cold," Josiah said. "You haven't regained your strength yet. You need more rest."

Cassie laughed. "More rest? I slept nearly forty-eight hours. How could I possibly need more rest?"

"Even so, that whole nasty episode took its toll. You look pale."

"Maybe. But tonight I'm giving you back your bed. I'll sleep someplace else."

"Don't be silly, you and Cole keep the bed. The cot is good enough for me."

"Cole?" She stopped walking.

Josiah tried to hide his smile. "Yes, Cole spent both nights with you. He was terribly worried."

Cassie's feet began to move again, but her thoughts were stuck on Cole sleeping with her. Two nights? What must Josiah think?

CHAPTER TWENTY FIVE

The floor was as good as done. Cole laid the hammer down and stood to admire the job. He strolled from one side of the large surface to the other, stomping his heel on this place, pressing his toe to that, feeling proud of himself as he visualized what the cabin would look like finished.

Where he stood would be the main room large enough for cooking, eating, and sitting. He turned toward the back where he'd build two bedrooms. The loft would hold one large bedroom facing the lake and one small at the back facing the mountain. Everything was coming together even quicker than he had imagined. The rest of the things would arrive any day, and in no time at all, they could move in.

He cast a quick glance at the sky, grateful the weather was holding. For once, he could find good reason for a dry year. He tried to picture what the lake would look like covered with snow and imagined how beautiful the view would be from upstairs where he and Cassie would sleep. At least he hoped they'd share it. He still wasn't sure about her feelings.

Cole's worries over sleeping arrangements vanished when Cassie and Josiah arrived at the building site. He stood in the middle of the golden pine floor, unaware of the pride beaming on his normally stoic face. His attention was focused strictly on Cassie.

She took her time looking at all the changes; the singed trees, the hole where the privy would go, the mountain of supplies, and finally the new floor. He waited anxiously for a response as her face conveyed her grief, anxiety, gratitude and excitement. She put out her hand, and he pulled her up next to him.

She gazed into his eyes for a moment before turning to look at the lake. "Will there is a window?"

"Yes, two big windows in the main room here on either side of the door, and one each in the two bedrooms at the back." He pointed with his outstretched arm as he breathed in the fresh-scrubbed fragrance of her hair. "The loft will have one large window facing the lake and a smaller one in the bedroom facing the forest."

"There will be a loft?"

"Yes." He wanted to tell her that their bedroom would be up there, with a window seat for her look at the lake while drinking her morning coffee.

"The floor is so big."

"The cabin will be big."

She shielded her eyes from the sun with her hand and looked up at him. "I'll never be able to repay you."

"Don't worry about that right now." His voice came out husky with emotion. He wanted to pull her into his arms and tell her this had nothing to do with paying anyone back, that he wanted this to be a home they would share forever, but that was something he planned to tell her in private.

Before he could say anything more at all, Storm whinnied from the corral. Lady whinnied next, followed immediately by the other horses. Cole and Cassie looked over to see two wagons pulling into the clearing.

Austin, Ginny and Victoria were in the smaller one, with Ring perched behind them on top of a tarp covering a mound of something inside. Tied to the back was a pretty, brown and white pinto colt. John Brewster drove the second wagon, loaded with hay and grain and two caged hens. Brew's mare and a fat cow brought up the rear.

All at once Ring spotted Cole and jumped to the ground. Barking excitedly, he landed both front paws on Cole's chest as he and Cassie stepped down from the new floor. Cole commanded him to sit, and Cassie bent over to give him a hug. Victoria jumped down from the wagon seat before Ginny could grab her. She threw her arms around Cassie, then quickly turned and hurled herself at her father. Cole was so shocked at her unexpected behavior he swept her up without thinking.

She wrapped her arms around his neck and started babbling rapidly about the spotted colt. "Isn't he beautiful Daddy? Austin gave him to me. I can't ride him yet, he isn't broken. But Austin said you would do it. And you would teach me how to ride. He and Ring are already good friends. And he likes me too. He lets me feed him oats right out of my hand. Ginny showed me how. I just hold my hand real flat, like this." Her small hand shot out under Cole's nose, palm up.

"That's great, Vic…"

"And he doesn't even bite me or anything. It tickles sometimes, but I don't move. His name is Ghost Dancer. I just call him Dancer. Yarmony brought him and four other horses to trade for cows. Yarmony is a Ute Indian. He's not scary or anything. He's nice. Austin decided I need a horse and let me pick the one I wanted. Dancer was the prettiest and the smartest."

Cole laughed out loud. It was all he could do to keep up with her excited chatter. But she'd called him Daddy. And she'd jumped into his arms as if it were the most natural thing in the world. He slanted a look at Cassie, who was smiling at them with tears in her eyes.

Ginny and Austin walked up, equally pleased. Austin and Cole shook hands. Ginny greeted Cole then turned to Cassie, and the two women embraced.

"Look at you," Cassie said, pulling back a step and staring at Ginny's protruding abdomen. "You're so big already."

"I know," Ginny laughed and spread her hands lovingly over her rounded middle. "I'll feel like a barn by Christmas."

"What are you doing here?"

"Things slowed down enough that we could leave Ollie in charge of the two new ranch hands. Austin fixed up the wagon so we could camp in it. Dan's coming too and bringing more help. They should be here any time to help build the house."

Cassie shot a questioning look at Cole. He smiled and shrugged his shoulders.

"Cassie," Ginny said, taking hold of the old shirt Cassie wore. "I've never seen anyone with less care of her attire. What happened to the dresses I sent you?"

The laughter in Cassie's voice disappeared as she began to explain, ending with, "Everything's gone, Ginny. The dresses, my new clothes, even the pretty dishtowels and mirror you gave me."

Ginny gave her an encouraging smile and another big hug. "Never mind, my dear friend. Those were only things, and things can be replaced. I'm just grateful you're all right."

Cole listened to the exchange, grateful Ginny had come. It would be good for Cassie to have her around. Although, with Ginny and everyone else here, he didn't know how he'd ever get any time alone with her.

Victoria became restless when she lost her father's attention. She wriggled out of his arms and bolted toward the back of the wagon where the new horse was tied. Cole started after her, but Brew scooped her off the ground and tossed her in the air, wincing a little at the effort. "You know better than to go near that colt without a grownup, little miss. How many times have you been told?"

The five-year-old looked momentarily contrite. Then she giggled. "Do it again, Brewster."

Brew tossed her in the air again, and she squealed with delight. "I'll watch over her," he said to Cole.

"You sure you're up to it, old man? You look pretty stiff to me."

"Not so stiff I can't handle a little fuss-budget like this." He settled Victoria in the curve of one arm. "I'm better. Ginny's been spoiling me. I plan to visit Hot Sulphur Springs after we get this house built. I've heard that the healing properties in the hot pools will do me a world of good." He gave the little girl an affectionate squeeze. "Come on, tyke. Let's go see that colt."

Austin clamped a hand to Cole's shoulder. "Looks like you're making a lot of progress." He nodded toward the new floor.

Cole glanced again at his daughter. "Yeah. In more ways than one, it seems. Thanks, Austin, for everything; Victoria, the colt, bringing Ginny. It means a lot to Cassie and me."

"It's the least I can do. Building one puny cabin isn't anything compared to all you've done for me." A slow smile spread across his face. "It's good to see you settling down. You look like you're enjoying the hell out of all this hard work."

Cole held up a blistered palm. "Yeah? Well, my hands tell a different story. Poker is a lot easier on 'em. Come on, I want you to meet Josiah."

The afternoon passed quickly as everyone pitched in and expanded the camp to include the newcomers. When everything was situated, everyone went to Josiah's for supper. Ginny brought along a basket of food she had prepared, and combined with Josiah's offering, the group feasted on fried chicken, ham, trout, boiled potatoes, corn, green beans, sliced tomatoes and sourdough bread. For dessert there was raspberries, cream and sweet cake for those who still had room.

Throughout the meal, Cassie watched the continued affection between Cole and his daughter. Ginny had explained about Victoria's fever and the get-acquainted time it had given Cole with her. It obviously had paid off. Even now Cole could hardly put a bite of cake in his mouth because Vicky was so bent on chatting about her horse and the things she'd done at the ranch.

"Isn't it wonderful?" Ginny whispered in Cassie's ear, nodding to the pair. "When the two of them got back from Georgetown, I noticed immediately that Victoria was more comfortable with him. We worried about what her reaction would be when he immediately left her to ride up here. But outside of being a little withdrawn at first, she did fine. We just left her alone the first morning, and she was content to focus all her attention on Ring. That animal is something else. He stayed beside her every minute."

"That's the way they've been from the beginning. He's adopted her."

"And he's as big as she is. Which reminds me. I may have done something you won't like." Ginny looked repentant. "Victoria seemed the most vulnerable at night, so I gave in and let Ring sleep on the bed with her."

Cassie smiled sheepishly. "You aren't to blame for that bad habit, Ginny. It was started in Georgetown." Cassie didn't offer the reason why, but her cheeks burned with the memory. She was also concerned that she hadn't noticed Vicky was coming down with something. She never would have left if she had. "I wonder why she got sick?"

"I guess she was just run down. She's been through a lot." Ginny glanced over at Cole and his daughter, then back at Cassie. "You all have. It's a wonder all three of you aren't flat on your backs."

"Tough stock, I guess," Cassie said, but inwardly shook her head. Tough? She'd just gotten out of bed after two days of collapse. She didn't feel tough at all right now. "Tell me about the pinto. He's beautiful."

"Isn't he? When Austin saw how attached Victoria was to the dog, he got the idea about getting her a horse. Austin's developed a friendship with Yarmony. He's a sub-chief with the Uintah Ute's and has become a frequent visitor. The last time he stopped by, Austin told him we were interested in purchasing some horses. He showed up the other day with five. Victoria seemed drawn to the pinto, so Austin gave him to her." Ginny looked again at the five-year-old who was now sitting on her father's lap, slipping bites of food to Ring. "We knew she was excited, but we were just as surprised as you and Cole over her exuberant outburst this afternoon."

"I'm so grateful to see her like this, Ginny. I think Cole was afraid she'd never warm up to him. And he loved her at first sight."

"Well, he doesn't have to worry anymore. She seems perfectly at ease with him now. And you're wonderful with her."

Cassie's heart overflowed with love for the little girl. "I'm crazy about her. We hit it off right away. Actually, we clung to each other like two ship-wrecked souls. She needed a safe person to hang onto, and I needed someone to need me."

"You make a wonderful family. The three of you look like.... What is it? Why the sad look?"

"The way you said 'family.' I'm afraid to reach for that, Ginny."

"Why? I know you lost your family, Cassie. But that doesn't mean you can't have another one. It's obvious how much you and Cole care for each other."

"Is it? I know how I feel about him, but I'm not sure he feels the same way."

"Cassie, Cole's attraction to you is glaring."

"Attraction! That's just it. I know he's attracted to me. But he's also attracted to Ruby. You should see how he is with her. And who knows how many others. Besides…"

"Besides what?"

"Ruby's…white."

"I don't believe it," Ginny's whispered voice raised in exasperation. "You're not still worried about your Indian blood? Cassie, I know Cole Adams. He may be a lot of things, but he certainly isn't prejudiced. And you can forget about other women. I've seen him with Ruby and with others as well." She wiped her mouth with a napkin. "His feelings for you are completely different."

Ginny suddenly jerked around as Austin nudged her with his elbow. "What are you two whispering about?" he asked none too quietly.

All eyes at the table turned their way. Cassie could feel her face heat. Ginny choked on the bite of food she'd just placed in her mouth. Austin patted her gently on the back.

Cole's brow arched. He gave Cassie a droll look. "Don't you ladies know it's impolite to whisper at the supper table?"

Cassie stared back at him, mortified with the thought that she and Ginny could have been overheard. Vicky saved the moment by climbing off her father's lap and onto Cassie's.

The five-year-old placed her hands on either side of Cassie's face, making sure she had all her attention, then promptly began reciting all of the things that had taken place on the ranch; the skunk that had gotten in with the chickens, how she had helped Ginny milk the cows, how she'd beat Austin and Brewster at poker more often than they'd beat her, and the visit from the Indians. She ended with a repeat of Ghost Dancer's wonderful attributes.

After dessert, tea and brandy were served. Josiah and Brewster played checkers while the rest continued their conversations. Vicky finally ran out of steam and fell asleep in Cassie's arms.

Later, as everyone got ready to make their way back to the campsite and their particular beds, Cole transferred his daughter to his own arms. Cassie felt left out and silently wished she could go with them. But she could only manage to say how grateful she was for Cole's and everyone else's help.

The moon was high in the sky by the time Cole tucked his daughter beneath a pile of blankets on top of a warm buffalo robe inside one of the tents he'd bought in Georgetown. Ring slept pressed up close to the little girl. After a quick wash in the lake, Cole climbed in next to her. His breath sent puffs of vapor into the cold night air as he stared into the welcome darkness, glad to lay his tired body down for rest.

As usual, whenever he stopped all physical activity, his thoughts veered to Cassie. Her absence was tangible, and his need for her was raw. Damn it all. She had practically turned her back on him when he tried to talk to her as everyone was leaving, dismissing him with words of gratitude for all he had done and was doing. He didn't want her gratitude. He wanted her. But he hadn't been able to utter a word with everyone else standing around gawking. So he'd stood there with a sleeping Victoria in his arms, feeling abandoned and like a damned fool.

Damn that stubborn woman. Damn everyone else for hovering around all night. Damn him for not being able to think of a better way to handle things. He flipped to his side and pounded the hard ground with his fist. Ring's head lifted and the yellow-gray eyes stared through the dark at him. "Go to sleep, Ring," he growled.

The next morning brought a flurry of activity. Josiah looked and felt stronger and added his assistance to the construction of Cassie's new home. In the afternoon, Dan rode up with three loaded-to-the-hilt freight wagons and three more men to help with the building. Cole stopped working long enough to oversee the unloading of the wagons, critically inspecting each item as it came off. When he was satisfied that everything he'd purchased had arrived in good condition, he covered it with tarps and went back to work.

Austin, who had been trained as a carpenter before he came west, took charge; issuing instructions to the others as needed. With so many added hands, the construction time was shortened considerably. Each day gave way to another in rapid succession for the busy group. And everyone was grateful for the weather's cooperation. The nights were frigid, but the sun, within an hour of its appearance, chased away the frost.

Cassie was completely spellbound as her new home materialized before her eyes. Consequently, she had difficulty staying out of the middle of things. She found one excuse after another to ask a question or offer refreshments. Every time she got too close, Cole shooed her away, his mood becoming gruffer with each passing day. The only thing she was allowed to do was help gather stones for the fireplace. Vicky helped too, and so did Ginny, insisting, when Austin and everyone else made a fuss, that she was a rancher's wife, not some fragile flower.

After the rocks had been collected, Cole gave Cassie the measurements of the new windows and several bolts of fabric. So late afternoons found the two women sitting on a blanket beneath an aspen tree, cutting and stitching. Cassie's attention constantly catapulted from the curtains, to progress on the cabin, to Vicky, who seemed to always be headed for the corral.

She also made herself useful by tending to an occasional minor injury. And each evening she concocted hot poultices out of mashed, stinging-great-nettle leaves for Brew's rheumatism. The easing of his pain and stiffness brought relief to them both. Brew could move around better, and Cassie didn't have to feel guilty watching him limp in pain while he helped build her new home.

At bedtime, everyone retired to his or her individual spots for sleep. And each night Cassie lay on the cot in Josiah's cabin, miserable because she wasn't sleeping where she wanted to be. With each new day, her ache for Cole grew. She longed to feel his arms around her, to talk privately with him, to find out what thoughts lurked behind the strange looks he gave her. But there was never a moment to spare. Everyone was working at top effort in a race against the weather.

Once the walls were up and the roof was in place, Cole, Josiah and Brew filled the chinks between the log walls, applying the same lime, sand, and water mixture they had used in building the fireplace. The other men moved on to the construction of the privy and a small barn for the animals.

By the end of the second week, the new home was given the finishing touches. Cassie's excitement could hardly be contained when she watched the men carry various furnishings inside. There was an oak table and six chairs, an oak sideboard, a beautiful mirror, a settee upholstered in a rust-colored fabric, two wooden rocking chairs, three dressers, three room-size rugs, six lamps, a dry sink, and a Columbine cooking stove. Her previous worry over sleeping arrangements returned when she watched the assembly of only two brass beds. She avoided Cole's eyes as he and Austin carried the larger bed up to the front bedroom in the loft and deposited a fluffy feather mattress on top. The smaller bed was placed in the other upstairs bedroom, and Vicky pounced on top of it when she was told it was hers.

Cassie couldn't face the idea of bedtime and what would be involved with solving that puzzle, so she busied herself with unpacking and putting away all the new possessions. The opening of each trunk and package was an exciting task. She couldn't believe Cole's foresight and planning. He'd purchased cooking implements, pots and pans, pillows, linens, blankets, quilts, dishes, eating utensils, a coffee grinder and coffee pot, a barrel of kerosene, lamps, buckets, rope, and odds and ends of little things like string, matches, wicks, candles, liniment, medicines, bandages, and writing supplies. There were several crates of canned foods, and barrels and crates of food staples including coffee, tea, cornmeal, rice, salt, pepper, sugar, flour, baking soda, dried beans and fruits, cured ham, dried beef, and salted bacon. He had even purchased extra winter clothing for her and Vicky along with fabric for dresses.

Why? The question formed itself in Cassie's mind again and again. Why was he doing all this? He hadn't spoken one word to her about his intentions, and she was left to wonder and guess. Was it all for Vicky, as she'd overheard him say to Ruby? Was he so impressed with the relationship she had with his daughter that he'd go to this elaborate extent to keep them together? No, that couldn't be it. Vicky was becoming just as open and affectionate with Cole. Maybe he was afraid to be alone with his daughter. Maybe he wanted a mother for her. Maybe he didn't feel his former environment would be a good place to raise his daughter. If he loved Ruby, why didn't he build a home away from the gambling hall? Wouldn't Ruby leave her business? Did she want Cole but not his daughter?

The questions never found answers, and Cassie was left with nagging doubts. So she stuffed them away with the rest of her concerns and misgivings about Cole Adams and concentrated on the happiness of the moment. He and Vicky were here with her now. He had used his time, effort and money to build her a new home. And whatever his reasons, Cassie was grateful and felt overwhelmingly in his debt.

Before she knew it, it was past time for lunch and all work ended. The group was in high spirits as they gathered together for the first time in the large main room. Laughter and loud male voices punctuated the festive atmosphere. There was plenty of light from the two big windows, but Cole still insisted on lighting the large chandelier that hung above the table. The men sat crowded together around the oval table, sharing tales of woe about a banged thumb, a stiff neck, a smashed toe, a skinned elbow, aching backs, and arrogance-filled anecdotes over each one's particular contribution to the building of the new home.

Ginny dropped the last of the peeled potatoes in the pot of water on the stove and turned to lean against the shining surface of the new sideboard. She wiped her hands on the towel tied around her bulging middle and watched Cassie bend over to check the beef roast in the oven of the new stove. "Cassie, you've worn that smile so long it must be permanently fixed by now."

Cassie's face was already pink from poking it into the hot oven yet she still managed to blush with sheer happiness. Just as she opened her mouth to comment, she saw Ginny's hand go to her abdomen. "What is it?"

"The baby just walloped me a good one." Ginny's face beamed. "There. He did it again."

"Can I feel?"

"Give me your hand." She positioned Cassie's fingers just so, and they both waited. After a few seconds, they smiled at each other.

Ginny said, "I never realized it would feel so strong."

Cassie nodded, feeling joy for her friend. "Me either. It's amazing isn't it?

"Yes, it is. Cassie, I'm so happy. My life is so different from what it was such a short time ago. Sometimes I have to pinch myself to see if I'm dreaming."

"I know what you mean. I've been feeling the same way these past two weeks. When Zeb and Dalton carried me away from Kentucky, I was so sick and sick-at-heart, I couldn't imagine I'd ever feel happiness again. Yet all of you have come to mean so much to me. And now this…" Her eyes roamed dreamily over the room and everything and everyone in it. "You've given me a home. I don't know how I'll ever repay everyone."

"Cole has given you the home, Cassie. All the rest of us did was help put it together, just as he did for Austin and me. And, if I know Cole, he isn't thinking in terms of repayment. He did this because he cares so much for you."

Cassie looked at Cole, her heart bursting with love for him. She wanted to believe it and started to tell Ginny so, but a commotion outside stopped her.

CHAPTER TWENTY SIX

Cassie stepped to the front window and was amazed to see what looked like a small army riding along the lakeshore toward the house. There were at least twenty riders, making no small amount of racket with whoops and hollers, laughter, singing and whistles. Whoever they were, a party was in progress.

Ginny joined her at the window. Cole, Austin and the other men stepped outside onto the wide porch. When the revelry drew closer, Cassie spotted Ruby, resplendent in a beautiful emerald riding habit and sitting proudly on a prancing white horse. Cassie and Ginny stepped through the doorway as Ruby stopped her horse in front of the porch. The crowd filled in every possible space around her. They were all men, every age, size and shape, and all smiling as they stared bug-eyed at Cassie.

Victoria jumped off the porch and ran around greeting the newcomers. The beautiful Ruby climbed off her horse and gave the little girl a hug.

Cassie grabbed hold of the porch railing. Her stomach flipped over. She tore her eyes away from Ruby and Vicky and glared at Cole. There was absolutely no expression on his face, but his midnight blue eyes bored intently into hers. Something ominous was happening, and she wasn't sure she wanted to find out what.

But Austin did. "What the hell's going on, Cole? It looks like half of Georgetown is here and you don't seem surprised."

Cole opened his mouth to speak, but Vicky beat him to it. "We're going to have a party, Daddy. Ruby says this is a wedding-party."

The porch started to wave under Cassie's feet. Nausea rose with such force she had to slap a hand over her mouth to keep from retching. She ran around the side of the veranda, jumped down and made it to the trees behind the cabin in time for what felt like her whole insides to come up. When the spasm passed, she braced herself and fought for breath.

For the past two weeks, she'd fooled herself into thinking that Cole had done all of this for her. That he'd planned to stay here with her. But the dream was over. Cole was marrying Ruby. Oh, Great Spirit, she prayed under her breath. How can I get through this? How can I face him? How can I face any of them?

"Cassie?" Ginny called as she hurried to Cassie's side. "Oh my God, you're sick." She cupped a cool hand against Cassie's brow.

"I'm...all right." But she wasn't all right and never would be again. And after all the talking she'd done to herself, all the cautioning, trying to prepare herself for this very happening, she couldn't understand how it could hurt so bad. She wanted to wail and scream and tear her hair. "Ginny, please, I just need to be alone for a..." Another wave of nausea bent her forward. Her stomach heaved, but nothing came up.

When she straightened, Ginny took her arm. "Cassie, you look like you're going to fall down. Let me help you into the house."

"I'll take care of her, Ginny," Cole said from behind. "Please help Austin entertain our guests."

Ginny spun around to tell Cole what she thought of him and his orders and his guests, but his scowl changed her mind. "You better have a good explanation for all of this, Cole Adams," she said and marched off.

Cole pulled Cassie against him and wiped her face with his handkerchief. "What's the matter with you?" he demanded.

She wanted to yell at him to go away and leave her alone. She was hurt beyond words and humiliated to have him see her like this, but another swell of nausea wrenched the words from her mouth and she fell forward again. She heaved and heaved, but her stomach was as empty as her heart and soul.

Cole steadied her with one hand on her forehead and the other around her waist. When the empty retching finally stopped, she collapsed back against his solid frame and finally managed to mutter, "Leave me be, Cole."

"Leave you be? Are you daft, woman? You can't even stand." He swept her into his arms and started for the house. "Talk to me. Why are you so sick?"

"It's nothing," she mumbled against his neck.

He carried her in the back door and up the stairs to the loft. He laid her gently on the bed. She rolled away from him, hiding the tears that threatened to spill. He sat down next to her, hooked a hand over her shoulder and turned her back.

"Please, tell me what's wrong. I'm worried about you."

The concern in his voice was her undoing. How could he act so soft and caring after audaciously inviting Ruby up here? Sudden anger erupted with the same force as the nausea. "Go away, Cole."

"Go away?" He threw up his hands at the quicksilver change in her condition. "I'm not going anywhere. Especially not until you tell me what's going on in that head of yours."

Cassie sat up and tried to scoot around him and off the bed. But he pulled her onto his lap and held her firmly.

"What in tarnation is wrong with you? First you're sicker than a dog. Now you're hopping mad. You have some explaining to do, and neither one of us is leaving this room until you do."

"I have some explaining to do? It seems to me the facts speak for themselves. You're gettin' married, and I don't care to be a part of it. I'm going to Josiah's for the night."

His anger matched hers. "You aren't going anywhere. And neither am I. This is my home too."

The sharply spoken words turned her wrath back to slicing pain. "You mean you'll be wantin' the cabin after you're married?"

Cole looked liked she'd slapped him. His arms went slack, allowing her to escape. She backed away until she bumped into the dresser. He looked at her as if she'd lost her senses. "Of course I want to live at the cabin. Where the hell else would I live?"

"I thought you'd go back to Georgetown." She wrung her hands, wanting desperately to get this horrid confrontation over with before she started wailing like a baby. "Well, you better not expect me to move out. Cause I'm not. Not now, not ever."

His mouth fell open. He gaped at her a full minute. Then his eyes narrowed to mere slits. "What in the hell are you talking about? I already told you, you aren't going anywhere."

The absurd remark brought her anger back. She braced her hands on her hips and moved in front of him. "What are you talking about? I'm certainly not going to live with you and… and her. And you can just get that pigheaded, overbearing look off your face. You may have saved my life, but that doesn't mean you can use you're domineering ways on me."

"Cassie, you're making me crazy." Cole stood and loomed over her. He gripped her shoulders with both hands. "I don't know what's going on in that beautiful head of yours, but you're obviously jumping to some wild and very wrong conclusions. Now calm down and listen. I'm not marrying Ruby."

"You're not?" Her anger gave way to uncontrollable shaking.

"No. Listen carefully, please. I know you want to handle your own problems and take care of yourself. But you need me. You really do. And I need you too. That's why I've chosen to handle this marriage the way I have. With that independent streak of yours, I figured there was no way you'd give me a simple yes if I asked you. So before I left Georgetown, I arranged for the

Judge to come up here, hoping you'd see the light. I haven't had a spare min-ute to get you alone, otherwise this wouldn't have come as such a shock. My timing was pretty good though, if I do say so myself." He smiled and softened his voice, "I love you Cassandra O'Brian and I'm praying you love me to. But whether you do or don't, whether you're sick or not, you're going to marry me, and you're doing it today. I'll make it part of the stupid debt you think you owe me if I have to. So what do you think? Please put me out of my misery and say yes."

If Cole hadn't had such a firm hold on her, Cassie would have gone to the floor. "Me? You want me to marry me?"

He gave her shoulders a slight shake. "Of course, you. Today. No excuses, no arguments, and no more crazy talk. We're getting married. I've done every-thing I can think of to be worthy of you. I've changed my whole damn life and I'll gladly do it again. I'll give you anything you ask for, anything. I know the cabin isn't much, but it's adequate for now. I'll enlarge it if we have more children. You do want more children don't you?"

"But why would you want to marry me if you love Ruby? I heard the two of you talking through the door." Cassie was so befuddled, she spoke more to herself than to Cole, oblivious to the confession she was making. "You said you were going back to the lake because it would be good for Vicky. I didn't think you would ever want to marry someone like me because...because I'm a half-breed."

Cole's normally stoic face registered a mixture of responses -- sadness, remorse and a little anger. "You seem to have selective memory. I told you before that not everyone is concerned about a person's breeding. I don't care who or what you are, or who or what your family was. And it doesn't say much about your opinion of me to think I would."

He looked away. A muscled tensed in his jaw. Then he took a deep breath, let it out, pinned her with a firm look and said, "The next time you eavesdrop on somebody's conversation, stick around long enough to hear the whole thing. You would've heard me give the same speech to Ruby."

It was quite a mouthful for a man of few words. Cassie appreciated that fact. And he was right. She should have known better than to think he would be so shallow. She had obviously transferred her own self-doubt onto him. But it still didn't address her concerns about his feelings for Ruby.

Cole seemed to know what she was thinking. He lowered his head until his mouth was mere inches from hers and said, "Cassie, Ruby is a friend, a good friend, but only a friend. We go back a lot of years, and she tends to get possessive. But that's all she's ever been to me. You're the woman I love. You and only you."

"You love me?"

"Yes. Haven't I done everything in my power to show you?"

He eased his hold on her arms, but didn't let her go.

Cassie thought about everything he'd said. Seeing it all in this new light, she knew without doubt that he was telling her the truth about his relationship with Ruby. Not once had he ever treated Ruby like anything but a good friend. And here he was, now, confessing his love for her and acting like she should have known it all the time. And she should have, she admitted. Her Da had seldom used words to express his affection to her mother or herself. But he'd expressed love in his every gesture and every action. Just as Cole had done for her. She had been so wrong about everything.

"Well, what about it?" he prompted, when she continued to stand there, looking witlessly up at him.

"What about what?"

"Are you going to marry me willingly or do I have to force you?" There was the slightest hesitation in the threat, emphasized by grave apprehension in his cobalt eyes.

Her senses returned with a feeling so warm she felt like she glowed from head to toe. "You don't have to use force, Cole. I'll marry you, and Victoria too."

His sigh parted her hair. "Thank God."

He possessed her mouth with weeks of stored up need and passion. She wrapped her arms around him and opened to take it all in. When she sighed with pleasure and surrender, he deepened the kiss. And she kissed him back with all the pent up love she had to give. The moment turned into minutes, and still they clung to each other, reveling in joy and relief. But the fact that people were waiting must have reached Cole. On a moan he pushed her away from him.

"We'll finish this later. Now wash your face and get yourself ready. I'll get the Judge."

"Cole…"

He stopped at the door and spun back around. "Yes?"

"Why is Ruby here?"

His lips curved into a sheepish grin. "She's the organizer of the wedding party. I'm sorry about that part, Cassie. Everything got blown out of proportion. Ruby and the Judge got together and before long, everyone wanted to be included. He shrugged, then took three long steps back across the floor and kissed her again. "I'm not the only one charmed by your spell. You left a throng of admirers behind in Georgetown."

After he was gone, Cassie flopped down on the bed and tried to assimilate all that had happened. Ginny found her in the same spot ten minutes later. "Can I come in?" she asked, peeking her head around the door.

"Aye." Cassie took a deep breath and let it out. She stared wide-eyed at her friend.

Ginny fairly beamed with delight. She came all the way into the room carrying a brown paper package and laid it on the bed next to Cassie. "Is there going to be a wedding?"

"It seems so."

"You aren't acting very happy about it."

"I'm overjoyed somewhere inside. It just hasn't worked its way out yet."

"Cole does have an unconventional way of handling things doesn't he?"

"Aye, he does that. It's one of the things I love about him, I think."

Ginny grinned at Cassie's bewilderment. "There's quite a mob out there waiting for you. Don't you think you should get dressed?"

"Dressed?" Cassie looked down at the simple, unadorned, navy blue frock she was wearing, one of the several Cole had purchased. "Won't this dress do?"

Ginny shook her head. "You're the only woman I've ever known who is completely unconcerned about clothes. You can't get married in that, silly." She pointed to the package. "It's from Cole. He asked me to give it to you."

Cassie glanced at the package. "He did? Why didn't he give it to me himself?"

Ginny laughed. "Cole is in a sorry state right now. I've never seen him so flustered. Hurry up and open it. I'm dying to see what it is."

Cassie untied the string and parted the paper. She and Ginny gasped at the same time. "Oh, Ginny. Would you look at this." She delicately lifted the glorious dress and held it against her. It was one long, shimmering line of ice blue satin. Ginny clasped her hands together. "The color is perfect for you. Cole obviously had your eyes in mind when he bought it." She rustled around in the package, looking for something else, but came up empty handed. "Isn't that just like a man. No shoes or anything else to go with it. Wash your face and pinch your cheeks, while I see what I can come up with."

After Ginny left, Cassie did as she was told. She pulled her dress off and tossed it on the chair in the corner. As she reached for the beautiful dress Cole had bought her, a sharp rap sounded on the door. "Come in, Ginny."

"It's not Ginny," said a sultry voice. "May I come in anyway?"

"Aye." Cassie held her wedding dress in front of her as Ruby opened the door and stepped into the room. The beautiful redhead had changed out of her riding garment into an unassuming peach-colored dress, cut surprisingly very modest. Still, everything about the woman commanded attention. "I wanted to talk with you for a minute, if you don't mind."

"I don't mind," Cassie lied. "Would you like to sit down?" She motioned to the only chair in the room, but it was covered by the dress she'd just taken off.

Ruby tried to smile, but failed. "I don't need to sit. This won't take long." She cleared her throat and gave Cassie a direct look. "I want to apologize. I've behaved reprehensibly toward you and I'm ashamed of myself for it."

Cassie wasn't sure she could take one more shock today. This candid apology was the last thing she'd expected to hear. "Ruby, you don't have to..."

"Yes, I do." Ruby folded her hands together in front of her and continued. "I have been insanely jealous of you since the day we met."

"Jealous? Of me?" Cassie plopped on the bed; the dress slithered to her lap, forgotten.

"Yes. You see, Cole means a lot to me. He happened along when I needed a friend desperately and over time he became more like a brother than a friend. I guess I got pretty possessive. After you came into his life, he was never the same. When I met you, I could understand why he was so smitten. You have a special quality that is quite rare. And it isn't just your looks, although you're certainly attractive."

When Cassie opened her mouth to respond, Ruby stopped her with a raised hand. "Please let me finish. At first, I felt like you were stealing him away from me. I was angry. And hurt. I wanted to strike out at you and Cole. But I've had time to settle down and see the folly in that. Cole and I had... have a damn fine friendship. Too fine to throw away over something as petty as jealousy." She cleared her throat again and her striking features shone with hopefulness. "I guess what I'm trying to say is I'd like to have you for a friend too, if that's possible."

Cassie was moved as much by the sincerity reflected in Ruby's hazel eyes as her words. And she was hugely grateful to hear Ruby admit her claim on Cole was truly only friendship. She reached out her hand. "I would be honored to be your friend, Ruby."

Ruby's smile widened into a big grin. She batted Cassie's hand away and surprised her further by embracing her in a quick hug. Then, with a spurt of laughter, professed, "I do believe you are the first woman I ever hugged in my life."

The next twenty minutes moved in high-speed for Cassie. Ginny came back in and helped her into the splendid dress and a pair of cream-colored shoes, only slightly too big. Cassie tried to look at herself in the mirror, but Ginny wouldn't let her move as she fastened what felt like a thousand tiny pearl buttons up the back of the dress.

Ruby left the room, but returned a few minutes later with a carpetbag of assorted female items the likes of which Cassie had never seen before. Ginny began working on the buttons running up both sleeves from wrist to elbow. Ruby worked around her, first touching puffs of this and bits of that to Cassie's cheeks, eyes and lips, and used something hot and sizzling on her hair.

Ginny finished first and stood back to watch, resting her arms across her protruding abdomen. When Ruby stepped back, both women admired the results.

"You look like a fairy tale princess," Ginny whispered.

"There's been a more stunning bride," Ruby agreed.

When Cassie turned and looked in the mirror, she scarcely recognized the woman staring back at her. She had never thought of herself in terms of beautiful, or lovely, but Ginny was right, the silvery-blue satin made her look regal. It set off her dark hair and grey eyes beautifully. She dipped and stretched and twisted this way and that, trying to see as much of herself as possible in the mirror.

The sides of her hair had been lifted into loose curls and somehow secured at the top of her head. Blue and pink wild flowers were twisted to form a crown. The back of her hair fell in burnished waves to skim the top of the slight bustle on the back of the dress. Turning back around and bending closer to the mirror, she was in awe at the transformation. "So this is what a bride looks like."

She fingered the coral and turquoise stones hidden beneath the high neck of the dress, wishing with all her heart that her mother and great-grandmother could see her. And just like that, she felt their presence as strongly as if they'd entered the room, smiling their approval and their joy. She blinked back hot tears and swallowed hard.

"Now, now, none of that," Ginny said through her own tight throat. She gave Cassie a quick squeeze. "You'll have us all bawling. Let's see now, something borrowed...my shoes. Something new...your dress. We need something old and something blue."

"And a half-pence for her shoe," Ruby chimed in, producing one.

Ginny laughed. "Where did you get that?"

"I collect coins, especially old or foreign. My customers know this, so somebody's always dropping one in the jar I keep on the bar."

Her hand disappeared into the carpetbag on the bed. A moment later she pulled out a pale blue hanky trimmed with lace gone yellow with age. "It was my grandmother's."

She presented it to Cassie almost reverently, her eyes wistful. "I hoped to carry it on my own wedding day, but..." She shrugged her shoulders and left the statement half-finished.

Cassie accepted the pretty hanky, deeply touched by the fact that Ruby had thought to bring it. "Thank you." She squeezed Ruby's hand affectionately. "You're already a good friend.

"That takes care of blue," Ginny said gaily, trying to return the mood to a lighter one. "The hanky would work for something old too, unless you have something else."

Cassie placed her hand against the stones hanging beneath her dress, feeling a wondrous surge of happiness. "My necklace. It's very old."

"Good. We're all ready, then."

Ruby opened the bedroom door. "I'll go put the nervous groom out of his misery."

Cole adjusted his tie a fourth time as he walked around the perimeter of the wide veranda. He felt like a bevy of quail had taken flight inside his stomach and was certain he'd be the next one vomiting in the bushes if they didn't get this wedding over with soon.

What could be taking those women so long?

He'd nearly lost it when Austin told him Ruby had gone in to talk to Cassie. He would have stormed in after her if Austin hadn't stopped him. Ruby had assured him that she had resolved her feelings and was happy for him. But this thing could still blow up in his face if something hurtful was said to Cassie.

What if she was still reluctant? He'd threatened to use force, and was prepared to do so, but in truth, he hated the idea of pressuring her into it. He wanted her to be as willing and excited as he was.

He paused at the porch railing and looked out at the crowd of high-spirited men in the yard, some sitting on the ground, some standing, some sprawled in the few chairs Austin had brought out of the house, all of them drinking from flasks and jugs they'd brought along for the occasion. The whole situation was ridiculous, but Ruby had told him that no force on earth would stop them from coming. Not since Joe Weber's big silver strike soon after he'd encountered Cassie in the street and gotten her wishes of good luck had they come up with a better excuse for a shindig. And what better reason now than the wedding of the "silver-eyed angel" who'd brought him luck?

Thankfully, the late afternoon sun was still warm, but if those women didn't get a move on, they'd have to hold this affair inside. And he wasn't at all thrilled about that.

Just as the last of his patience drained away, the door burst open and Ruby stepped out. "Here comes the bride," she announced in a loud voice.

The bride appeared a couple of minutes later, but was so thrown from the enormous cheer that greeted her; she stepped back into the house smack into Ginny. Ginny laughed and pushed her back outside.

The wedding party whooped even louder at this, but Cole couldn't have made a sound just then if his life depended on it. Cassie always looked good to him, in whatever she did or didn't have on; even Dalton's baggy clothing. But he wasn't prepared for the vision standing self-consciously before him. She seemed to be glowing. Her silver gray eyes looked even larger than usual. The dress was perfect for her, just as he'd known it would be when he spotted it in a Denver shop window. He'd impulsively bought it and tucked it away; never dreaming it would be her wedding dress. But he was glad for it now. The ice blue satin shimmered divinely over every curve before draping softly to the porch floor, creating a look of virginal seductiveness. Which only made him want to tear it off of her. Later, he promised himself, and then wished he could put blinders on every whistling, whooping, gaping-eyed miner.

Victoria came up and took hold of Cassie's right hand. "You're beautiful." The little girl had insisted on wearing a pink velvet dress, and Cole had helped her clean up and put it on. Then Ruby had tamed her dark curls into a cascade down her back.

Cassie gave her an adoring smile. "You're beautiful too, love."

"We're going to get married, aren't we?"

"Aye that we are. Is that all right with you?"

"Yes. Cassie, when we're married, will you be my momma?"

"If you want me to."

"I know you won't be my real momma. But I'd still like to call you momma."

Cassie looked up at Cole. "Is that all right with you?"

"Very much so," he answered, still glad he had a voice. After his parents and his siblings had all died, he never imagined having a family again. He was grateful God had had other plans.

He stepped close to Cassie and took her left hand in his. "You're about to become my wife," he whispered in her ear.

"Aye."

"You won't be sorry. I promise."

"I know that, Cole. And I'll work very hard to make you happy."

"Cassie, just having you in my life makes me happy. Although there is one thing I need from you."

Her winged brows arched at the seriousness of the coming request. "What is that?"

"A promise that you won't ever let that independent streak of yours take you away from me. I couldn't bear to lose you."

"You could never lose me, Cole. I don't want independence, not in the way you're thinking. I only functioned in that manner for survival. You should understand that. You perfected it, remember?"

"I remember. But life is more than survival to me now. I could never go back to living that way."

"Nor could I. You and Victoria are my life. I love you with all my heart."

Cole's throat constricted. He hadn't realized how much he'd needed to hear those words. He felt like he'd just been given the moon and stars and all their glories. He smiled at both of his girls, thinking about how much his life had changed and knowing he'd never need anything else the rest of his days. He was the happiest man on earth. He bent closer to Cassie's ear. "You never answered my other question."

"What question was that?"

"I want to have more children, Cassie. Do you?"

"Aye. Especially if they are anything like this one." She nodded at Vicky, then dropped Cole's hand to pull his head down and kiss him long and hard.

Another cheer resounded from the gawking crowd.

Cassie blushed and stepped back. "You better hurry up and marry me Mister Adams because I have something very important to tell you."

EPILOGUE

Spirit Lake, September 30, 1874

Cassie lay with her head on her husband's lap. A soft breeze caressed her face. Cole's fingers combed lazily through her hair. Overhead in the sapphire sky, figures and patterns in billowy white gathered, circled and scattered in a never-ending display.

"I see a ship."

"Hmmm?" Cole kissed her sun-warmed brow.

"The clouds. One of them looks like a large ship... Well, it did. It's already become an elephant...no, even that's gone."

"My wife has a very vivid imagination. Clouds that look like ships and elephants?"

"Not just ships and elephants. Since I've been lying here, I've seen a mountain range, twin whales, a camel, even a herd of buffalo."

"An entire herd. Imagine that." He tugged playfully on a lock of her hair.

"You doubt me? If you were lying here, you'd see pictures too."

"I would love to put my head in your lap," he drawled. "Want to trade places?"

She pretended to ignore the seductive tone in his voice and shook her head. "No, I don't want to trade. I'm quite comfortable, thank you."

Comfortable couldn't come close to describing how she felt. This day, this place, this man, everything in her life was more than she could have ever wished for. Great Spirit had blessed her with enough riches for a lifetime. She held up her hand and looked at the gold band Cole had placed there exactly one year ago today. It captured the sun in tiny twinkling shafts. Cole's grin appeared in her peripheral vision.

"Happy?" he asked.

"Happier than a body has a right to be. Are you?"

"My life is complete, Cassie. I'm the most fortunate man on earth."

She beamed at his words, knowing they didn't come easy for him, nor did they come very often. But he showed her in countless ways how much he cared for her, and she returned his love in every way she could think of. They had both lost their families, but together they had created a new family and the future was bright with hope and promise.

Childish laughter turned their interest to the other blanket only a foot away. Ring crouched next to Victoria, half off and half on the blanket. His tail swished back and forth, every stroke hitting the little girl square in the back. His focus was intent on the two small bundles wrapped in matching knit blankets. Victoria dangled Cole's pocket watch by its chain over one, then the other. "Kristina smiles at me all the time, but Katy's still stingy with her smiles."

"Keep trying, love." Cassie encouraged. "If anybody can get that little sourpuss to smile, it's her big sister."

"You knew all along didn't you?" Cole asked, drawing her attention back to him.

"Knew what?"

"That you were giving me two more daughters."

She snuggled more comfortably against him. Opportunities for complete relaxation were rare in this remote life they'd carved out together, especially since the twins had arrived, and she wasn't going to waste a minute of it. "I was fairly certain the child I carried would be a girl. I had no idea there would be two. That fact surprised me as much as it did you."

"How did you know it would be a girl?"

"It has been the way of my mother's family for many generations. The firstborn is a girl. My mother, grandmother, and great-grandmother only had one child each; a daughter."

Cole scowled down at her. "Is this your way of preparing me to live the rest of my life surrounded by nothing but females."

"Would that be so bad?" She poked him hard in the ribs with a finger.

He flinched, then grabbed her hand and pulled the offending finger into his mouth. He sucked and kissed on it until her eyes closed in sensual pleasure. Then he nipped the tip with his teeth, and her eyes flew open in outrage.

"Serves you right." He kissed it again and said, "I've learned how to tame this female, I guess I can figure out how to deal with a whole houseful."

"Before you feel too put upon, let me tell you I have male ancestors, too. Running Deer had six brothers; the youngest were two sets of twins. Don't look so panic stricken. That doesn't mean all of our children will arrive in pairs. I just wanted you to know that Ginny isn't the only one capable of producing a son."

"Hmmm…" Cole's eyes strayed in the direction of the house.

"That news displeases you?"

"No." He looked back down at her. "It pleases me no end. I was just trying to decide the best way to expand the house."

"I don't think you need to jump right up. It'll do fine for a while. Let's concentrate on the three children we have."

Reaching up to smooth a stray ebony curl off Cole's brow, Cassie's eye caught a glint of light in the tree. She shifted her head slightly and saw the sunlight reflect off of something silver.

The knife! She scrambled to her feet. The silver-handled knife Zeb's brother had used to mark the location of his buried gold. She would never have seen it if the handle and the sun hadn't been in the precise angle to her and each other that they were. Her heart beat a little faster as she realized how close Zeb and Dalton had been. How many times they must have ridden right by it.

She stood on tiptoe to reach the handle, but it was too high and buried to the hilt.

Cole watched her struggle for a minute then got up, yanked it out and handed it to her with a knowing look. "It's the knife Zeb was searching for, isn't it?"

"Aye. I'm sure it must be."

"Are you going to write him about finding it?"

Cassie turned the knife over in her hand. Would Zeb even want to know? He certainly didn't need the money. Dalton's family was wealthy. She'd written Dalton twice since her marriage and received the same number of letters back from him. The first held news of how much he was enjoying college and the young women he was dating. His last letter had congratulated her on the birth of the twins, then he'd gone on to assure her that he and his grandfather had finally mended their bad feelings and that Zeb was well and happy.

Would news of the found burial spot be welcome or would it stir up old pain and hard feelings?

"I don't know," she finally said. "Maybe the gold is worth more where it is." Indeed, the real treasure marked by the knife was in her husband's smile, her children's laughter and in the joy and security of her home.

Zeb left these hills thinking he hadn't accomplished his mission. But she knew differently. His quest was completed the moment he brought her to this glorious place, a place more valuable than all the gold in the world: Her home.

And she would be forever grateful.

Maybe she would write… and tell him just that.

The End